4.95

Year Zero

Year Zero

Brian Stableford

Five Star • Waterville, Maine

First Edition in the United States.
First Printing: April 2003

Published in 2003 in conjunction with
Tekno Books and Ed Gorman.

Set in 11 pt. Plantin.

Printed in the United States on permanent paper.

Library of Congress Cataloging-in-Publication Data

Stableford, Brian M.
    Year zero / by Brian Stableford.—1st ed. in the U.S.
      p. cm.
    ISBN 0-7862-5333-9 (hc : alk. paper)
    1. London (England)—Fiction. I. Title.
  PR6069.T17Y43 2003
    823′.914—dc21   2003040866

Year Zero

1

When Molly bumped into Elvis at the cheese counter at singles night in the local supermarket, you could have knocked her over with a feather.

"Are you *him*," she asked, "or do you just look like him?"

"Ah'm *him*," he admitted, in a laid-back drawl undercut by awkward anxiety.

Molly still had her doubts. He didn't look a day older than he had in *Viva Las Vegas*, and she was pretty certain that he'd got very fat before he'd supposedly died because of all the junk food he ate. She sneaked a look at the stuff in his trolley, and was surprised to see that he'd stocked up with fresh fruit and veg before coming to collect his Camembert and Port Salut. Even the bread was wholemeal. All in all, he was putting on a better show than she was with her frozen pizzas and mild Cheddar slices—which weren't the ideal goods to be seen with on singles night, when image was everything.

Molly hadn't actually known that it was singles night when she'd set off from the B&B—she wasn't a Sainsbury's regular and didn't even have a loyalty card—but when she'd found out, she couldn't help wondering whether fate was taking a hand in her affairs. She'd been forced to spend New Year's Eve at the B&B instead of going to Trafalgar Square because it was the only way she could get permission to see in the new year with Christine. Some said it was the new Millennium, of course, but Molly knew better than that—and so had Adam, the new boyfriend that Francine had pinched from little anorectic Annie. When Mr. Jarvis had picked up Christine at one in the morning and Francine had passed out from the combination of drugs and booze, Molly and Adam had had a long and only slightly drunken conversation about the absurdity of regarding the end of 1999 as the end of the Millennium.

"It's a whole year short by a proper count," Adam had agreed, when Molly had put the point to him, "but it's absurd in any case that we should still be saddled with the historical burden of the Christian Church's bad calculations." He had gone on to argue that the world would have done far better to agree with its ill-coded computers that the coming year was year zero rather than trying to rewrite all their software to make them admit that it was actually 2000. "We could all have made a fresh start," he had lamented, "and we could certainly do with one, couldn't we?"

Molly had been impressed. She had decided there and then that she would refuse point blank to be Y2K compliant, and would instead use whatever opportunities year zero provided to make a fresh start and turn her life around. She reckoned that there were unlikely to be many people this side of Serbia so direly in need of starting over with a clean slate. She had to admit that Francine and Annie might have been equally strong candidates had they not gone to sleep immediately after midnight, but fact was that they had and she hadn't —and here she was in Sainsbury's on singles night, and here was Elvis, as large as life and twice as natural.

Getting herself a man hadn't been number one on Molly's fresh start wish list—in fact, she hadn't thought to include it all, having spent far too long on the game to have any romantic illusions left—but bumping into Elvis five days into year zero surely had to be an omen of sorts: a promise of new and extraordinary things to come. She was determined not to muff the opportunity that fate had laid on.

Fortunately, she had always been a good listener.

Elvis explained to Molly that he'd faked his death in order to take part in the clandestine clinical trials of a new immortality serum whose makers intended to reserve its use to the fabulously rich and the richly deserving. The entire experimental sample had recently been brought over to England because secret agents of the Federal Drug Authority had figured out where their Californian hideaway was, probably because Charlie Manson had opened his big mouth once too often. Howard Hughes had fixed it for Elvis and Patsy Cline to stay with Bob Maxwell and Lord Lucan, although the safe house in Herne Hill wasn't really big enough for the four of them, with Maxwell being such a boorish type.

"Patsy normally does the shopping," Elvis said, mournfully, "but she ain't feelin' too good right now."

"Heartsick, I suppose," Molly said, thinking that she probably knew exactly how poor Patsy felt, having been called crazy herself, and not just because of being sectioned a couple of times. "I don't often come here myself, but I wanted to do something different, just to break a habit."

In answer to her subtle probing, Elvis explained to Molly that the serum tests had been an unexpectedly long haul, with several prototypes not quite living up to expectations, but that the latest version really seemed to be getting down to the nitty-gritty. It tasted like scouring-powder but it was doing him so much good that he was just about back to his physical peak.

"Good Es used to taste a bit like scouring-powder too," she observed, wistfully, swiftly adding "or so it's said," because she remembered hearing it rumoured that Elvis's private self-indulgences hadn't been quite in keeping with his publicly-expressed opinions.

"Ah'm surprised you remember me," Elvis observed.

"Most of my fans are a little older nowadays."

Molly wondered whether that was intended as a compliment. She'd been born in May 1968—conceived in the hottest part of the Summer of Love, her mother had told her before sodding off to God-only-knew-where—but she certainly couldn't pass for any younger than she was. On the other hand, Elvis had been reported dead by the time she reached puberty, so it wasn't entirely surprising that he thought she was younger than the average necrophilic fan.

As the conversation progressed, Molly gradually realised what a marvellous freak of chance their meeting was. Elvis hadn't known that it was singles night at Sainsbury's, because Patsy hadn't tipped him off. None of the local harpies had been quick enough to lock trolleys with him because they were mostly hanging around sherry and spirits hoping to catch a few slummers down from Chelsea, so Molly had had a clear run. It was exactly the kind of thing she needed to get year zero off to a flying start, even if she still had to give top priority to getting Christine and Angie back from the Jarvises, just as soon as she'd kicked the Prozac and tranks and found herself a real job.

"Look, Elvis," she said, "I'm not being funny or anything, but I really think you ought to stick with me at least until we get through the checkout. A good-looking guy like you could easily get mobbed even if nobody else recognises you, because just being here on singles night puts out all the wrong signals to the slags from the local estates. *Your* address might be Herne Hill, but where we're actually standing is definitely Brixton." She paused for breath and a moment's consideration, then decided that if she were in for a penny she might as well be in for a pound. "In fact," she continued, "if I were you, I'd stick with me all the way back to the B&B. You don't have to come in for coffee, of course, and it wouldn't be Gold

Blend if you did, but you'd be safer going home from there than you would if I left you drifting hereabouts—honestly!"

She was sure that she could have put it better, but once Elvis had had a good look round and had seen what was lurking behind the yoghurt counter, his natural paranoia came to the rescue.

"Ah'm with you, ma'am," he said.

And he was, all the way to the front door of the B&B— though not a step further.

2

Molly and Elvis had agreed to meet in Sainsbury's again the following week, at the cheaper end of the wine lane. She wasn't sure that he would turn up, even if Patsy wasn't feeling any better. After all, being an authentic aristocrat, Lucky Lucan was probably the kind of guy who'd take his turn at the shopping, even if the likes of Captain Bob wouldn't. *Noblesse oblige,* wasn't that what they said?

As it turned out, though, there he was, a little careworn but still pretty tidy and trim—and not a rhinestone in sight. They chatted together for an hour or more, passing the tinned tuna and baked beans so often that Molly almost felt embarrassed, even though she'd made sure this time that there was nothing in her trolley anyone would have looked down her nose at if she'd been in Marks & Spencer's.

Molly told Elvis that although she was far too young ever to have been a true fan of his, she'd really loved all the films —especially the one in which he sang "Teddy Bear." Since the kids had been taken back into care, of course, watching films on TV was pretty much all she had been doing during the day before resolving to make her fresh start. The B&B actually had cable, so she, Greta and Francine could watch the ones on Bravo and TNT as well as all the ones normal people got to see, always provided that one of them was quick enough to grab both remotes and brave enough to stand firm against Gloria the spitting schizo, who claimed to hate "unreal drama" and always wanted to watch "Jerry Springer" or the "Live! TV Agony" programme instead.

Molly didn't explain *all* of this to Elvis, of course; she didn't want him to think that she might be the kind of person who was so desperate for a little human warmth that the fictional characters in soaps and movies had become not merely imaginary friends but her entire social life. She did explain, however, that she wasn't a regular at singles night in Sainsbury's or anywhere else, because she wasn't the kind of shallow person who could be satisfied with an endless sequence of one night stands. She also told him that she was usually far too shy to strike up conversations, although that was stretching the truth a bit too far even by her elastic standards. She tried to impress upon him how special he was, even to someone too young to have been a real fan.

"I always loved the kind of music that could lead a girl astray," she told him, truthfully, "and I always knew that you were the one who'd started all that off. I always knew that you were the first source of everything I held dear. I always knew that you were more than just a man: a force of destiny incarnate."

"Ah wouldn't say *that*," Elvis said, modestly. "Ah allus felt different, even when ah warn't no more than knee-high to a cricket, but ah ain't no angel."

"Angels are probably over-rated," Molly assured him. "The man who gave rock'n'roll to the masses is my idea of a messenger from infinity."

While they were on the way back to the B&B, Molly explained that in England cricket was a game, rather like baseball—except, of course, for the bouncers and the LBW rule. Elvis held up his end of the conversation by explaining the ins and outs of being a guinea pig for an immortality serum, and his reasons for becoming involved with the project.

Fame was all very well, Elvis explained, but it forced you

to live life at such a pitch of intensity that it almost became unbearable. When he'd been the king he'd felt all the time like a moth zooming back and forth across a candle-flame, just asking to get his wings singed. He'd decided readily enough, when the Faustian bargain was offered by a Mephistophelean biotech company, that he wanted to sign on the dotted line, in good red blood. He wanted his life back—and that meant getting his *youth* back because, when you came right down to it, youth was the one and only place where life was really *at*. He'd always thought that second chances were something even money couldn't buy, even from angels, but he'd underestimated the pace of technological progress and the ingenuity of genetic engineers. Second chances *were* available, to those who were truly deserving, and a clear shot at one was worth almost any sacrifice.

Molly knew what he meant. She had always known that not everyone who arrived at the age of thirty looked back with such fierce regret at the time when they were seven-teen-and-a-half, but she suspected that there were plenty who did, and that broken-down whores were far from being a majority among them. In her heart of hearts, she knew that rigidly-applied logic would force her to concede that even if she could have another shot, knowing what she did now, she probably wouldn't be able to do any better, but rigidly-applied logic was no longer an issue. This was year zero, after all, and the momentum of the past could be dodged, if only you had the trick of it.

If any emissary of the Devil had offered Molly the chance to get into the clinical trial along with Patsy and Elvis she would have opened a vein right away, but she knew better than to ask. She wasn't rich, and she wasn't deserving—yet.

When they eventually parted, Molly said to Elvis: "I hope you won't mind me saying so, but for someone who's been thoroughly rejuvenated by the elixir of life, you're looking just the teensiest bit peaky. A little thinner than you were last week, if my judgment can be trusted."

Elvis admitted that the newest version of the serum had just begun to throw up one or two unexpected side-effects, and that he had indeed lost weight.

"Believe me, honey," he said, "it ain't nothin' they cain't take care of. These guys are the best." He said it with the air of a man who'd grown used to expecting the best, and used to expecting that the best would be provided.

"I hope you're right," she said, "for all our sakes."

She couldn't help remembering the endless catalogue of her own side-effects when the drugs they'd given her when she was sectioned had interacted with the ones she hadn't been prescribed, and how even her side-effects had begun to have side-effects. "Unexpected synergies" was what the doctor at the Maudsley had called them—by which he meant that she was taking so many damn drugs they were interfering with one another in a manner which was almost as promiscuous as her sex-life. She was past all that now, of course. She was a survivor, perhaps not so very unlike Elvis in spite of the difference in their years and the sharp contrast in their life-chances.

Again, Elvis saw her to the door of the B&B. This time, she invited him in, but he was too much of a gentleman to accept. She knew that it was because he was a gentleman and not because he didn't want to see her again because he was prompt enough to answer when she asked if she'd see him again.

"Ahm busy almost every day," he said, with authentic regret, "but I kin manage the same time an' place, even if I don't have the shoppin' to do."

"It's a date," Molly said.

That night, as she lay in bed, she actually put down her paperback long before its soporific effect had taken hold and took time out to wonder where the relationship might be going. It was a long time since she'd had occasion to do that, but she hadn't lost the knack. All the old self-doubts were waiting in the wings of consciousness to fall upon her, but she wasn't about to give in to them. This was *year zero,* and if that were to mean anything she had to keep all her former tormentors at bay.

Unfortunately, it wasn't just the self-doubts she had to contend with. There was also the question of what her social worker, Elizabeth Peach, might think. She was the one who would have to start the ball rolling if Molly were to stand any chance of regaining custody of her kids, and Elizabeth Peach wasn't the kind of person to approve of her clients having affairs with rock musicians, even successful ones—and especially ones that were generally supposed to be dead.

Molly realised that making a fresh start might not be as easy as she had hoped, even if fickle fate really were on her side.

3

When Molly met Elvis the following week, at the muesli-and-bran-flakes end of Breakfast Cereals, she was immediately struck by the fact that he was looking more than a little peaky indeed. In fact, he looked like the landlord after a particularly protracted bout with Gloria or the manic-depressive in the first floor back. There was a distinct greenish tinge about his face and he was so thin as to be almost emaciated.

"Are you sure you're eating properly?" she asked, checking out his trolley suspiciously. The smoked salmon and champagne were reassuring in their way, although she had a sneaking suspicion that they were probably for Lucky and the Captain. Molly didn't know whether she ought to be worried about the presence of the bumper pack of grillsteaks, the Goodfellas pizzas, the chocolate digestives and the breakfast cereal that she insisted on thinking of as Coco Pops no matter what was printed on the packet nowadays. The digestives were probably Patsy's, and even if some of the rest were Elvis's she could take some comfort from the fact that the shelves were packed with even worse excuses for nourishment.

"Ah'm fine," Elvis assured her. "Ah'd-a stayed home if ah warn't." As if to reassure her, he picked up a 750-gram packet of the own-brand DeLuxe Muesli which boasted that it contained a minimum of thirty percent fruit and nuts. Then he steered in the direction of the yoghurt counter, conspicuously ignoring the battered fish.

Elvis went on to explain that the new immortality serum

was working a little *too* well. Molly didn't understand all the technical details, but she figured that he was a little hazy on that side of things himself. In fact, he probably knew less than she did about active liposomes and free radicals because he rarely watched the ads on TV and never read *Marie Claire*. She gathered that although the serum had dutifully conferred immortality on Elvis's own cells, and had done a really ace job of smartening up his innards as well as smoothing out his wrinkles, the bacteria and nematodes that were normally resident in his body had begun to mop up the elixir with everincreasing alacrity. When it came to internal parasites and passengers, apparently, superstars were no more abundantly-equipped than everybody else, but that was quite abundantly enough. Apparently, the consequence of sharing in his biotech bonanza was that Elvis's hidden companions were enjoying something of a population explosion.

"It's just a glitch, the scientists say," Elvis lamented. "There've been glitches before. Ah could tell you some stories . . . but ah trust these guys. If it warn't for them, ah'd either be dead already or sixty-four years old and wearin' every one o'them in the bags under my eyes. Don't you worry your pretty little head none."

It was the first time Elvis had called her pretty. Molly knew, of course, that he didn't really mean it. She had been *sort of* pretty once, but that was before the creases had begun to set in around her eyes and her mouth. She was almost exactly half his age, but if any of the other singles night shoppers ever condescended to notice them they'd leap to the conclusion that she was the older of the two. The fact that Elvis didn't look at all well didn't make him look a single day *older*. Molly quailed at the thought that he might one day get to see her stretch-marks—but once she'd done quailing she felt a peculiar kind of naughty thrill, because she really did want him to see her stretch-marks some day soon—always provided that his present condition was only temporary.

In the meantime, it was really nice that he was being so polite.

"Well," Molly opined, "there *is* a limit to the trust you can put in doctors. Believe me, I know. I dare say you have the very very best, but they're only doctors when all said and done, and all doctors are alike in some ways. For instance, they tell you over and over again that things will be all right, even if they know bloody well that they won't. There are some things, you see, that are simply beyond the reach of medical wisdom. Ask Patsy—*she* knows."

Elvis groaned when Molly said that, and Molly wondered whether it had been a bad move to bring Patsy's name into what as supposed to be an intimate *tête-à-tête*. If she had learned one thing from all she'd been through, it was that one should never, never, never start talking about other women to blokes that one fancied. It led so easily to their making unfavourable comparisons. Annie had probably talked about Francine to Adam, with the inevitable result that Adam had defected. It probably hadn't helped, of course, that Annie had an unfortunate habit of slashing her wrists and breasts with razor blades as well as a long-held ambition to starve herself to death, but it wasn't until Francine had alienated Adam's affections that Annie had started going on about being abducted from her bed by little grey men in flying saucers.

Luckily, Elvis let the subject drop, and began reminiscing about the good old days, and why *Blue Hawaii* was a much better film than the critics had ever give it credit for, and what a compliment it was to have your nether regions deemed too obscene to be seen on the Ed Sullivan show.

Molly had actually seen Elvis on the Ed Sullivan show,

thirty-five years after the event, thanks to VH-1 buying up all the old tapes, although the first time she'd flipped into it while channel-surfing she'd mistaken Ed Sullivan for Richard Nixon and had only paused because she couldn't figure out what on Earth had happened to the ex-president's neck. She hadn't much in the way of nostalgic memories to offer in return for Elvis's Hollywood reminiscences, but she tried her best not to be entirely reduced to such empty conversational interpolations as, "Oh yes, I saw that one," and she managed to bite her tongue on the only occasion that the fateful words, "I wasn't even *born* then!" rose unbidden took her lips.

Fortunately, Elvis didn't seem all that curious about her past, so Molly didn't have to get too close to memories of the more uncomfortable kind. When she showed him the pictures of her kids that she carried in her purse, he barely glanced at them.

"Christine's fifteen now," she explained, wondering why it sounded as if she were apologising. "I had to go to Tooting the day before I first met you to deliver her present. She's with temporary foster parents—the Jarvises. Angie's growing up too—nearly twelve. This picture's two years old, but I haven't got a more recent one. The Jarvises probably have, but they wouldn't give one to me if they had."

"Ah've got a daughter o'my own," he told her. He sounded faintly regretful, but Molly assumed that it was only because of the thing with Michael Jackson. Men always had a problem with their daughters' boyfriends. Sometimes, she thought that it was perhaps as well that her own father had never known that she existed—assuming, that is, that the Old Witch had been telling the truth about that.

Elvis was just as sweet as ever when he said goodnight outside the B&B, although he was obviously in some discomfort. Although Molly felt guilty about thinking it, she couldn't help thinking that he wasn't quite the man she'd imagined him to be. She didn't invite him in, and he seemed a little disappointed about that, but she did let him kiss her. It wasn't nearly as nice as she'd hoped it would be, but she knew that she had to make allowances. He was ill, after all. When the doctors had sorted him out properly, he'd be back to his best, and that would be the time to explore further possibilities.

4

The following week, when Molly met Elvis in Frozen Foods, between the crinkle-cut chips and the chopped spinach, things had obviously got a lot worse. Her heart sank when she saw him, although she had been nursing the fear all week that this was the way things were bound to go.

It seemed almost as if Elvis was visibly rotting. His cheeks were a terrible shade of putrescent grey, and his breath stank. Even so, he was still cheerful. He assured Molly yet again that it was just a snag that the scientists had to work out, and that he wasn't in the least worried.

"After all," he said, "it ain't as if ah can die, now, is it? Ah'm immortal, right? There ain't nothin' the viruses an' all the other parasites can do to *me*. Anyways, you should see the others. The Cap'n looks as if he really had been sleepin' with the fishes for a fortnight."

Molly was almost tempted to ask whether the temporarily baffled biotechnologists couldn't have laid on somebody to do the shopping for the household, but she knew that Elvis hadn't really come out to replenish the safe house's larder. He'd come to meet her—the groceries and Patsy's incapacity were just the excuses that he gave Bob and Lucky for regularly jeopardising their cover.

Molly couldn't help remembering the way they'd exchanged that first kiss a week before. Even though it had just been a peck on the cheek, the persistent memory of it had put a real dent in her hopes for the future of the relationship. She had realised, on due reflection as she lay sleepless in bed, that his skin had felt curiously fluid and that it had tasted ever so faintly of mould. He hadn't mentioned fungus when he'd been explaining the problem of the immortal parasites but she supposed that everything was included in the immortality deal. As they negotiated the corner that took them past frozen pavlovas and chocolate fudge cakes, Molly was struck by the horrible irony of Elvis's situation, and what it might signify for the future of the whole human race. If the quest to secure human immortality merely managed to preserve and empower all the myriad forms of human corruption, then living forever would be a far greater challenge than dying, and the possibility of getting bored after the first thousand years or so would be the least of an apprentice immortal's problems.

On another occasion she might have been able to follow this train of thought to an interesting terminus, but for the moment she couldn't quite bend her mind to matters of philosophical speculation. She knew that she had more inti-mate, if not more important, things to consider.

What if Elvis wanted to kiss her again tonight? What if he wanted to come up to her room and fuck her brains out? They were, after all, on their fourth date, and even immortals couldn't be expected to wait forever. Would she be able to bear it? Should she even try?

Molly realised as she posed these questions and paused to pick up a small packet of lard that the answers were already inherent within them. If such uneasy thoughts even needed to be raised, the end had to be in sight.

"An' it ain't just us," Elvis drawled. "If'n you think *we* look bad, you should see Al Einstein and Siggy Freud. Ah bumped into'em last week at the clinic. Whoo-*ee!* Ah've told the big guys over an' over that they shouldn't have gotten so deep into charity work, an' so has Howie, but ah guess it's understandable they have this thing about their brother egg-heads."

"Of course it's understandable," Molly said, feeling a slight pang of irritation. "After all, without in any way questioning the value your own contribution to twentieth century culture, I must say that I couldn't possibly have much respect for people who'd try to save the likes of Robert Maxwell and Howard Hughes while blithely allowing Einstein and Freud to be committed to oblivion. Mind you, I'm a little bit surprised to hear you mention Einstein's name, because there was a programme on 'Discovery' only a couple of weeks ago about a man—Japanese, I think he was—who was trying to find out exactly what had happened to his brain, which had been put in a glass jar after he was buried."

"It was a fake," Elvis explained. "Brains are a dime a dozen. Sex-appeal is somethin' else."

Unfortunately, Molly thought, Elvis's sex-appeal was no longer very evident—and now that she was forced to confront the issue, his brain hadn't seemed much to write home about even on that first magic night when they'd met by the cheese counter. What was so special about Port Salut, when all was said and done? It might have a fancy orange rind but it was right there on the shelf, just like the mild Cheddar and the Dairylea slices.

Even while Elvis was walking her home that night, Molly knew that her dream had begun to fade—that this wasn't the turning-point in her life that she'd hoped it might be. It wasn't Elvis's fault—he really was doing his best, and underneath it all he was a really nice guy, but it just wasn't right for *her*.

"Ah was better in *Jailhouse Rock*, o'course," Elvis observed, with the half-hurt, half-apologetic air of a man who had just realised that his audience had lost the thread of his argument.

"Loved it," Molly said, tokenistically. "*Kid Creole* too. Loved them all."

"Ah was young then. *Really* young."

"I wasn't even born," Molly answered, hardly feeling the half-hearted reflexive nip of her teeth upon her tongue. She was immediately swamped with guilt. There was nothing wrong with Elvis that wasn't part of the essential human condition. Perhaps he was exhibiting his corruption a little more clearly than most, but the only difference between him and any other man was that he had lost his balance slightly. It wasn't even a *man* thing. Exactly the same nematodes and bacteria were patiently keeping house inside her own tissues. Her blood and skin were swarming with uninvited guests too. It wasn't Elvis's fault that he wasn't the ideal man. It was the ideal man's fault that he wasn't Elvis—that even the best man imaginable wasn't really the wellspring of all that was good and exciting and musical. If Elvis was only a symbol of the music, then the music too was only a symbol for something more basic and deep-seated. Music only had the effects it had, on her and everybody else, because it stirred up something inside. It stirred up lust and melancholy, a sense of the sublime and a sense of the ridiculous. It made your ribs reverberate and your heart beat more assertively, and it blotted out so many niggly parasitic distractions and irritations, but no music ever heard or imagined—not even the mythical music of the spheres—could ever be anything but a reflection of the human soul. And what was the soul, if you weren't a religious nut, but the sense of being yourself and not the person the rest of the world wanted you to be?

"I'm trying to get my kids back," Molly told Elvis as they walked back to the B&B. "I've seen Liz Peach, and she thinks I've got a chance. She's a social worker, of course, so she would say that—the lying bastards never say anything likely to upset you—but I think she's telling the truth. I mean, it's not as if I'm Francine, am I? Nobody but a lunatic would trust Francine to look after her kids, but I'm not like that. I'm capable of starting over. I've already kicked my worst habits, and I'm working my way through the bad ones. I know that the world and his wife—especially the wife—think that you can't really start a new life without a new man, and that a man is really all you need, but it's not as simple as that. If I were to stand face to face with the Devil himself and the Devil were to tell me that if I didn't toe the line he'd see to it that I never had another man as long as I lived, I'd tell him that if that was the worst he could do to me, I'd take my chances. I mean, you have to, don't you? You have to get your priorities in order, and we're already out of January and into February and even though it's a leap year, year zero still only has three hundred and sixty-six days in it and I can't afford to let whole weeks go by just *waiting*. It's not you—you have to believe that. You're great. You're the king. If there were any man alive for me, you'd be him, and if there were any man who'd ever lived, you'd be him too. You really are *the king*. But I'm not sure that I can do this, Elvis. It's just not right *for me*."

Elvis explained to her that it was just like Hollywood, where everything worked to a standard three-act formula. In every movie, he said, there was a point where the hero—and he, of course, had always been a hero, even in *Jailhouse Rock* —was delivered into the pit of despair, where it seemed that everything was lost and that his dream had become impossible of fulfilment. But that was just a phase that all heroes had to pass through, because that was the moment at which every true hero reached into himself and found the hidden reserve of strength of character that would carry him through to victory—and from that moment on, there was no way to go but up, until everything was settled and right and lit up like Las Vegas.

"Jus' give me a chance," he begged. "Jus' one more chance. Ah can be what y'want me to be. Ah'm much better than I seem right now. Jus' give me a chance to prove it."

They didn't kiss when they said goodbye, and the way Elvis's shoulders drooped as he trudged away into the darkness made Molly suspect that for him too, no matter how things worked in Hollywood, a lovely dream had begun to die.

5

Molly was surprised to see Elvis the following week, given the appalling condition he was in. She was astonished that Bob, Lucky and Patsy had let him come out to do the shopping—so astonished, in fact, that she figured that they couldn't possibly have any idea that he was here. Nevertheless, he was right where he'd promised he'd be, next to the dumpbin where they put the goods that were past their sell-by dates so that old age pensioners could pick them up dirt cheap.

His trolley was empty, and he was showing no interest at all in the goods on the shelves, so it was perfectly obvious that he had made the trip just to see her. He still wanted his one more chance, even though he must have known that it was absolutely hopeless. He couldn't accept fate, because he was a hero.

In view of that, as well as everything else, Molly felt that it would be terribly unfair to string him along, so she decided to come right out with it.

"Look, Elvis," she said, "I'm sorry but it's just not working. Liz Peach says that I only have a chance of getting my kids back if I can demonstrate to everyone's satisfaction that I'm back on an even keel. She says it's okay to keep taking medication, provided that it's on prescription, but that everything else has to be squeaky clean. The right kind of job would be good, but the wrong kind of man would be as fatal as the wrong kind of speed. From now on, the only whizzing I'll be doing is round and round the aisles of the blessed with a fully-loaded trolley, and not on singles night either. It's not *you*—it's just that this isn't the right time for someone like me to get involved with *anybody*. Friends would be okay, but even they'd have to be the right sort. The way Liz Peach sees things, nothing short of an angel is safe company for me right now, and you're a guy whose pelvis was once regarded as an instrument of the Devil from the buckle to the tongue of the Bible belt. I can't see you again. It's over."

He protested, of course. In fact, he protested with an eloquence and fervour that she'd never seen in him before, not even in the very best of his films. For just a few moments, she could almost have believed that he'd meant every word of "Heartbreak Hotel."

Elvis told her that there was always a let-down effect when a person met an idol, whether the idol turned out to have feet of clay or not, because what getting to know someone actually *meant* was that you had to relate to them as a normal human being, not as something altogether outside the ordinary run of things.

"Tell that to Lisa Marie," Molly said, although she bit her lip afterwards, in case it sounded too cruel.

As it happened, Elvis didn't understand what she was getting at. He decided to play the sympathy card. He told her that his eyeballs were full of immortal worms. He told her that he couldn't watch the TV news any more because the picture was just a blur of meaningless colour, and that the world was gradually going the same way. He told her that he couldn't sleep and couldn't eat, and that he was just about at the end of his tether with all the immortal parasites devouring his guts as fast as he could grow them back. Without the thought of her to sustain him, he said, he would be a goner. Without the hope of winning her heart, he would have nothing to live for.

"That's not fair," Molly told him, in an injured whisper.

"You can't put that kind of responsibility on another person's shoulders."

He wasn't an unreasonable man, and he apologised for having temporarily forsaken his dignity, but he didn't let up. He just changed tack again. He told her that she had to look beyond the image and the artifice to the lonely human soul within, with sympathy and understanding. He told her that she had to do that, not for his sake but for her own. He told her that she mustn't be afraid of life, that she too had to reach into herself in search of the hero within. He told her that for the sake of her own personal fulfilment she had to make the effort to appreciate that underneath all the glamour and the glitz there was nothing that mattered except a vulnerable human heart, beating in harmony with her own.

"That's half right," she replied, doggedly. "Beating, yes—harmony, no." It didn't seem right to add a comment to the effect that those four words summed up her whole life, although it would certainly have added a delicate spice of wit to what was turning out to be a rather painful conversation.

Elvis protested some more, and then he started pleading again. It was all rather ignominious, and Molly became embarrassed on his behalf. Fortunately, with it being Sainsbury's, and Brixton, none of the passing trolley-jockettes paused to give them a second glance. Molly couldn't help wondering whether it would have been any different if they'd been in a KMart in Tennessee.

To cut a long story short, Elvis fell apart—but Molly just kept on telling herself over and over again that it wasn't her fault. She had her own life to lead, her own destiny to seek, and there simply wasn't room in her life just now for an immortal superstar and all the immortal corruption he was carrying around inside himself.

In the end, he became too annoying to be borne a single moment longer.

"If I were you, Elvis, I'd try to pull myself together," Molly advised him. "I know you've been hurt—wounded, even—but you have to be strong. It's not the end of the world, you know. Mortal or immortal, worm-eaten or worm-ridden, idol or idler, life is what you make it. That's my philosophy, at any rate."

It was, too. At least, it was *now*. This was year zero, and it was February. Saint Valentine's Day was already in the past and Easter was on the horizon. It was time to think of more serious matters, to try to get the big picture into focus. She was sorry for Elvis, but he was responsible for himself, and if he couldn't take are of himself, who could? The simple fact was that she didn't love him and she couldn't include him in her plans—but she couldn't help feeling a distinct thrill of triumph when he finally admitted that she was right and agreed to disappear.

6

The first time Molly saw the angel, he was standing in the middle of the pedestrianized precinct at the end of Stockwell Road. There was no mistaking what he was. He had wings like a great white eagle, whose pinion feathers were touching the ground although the tops of their great furled arches extended a foot and a half above the circle of light that rimmed his head. It wasn't a comedy halo like a battery-powered quoit, but a solid disc half as bright as the winter sun. He was dressed in a dazzling-white robe that hung loose from his broad shoulders to his sandaled feet. He looked slightly puzzled, but only in an intellectual sort of way—more curious than alarmed and not in the least discomposed.

No one was paying any attention to the angel, even though the passers-by had nothing more pressing to do than was normal for a Tuesday morning in February. The shoppers and the truanting kids saw him all right, but they wouldn't look directly at him and they made detours to avoid passing within arm's reach of him. He couldn't have alienated so much attention if he'd been carrying a clipboard, a blue pencil and a sheaf of questions about sanitary protection.

Molly almost paused—but during the little margin of hesitation which might have realised the *almost,* she lost heart and quickened her step, just like everybody else.

Later, she told herself that she'd had to do it. She couldn't afford to get involved in anything dodgy. She'd kept the affair with Elvis secret, of course; if she'd told anyone it would have got back to the Social Services. Not that she'd have been sec-

tioned again—you practically had to kill someone to get sectioned these days—but it would have come up when the next
group meeting considered the possibility of restoring custody
of the kids. The only thing likely to have a worse effect on the
average group meeting than the news that the client thought
she'd had a fling with Elvis—even one that had never got as
far as actual penetration—was the news that the client
thought she'd been visited by an angel. The entire audience
for "Touched by an Angel" was probably made up of social
workers, who presumably figured the show as the ultimate
wet dream but couldn't believe a word of it. It was very popular in the States, they said, but so was Elvis; neither played
quite as well in Brixton, even on what the local Estate Agents
called the "Dulwich fringe."

Even so, she regretted falling into step with everybody else
and pretending that the angel wasn't there. It was cowardly.
It was no consolation to think that angels' missions were
probably supposed to work that way. In all probability,
nobody ever stopped to speak to an angel except the person
the angel had come to see. There would be a certain propriety
in that—and if angels couldn't maintain propriety in this god-
forsaken world, who could?

When she saw the angel again, he was standing outside the
old Salvation Army Temple. There was a split second when
she didn't quite recognise him, but the face was unmistakable
even though everything else about him had changed. His
wings were only half the size they had been, and were now
patterned like a pigeon's. The nimbus was gone, although his
hair was still luxuriant and golden blond. The white robe was
gone too, unless its trailing hem had been tucked up above
the knee so that it could remain hidden within the
tan-coloured raincoat he was wearing—which seemed
unlikely, given that the bottoms of a pair of grey flannel trou-

sers were clearly visible, their turn-ups resting on brown suede loafers. He still seemed a trifle bewildered, and discomposure was beginning to creep up on him now.

The benches where the down-and-outs hung out were crowded, but none of the alkies was looking at the angel. They couldn't have treated him with more disdain if he'd been a Tory councillor down from Westminster on a fact-finding tour.

Molly had thought for some months after it closed that the alkies kept returning to the Temple out of habit and sentiment, but Francine had eventually let her in on the secret that it was just round the corner from the lock-up where the local white van man stored the bottles and cans he shipped in from Eastenders three times a week. It was the cheapest source of strong cider for miles around. The white van man was called Lucas but the alkies called him Saint Luke because he allowed them to buy at wholesale prices without a trade card. The local crackheads looked upon the alkies with naked envy, knowing full well that their prices went up as their dependency increased—but their supplier insisted on being known as Saint John anyway, just for form's sake.

Again, Molly almost stopped when she saw the angel, in spite of the fact that he was hanging about in a place where she usually quickened her paces in order to minimize the deluge of cackling abuse. Again, she couldn't quite bring herself to interrupt her stride.

The down-and-outs weren't in the least bothered by the fact that the angel could overhear them; they made all the usual remarks. They knew where Molly lived, and in their estimation—which was not unrepresentative of the world's —that automatically made her a career whore whose current hundred-per-cent dependency on the social only signified that she was too ugly to get the kerb-crawlers to stop. That was what they called out, anyhow, although an alky would have to have very few memory cells left to be oblivious to the fact that kerb-crawlers would stop for anything in a skirt and heels, provided that she a hole at the right height.

Molly never rose to the bait, as Francine some of the other residents of the B&B were wont to do, but on this particular occasion she couldn't suppress a blush. It was not on her own behalf that she suffered embarrassment but on behalf of the angel. It wasn't much of an advertisement for humankind that the Sally Ann had had to close its Temple, or that all the street scum in the neighbourhood gathered there to take what advantage they could of their friendly neighbourhood smuggler, or that the very same street scum were prepared to pretend that the only thing stopping her from pulling down her knickers for them was that they had better things to do with their money.

Given that the real Millennium was only ten months away, Molly would have thought that even the down-and-outs would have wanted to put on a *bit* of a front while the eyes of Heaven were upon them, but no. The alkies had long since given up on propriety—and, she supposed, everything else.

The third time Molly saw the angel he was sitting at a two-seater table crammed into an alcove in the public library. He was reading the *Independent*. Of his wings there was now not the slightest trace, and his raincoat, although it couldn't have been cheap—if, in fact, he'd purchased it instead of miraculously spinning it out of some mysterious utility fog—was stained, as if he'd been sleeping rough. His hair was mousy brown, just beginning to thin at the back. In spite of all this, there was no hesitation in her recognition. She'd seen him twice already, and she hadn't forgotten the finely-sculpted lines of his face. Three days' worth of stubble couldn't hide the fact that he was the most beautiful man presently in the world. Elvis would have wept in envy, even before the immortal worms got to work on his insides.

Molly looked away as soon as she saw him, but she'd already taken note of the fact that the only empty seat left on the entire ground floor was the one opposite the angel, and she knew before she went up the stairs to REFERENCE that there wouldn't be any room up there because of all the kids from the college filling in their free periods. When she got to REFERENCE, she went over to the encyclopaedias. She hesitated over the *Britannica* and the *Catholic Encyclopaedia*, but in the end she took the *Encyclopaedia of Fantasy* off the shelf. It seemed, on the whole, to be the most sensible place to look up ANGELS.

She read through the article, committed a handful of names to memory and then went back down to the card-catalogue to check whether the books were in the lending stock. She always used the card-catalogue instead of the computer because it felt nicer. She'd hoped the library might at least have *The Revolt of the Angels* or *The Wonderful Visit*, but they didn't. Out of print, out of mind. What they did have back in REFERENCE, however, was a two-volume edition of *Old Testament Apocrypha and Pseudoepigraphia*, so she went upstairs again and hauled out the unwieldy volume containing the *Book of Enoch*. Then she took it downstairs, planted it on the table at which the angel was sitting and plonked herself with almost-equal emphasis in the vacant chair.

7

It didn't occur to Molly to wonder whether the angel might be reading the *Independent* as a matter of choice. She'd spent enough time taking advantage of the free central heating to know that no one came into the library because they were keen to find out what was happening in the world. The ones who were so desperate to get in that they would be queuing up at opening time always grabbed the *Sun*, the *Mirror* and the *Mail* first, then the *Express* and the *Guardian*. Then the ones who were pretending hardest that they were really earning their Jobseeker's Allowance would grab the *Times*, the *Telegraph* and the local rag. The *Independent* was always the last to go, left for the attention of the poor sucker who had no choices left.

She had opened her own book and read the first four pages of *Enoch*, including the footnotes, before the angel finally condescended to lower the *Independent* sufficiently to let his eyes peep over. She waited a full three seconds before raising her own head so that she could meet his curious but mildly suspicious gaze. The angel's eyes were the bluest she had ever seen. They were bluer than the bluest sky on the brightest summer day there had ever been. They were the only thing left which would have immediately informed the most casual observer, seeing him for the first time, that their owner was, in fact, an angel.

To show off her erudition, Molly had already prepared an apposite quote. She wasn't entirely sure which James Bond book it came from, but thought it was probably **Goldfinger**.

"Once is happenstance," she said. "Twice is coincidence. Three times is . . . are you looking for me, by any chance?"

"No," said the angel, too bluntly to allow her to savour the music of his voice.

"Oh," said Molly, wondering whether she ought to be relieved or hurt. "Well, if you'd care to tell me who you *are* looking for, maybe I can help. You don't seem to be having much success on your own."

"I'm not looking for anyone," the angel said. He didn't seem particularly well-spoken.

"No message to deliver?" Molly queried. "No mission to carry out?"

"No," said the angel.

"You're just not playing the game, are you?" Molly said. "What's the matter—don't you have TV in Heaven?"

The angel lowered the *Independent* and displayed the entirety of his incredibly beautiful but unshaven face. He seemed to be trying to formulate a question. Molly guessed that she was the first human being he'd talked to, and figured that she ought to help him out.

"Well," she said, "if you haven't come to deliver a message, and you aren't here to befriend and redirect some poor unfortunate who's on the brink of making a morally disastrous decision, what *are* you doing way down on *terra firma*?"

The angel didn't even blink. "I fell," he said.

It wasn't what he said that bowled Molly over but the way he said it. She'd spoken lightly, as if the whole thing were a joke, not because she thought it was but because that was the only way she knew of dealing with a situation she'd never encountered before. He could have said exactly the same words in that sort of way and it would have been funny. It *could* have been pure stand-up, the kind of thing that got Eddie Izzard a big laugh—but it wasn't. It was deadly serious.

Even though Molly was sitting there with the *Book of Enoch* open on the desk, its pages well-nigh tabloid-size, it didn't even occur to her to connect "I fell" with the war in Heaven or **Paradise Lost** or the angels which had begat the Nephilim on the lucky daughters of men. She had heard "I fell" spoken in exactly that manner, in exactly that tone, by neighbours in the bedsit, by companions in group and by fellow shelf-stackers on the very few occasions when the temp agency managed to get her work in spite of her record, her history, her lack of a proper address, and her general Oxfam-dressed appearance.

Oddly enough, she couldn't quite remember whether she'd ever said it herself. She'd certainly sported the bruises more than once in the hectic days when she'd copped for the kids, so she knew it wasn't a lie. It never was a lie, although everyone always thought it was. Even when you got a push in the back, or a fist in your face, it wasn't a lie. The fact that an angel could say it certainly proved that, even if it proved nothing else.

A few more minutes passed before Molly recovered herself sufficiently to say: "When you say *fell*, you do mean from Heaven, I suppose—not from the Land of Dreams, or any cop-out along those lines."

"From Heaven," the angel confirmed. Nobody with eyes like those could be capable of copping out, any more than he could be capable of copping for a couple of kids.

Molly took the angel round the corner to The Greasy Spoon, whose proprietor hadn't quite got to grips with the concept of irony when he'd changed its name from The Bistro. She offered to buy the angel something to eat, but he told her that he didn't need food *as such*. She ordered the all-day breakfast and a pot of tea for two.

"I shouldn't really have to do this," she explained to him,

figuring that he had to be pretty innocent in the ways of the world if he'd had to make do with the *Independent* since his arrival. "Being in a B&B, I ought to get breakfast *included.* That's what the second B stands for, after all—but standards have slipped down here. On the other hand, it's better than a lot of places. The girls on the game are very good about only doing it in alleyways and cars, for the sake of the kids, and we've all got our own sinks and electric kettles, and the loos aren't that bad, considering, and the TV in the sitting room is always replaced the day after it gets nicked, and we've got cable. I'm in the smallest room, of course, but you could say that I'm in the lap of luxury compared to most, because my kids are still out to foster. Unfortunately, just about the last way you can score any points when you get that close to the bottom is to get your kids back, so I'm actually reckoned to be not yet off the mark, even though I've kicked everything but the Prozac and the over-the-counter tranks disguised as anti-histamines. Some would say that my brain chemistry is fried anyhow, but I don't think so—and at least I've got guts, to say that to an angel. I have the breakfast at lunchtime because it's cheaper than anything actually called *lunch* and if you only have one real meal a day it's better to have it in the middle. Can't cook in the rooms, you see, except for cup-a-soup and other just-add-boiling-water crap, and who can stomach that? What's Heaven like, exactly?"

"It's not *like* anything," the angel said, unhelpfully.

"Nice gardens? Pleasant weather? Bright light?" Molly prompted, figuring that any hint at all would be better than nothing, and that she really ought to try to bring the angel out of himself a little. If he hadn't been sent to deliver a message, the fact that he had accepted the lunch invitation, even though he didn't need food *as such,* suggested that maybe he had been sent as some kind of *test.*

"None of that," he said.

"*None* of it! What about singing? Surely you were in the choir. Doesn't it get boring, just bathing in the presence of God, century after century?"

"No," he said. "There's no time in Heaven."

"No *time?*" Molly hadn't been expecting that. "What keeps everything from happening at once then?"

"Nothing," he informed her, calmly. "Everything does happen at once." He sipped his tea but it was still too hot, and probably too sharp for his celestially-softened palate.

"You'd better put some sugar in it," Molly said, passing him the thing that looked like a giant salt-cellar with a chimney. "That's a bit rotten, don't you think? The preachers promise eternity. Don't you think the dead might be a little disappointed when they get there and find that their stay is considerably shorter than a split nanosecond? If Saatchi and Saatchi tried that, the Advertising Standards Authority would be down on them like a ton of bricks."

"It's not *shorter* than anything," the angel said. "You have to set aside that whole way of thinking. Paradise isn't a *place* at all. The human imagination is too narrowly attuned to mere existence to encompass its essence."

Molly couldn't help but wonder whether she'd first caught sight of him just too late to see the clipboard and blue pencil disappear.

"So what did you do?" she said.

"We don't *do* anything," he began—but she immediately saw that he'd got hold of the wrong end of the stick.

"I said what *did* you do," she reminded him. "I've given up fishing for descriptions. I mean, what did *you* do to qualify for the drop? With Lucifer it was pride, with the fathers of the Nephilim it was presumably lust. That still leaves five deadly sins untapped by angelkind. *Please* don't tell me it was sloth."

The angel made a face. He'd obviously put too much sugar in the tea. "I fell," he repeated, in the same stubbornly heart-melting fashion. It wasn't a lie. Whatever he was covering up, whoever he was protecting, it wasn't a lie.

Molly sighed, but she didn't have the heart to be sarcastic. "So what are the other fallen angels doing these days?" she asked. She was genuinely interested. "According to Enoch, they taught mankind the fundamentals of technology and civilization, but the skills they passed on must have become obsolete ages ago. Unless, of course, they got more out of government retraining schemes than I ever did."

"I don't know," he said.

"But you're hoping to make contact, right? Or maybe not. I mean, if the fallen angels are all in Hell, you'd probably rather stay here. Always assuming, of course, that this isn't Hell and that I *am* out of it. That's Mephistopheles, you know." She felt slightly ashamed of showing off, especially as she'd only seen the *Dr. Faustus* movie with Richard Burton, way back in the days when she'd had the falling habit herself. At least she'd always had her own TV in those days; the only way to keep a TV was to have a bloke around who could nick someone else's when your own got burgled. Sometimes, she wondered whether there were any real victims any more, or whether there was just a vast population of knocked-off TVs that were kept constantly in circulation by the beating heart of larcenous intent. The ones that kept reappearing in the sitting room certainly hadn't come from Comet.

"I don't know anything about Hell," the angel said, stuffily, "but I know this isn't it."

Molly could see that it was going to be hard work getting any more out of him. She was half-inclined to drop it and go back to ignoring him, just like everybody else. Hadn't she already told herself that it was the sensible thing to do? But she couldn't rid herself of the nagging suspicion that even if Elvis hadn't been what she needed to get year zero off to a flying start, the angel might be.

"If you're not going to drink that tea," she said, in the end, "you might as well give it here and sod off."

8

There was a long pause while the angel considered his options. In the end, he decided not to give her the tea. He forced himself to drink. After two or three further sips, he seemed to get used to the sweetness. The colour of his eyes was like a sky looking down on someplace as far away as Molly could imagine—and she was not an unimaginative person.

"Well," Molly said, even though she knew it would make her sound like a social worker, "if it's nectar you want, you'll have to get up again, won't you? It's the only way to get over the falling habit—believe me, I know. Stick around here, and it isn't just the tea that will go from bad to worse. It won't be just a matter of losing the wings and your raincoat turning into something a flasher would be ashamed to open up. I saw what happened to Elvis when the serum got to work, and it wasn't a pretty sight." She figured that it was safe to mention Elvis to the angel. If you couldn't trust an angel not to shop you to the moral guardians of society, who could you trust?

The angel still didn't reply. He was now so deeply absorbed in the tea that he was at risk of becoming obsessed, and Molly began to wonder whether it had really been a kindness to tell him to sweeten it. Fortunately, she was spared the temptation to offer him a sausage or a bit of fried bread. She'd been hungry. Conversation always gave her an appetite—*real* conversation, that is, not the kind of chatting that the women in the B&B went in for.

"Of course," she said, figuring that if she were going to come on like a social worker she might as well go the whole hog, "you have to *want* to get up again. Nobody can help you if you won't be helped. Maybe you'd be happier down here on Earth. There's not much to recommend it, I suppose, but we do have *time*—all the time in the world. Places too, though rumour has it they're not as various as they used to be. Look, you're not exactly making this easy for me, are you? I mean, I'm trying to do you a *good turn* here. Who knows—this may be my last chance to qualify for Heaven? You could at least pretend that you're interested. Think of it as an episode of 'Touched by a Human.' I can only do so much—at the end of the day, it's up to you."

"Yes," he said, betraying a hint of positivity for the first time. "I can see that. But it's hard for me too."

The tone of his voice melted her heart all over again. The words *I fell* echoed in her mind, and echoed and echoed.

"It's okay," she said. "If you guys really did teach us the fundamentals of technology and civilization, we owe you one. Like they say in America, if you can't pay back, pay forward. Between the two of us, we'll get it figured out. You lucked out—hardly anyone around here spends more time in the library than me, and I don't just *pretend* to read. You can come back to the B&B with me if you like, but you can't stay the night. It's the rules, and I can't afford to get chucked out, for the kids' sake." She was telling the truth about not pretending to read. She loved the **Penguin Dictionary of Quotations**, where Oscar Wilde had observed that it was better to be beautiful than good, but better to be good than ugly. If the beautiful angel wasn't going to cuddle her, she could at least pretend that it was her decision, her choice, her ruling.

"I understand," he said, although it wasn't at all clear what he understood—or was prepared to pretend that he understood, given that he probably didn't know anything at all about anything outside of a Heaven which wasn't a place and didn't even have time.

"Okay," she said. "Let's go."

The alkies didn't say a word when Molly and the angel walked past the old Salvation Army Temple, but that was probably because the cider had taken the edge off their wit. There was no sign of Saint Luke or his boozemobile but the down-and-outs had obviously experienced a visitation. They weren't as blissful as crackheads blessed by Saint John, but they weren't as mean as they were when they had hangovers.

There were five pre-schoolers playing on the stairs at the B&B, and a couple of the mums popped their heads out to make sure that the visitor wasn't an obvious child-molester, but neither passed any comment on the unlikelihood of Molly keeping company with an angel. They just stared, with eyes the colour of dirty dishwater—eyes incapable of reflecting anything but the dullest winter sky.

The angel was appropriately impressed by the tidiness of Molly's room, although it represented a very modest victory over the forces of chaos. She'd moved the wardrobe to cover up the corner where the mould kept growing on the wall, and she'd put the rug she'd salvaged from a skip over the shiny grease-patch on the carpet. The bed was made and there wasn't a single item of clothing draped over the back of the chair. Only the curtains were seriously disgusting, and she couldn't be expected to take *them* to the launderette. The angel didn't even glance at the curtains; a true representative of the Good, he let his eyes wander over the piles of books stacked—*almost* neatly—under the window, at the foot of the bed and all around the sink.

"Burglars never pinch books," she told him. "No point. And before you ask, I haven't read them all. I picked most of them up going through the boxes people leave at the side when the recycling bin gets too full, and I always figure it's better to take the ones that you might never get around to reading than leave anything you might regret not having picked up when you run out of ones you're actually keen on. Anyway, big thick paperbacks make bloody good draught-excluders."

The angel turned to look at her, more appraisingly than before. Molly was alarmed to note that the summer sky had already begin to fade from his eyes. At what point, she wondered, would he pass the point of no return? And what would happen to him then? Would he have to fight just to hang on to human status? *Could* he hang on to human status, if that became his fallback position, or would he just keep on sliding, all the way to Lucifer and Hell?

When the angel sat down on the bed, slumping like Annie after a bad abduction experience or Francine after an extra-generous hit, Molly knew that she had her work cut out, but it was too late to complain. She'd already accepted the responsibility.

Maybe, she thought, this was the best way to make a new start—not by grabbing something new for yourself but by doing something new for someone else. Maybe, in the great cosmic scheme of things, you were supposed to build up a little moral credit before you could get the go-ahead to turn your own life around. If so, this was going to even more imagination and ingenuity than letting Elvis down gently.

9

"I suppose you've tried praying?" Molly said, dispiritedly.

"I've *tried*," the angel said, "but I seem to have lost the knack." He looked up at her with his wonderful blue eyes, as if he were expecting a sympathetic pat on the head. Molly had to resist the temptation to join him. Now that he'd taken his raincoat off, his relatively unspoiled suit made him look way too good for this kind of environment, and she couldn't bear the prospect of seeing him flinch and move away if her cellulite should accidentally come into contact with his thigh.

"I think I tried it myself once," she said. "Way back when. It didn't do any good, even though I was still a virgin and didn't understand the chorus of *Ebenezer Good*. Maybe I couldn't take it seriously enough—but lack of faith is one problem *you* shouldn't have. I suppose there's no point in asking what God's like. He's not *like* anything, is he? He just *is*."

"That's right," said the angel.

"Thought so. You haven't a fucking clue, have you? Down here, you're completely out of your depth."

Because she was looking him right in the eye she saw the colour weaken when she pronounced the obscenity, and was stricken by the terrible thought that if this *was* a test, she must be more than half way to failing by now whether she stooped to further obscenity or not. She was suddenly struck by a sense of awkward urgency. This was Earth, after all, and time was of the essence here. The angel probably couldn't stand much more exposure to the forces of change and decay—and as soon as she'd condescended to notice his presence in the world she'd become time's accomplice, aiding and abetting its patient assault on his divinity. If she wasn't part of the solution, she was part of the problem. She couldn't just wash her hands of this one.

As that revelation roughly took hold of her, Molly felt that she would have given anything in the world for the answer to the angel's problem to be easy. Love would have been *so* easy, but she already knew that it wasn't even worth a try. She knew beyond the shadow of a doubt that if she could only get the angel to take the least little bit of pleasure in her, she could do it with love and not just with lust, but she also knew far better than he did—with luck, far better than he ever would—where the limitations of reality lay.

It had been easier by far with Elvis. Elvis, immortality serum or no immortality serum, had already been finished. The angel, God bless him, hadn't even started. No matter what his timeless experience in Heaven had been like, and no matter what it was that had caused God to knock him down, the angel hadn't even begun. Molly supposed that you had to get used to being in time before you could get to grips with beginning, and that the angel simply hadn't had long enough, or help enough, even to think about what it would *mean* to pull himself back together.

"Well," she said, slightly startled by the desperation in her voice, "there are a few more things that aren't even worth trying. I think we can take it for granted that Prozac isn't the answer in this particular case, and Freudian analysis wouldn't get us anywhere even if we had the time. We need a fix that's quick, but one that isn't chemical." She nearly added *and doesn't involve fucking* but she caught herself in time. She didn't want to labour the point, or deepen the blue of his eyes any further than it was already deepened. Hastily, she added: "It might help if you could bring yourself to tell me exactly why you stand in need of absolution." No sooner had she said it, however, than she jumped to the conclusion that it probably wouldn't.

"I fell," said the angel, yet again.

There was nothing in the least infuriating about the repetition, because the pathos wrapped up in the remark was still undergoing a stage-by-stage metamorphosis that had not yet reached its heart-rending end.

That had to be the key, Molly thought. That had to be the vital clue, the vital cue, the vital Q to which she was required to find the A.

"I'm stupid, aren't I?" Molly whispered. "You keep telling me what the matter is, and I just keep missing it. I keep getting hung up on the questions that don't have any answers, like where you fell from and what made you fall, but the real point is that you're *still falling,* faster and faster, into time and into place and into the vortex of creation. Of course you don't know *why,* because there is no *why* in Heaven. All the worldly whys are in Hell, aren't they? Every last one."

"I don't know," said the angel, proving her point.

Molly realised that when she had first seen the angel he had been over six feet tall. Even in the library he'd topped five-seven, but now he was no taller than she was. In a matter of hours, he'd be no bigger than a child, but he'd still be too old to grow wings and fly, even in his imagination—and her presence was making it worse. Her nearness was accelerating the process. She was a carrier of time and place, and she was furthering the angel's infection with every breath she took, but she knew that it wouldn't do any good at all to send him back out on to the street. There were five billion people in the great wide world, and they had thousands of years of history in them, and the people closest to hand were as riddled and

50

raddled with contagion as all the rest.

In spite of her resolution, Molly sat down on the bed, next to the angel. He didn't reach out to her, but at least he didn't move away. He wasn't afraid.

She closed her eyes, as if she were a little girl confronted with a birthday cake or some other everyday prodigy, who had to close her eyes to make a wish if she were to stand any chance at all of making it come true.

"I'll tell you a funny thing about the human brain, Mr. Angel," she said, speaking out of the darkness. "There are any number of ways to jolt it out of everyday misery, and all of them work for a while, but you can never get more than the merest delusory glimpse of Heaven. If you do something like heroin the brain just stops producing happy chemicals of its own, so when you try to give it up you just go crazy. It's different with Es and acid, but not so very different. Whatever the stuff gives you, you stop giving yourself, and when you stop doing the stuff because the effect's worn thin, you've lost it. People think it's just drugs, but it isn't. It's the same with everything you do that allows you to grasp the merest atom of delight. Fucking, dreaming, reading, kids . . . everything. Whatever gets you an inch nearer to Heaven only tantalises once or twice, and then it starts to become as ordinary as anything else, and leaves you without the ability to do it for yourself if you don't get the fix—and if you can't handle that, you just go crazy.

"I don't have the slightest idea what Heaven is really like, Mr. Angel, and I can't tell you anything about Hell, but I can tell you this: if you intend to stay here, you have to be able to handle it without going crazy. You have to realise that everything you try, everything you do, and everything you think of will only seem to work once or twice, and that the best you can hope for afterwards is that things will stay *ordinary*. If you can't help going crazy, everything you think and feel and do thereafter will be a matter of trying to get back to the beginning, of trying to hold on without shrinking any further and losing any more—because time leads nowhere except death, and you just have to learn to handle that, and get what you can out of a world without a Heaven. If you came here thinking that time heals, forget it, because time *wastes*. If you came here looking for a place to be, you shouldn't have bothered, because there's no place like home—and I don't mean that there's no place *like* home, I mean that there's *no place* even remotely like what you'd really like to think of as *home,* but you have to get used to that and make do with what there is, one way or another. You just have to *get used* to it, and *make do with what there is,* or else you get crazier and crazier and crazier until there's nothing left at all. Down here, you have to accept things as they are if you want to make a new start, because there's no other way to *begin.* Even in year zero, you have to see things as they are. There's no other way, except to oblivion.

"So if I were you, Mr. Angel, I'd stop fucking around down here where you don't belong and go back where you came from, where you don't have any time to waste or any place to call anything. It doesn't matter how or why you fell —what you have to do is get up again, while you still can. If you don't, you'll become just as human as the rest of us, and the only way to get up will be the hard way. That's the choice: either you get back up, *right now,* or you stay here and rot. Just *do it.* I know it's the most difficult thing in the world, but that's all there is to it, and all there can be to it. It's what all of us have to do, one way or another. I'm going to open my eyes now, *and I want to see you gone.*"

Molly knew, even before she opened her eyes, that the angel would be gone, and so he was—because he was still an angel, even if his wings had gone into hiding. She had pronounced far too many obscenities to sustain the sky in his eyes. She had shown him darkness, and she had scared him as shitless as only an entity who didn't need food *as such* could be.

She wished that someone had done as much for her, way back when, although she knew perfectly well that she wouldn't have been able to take it in. Whatever else she'd been, she was no angel—but whatever she'd been, this was year zero and she was now the kind of person who could touch an angel and do him a good turn. She had to be. There wasn't any other option left.

She also knew, though, even before she got down to the serious business of planning the rest of her day, that she would probably never know *for sure* whether she had passed the test, if it actually had been a test, or whether the angel really had decided to go back to the place from which he had fallen instead of all the way to Hell. In her experience, people mostly did go back to the place from which they had fallen, if they only could—and she now had no good reason to suppose that angels were any different—but sometimes, like little anorectic Annie, they simply couldn't.

That was why, when people like her said, "I fell," it was hardly ever a lie—but that was why people like her who still had it in them to get up again did get up, even though they had no way to do it but the hard way.

10

When the silver light first came creeping through Molly's window at half past midnight, she naturally assumed that it was a sign from Heaven, to reassure her that the angel had got home.

When the duvet slid away and she rose into the air, levitated three feet above the dirty sheet, she took it for a miracle. Even when she floated out of the window, which had opened of its own accord in spite of the fact that the sash was nailed shut, she wasn't in the least anxious. Not that she'd expected any kind of recompense for helping the angel out, of course; she'd had far too much experience of life to expect that virtue would ever be rewarded, even in Heaven.

When she saw the slowly-rotating saucer-shaped UFO hovering above the B&B, however, she realised that Heaven had nothing to do with it. It was just another bloody abduction. Francine, who seemed to have got so far into the habit of pinching everything Annie had that even Annie's death hadn't stopped her, had been telling anyone who would listen about her own abduction experience for a fortnight.

Like everyone else, Molly had assumed that Annie and Francine were out of their minds—and Francine's highly-coloured protestations about what the men in black had done to her after her return to Earth had made that conclusion seem perfectly secure—but now that she was actually being sucked up into the belly of the saucer, she had to concede that maybe Annie and Francine had been entitled to get excited.

Oh well, she thought, as the aperture closed soundlessly behind her, *I might not have had as much recent practice as Francine, but once you've been on the game you never lose the knack. There's nothing so very terrible about a rectal probe.* She was just trying to put a brave face on it; Molly hadn't forgotten that Annie had carted off to the hospital only a couple of days after her last abduction experience, when her HIV finally went full-blown. Annie had been dead within a week, having already shed most of her flesh and all of her resistance. Opinions in the B&B had varied as to whether the UFO or the world was to blame; Molly had come down on the side of the world.

The advantage Molly had over Annie and Francine was that she'd had the chance to hear both their stories several times over. The salient details had been traced and retraced so often that she knew exactly what the score was. When the little silver guys with the big almond eyes came to peer down at her, she just smiled and said "Hi," and when the cold probe went up her arse she didn't bat an eyelid. She didn't gag when they slipped the wriggly things into her more accommodating orifices and she didn't writhe when they attached the electrodes to her scalp. If she hadn't been incapable of speech by that time, she might even have apologised for the fact that her brain had been worked over by all the LSD and Es she'd done while she was heavily into the rave scene, but she knew they'd probably figure it out by themselves. If they didn't like it, they ought to go fishing in better neighbourhoods.

The only real surprise was that the aliens injected the biochip into her left breast instead of the nape of the neck, where Annie and Francine had got theirs. That was bound to cause embarrassment, if anybody demanded that Molly show them the sore spot. If Francine could be trusted, somebody would—but Molly knew that she'd have the option of playing dumb. For some reason she'd never quite been able to fathom, men usually believed her if she played dumb.

Forewarned being forearmed, Molly knew that she only had to wait until the examination was concluded, and that she'd be returned to her bed safe and sound. According to Francine, who'd spent hours on the abductee helpline, only one subject in five got recalled for a more extensive examination, and six or eight months was a more common interval than the six days they'd allowed her and Annie. The silvery guys obviously had a heavy schedule—as you'd expect, if they were really trying to catalogue the whole human race before reporting back to Epsilon Eridani IV or Tau Ceti II, or wherever.

Molly estimated that the whole thing took about an hour, although she knew that her time-sense might have been cunningly distorted. The aliens could do that, according to the abductee helpline. On the basis of her research, Francine had assured Molly that the aliens were easily capable of ensuring that people would forget the whole experience, or remember it only fleetingly, as a dream, but that they'd stopped bothering since hypnotists had found a sure way to penetrate their deceptions.

"The reason I can remember it so very clearly," Francine had assured Molly a dozen times over, as well as everyone else who'd listen, "is that I'm an abnormally sensitive person. If I'd been able to get my regular fix I'd have breezed through the whole thing, but it's been slow out on the street since the local trainspotters started taking plate-numbers."

Molly had never thought of herself as an abnormally sensitive person, so she half-expected to have forgotten the entire business by the time she woke up again, but she must have underestimated herself, because she remembered every last detail.

Unlike Annie and Francine, of course, Molly would never have breathed a word to a living soul voluntarily. Unfortunately, she wasn't given that opportunity. She hardly had time to get her knickers on before the men in black came knocking at the door.

Molly knew that it had to be Francine who'd ratted her out. Francine was the only one in the B&B who kept her eyes resolutely fixed on the sky when she couldn't roust up any business, and the only one who had the phone number of Croydon's equivalent of Area 51. Francine was also the only one whose door didn't open, even by a crack, when the men in black started banging on Molly's door, proclaiming loudly that they were from the DSS Investigations Department. They obviously hadn't the faintest idea how to go about building a viable cover; everybody in the B&B knew the faces and inside leg measurements of the local DSS's ball-bearing secret agents, and everybody knew that civil servants couldn't arrest anybody who refused to be arrested, unless they had a warrant.

It wouldn't have been so bad if the men in black had looked like Will Smith and Tommy Lee Jones, but these were *British* men in black, and they had a thoroughly British idea of who the scum of the universe were. They had probably been to public school, although that didn't excuse the moustaches and the pin-striped ties. The senior man's moustache was a pencil-thin thing that would have suggested queerness if he hadn't been so obviously interested by the sight of the bare flesh above and below Molly's knickers; his junior had a bushier one whose lop-sidedness suggested that he hadn't quite mastered the art and science of Bic topiary.

From the moment the senior man bundled her into the back of the black Rover 2000, copping a feel of her bum in the process, Molly was absolutely determined not to co-operate.

She knew that it would be useless to deny everything, and risky to be economical with the truth, but it was a matter of principle. If they used truth serum there was every chance that they'd find out about Elvis and the secret experiments in rejuvenation, but Molly figured that they probably knew about that anyway. They wouldn't be interested in the angel.

11

Once they were under way, driving south at a very respectable speed—because all the commuter traffic was heading the other way—the man with the pencil moustache said: "I'm afraid that I had to lie to you back there. I'm not from the DSS, and you've no need to worry about your benefits."

"You don't say," Molly replied, insouciantly. "Wow, you really had me fooled. I'm so stupid. Francine only told me about your last visit seventeen times, and even from here I can tell that she was entirely mistaken about the pin-sized prick. Her sense of proportion goes right out the window when she's full of dope—so to speak."

"I can understand your being annoyed," the man in black admitted, his voice becoming even more treacly although he must have figured out that he was being subtly insulted, "but this is a matter of national security. More than that—the future of the entire human race might be at stake."

Thanks to her brief encounter with the angel, Molly knew that the virtuous members of the human race didn't actually have a future *as such,* on account of there being no time in Heaven, but she wasn't about to tell that to the man with the pencil moustache. Her first priority, she figured, was to avoid the possibility that they'd do an amateur mastectomy in order to recover the biochip. Her tits might not be her best feature, but she didn't like the idea of not having a matching pair.

"Well," Molly said, defensively, "I expect you've heard it all before. Haven't we all? Unfortunately, it's all a bit vague. Big round thing with lights around the rim, slowly rotating.

59

Beam of light comes down, then I'm floating up into the belly of it—rather like being born, only backwards. Little guys with big eyes staring at me all the time. The memory's fading already, to tell you the truth. If you hadn't come for me, I'd probably have thought that it was all a dream, courtesy of a dodgy kebab and Francine's fairy tales."

"It was no dream, Molly," the man with the pin-striped tie assured her, "and Francine's story was no fairy tale. We've known about the aliens since Woking in 1897, although the bloody Americans wouldn't take a blind bit of notice for fifty years, until they got a crasher of their own. They even accused us of faking the autopsy record, just because we hadn't got it on film. Who were we supposed to get in—Georges Melies?"

"Is *that* how it's pronounced?" Molly said, trying to sound irredeemably dopey. "Well, I wish I could help, but it's all *very* hazy. They probably drugged me. I'm really not sure how much of it really happened and how much was just suggestion, from hearing Francine's story over and over and over and . . ."

"I understand," said the man in black, hurriedly. "It's not uncommon for abductees to be disorientated. We can put you under hypnosis, if that will help."

"They tried that last time I was in the Maudsley for treatment," Molly told him, blandly. "The hypnotist was very nice. He specialized in breast enlargements, I think, when he wasn't doing his bit in the bin. I was a *terrible* subject. He said that I was constitutionally unable to relax because of what speed and ecstasy had done to my nerve-ends. I'm sorry, but I really don't think I'll be any use to you."

"Are you a regular drug-user?" the man in black inquired, in the slightly defeated manner of a dedicated seeker after truth confronted with the witness from Hell.

"I had to give it up a couple of years ago," Molly admitted. "The doc told me that if I carried on, I wouldn't have enough self-control left to keep from wetting the bed at night. I'm straight now, apart from the Prozac and the tranks—but I'd rather you didn't tell anyone about the tranks. I buy them over the counter at Boots, pretending they're for an allergy. Not that I'm not allergic, you understand—it's just that the allergy's not the real reason I buy the tabs. Did you know that all the best antihistamines are also major tranks, on account of being chlorpromazine derivatives?"

"No," said the secret agent, glumly. "I didn't."

"I'm afraid I won't be *nearly* as much use to you as Francine was," Molly said, with a sigh. "She's so much younger than I am, and she gets out so much more. Isn't it a pity the aliens never abduct intelligent people like you?"

That was a step too far. Molly knew from bitter experience that even civil servants could spot a wind up eventually, and that they never liked having the piss taken out of them, presumably because they were too tight-arsed to have any to spare.

"Don't mess us about, Molly," her interrogator growled, still using her first name because he wanted her to think that they knew *everything* about her, although all they really knew was where she lived. "This is serious. The greys have been watching us for more than a hundred years, and we have reason to believe that they're about to move to the next phase of their plan."

"They seemed more silver than grey, actually," Molly observed.

"Only when the light's bright," he countered. "We suspect that they're worried. We think they've been expecting us to wipe ourselves out for the last fifty years, but now that the collapse of communism has reduced the probability of nuclear war to one in a million they might be considering direct action. We think they might be preparing to use what they've learned about human physiology to engineer a doomsday bug. That's probably why they've stepped up the anatomy lessons lately. We think AIDS might have been a trial run, maybe even a failed attempt."

The Rover turned into an underground car park beneath what looked for all the world like any other Croydon office-block. You had to give *some* credit to British Military Intelligence, Molly reflected. The stupid Yanks had built a huge fenced compound in the middle of the Arizona desert, where it was bound to stick out like a sore thumb from any viewpoint in orbit, but anyone looking at *this* place from any angle whatsoever wouldn't be able to distinguish it from your average bog-standard insurance company. If only the spies inside could keep a little more closely in touch with the manners and mores of real DSS personnel, the set-up would be perfect.

Unfortunately, the room they took her to wasn't nearly as cosy or as user-friendly as an actuary's office. It might have been mistaken for a hospital operating theatre, except for the disquieting fact that the straps they used to secure her to the table after they'd stripped her were thicker and tighter than the ones in Torquemadam's Berwick Street Boudoir, where Molly had once done a demanding but fairly rewarding stint of dressing-up and domination.

The men in black had enough sensitivity to bring in female officers to search her teeth for new cavities and her cavities for new teeth, but that didn't make Molly feel any better about the ordeal. They put lead-lensed spectacles over her eyes while they X-rayed her head, but they didn't take any noticeable precautions lower down. They vamped a whole half-pint of blood and various other fluid samples, but so far as she could tell they didn't find the biochip. One of the female officers was kind enough to replace the filling that she had accidentally knocked out of one of Molly's molars, carefully and without any fuss, but the rest of the procedure seemed distinctly lacking in respect for her person.

When they were finished, they put a thin sheet over her, but she still felt awkwardly naked underneath it. She tried to go to sleep, but they weren't quite ready to let up yet.

12

When the two men with moustaches continued with the interrogation they read the questions from a series of forms, running through them at the double with quasi-military precision. There was nothing on the list about Elvis or angels, and if they had sneaked any truth serum into her veins it was obviously from a dud batch. She shaped her answers to give the impression that she was an unobservant, unintelligent and thoroughly confused person, but couldn't help feeling just a little annoyed by the ease with which the ruse succeeded.

"You didn't have to keep me strapped down once you'd taken the X-rays," Molly complained, when they finally set her wrists and ankles free and allowed her to gather the sheet around herself. "I could have answered the questions perfectly well while I was massaging my pins and needles."

"It's just routine," the man with the pencil moustache assured her. Like Molly he was putting on an act, but unlike Molly he wasn't succeeding. He was too transparent to persuade anyone with half a brain that he wasn't the kind of person to be stimulated by the process of strapping a woman down and tormenting her.

"We're truly sorry for the inconvenience, Molly," the agent went on, heaping lie upon lie, "but we need to figure out exactly what the greys did to you if we're to have any chance of finding out why. We're all in quarantine here until we're sure that you're not carrying any unknown viruses or prions. The important thing now is to think ahead. I suppose you know that they sometimes come back for a second look."

"Their procedures aren't exactly secret any more," Molly observed.

"On the contrary," the man in black replied. "The best place to hide a tree is in a forest, and the best place to hide the truth is in a mass of confused data. We think they let people like your friend Francine remember more precisely because they're irredeemable gossips and congenital liars. They favour trailer trash in the States for exactly the same reason. But we're just as clever as they are, because we know that they make the occasional mistake and we know that whenever they lift somebody with a little bit more common sense it gives us an opportunity. The question is, Molly, are *you* one of those people? Are you the kind of person who could help us—not just by tipping us off next time you catch a glimpse of them at work, but by keeping your wits about you if they come back? Can you probe them while they're probing you?" He didn't sound hopeful. He might as well have been reading off his crib-sheet.

Well, Molly thought, *I'm not doing such a bad job of probing you while you're probing me.* All she said aloud was: "I could try." She tried to sound woefully unconvincing, and she could tell that he took the bait—but there was still a gleam in his eye. Molly knew better than to be flattered by that. It wasn't her faded beauty that had turned him on.

"Okay, Molly," he said, brimming over with false generosity. "Consider yourself recruited. If they come back—and I say *if* because the odds are they won't, so you shouldn't worry too much—it would be a really good idea if you were to make a proper study of your surroundings. Forget the big staring eyes and try to concentrate on the walls and the equipment. Try to memorise any symbols you see. It'll be hard, because they don't write in any script you'll ever have seen, but if you can make accurate drawings of any symbols you see that'll be a great help. If they say anything to you—they probably won't, even if they do come back, but *if* they do—we'd really appreciate it of you could remember *exactly* what they say, even if it isn't in English. And if they put anything inside you, try to remember *exactly* where they put it. That's very important—it's nothing to worry about, but we do need to know."

"That's not going to be easy," Molly said, trying to imply that for someone like her all that remembering would be absolutely bloody impossible—although she was still offended by the ease with which he seemed to take the inference.

"You'll have to stay here for a while, until we get the report on the blood tests," he said. "Then I'll get someone to drop you at the station We'll even buy you a travelcard, to thank you for being so helpful. All zones."

"Wow," she said, faintly. "I can tell that *you* work for the government. The taxpayers' money provides you with a Rover, but all I get is a one-day travelcard."

He didn't laugh, and for a moment she thought she might have tipped him off as to her true state of mind, but then his avid eyes scanned her sheet-clad body again. "Is there anything I can do for you?" he asked, solicitously. "Anything you need?"

"Sleep," she said, firmly. "Lots and lots of sleep."

This time, they let her have it. It was a small enough victory, but a victory nevertheless.

The next day, when Molly returned to the B&B, she was told that Francine had been found dead in bed, having taken an overdose. There were, apparently, no suspicious circumstances. Molly had to agree with that judgment, albeit grudgingly. If ever there'd been a person likely to turn up dead in a

B&B bed having taken an overdose, it was Francine. It probably hadn't even been suicide, given that Francine was such a
dozy cow, although there wasn't any life insurance payout
hanging on the coroner's verdict. Francine's kids were still
with the foster-parents they'd gone to while Francine was last
inside, so there was relatively little mess to tidy up. Even a
non-paranoid person could have been forgiven, however, for
noticing the beginnings of a pattern. Little anorectic Annie:
abducted by aliens, then dead. Francine: abducted by aliens,
then dead. Molly: abducted by aliens . . .

Well, she thought, *there's bugger all I can do about it, even if
there's an angel in Heaven who owes me a favour.* She didn't
expect the favour to be returned. After all, Elvis might have
fallen head over heels in love with her, but he hadn't offered
to let her in on his immortality programme. Maybe that was
just as well, given the way the programme seemed to have
turned out, but it was the thought that would have counted.
It was a sad commentary on the deterioration of her looks
that no one had given her a better present than the man in
black's travelcard since she had turned thirty.

There was no funeral, as such, but when the formalities
had all been concluded and Francine's ashes had gone to
wherever unclaimed ashes usually went, Molly and the B&B
mums shared half a dozen bottles of cheap red that Julie had
bagged off the local white van man by way of commemorating
Francine's passing. Mercifully, Gloria the spitting schizo
wasn't around, although it was too much to hope that the
aliens had taken her too.

"At least we won't have to hear all that shit about being
abducted by aliens again," said Deirdre, when the drink had
overcome her inhibitions against speaking ill of the dead.

"Or that crap about men in black pretending to be DSS
investigators," added Julie, with a meaningful look at Molly.

"Everybody pretends to be DSS investigators nowadays," Molly said, airily. "They think it's an easier way to get into your knickers for free than pretending to be CID. What's the world coming to?"

"Rack and ruin," Julie admitted.

"*Crack* and ruin," Sheila improvised, cackling so hard she could hardly light her next cig.

"Completely fucked over," Greta agreed. "Or is that just us?"

13

Thanks to the wine, whose effects combined synergistically with her double doses of miscellaneous chlorpromazine derivatives and Prozac, Molly fell into a deeper sleep than was usual, and didn't even wake up when the aliens levitated her out of her bed and through the mysteriously-opened window. She would probably have slept through everything except the rectal probe if things had gone according to the same pattern as before, but they didn't. This time, the aliens took her to a different space, far less spare in its decorations and far less glaringly lit, and sat her down in a chair made out of something like foam rubber, which moulded itself to her contours and flowed right around her midriff.

"I am sorry," said one of the aliens, with a distinct west country accent and a slight lisp, "but we shall accelerate soon, and you will feel a force of four gravities for a few moments. You will be weightless thereafter. It is best that you are secure."

"Don't mind me," Molly said, sleepily. "I've been strapped into far worse contraptions than this." She didn't make the slightest attempt to study the hieroglyphic writing on the various green-glowing screens or the structure of the keyboard on which the alien's slender fingers were tapping —but the acceleration, when it came, pulled her back into the rubbery cradle with such horrid avidity that she thought her heart might give up. When the g-force vanished, she was extremely grateful.

"Bloody hell," she said, when she had drawn breath.

"Don't you lot have antigravity machines or anything?"

The grey—who really did look grey now that the light was more subdued, as the man in black had said—turned two vast night-black eyes to stare at her, in what seemed like a sorrowful manner.

"We are sorry about your friend," the grey said. "We were not responsible."

"Nobody said you were," Molly countered, warily.

"This whole project is getting out of hand," the alien observed, mournfully. "*O what a tangled web we weave, when first we practise to deceive!* I love Scott, don't you? Poetry appreciation is the only way to really get to grips with an alien language."

Molly thought that if the greys had really got to grips with English they wouldn't split infinitives, and would probably recognise brave Sir Walter for the doggerel-merchant he was, but she supposed that a certain unrefinement of taste was one of the penalties of dealing with the kind of people they usually dealt with.

"I suppose you know that the men in black have had me in," she said, cautiously. "They frisked me for viruses, but I don't think they found the biochip in my tit."

"Of course we know. We heard every word you said, and monitored every hormonal nuance of your psychosomatic response. We were grateful for your principled discretion. It's not every day we implant someone with your fine qualities."

"Maybe you should go hunting in more upmarket territory," Molly said.

"We used to," was the sad reply. "You humans have no idea how duplicitous your high-status individuals are."

"Oh, I think we have a pretty fair idea," Molly said. "Oxford and Cambridge were no good, then? I can believe that the entire population of Islington and Hampstead is way up the top end of the hypocrisy scale, but what about the Isle of Wight or Poole? Come on—there must be some nice people in *Poole.*"

"Nice," said the alien, dolefully, "is not our number one criterion."

Molly thought about that for a moment. She had never been one to harbour delusions of grandeur, even if she had been the last true love of Elvis's protracted life and the kind of person who could talk a fallen angel into getting right back up into the heavenly saddle, so she couldn't quite bring herself to believe that of all the people the aliens had abducted during the last 103 years she was the most worthy.

"What, exactly, do you want from me?" she asked, mildly.

"Actually," said the alien, "we'd like some advice. We feel that our presence here has become a little too confrontational, and we're not sure how—or even whether—we ought to continue the mission."

"Considering the way you've been carrying on so far," Molly said, figuring that if the biochip had her innards under such careful observation that they could read the testimony of her hormones there was no point in pussyfooting around, "I'm astonished that it's taken you so long to get self-critical."

"Oddly enough," said the grey, "that's exactly what we think about humans."

"I'll give you that one," Molly conceded, gracefully. "So —what *is* your mission, exactly?"

"Basically," said the grey, "we're trying to figure out who we'd like to be. We've been living a gypsyish kind of existence ever since our own ecosphere had a purple fit and reverted to cyanobacterial slime. We have the technology to nudge it back to complexity, of course, but there doesn't seem to be much point in simply recapitulating the same evolutionary sequence as before. It's not so much that we worry about making the same mistakes again as the feeling that if we just put things back exactly the way they were, we'd be deeply boring individuals. Wiser, of course—but somewhat stuck in a rut."

"Been there, done that, ripped off the t-shirt," Molly put in, helpfully.

"That's about the size of it," agreed the diminutive alien. "We figure that reconstituting the ecosphere should be a learning experience, existentially speaking. We can genetically engineer ourselves, of course, to be more or less any kind of humanoid, within reason, but it's difficult to choose. There do seem to be some advantages to the human model, provided that we could ratchet up the rationality by a couple of orders of magnitude, but we have to be careful. It's a big decision, after all, and even with our technology it's going to take a couple of million years to get our ecosphere back into good shape. We wouldn't want to get half way through and then decide that we'd rather be more like the Cetians or the Eridanians. We've been hanging around Earth for a long time now, waiting for all the wars to finish, so that we could find out what human life is like when things are going *well*, but to tell you the truth, we're a little disappointed. Some of us have begun to suspect that the human model is so utterly fucked up, hind-brainwise, that even a massive dose of rationality couldn't get it to a tolerable state of being. I know it smacks of desperation, given that you can hardly be objective, but we wondered whether *you* might have any thoughts on the matter."

Molly resisted the temptation to be flattered. She knew that it wasn't the quality of her mind that had enticed them to pick her as their agony aunt. They had picked her because she had been there, done that and ripped off the t-shirt, in more

ways than one. She was an also-ran in the human race: someone who had never been blinkered by privilege and had there-
fore got down to the existential nitty-gritty.

"Well," she said, very carefully indeed. "I'd have to think
about that. I wouldn't like to make an uninformed decision.
It would need a certain amount of research and analysis."

"That's a sensible approach," the grey conceded. "We
could help with that, if you'd be interested. We're on our way
to the mothership right now, as it happens—we had to move
it from the other side of the moon once Apollo got under way.
You won't be able to make any sense of the library, but there
are a dozen of us who speak reasonably good English. Mostly
American English, I fear—but I spent a couple of years
undercover in Devon."

Molly felt that it would be undiplomatic to mention the
beast of Bodmin. She was concentrating very hard on the task
of playing her cards *exactly* right.

"That would be a start," she conceded. "But there has to
be an element of give and take here. I'm not an ungenerous
person, as you presumably know, but what you're offering me
is, in essence, a *business proposition*. If I'm to help you out, I'll
need your full co-operation—and fair compensation."

"I quite agree," said the alien. "You work out exactly what
it is you want, and we'll see what we can do."

It was the offer Molly had been waiting for all her life. She
could hardly contain her excitement. She reached out a hand
to touch the grey on the shoulder. The skin was soft, not rep-
tilian at all, and in spite of the dim lighting she knew that it
was silver through and through, and that within the slender
torso there beat a heart of pure gold.

"Is there anything I can get you?" the alien asked, uncertainly. "Anything you need?"

"You have no idea how much," she answered.

14

Molly hadn't been back in her room for five minutes when the men in black kicked the door down and leapt through the opening. The one who'd interrogated her before had an automatic pistol in his right hand, and his sidekick was waving a pump-action shotgun.

When they found that she was alone in the room and that the window was nailed shut again they cursed, although they could hardly have been surprised. Molly could see Julie and Greta out in the corridor, mouths open to complain about the noise—but when they saw the men in black, the protests died on their lips. Gloria the spitting schizo wasn't so reticent; she went for the guy with the pump-action shotgun like a rottweiler on PCP. Things were seriously hairy for a few minutes, but the gunman had sufficient diplomatic flair to use the barrel of the gun to beat Gloria senseless rather than splattering her guts all over the wall.

By the time the senior man had pulled himself together, smoothed his tie with the barrel of his gun and turned to Molly with what he hoped was a winning smile, his cover was well and truly blown. Everybody knew that DSS employees had to go through courtesy training to make sure that they never used phrases like *motherfucking bug-eyed monsters,* whether they were talking about clients or not. His companion stared at Julie and Greta, intimidating them into a hasty retreat in spite of the lop-sidedness of his moustache.

"Thank God you're all right, Molly," said the man with the pencil moustache. "We were very worried about you.

When the tracking device we planted in your tooth told us that you were heading for the upper atmosphere, we thought you were a goner—and when it conked out five seconds after the ET told you that it was best to be secure we were sure you'd been rumbled as a spy."

"It was the sudden acceleration," Molly said, apologetically. "I guess I bit down a bit too hard."

They hustled her down to the car, looking daggers at the curious eyes peeping through the ground-floor doors. Molly favoured Sheila's kids with a little wave, figuring that it was the only goodbye she'd have the chance to offer.

The men in black continued to wave their guns around as they loaded up the car, and made a big show of making sure they weren't being followed as the Rover darted off into the night.

"The greys are gone," Molly assured the man beside her.

"I know that," he replied, gruffly. "It's the Americans I'm worried about. They always eavesdrop on our bugs, and none of *theirs* have been taken to the mothership for at least a couple of years. If they saw a chance to debrief you before us . . . well, let's just say that they aren't *gentlemen*."

"I don't know," Molly said. "Back in the days when I was supporting a habit, their tourists seemed to be a lot less interested in weird stuff than your average Old Harrovian—but I suppose I only saw the cream of the crop at King's Cross. The regulars on Jerry Springer don't have passports, do they?"

"You'd better concentrate on keeping your memories in focus, Molly," he told her, with a slight edge of menace in his voice. "It's going to be a long night."

He meant it, too. There was only a couple of hours to go before dawn, but by that time Molly was banged up in a windowless and mirror-walled room, flat out on a table that was just as liberally equipped with straps as the one she'd been on before. She'd been stripped again, then lackadaisically draped in a hospital gown that certainly wasn't fresh from the laundry. The "long night" went on all through the next day, and didn't come to an end until the day after that, by which time the female officers had delved a lot deeper into her than was strictly necessary to recover the biochip from her breast. They'd injected her several times and had vamped a full pint of blood. This time, the formularized interrogation was carried out in parallel with the physical, and eventually extended far beyond the scope of the printed questions.

"I'm truly sorry about all that, Molly," the man with the moustache assured her, when his colleagues had finally called a halt, cleaned her up, given her something for the pain and tucked her up in a clean and comfortable bed in a room with a nice bright window. "We didn't want to hurt you, but we couldn't use a general anaesthetic while we were still using the pentothal to question you. We didn't know that the aliens had the kind of technology necessary to scramble your mind like that. We didn't even know that they knew enough about us to make all that shit up. Elvis I can understand—nine out of every ten American abductees expect to meet Elvis, and three come back convinced that they did, but fallen angels from a Heaven where there isn't any time . . . Jesus, those guys are weird!"

"You know," said Molly, tiredly, "I'll bet you'd seem just as weird to them, if they could only get inside your head."

He laughed at that, but he was only trying to be clever. She already knew that he hadn't got a sense of humour—but he had taken off his tie. Obviously, he'd found that watching the interrogation from behind the mirror was rather tiring, although he didn't have a dull but insistent ache in a comprehensively fucked-up tit to remind him exactly how tough things had been at the sharp end.

"You knew where the biochip was all the time, didn't you?" she said.

"Of course we did," he told her. "We're not stupid. We just didn't want the greys to know that we knew, in case they came back for seconds. We figured that if it could do such a good job recording for them, it could do its bit for us too. Now that it's been somewhere none of our bugs ever came back from in working order, it's well worth our while to try to crack the code. Don't feel too bad about the way they fucked over your memories. You're still *compos mentis,* and you're not carrying any resident viruses you didn't have before, although I hope you'll forgive me for mentioning that you had rather more than your fair share before. We'll keep you under observation for a few days, but when you're well enough to leave you can put this behind you and move forward. The greys won't come back for you again—we're pretty sure about that, given that they must know that we have the biochip."

He wasn't sure about anything. He was just saying what he thought she wanted to hear.

"You know better than to repeat any of this outside, of course," he said. "You'd only be buying a ticket to the Maudsley, and you already know what *that*'s like. You might not like what we just did to you but I hope you're intelligent enough to understand why we had to do it. We're your friends, Molly, not your enemies—maybe the only friends you've got. I know what you're thinking—with friends like *those* and all that—but you have to get past that. It's us against them, Molly. Humans against aliens. We have to find out what they're up to, any way we can. You're a hero, Molly. Come the day we get rid of the nasty little buggers for good and all, you'll have played your part. Maybe we'll even be able to give you a medal. We can certainly give you a little better compensation than we gave you last time."

"Don't tell me," Molly said. "A second-class ticket to any-where in Network South-East."

"Better than that," he assured her. "Cash in hand. Enough to buy all the over-the-counter tranks you want, and then some—or a fully comprehensive detox, if that's what you'd prefer."

"I'm not really worth it," Molly observed, with heavy sarcasm. "I've been fucked too many times, in every orifice, to command a high price from decent men like you."

He looked at her sharply then, with naked suspicion. "Don't get smart, Molly," he said. "We know where you live. We'll *always* know where you live."

She wasn't stupid enough to parry that one. She had to let him think that he'd won for a little while longer.

"Are you feeling okay," he said, when he finally made ready to leave. "Is there anything you need?"

"Now that you come to mention it," she said, letting her tongue play momentarily upon her lips, "there is a little something you could do, if you really wouldn't mind."

15

The greys could have picked her up again any time after the first three weeks, but Molly wanted to make sure that she'd got the job done. She knew that the men in black would cotton on eventually, but she figured that it was worth keeping the ball rolling anyhow. The aliens didn't know how successful the men in black would be in extracting information from the captured biochip, because they didn't know how much the men in black already knew, so they hadn't been able to quantify the risk for her, but they'd assured her that if things *did* get sticky they could get her out in one piece. She trusted them.

When the Rover 2000 screeched to a halt beside her King's Cross pitch, she wasn't frightened. Indeed, she felt preternaturally calm as she totted up the days in her head, multiplied the days by seven, and multiplied the figure she got by a further fudge-factor in order to estimate the total number of people who'd so far been exposed. It wasn't huge, but it was big enough. London might no longer be *the* cultural and financial hub of the world, but a lot of wheels still turned around it.

The man with the pencil moustache bundled her into the back of the car and slammed the door behind him.

"You were supposed to be clean," he said, in a voice which had more terror in it than wrath. "We were all in quarantine till they told us you were clean. They *swore* you weren't carrying anything that hadn't shown up the first time, and that it was all common-or-garden shit. I thought it was odd that you'd gone back to the game, even though I never doubted for a moment that you were a slag through and through, but do you know what I told myself? I told myself that you were worried about the chunk we had to cut out of your tit. I told myself that you were anxious about still being *attractive*. But you *knew*, didn't you? You actually *knew*."

"You're the one who watched while they had me stark naked and strapped down, questioning me under pentothal," Molly pointed out. "Everything I know, you know."

"All that shit about Elvis and angels," he spat at her, as the wrath began to climb out of the terror. "It was all just *cover*."

"Oh no," said Molly, mildly. "That was all true. It was the plausible stuff that was the cover. Double bluff, you see— trees in forests, all that sort of thing."

"I was being *kind*," he yelled. "I was doing you a *favour*."

He actually seemed to believe it. He was enough of a public schoolboy to fool himself into thinking that he really hadn't fucked her for the sake of his own twisted power trip, but as an act of pure good-hearted charity. At least none of her more recent encounters had involved that level of self-deception.

"That's the difficulty, you see," she murmured. "How could they ever have decided, if they couldn't see us at our best? How could they ever have figured out what possibilities we had, unless they could get rid of all the crap that was obscuring the view? They didn't want to do it, because they're scientists at heart, and they have ethical as well as methodological reservations about observers interfering with the properties of that which is being observed, but it *was* the only way."

"It's going to kill us all, isn't it?" the man in black said, the fever of his paranoia having reached its final crisis. "AIDS was just the rehearsal, but this is the main event. How many people have you turned into carriers? They knew we'd already screened you for viruses and prions, so they just borrowed the protein coats from all the ones you were already carrying, and stuck new cargoes of DNA into every last one —and we fell for it. We took you in and we let you out, and we watched you go back on the fucking game, and we *were too fucking slow to figure it out*. You've helped them kill us all, haven't you?"

"Don't be silly," Molly said. "Why would I want to do that? Why would *anyone* want to do that? If they'd wanted the world, they'd have taken it a hundred years ago. You surely must have figured out that they wanted something much more difficult to obtain than *that*."

That took him aback, and a little of the wrath evaporated, along with a little of the terror. "You poor fool," he said, eventually. "They lied to you, didn't they? They lied to you, and you fell for it. No wonder they wanted someone like you —someone they could play for a sucker."

"No wonder," she agreed, mildly. "But you're not actually dead, are you, darling? You're not even dying, are you? Even when it's triggered you'll just feel a bit funny, hind-brainwise. It'll pass. Believe me, darling, it *will* pass, and you'll come out of it a much better person—so the greys say, and I'm inclined to trust them."

He groaned theatrically. He was evidently not a man much given to trust. It was probably the result of having spent his entire life immersed in various cultures of hypocrisy.

"Think of it as an adventure, if you can," Molly advised him. "I think you will be able to. Maybe not today, maybe not tomorrow, but one day. We have no idea what we might become, given the right sort of help—but it really will be wonderfully exciting. There are others like me, of course, on the other side of the Atlantic and the other side of the world. Not *exactly* the same, of course—been there, done that, didn't bother with the t-shirt—but fully-laden with similar cargoes. You may think you've been living in interesting times for the last forty years, Mister Man in Black, but you haven't seen the half of it yet, or even the tenth. Personally, I'm looking forward to it. They've assured me that nothing exciting will happen before I get back, so if it makes you feel any better, you can be certain that I'll be with you all the way. Wouldn't miss it for the world."

Perhaps the man in black was far enough gone to be getting past his panic, or perhaps it was his training reasserting itself. At any rate, he almost relaxed.

"What is it, if it's not the doomsday plague?" he asked, in the manner of a man who really wanted to know, and was at last prepared to listen.

"It's the stuff of saints and scientists," she said. "Vision. Ecstasy. Not the sort that fries your brain—more the sort that will bring it very gently to the boil, and simmer it till it's done. They couldn't promise that we'll love it—not all of us, at any rate—but they guaranteed that we sure as hell won't find it boring."

He wanted to know much more, and she would probably have been prepared to tell him, always provided that he'd asked politely, but as the Rover sped southwards over Vauxhall Bridge it was suddenly bathed in bright white light that poured down from above. The man in black knew exactly what *that* was.

"Don't worry," Molly said. "They haven't come for you. It's me they want."

"You were in on it all the way," the man in black whispered, as if he couldn't quite believe it even now. "You knew everything. You went along with it."

He didn't know the half of it. Molly might even have told

him that it had been *her* plan, not theirs, but he didn't give her the chance. The anger and the terror were making themselves felt again.

"I knew you were just a slag," the man with the pencil moustache went on, his voice rising in pitch as well as in volume, "but I didn't have you pegged as a traitor to the whole human race. What did they offer you, Molly? *What are they giving you in return?*"

"Just a travelcard," she said, as the window of the car wound down of its own accord and she floated out into the starry night. "They're on a tight budget too, and they've got a lot of work to do before they can trigger the psychological transmogrification of the human race—but their travelcard really is *all zones.*"

16

When Molly got back to the B&B after the aliens dropped her off, she found that her room had been let to a new tenant. She'd been gone five weeks, Earth time, although she'd only experienced two because of the relativistic effects of interstellar travel, and year zero was now almost half way through. She hadn't been any further than Altair, which was a lousy 15.7 light-years away, but the warp-drive had thrown a wobbly somewhere around Sirius B and the starship had got caught up in a sub-cee jam caused by a chronoclasm on the hyperspatial freeway. The landlord explained that ordinarily he'd have kept the room for her and carried on banking the giros, but that there'd been too many people looking for her to let him keep her absence a secret.

"What sort of people?" Molly asked.

"Y'social worker twice, the DSS—the *real* DSS, not the cowboys from Croydon—and a WPC. Askin' after y'daughter."

"Which one?" As far as Molly knew, both of her daughters were safe in the bosom of their oh-so-adorable foster family in Tooting.

"Dunno. Y'stuff's in two boxes in the cupboard under the stairs—what's left of it. Y'll need a car if y'goin' to shift them books, mind."

Molly told the landlord that she'd pick up the boxes when she could and hopped on a bus to the Social Services. She had to wait two hours before Elizabeth Peach could find a gap in her schedule, and the bad temper Molly had built up wasn't improved when the first thing the social worker said to her was: "Is that a *suntan?*"

If there was one thing social workers hated more than another it was finding out that their clients had been taking holidays, and Molly's current handler was an old timer whose last vestiges of conscience and goodwill had shrivelled after her divorce, five years before she ever clapped eyes on Molly. It would have been pointless to explain about the shortage of shade on 61 Cygni C VIII. In any case, Molly had always found that when dealing with the Social Services honesty was the second best policy, so the only reply she offered was: "No. What's up with the kids?"

"Christine's absconded," Mrs. Peach informed her. "We figured that she'd come probably looking for you, but we had to assume that if we couldn't find you, she couldn't either. That left us no alternative but to inform the police."

"Thanks a bunch," Molly said. "I suppose you know that I've lost my room at the B&B. Not that I'd have still been there, of course, if you'd kept the promise you made six months ago that as soon as you could find me a decent flat I'd be out of there—and then I'd have the girls back in no time."

"Well, that's all out of the window *now*," said Mrs. Peach. "We were trying so hard to find you, and for such a good reason, that one of the other women at the B&B mentioned something about travelcards and King's Cross. That wasn't in the contract, Molly. If you're back on the game that means you're back on the smack, and if . . ."

"I'm not," said Molly, shortly. "That's all over and done with. I've even kicked the Prozac. I'm clean as a whistle. I just need a place to live, and I can be a model mother." Molly could see that it wasn't going down well. It would only have made things worse to explain that the greys had sorted out her metabolism while they were repairing the mess the men in black had made of her left breast.

"It's not that easy," the social worker informed her, with an edge to her voice like a worn-out bread-knife. "All that's available is a thirteenth-floor flat in Arcadia House. It's not big enough for three, and even if it were, the case conference would have to address the question of whether Arcadia House is a fit environment. It might be a stepping-stone, but you'd have to stick it out longer than the last three tenants —none of them lasted a week."

Arcadia House was an authentic 1960s tower block, so old that it would have been in danger of becoming a listed building if it hadn't been so far down the list of sink estates as to be popularly known as "the Waste-Disposal Unit." In other circumstances, Molly might have preferred to sleep rough, but if she didn't have a solid address there was no way Christine would be able to find her if and when she decided to start looking.

"I'll take it," Molly said. When Mrs. Peach had made the call to the Housing Department, she added: "Could you possibly give me a lift with my stuff? There's a couple of boxes back at the B&B. The books and the frying-pan are a bit heavy."

She had to wait until Mrs. Peach came off shift, of course, but she got the lift she needed. Molly made sure that her old landlord knew exactly where she would be, in case anyone came calling. She used a red magic marker to write the flat number—1303—on the back of an old betting-slip and pinned it to the noticeboard beside the phone in the downstairs corridor.

"She might not come," the social worker said, once they were back in the car. "Did I mention that she'd been seen a couple of times with a man."

"A boy, you mean," said Molly. She had no need to ask

who had seen them. Christine's foster parents, Mr. and Mrs. Jarvis, took their pseudoparental duties very seriously indeed.

"No, a man. Two, actually, but not at the same time. One in his late twenties, maybe your age. The other about fifty, dressed in an old-fashioned trench-coat and a broad-brimmed felt hat. Ring any bells?"

Molly knew that Mrs. Peach was wondering about Christine's father, but whoever that had been was highly unlikely to have fitted either description sixteen years after the moment of her conception. Molly had to hope that if Christine had run off with anyone, it would be the younger one. The idea that she might have been entrapped by a comic-book child-molester was presumably the kind of paranoid fantasy which routinely haunted people like the Jarvises, but it certainly wasn't one that Molly wanted to entertain.

At Arcadia House even the OUT OF ORDER signs on the lifts were shrivelled by age and ill-use. Mercifully, Elizabeth Peach—who had been working out twice a week at her health club ever since the divorce, ostensibly to relieve work-related stress—condescended to carry the lighter carton up the twelve flights of stairs. Molly took care of the one with the paperbacks and the frying pan.

Molly was pleased to notice that the stink of stale urine abated somewhat as they climbed. By the time they reached the thirteenth floor it had faded away entirely, although it was replaced by another faint odour she couldn't quite identify.

The man from the Housing Department was already waiting for them outside the flat, nervously jingling the keys in his hand. Somewhat to her surprise, Molly recognised him—he moonlighted as a bouncer at the Netherworld. In spite of his obvious qualifications for the latter job, he was extraordinarily anxious to be away; he seemed deeply relieved when he was able to scurry away after handing over the keys. This did not seem to Molly to be a good sign. It was almost as bad, in its way, as the fact that her door was the only one in the corridor—there were nine others—that was not fitted with a steel security-gate. Such gates were theoretically illegal, on the grounds that Fire & Rescue found them almost as hard to force open as the local burglars if the need ever arose. Because the local burglars doubled as arsonists when frustrated, the need tended to arise on a regular basis, but the council turned a blind eye anyway.

Mrs. Peach seemed almost as pleased as the part-time bouncer to be able to depart again, although it was common knowledge that the local rude boys considered their mothers' social workers to be strictly out of bounds.

17

Molly had only just unpacked when the boy that the estate boss had sent to check up on her appeared at her door. Oddly enough, he seemed just as anxious as Elizabeth Peach and the man from the Housing Department had been, although his gang was presumably the thing of which the respectable citizens had been most frightened. He was only fifteen, of course —as soon as the gang members reached eighteen the local police fitted them up for the Scrubs in order to pay them back for all the trouble they'd caused while they were minors—but fifteen-year-olds were nowadays under just as much pressure as their seniors to act macho at all times.

The boy relaxed somewhat once he had looked Molly carefully up and down. She invited him in and stood meekly by while he checked out her luggage, or lack of it.

"I don't have a lot of stuff," Molly told him—which, roughly translated, meant *I'm not worth burgling*.

"If you need anything," the boy said, "just let us know. We usually hang out in the ground floor derelicts but you can leave a message at 349 in an emergency. Say it's for Dean. TVs and stuff come with the standard policy—third party fire and theft." That meant insurance against thefts committed and fires started by third parties in the gang; one thing that would emphatically not be covered was the possibility of being done for handling.

"Thanks Dean, but all I need for now is a few clothes," she said. "I'll try the Oxfam next to Kwik-Save when I nip out for groceries." She gave no hint of the fact that she was uncommonly flush because her benefits had been accumulating while she was touring the galaxy with the greys.

"We take commissions," Dean told her, but not very enthusiastically. He meant that he and his mates would shoplift to order, but she couldn't blame him for not getting overexcited at the thought of yet another trip to M&S. He was only offering because he had to follow orders.

"That's okay," she said. "Oxfam will be fine."

"You're not a tart, then?" the child commented, showing off his powers of deduction. "Perhaps as well. Tricks won't come up here."

"The stairs would be a disincentive," Molly conceded, although she was pretty sure that wasn't what he meant.

"You get a good view of the races from the window," Dean observed as he moved away, evidently feeling that he'd done his duty. "Better be careful not to see too much, though. Might be seeing you around, if you can hang on longer than usual."

"I'm a good hanger-on," Molly assured him. "I expect I'll be here for quite a while—and I *never* see things I'm not supposed to see." She was trying to reassure him that she wasn't available for witness duty—which was what he'd meant when he'd warned her to be careful—but he seemed to take it differently.

"I hope you don't," he said, as he disappeared through the door, "but you probably will, no matter how hard you try." It wasn't a threat, and it wasn't *quite* a warning. It was mostly just a doleful comment.

When she went to close the door behind the boy, Molly finally recognised the odour lingering in the corridor. If it had only been sulphur she'd have cottoned on sooner, but the sulphur was partly masked by something much sweeter, like warm molasses. The odour was still there when she popped out to Kwik-Save to lay in supplies—and by the time she returned, it was even stronger.

The music started at nine o'clock, while Molly was making a fried egg sandwich. It wasn't particularly loud, and it wasn't the kind of drum'n'bass stuff that mimicked the effect of a migraine if you listened to it long enough without being stoned, but it was unsettling nevertheless. It seemed strangely sinister, although Molly couldn't quite figure out why. The best she could do when she tried to put a name to it was that it was the kind of music you'd use for charming very large and extremely poisonous snakes, although she wasn't quite sure how that conviction had come into her head.

By the time she'd finished the sandwich, with the music still echoing insidiously around her walls, the races got under way. She went to the window to watch. Either the twockers had gone all the way up west or they'd struck exceedingly lucky, because they'd brought back something a lot sexier than the average salesman's fleet car: a low-slung two-seater sports job.

As a lifelong non-driver Molly didn't know enough about cars to be able to tell a Lamborghini from a Lada, but it was easy enough to see that this one had far too much under the hood for the pursuing pandas. She didn't know the ins and outs of the track—or even where the main circuit was supposed to be, given that it was a purely theoretical construct engraved upon the local streets by the teenage imagination —but she could tell by the way the vehicles cornered that the pursuers and the pursued were giving it their all.

It might have been fun if it hadn't been for the thing that suddenly popped up out of nowhere to leer at Molly through the window.

The thing had red-glowing eyes and fangs like a sabre-toothed tiger, a nose like a bat and ears like a hog. Its body was like a gibbon's but the hands at the ends of its anorectic arms were like sharply taloned claws. It had six limbs in all, the extra pair being wings, more like a pterodactyl's than a bat's.

It was extremely ugly, but its appearance was not quite as intimidating as that of the inhabitants of 61 Cygni C VIII— who had turned out to be very amiable—and nowhere near as strange as that of the cloud-dwellers of Procyon XXI. While it stared lasciviously at Molly, Molly stared insouciantly back, but it wasn't built for hovering and soon had to dive away into the darkness.

Well, Molly said to herself, under her breath, *it's a good job I wasn't moved here six weeks ago.*

By the time the joyriders had abandoned the two-seater Molly was absolutely beat, so she figured that she might as well have an early night. She pulled her sleeping bag out of the box. In spite of the music she fell asleep almost as soon as her head hit the bundled-up coat she was using as a pillow, and didn't wake up until something brushed her face.

The bedroom curtains were far too tatty to keep out the ruddy light of the cloudy night sky, but as soon as she opened her eyes Molly realised that the darkness was nowhere near as deep as it should have been. The ceiling seemed to be leaking silver tracery into the air, whose threads coiled about one another in serpentine fashion, like moonlit cigarette smoke blown into the catchment of a slowly-turning fan.

While Molly watched apprehensively, the swirling light began to form suggestive shapes—and what the shapes suggested to Molly were human figures writhing in cages of icy flame. Their limbs and torsos thrashed and quivered, and their eyes were pits of infinite darkness set in brightly-agonised faces. It was like something out of *Poltergeist,* although Molly didn't have a TV set and Arcadia House presumably hadn't been built on a graveyard.

The eerie music was still playing in the background, not loudly but insistently and ominously. The ghosts, if that was what they were, were moving in time to the rhythm, although no one would have called what they were doing *dancing*. The cloud-dwellers of Procyon XXI, by contrast, had most certainly been dancers, and their accompaniment had been a far more convincing rendition of the music of the spheres.

This, Molly knew, was fakery. It was very clever, but it wasn't authentic. She watched until the ghosts faded out, and then she relaxed—but only slightly. She had the feeling that there was more to come. Almost immediately, there was a knock on the bedroom door.

18

Molly had carefully secured both the locks and the deadbolt as soon as she'd got her groceries back from Kwik-Save, so nobody should have been able to get to the bedroom door without battering down the main one.

Although she was naked, except for her knickers, Molly immediately got out of bed and moved towards the door, sweeping her arms back and forth about her head as she went. The sinuous threads of light resisted slightly, like fresh spiderwebs, but they didn't hold her back.

When she opened the door she found a quasi-human figure standing there, softly lit from behind. A fleshless skull peeped out of a capacious hood mounted atop a voluminous black robe, while two skeletal hands displayed a huge scythe. The edge of the scythe-blade sparkled in the uncanny light.

Molly had taken a few self-defence lessons after her second rape, and she'd taken care to remember the flashier moves. She reached up to take the haft of the scythe in both hands, and immediately fell backwards. As soon as her back hit the threadbare carpet she brought her feet up hard into the costumed joker's midriff, intending to throw him head-first into the iron rimmed bed.

The move was more successful than she'd hoped. The skeletal figure weighed no more than a child of ten, and when the skull smacked into the bedframe it shattered into a thousand pieces. The rest of the bones immediately fell apart, sending the folds of the black robe cascading down upon Molly's tanned and unprecedentedly lithe body.

When Molly got up again she shook the bones out of the robe, making sure that all the shards were gone before she put it on herself. She picked up the scythe and marched to the front door of the flat. When she found it still triple-locked she went to get her keys, then let herself out.

It only took a moment to ascertain that the music was coming from the door opposite—the nearest of the nine that were sheltered by iron gates. She stepped across the hallway and used the top of the scythe's shaft to pound upon it.

The music stopped, and there was a pause of at least thirty seconds before someone shuffled to the door. Molly heard two keys and a deadbolt turn, then the door opened by the merest crack. A single bloodshot eye peered out at her from a point some four or five inches below her own eye-line. The occupant of the flat made no move to open the security-gate, being perfectly content to peer at her through the grille.

"Is this *yours?*" she demanded, brandishing the scythe fiercely.

"No," said a small voice. It was probably male, but she couldn't be absolutely sure.

"Well, *whose is it?*"

"Death's?" the small voice guessed, suggesting that its owner knew only too well what kind of visitation she had just received. Now that the music was off, another faint sound was emanating from the depths of the flat, like the buzzing of a swarm of flies.

"Well," said Molly, again. "Next time you see your friend Death, you tell him that he'd better come collect it *real soon,* or I'll trade it to the lads downstairs for some cutlery I can *use.* While you're at it, you can tell your pet that he's the worst excuse for a parrot I've seen this side of Wolf 359. And while I'm here, I might as well tell you that if you'd only change the fucking record once now and again, your phantom snakes probably wouldn't be swarming all over my place *interfering with my beauty sleep*. Okay?"

"Um," said the small voice.

"Is that um as in *I'm really very sorry* or um as in *it definitely won't happen again?*" Molly wanted to know.

"Errrgh," said the small voice, uncertainly.

Molly decided to take that as a yes to both questions.

"Good," she said. "And good night." She turned on her heel and marched back into her own flat, closing the door as firmly as she could without actually slamming it. She locked it as tightly as before and went back to bed, stepping carefully over the remnants of the skeleton after she'd divested herself of the robe.

When she woke up in the morning the broken bones were gone, but the black dressing-gown was still hanging on the hook on the back of the bedroom door. The scythe was where she'd left it, propped up against the cooker. She made herself some coffee before she went to the window to greet the morning sun but the grill on the cooker wasn't working so she couldn't make toast.

The burnt-out husk of the two-seater hadn't been collected yet. Either police thought that there was no great hurry or they figured that it was now the sole responsibility of the owner's insurers.

Molly had just put the kettle back on the gas for a second time when there was a knock at the door. She couldn't suppress the sudden hope that it might be Christine, or a social worker bearing glad tidings thereof, but when she had wrestled the door open she saw that it was only three old people, two male and one female.

Superficially, they seemed like the oldest people she had ever seen, but she could tell that there was more to them than met the everyday eye. Their hidden depths were sufficiently well-concealed that her eyes couldn't quite fathom them, but her wide experience of the extraordinary allowed her to be immediately aware of an awful lot of things that they *weren't*. One of the things they weren't was human; another was nice.

"And which of you gentlemen would be Mr. Death?" she asked, ironically.

"We're sorry about any inconvenience you might have suffered," said the taller of the old men, insincerely. "May we come in?" His ash-grey suit certainly hadn't come from Oxfam, or M&S, or any place that the men from darkest Croydon were likely to shop.

Molly stood aside to let them pass. The female led the way. Her ankle-length dress was silvery in hue, its delicate texture not unlike the skin of a baby grey, and her slippers looked as if they might be made of porcelain. The shorter and stouter male was comparatively underdressed, having no jacket, although his red velvet waistcoat was spectacularly tasteless. The spokesman's lounge-lizard outfit was topped and tailed by a bow tie and spats; if he'd been funny he could have stepped out of a P. G. Wodehouse novel, but whatever he was—and it wasn't easy to put a name to it—funny definitely didn't cover it.

The set of chairs that went with the table in the kitchenette was one short, so there was only one to spare once the female and the shorter male had sat down. Molly and the taller masquerader eyed one another carefully, neither wanting to accept any positional disadvantage. The kettle was boiling, and that gave Molly a chance to turn away with the contest still unsettled.

"Coffee?" she said, blithely. "It's only instant, I'm afraid. I'm Molly, by the way."

The unhuman visitors didn't introduce themselves and made no reply to the offer of coffee. Like little Dean they were trying to look hard as well as sinister, but like little Dean they hadn't got the wherewithal. As soon as Molly condescended to meet his gaze again, the tall one said, "Who are you?" in a conspicuously frosty voice.

"I just told you," she reminded him. "My name's Molly. You don't have to worry about me. *I'm* not the neighbour from Hell."

The female and the shorter male started visibly at that. Molly guessed that it had been the short one who had answered his door to her the previous night, although his eyes were no longer unduly bloodshot.

"We know *that*," the short one countered. "The point is, where *are* you from—and what do you want with us?"

"I just want to be a good neighbour," Molly assured them all. "But in my book, that means no nocturnal visitations of the carnival kind. I do hope you won't take this amiss, but I really don't want this affair to escalate. Judging by your first three shots, things could get rather grisly if you decided to try much harder. To be perfectly honest, I'd rather you didn't. It's not for myself, you understand—there's nothing much that I haven't seen before, and worse—but I have two children who might just be allowed to come and live with me if I can only persuade Social Services that it's safe enough and not too cramped. For that reason, of course, I'd be perfectly happy for you to go on frightening the pants off everybody else—so if, by chance, you're only doing it for fun you needn't feel deprived."

The imitation man in the grey suit didn't bat an eyelid, although Molly could tell that the prospect of having two children move into the corridor was far from welcome. He didn't venture any immediate reply when Molly stopped speaking; he seemed to be thinking hard about what to say next.

"I take it, then, that you're *not* doing it for fun," Molly said, by way of a prompt.

"No," said the female, softly. "We're not."

19

"Is it gang kids you're worried about?" Molly asked. "Are the cheap tricks intended to deter would-be burglars?" she knew that it couldn't be the right answer—for one thing, the tricks weren't cheap, and for another, she'd got enough out of Mrs. Peach to know that her rapidly-deterred predecessors hadn't had any gang material in tow—but she figured that she might as well try to get warmer by degrees if her mysterious visitors were intent on not giving her a straight answer.

"Who sent you?" the tall one asked, sharply. He was reluctant to concede that she had as much right to ask questions as he did.

"The same people who sent the last three people you scared off," Molly replied, with equal sharpness. "Who did you *think* sent me?"

"We were rather hoping to take over the entire floor," the female said, ignoring the tall one's censorious glance. "We had no trouble getting this far, so it's a little disappointing to trip up at the last hurdle. Our friend would have been in if you hadn't suddenly jumped the waiting list. We *could* help you to obtain other—and better—accommodation if you wish. You've seen a small sample of what we can do. That was crude, of course, but we can be subtle too. Given that you're so resilient, we're prepared to work with you rather than against you, always provided that we could come to a mutually acceptable arrangement." By the time she'd finished her tall companion was looking daggers at her, but she was just cutting through the bullshit.

"I'm very discreet," Molly assured them. "Who, exactly,

are you hiding from?"

"Who told you we were hiding?" the short one asked, in frank amazement.

His taller companion groaned. "I *told* you we shouldn't have let him come," he complained to the female. To Molly, he said: "You really don't want to know. The last thing you need is for our enemy to decide that you're an enemy too."

"I have friends in *very* high places," Molly told him, cockily. "I may not look like much, but you already know that I don't scare easily. I wouldn't call in my favours for anything trivial, of course, but even if the Devil himself were to come after me . . ."

She paused then, because even the tall one couldn't help flinching visibly at that name, while his two companions were stricken with expressions not unlike the one she'd noticed on the face of the Housing Officer-cum-nightclub bouncer.

"Oh," she said, as the one in the grey suit finally condescended to sit down on the empty chair. "It's *that* bad, is it?" She remembered the fallen angel she'd sent back up to Heaven, and tried to imagine what he'd have looked like if he'd stuck around—not just for another few days, but for a *very* long time. Then she remembered the odour of brimstone and treacle that had haunted the corridor on the previous evening, and the sound of buzzing flies that she'd heard in the short one's flat.

The reason they only *looked* human, she realised, was that they were demons—presumably renegade demons, if they were in hiding from their old boss.

When none of them had said anything for a further half minute, Molly got three extra cups and began to spoon coffee out of the jar.

"Well," she said, as she turned the gas back up to pep up the cooling water, "now that I know the worst, you might as well tell me everything, mightn't you?"

It wasn't that easy, of course. Even when the coffee had loosened them up a bit the tall one continued to be recalcitrant, deploring the fall of every nugget of information that his companions let slip. The smaller one, on the other hand, admitted when charged that they were indeed demons. The tall one's swift corrective assertion that they were very *minor* demons didn't seem convincing to Molly.

The female added that all nine of the heavily-defended rooms on the thirteenth floor were occupied by what were, in essence, draft-dodgers who had given up the thankless business of temptation centuries ago. His Satanic Majesty apparently hadn't bothered to take them to task for their negligence because they'd been virtually redundant by that time, humankind having become so addicted to sin that they no longer required prompting, but circumstances had recently changed. Rumour among the fallen apparently had it that summonses had been sent out requiring all "reservists" to report back to Hell for retraining.

"Retraining as what?" Molly wanted to know.

"We're not sure," said the shorter male demon, sourly. "Tormentors, maybe." He gave the impression that he could imagine fates worse than torment duty.

"Hell's not like Heaven then," Molly said. "It's not timeless."

The smaller demon, who had evidently never mastered the art of self-control, looked utterly flabbergasted. "How do you know that?" he asked.

"An angel told me," she said, trying to imply that it wasn't the only thing the angel had told her, although it very nearly was. "He fell, but only for a little while. He wasn't too proud to get up again—unlike your glorious leader, if Milton can be trusted."

"Milton was a fantasist," the tall demon told her, sharply. "Almost as bad as that charlatan who wrote the *Book of Enoch*. Lucifer didn't fall—he *absconded*."

Molly thought that over for a minute or two while she finished off her coffee and wished she had an electric toaster. She could see how it might happen. God, presumably, was loving in much the same way that the Jarvises were loving, and every bit as jealous. There'd been a case a few years back of two foster parents who'd done a bunk and gone on the run when they were told that they wouldn't be able to adopt the two girls they'd been fostering, and Molly had always suspected that the Jarvises might have been capable of something similar come the day when they were notified that Molly had been cleared to take Christine and Angie back. The Jarvises didn't actually loathe and despise Molly—at least, not openly—but they certainly thought she was the spawn of the Devil. Perhaps she had more in common with the thirteenth floor tenants than she or they had realised.

"There wasn't a war in Heaven, then?" she said, eventually. "The archangel Michael leading the heavenly host in his chariot of fire and all that stuff?"

"Wars take time," the tall demon pointed out. Molly knew that she ought to have thought of that, and tried to think ahead so that she wouldn't make any more silly mistakes. Perhaps absconders from Heaven were pursued once now and again, but only in a cursory fashion. At the end of the day, God would probably take the view that the ingrates deserved whatever they got, and probably took immense satisfaction from the fact that they would get a rude shock when they found out what the real world was like. It wasn't really surprising, she supposed, that disaffected angels quickly became demons, dedicated to temptation or torment. What could possibly become of Christine, if she couldn't find her way to

Molly? What alternatives were there to whoredom and theft, once Jarvisite paternalism had been tried and found too cloying to bear?

"You aren't, by any chance, Mephistopheles?" Molly asked the tall one, on a whim. She darted a glance at the smaller male's face, figuring that it would light up if she scored a hit. She was rewarded by a full-blown beacon.

"What if I am?" the taller one retorted, tiredly. "Goethe was just as big a liar as Milton."

"I suppose that means that you're not prepared to trade me all the knowledge in the world for my immortal soul," Molly said, trying to sound equally languid.

"In case you haven't noticed, my dear," the tall demon said, with more lamentation than spite, "we're both living in somewhat reduced circumstances. If you had an immortal soul, it certainly wouldn't be a collector's prize, and like most people my apparent age I don't know *anything* any more. We just want to be left alone, to enjoy our music and our books —and one another's company, of course."

He sounded distinctly unenthusiastic about the last item, but Molly knew that it was a double bluff. Even the young couldn't really cut it on their own, no matter how hard they thought they were or tried to be, and no matter how resentful they were of the helpful efforts of their peers and parents. She thought that she understood exactly how the renegade demons must feel—and how Christine must feel now that she had flown the paradisal nest of Jarvisworld.

20

"I can sympathise with your difficulties," Molly told the visiting demons, when they'd all become much better acquainted and were feeling far more relaxed, "but as it happens, I know something you don't. The world is about to enter a brand new era of vision and ecstasy. Humankind is about to undergo a leap of mental and moral evolution. The greys are scientists at heart, and they like to proceed with caution, but the plan's already well under way and it's just a matter of time till they activate the trigger. That might well be why demons are being called in for retraining. After all, once you strip away all the superficialities, demons are just an ugly projection of the darker side of human yearning for moral order."

Mephistopheles had loosened up, but he looked as if he was going to get furious all over again about that, and his male companion was frankly appalled, but the old lady laughed aloud. "There you are, boys," she said, "the unpalatable truth, straight from the victim's mouth. Who's tormenting whom, hey?" The old lady had already told Molly that she was Lilith from 1302, and that the oafish demon from across the way was Beelzebub. Mephistopheles had been lying about their being mere rankers. Belial was next door on the right in 1304, Balberith in 1305, Ashtaroth in 1306, Belphegor in 1307, Astarte in 1308 and Samael in 1309. Asmodeus was in 1310, but Lilith told Molly not to expect to see much of him, because he didn't get out much nowadays.

Lucifer must be very lonely in Pandemonium, Molly thought,

*if that's really where he is. Almost as lonely as God—but that's
what happens to unhumans who deal in absolutes.* When the time
finally came for her to show her new friends the door, she
said: "I'm very pleased to meet you all, and I'm sorry about
your friend not being able to move in just yet, but I really do
need to stay where I can be easily found, at least for a while. I
hope we can all get along."

"Oh, I think we can," Lilith said, blithely ignoring the
stare of resentful disapproval that Mephistopheles directed at
her. "Perhaps we can even help one another a little, the way
neighbours should."

"I'd like that," Molly said, reflecting that even though this
was the first time in her life she'd had literal neighbours from
Hell, it might also turn out to be the first time she'd ever
really got away from the metaphorical kind. The demons
might not be nice by nature, but they did seem capable of
compromise, and her galactic holiday had put her in an optimistic mood.

It had been such a strange day that Molly felt like treating
herself, so when darkness fell that evening she decided to
walk the half-mile to the nearest fish-and-chip shop and have
a proper dinner for once. She even treated herself to a can of
Diet Tango, although she had to slip that into her pocket
between sips in order to have a hand free for the chips. She
had to eat while she walked; if she'd taken the food wrapped it
would have gone cold by the time she got it back to Arcadia
House even if no one decided to take it off her.

Although the sky was aglow with dimly-reflected light the
streets through which she walked were stubbornly dark, most
of the streetlights having been shattered by marksmen practising for the next riot. The weather was mild, so she didn't
hurry.

When Molly finally rounded the corner that brought her in

view of her new home she stopped. There was a big black saloon a hundred yards away, at the end of the path that led to the door of Arcadia House. For one horrible moment she thought it might be a hearse, and couldn't suppress the irrational fear that Christine might be coffined in the back—but then she realised that its engine was running and that the driver, whose head was hardly visible above the dashboard, was warming the engine with brief applications of the accelerator.

She recognised Dean, and figured that it must be his turn to run the imaginary maze. He was presumably waiting for the police to arrive. Molly hoped that his legs were long enough to give his feet adequate control over both pedals.

Relaxing, Molly paused beneath one of the rare illuminated lamps to finish off the last few chips and screw up the greasy paper. Then she saw something else from the corner of her eye and her heart leapt. She immediately looked sideways, but the slender figure was already moving away.

"Chris!" she called out. "Chris, it's me!"

The slender figure kept moving, and for a moment Molly wondered whether it really was her daughter—but the shadow was heading directly for Arcadia House.

Molly ran after the fleeing form, calling out the name for one last time before accepting that the other wasn't going to stop. *She doesn't recognise me!* Molly thought. *Poor kid doesn't recognise her own mother!* It was, alas, only too plausible.

As the runaway's great loping strides consumed the distance between the corner where Molly had thrown away the paper ball and the vast sullen mass of Arcadia House, the fleeing figure was suddenly caught in silhouette by the glare of two headlights. Molly felt even more certain than before that it was Christine.

Molly realised that the headlights belonged to a panda. As

the police car turned the corner the twin beams ran along the side of the saloon and she saw their light reflected from the sweaty sheen on young Dean's mahogany cheeks. She realised then that it wasn't Arcadia House that Christine was running towards but the big black car: not the Waste-Disposal Unit but the death trap.

"No!" Molly yelled. "Don't get in!" In the absence of any response, and the awful certainty that there would be no response, she increased her own pace markedly. She hadn't been working out the way Elizabeth Peach had, but the greys had tuned her up pretty well and she was sure that she could give the social worker twenty yards start and still beat her over a hundred. Unfortunately, Christine had had more than twenty yards, and by the time that Molly was in a position to reach out to her, her beloved daughter had actually taken hold of the handle of the rear door of the saloon. The car was already in gear and moving.

The next few seconds were dreadfully confused. Impossible as it seemed, the shadow Molly had been pursuing not only managed to slide into the back seat of the accelerating car but somehow contrived to snake out an absurdly long arm, whose taloned claw seized the wrist of Molly's hopelessly-extended right hand and yanked her into the darkness as if she weighed no more than a little child.

The door slammed shut behind her, and Molly caught sight of Dean's young face reflected in the rear-view mirror. His eyes were wide and staring, as if mesmerized, and although she was looking right into them, Molly knew without the shadow of a doubt that *he* couldn't see *her* at all. He was looking right through her at the headlights blazing in the rear window. His foot was flat to the boards as the saloon roared away on to the imaginary racetrack, but it could only be the desperate need to seem *hard* that was keeping it there, because there was nothing in those stark unseeing eyes but terror.

Molly wanted to yell Dean's name now, but it stuck in her throat. Instead, she swivelled her gaze to look at the monster who had hauled her into the death trap.

21

For a fleeting instant the monster showed her Christine's face again, but that was just to taunt and torment her. He had no intention of trying to keep his true identity secret, and he obviously took great delight in being one of the few entities on the planet that was instantly recognisable even to people who'd never met him before, or ever dreamed that he actually existed.

Unlike the flying creature that had leered at her the previous evening, this was no mere comic-strip caricature. This was the genuine article, and there was nothing sweet to take the edge off his sulphurous breath. He looked more like Giger's *Alien* than anything out of Hieronymus Bosch, but that was just the zeitgeist; the point was that he was the foulest thing that any merely human eye had ever beheld, or ever could. Molly knew that this was the essence of his challenge, and that she had to keep looking, or she'd lose.

"Well, well, well," said His Satanic Majesty, sarcastically. "If it isn't the apprentice redeemer."

The saloon roared into the first of many tight turns, flinging Molly against the hairy and horny body of her naked captor. He still had hold of her right wrist, so she only had her left to use as a buffer, and it wasn't enough. She *felt* him chortle. She tried to throw up in his lap, but she still couldn't get anything past the knot in her throat. His other talon seized her by the neck and held her head still, no more than six inches from his awful visage. His eyes weren't red or yellow, the way they usually were in cinematic images, but that didn't make their glare any less intimidating. Looking into them, Molly knew that she was looking right into Hell. One of her rapists had held her exactly like that, for a moment or two, but his eyes had been pale imitations of the real thing, and so had the rest of him. The game was, however, to endure the touch and the smell—and even the taste, if it came to that —as well as the sight and the sound.

"Oh yes," whispered the Archetype of Evil, beginning the challenge of sound, "it's lonely in Pandemonium, you smug little bitch. It's all so easy, isn't it, when you're friends with Elvis and the visitors from outer space? You do a little favour for a fallen angel, and suddenly you're not the little smear of shit you always thought you were. Oh no! You're not even content with being on top of *this* fucking world—*you* have to go tripping off round the Milky Way after telling the poor little fuckers in the saucers exactly how to save themselves from all that awful alienation. The sky's not the limit for *Molly,* is it? She can make judo moves on Death and make friends with the whole fucking hierarchy of Hell. So I'm just an ugly projection of the human yearning for moral order, am I? And you, of course, have just reinvented the whole bloody issue, thus rendering me utterly redundant. Well, thank *you,* you stupid little cunt—and welcome back to the *real world.*"

The headlights of the chasing panda were astonishingly bright. They filled the rear windscreen with angry light, and all the dust motes in the stale air at the rear of the car danced like damned souls in Hell. A single beam of even brighter light reflected back from the rear-view mirror, and although Molly could no longer see Dean's staring eyes she could imagine the fear that was in them. Not fear of the Devil, of course, but something worse: the fear of not being *man enough,* at fourteen, to be a winner in the human race. He was too short to be able to work the floor-pedals properly, and too raw to deal with the power steering.

Molly tried to speak, certain that she could find an answer if she could only loose her ever-reliable tongue, but the knot in her throat had gripped her vocal cords as tightly as Lucifer's talons had gripped her neck and wrist. Although the car was lurching this way and that, almost lifting its wheels from the ground every time it cornered, Molly's momentum was momentarily stifled. Somehow, she had to get it back, for poor lost Christine's sake.

"Did you really think that your daughter would come running back to *you?*" the Devil asked, still speaking in a hoarse stage-whisper. "Do you really imagine that she could give a damn about a mother she's hardly known? Do you want to know what your daughters think of you, Molly? Of course you don't—which is exactly why I'm going to tell you. They think you're a *joke*. They think you're *pathetic*. They think you're the only person in the world more embarrassing than the holier-than-thou Jarvises. Christine would rather be in the back seat of a car with a novice joyrider than anywhere in the world with *you*. And do you know how much difference it would make if she knew that you'd dumped Elvis, saved a fallen angel, showed the greys the way to go and taken pity on every clapped-out demon on the face of the planet? *None*— and I don't mean that approximately, Molly. Absolute fucking zero."

It was very strange, Molly thought, that the Devil's voice was as clear as it was, given that the panda's siren was wailing like a banshee and the saloon's engine was howling like a hellhound. More surprising than that, however, was the fact that she could hear another, even more muted, sound beneath and beyond that screaming cacophony. It was the sound of sobbing. She knew it wasn't her own sobbing, because she couldn't even whimper. And if there were tears in

Dean's eyes, then the stupid child wouldn't even be able to see.

Molly kept her own tearless eyes fixed on the Devil's. She inhaled the stink of his breath, and when he reached out an obscenely long tongue to lick her lips, she tasted him too. When he thrust the slimy tip of the tongue into her mouth, she didn't try to bite. That wasn't the game. The game was to wait. She'd been through it twice before, and she knew. It was all a matter of keeping your head, not just now but after-wards. No matter how hard you fell, you had to get up. You couldn't afford to be proud. You couldn't afford to pretend to be more manly—more *human*—than you actually were.

"I suppose you think I'm going to leave you here," the Devil said, "but I'm not. I can work in mysterious ways too, you know. Anyway, I want you to deliver a message for me. I want you to tell those snivelling idiots up on the thirteenth floor that *I don't need them*. I want you to tell them that I wouldn't take them back if they came crawling on their hands and knees licking shit every step of the way. I want you to tell them that I have some *real* soldiers now, and that they're wel-come to spend their pathetic twilight time indulging all the not-so-deadly sins that they couldn't even peddle to needy morons. I want you to tell them that the very thought of them makes me *sick,* and I hope they rot in pain and filth and misery until they can't bear it—and that they won't be able to stop. Not that I expect you to play messenger for nothing, of course. Old Meph may not know anything any more, but I do, and I'm more than happy to let you have the first sample for free. You'll see your precious Christine again, but she won't come near you until the need is exploding in your worthless soul, and you won't get any joy out of seeing her until you've been a hell of a lot further than Altair trying to make it up to her. Now, you worthless cunt, get out of here before *you* start to make me sick. I have a little job to do."

Molly had never turned away, never given in. She wasn't cocky any more, but she was still in the game. Suddenly, she got her momentum back.

This time, as the saloon cornered, its nearside wheels really did part company with the ground—and Molly hurtled headlong into the door behind the driver—which obligingly swung open in response to the impact, throwing her out into an apparent eternity that was really only time.

Molly felt herself tumbling in empty space, enjoying a precious moment of weightlessness before gravity's empire gripped her. When it did grip her, though, it did so with almost as much fervour as the Father of Lies.

22

Molly knew that it was going to hurt when she hit the pavement, and it did. She didn't mind as much as she might have, partly because the shock cleared her throat and partly because she was desperate to see what would happen to the car and its driver.

She knew already, of course, but for once she would have loved to be proven wrong, and she still had hope. Even after the box had been forced well and truly open, she thought, she was still entitled to hope. Even draft-dodging demons were still entitled to hope, although Molly knew that God and the Jarvises would probably have disagreed about that.

The big black car that looked like a hearse must have hit the wall at ninety miles an hour. It wouldn't have mattered a damn whether Dean was wearing a seat-belt or not, although he probably wasn't because it wouldn't have been macho. The fact that the Devil was riding with him undoubtedly made a difference, though, because the petrol tank went off like a bomb, and Molly knew that that never *really* happened, in spite of what the movies liked to imply.

Molly was knocked flat on her back by the blast, and she stayed there for some considerable time while the crowd gathered around her. The night air didn't taste clean, but it tasted a lot cleaner than the Devil's tongue. Nobody offered to help her up, but that was because niceness was an unaffordable commodity on estates like this one, on every floor of every dark and dour block.

By the time Molly had pulled herself to her feet the crowd

was melting away again in response to the arrival of the uniforms. Molly couldn't be bothered to make herself scarce. She just stood there, fondling her bruises, until a WPC said: "I don't suppose you have any idea who was driving?"

"Dean and the Devil," Molly replied, unable to suppress the temptation to tell the whole truth.

"Dean who?" the WPC asked, wearily.

"Don't know," Molly admitted. "You might try 349 Arcadia House, seeing as it's an emergency."

"Are you all right?" the WPC asked. "The car didn't clip you as it went past, did it?" She sounded like someone who didn't want to be put to the bother of calling an ambulance.

"I'm fine," said Molly, surprised to find that even though she'd finally managed to start sobbing and in spite of all she'd been though, she really was all right. "It takes more than an indecent assault by Absolute Evil to rattle me."

"Better get off home, then," the WPC said. "Nothing to see here."

"Yes," Molly agreed. "Best get back to the thirteenth floor."

She realised, as she stumbled away into the shadows, that she *had* been getting a bit above herself lately. Perhaps she had needed reminding that even if you could make judo moves on Death, and shatter him into tiny little pieces, and steal his dressing-gown, and make friends with the entire hierarchy of Hell, you couldn't actually put a stop to cold and decay and torment and temptation. That much of what the Devil had said was true—but as for the rest of it . . . well, he seemed to know about her little excursion to Altair, but he hadn't said a word about the impending uplift of humankind by the greys' psychotropic viruses. She had to keep it in mind that the Devil was a very old-fashioned sort, whose imaginative horizons weren't as broad as her own. She knew that she needed to keep that in mind no matter how bad things became before the greys could trigger the uplift.

Death will always get up again, Molly thought. *No matter what moves you make, he'll always be back. But the only thing you can do in answer to that is to keep on getting up again yourself, and keep on coming back. Next time, it really will be Chris, no matter what the Father of Lies says. I'll find her, one way or another. I'll settle up with her, whatever it takes. I'm her mother, after all. Whatever trouble she's got herself into, I can get her out —and if I can't, I can see her through it.*

When Molly got back up to the thirteenth floor, Lilith and Mephistopheles were waiting for her in the corridor. All nine of the security gates stood open behind them, and at least half the doors were already standing ajar.

Nobody called out, but the other demons began to emerge, one by one. It wasn't just the crippled Asmodeus who had trouble making progress, but these were individuals who knew how to cope with frailty. They weren't pretty, and they weren't nice, but they had learned to get by with torment and temptation. If there was any way to come to terms with being older than anyone dared to imagine, the demons had mastered it.

"It was *him*, wasn't it?" Lilith said.

"Yes," Molly admitted.

"What did he want?" Mephistopheles demanded.

"He wanted a little chat with me," Molly said, trying her damnedest to sound casual. "He thinks I've been getting above myself, lending a helping hand to recently-fallen angels and recruiting little grey men to uplift the human race to a new level of rationality, visionary power and hedonic potential. Oh—and he also asked me to give you all a message."

"What did he say?" Mephistopheles said. Molly could hear the fear in his voice. The others shuffled a few paces closer.

"He said that you don't have to worry about the ugly rumours," Molly said, with utter conviction. "He said that you've all done your bit, and that he's very grateful. He said that you've all earned a little peace and quiet, and that the bottom has dropped right out of the tempting and tormenting game anyway. He said that he wishes you all well, and he hopes that everything works out for you."

"Did he?" said Mephistopheles, wonderingly. "Did he really?"

"Word for word," Molly assured him.

Molly had the impression that Lilith wasn't quite so easily fooled, but the old lady wasn't about to look a gift horse in the mouth. When Lilith smiled, and turned to show her smile to the others, they all smiled with her. They were old and decrepit and they were living in the Waste-Disposal Unit with all the other neighbours from Hell, but they still had hope. For them, as for her, this was year zero—a time of new beginnings brimming with potential.

Molly might have smiled with them, if it hadn't been for Dean and Christine, but at least she wasn't crying any more.

"He said that he can work in mysterious ways too," Molly told the renegade demons. *And why not?* she added, purely on her own behalf. *When all's said and done, why the hell shouldn't he—and why on earth shouldn't we?*

23

As soon as she was properly settled into her new home, Molly called the Jarvises and arranged to visit Angie. Molly didn't know why Angie hadn't done a bunk too, although Christine probably hadn't given her the choice. What fifteen-year-old in her right mind would want to go on the run with a twelve-year-old?

Overshadowed as it was by Christine's seemingly-total disappearance, the visit was even more difficult than previous ones. The Jarvises broke all their previous world records in the delicate sport of being scrupulously polite and superficially pleasant while still contriving to imply that Molly was a worthless piece of human scum who would do everybody a favour by falling dead into the Thames and not being washed up this side of Sheerness.

Mrs. Jarvis had obligingly laid out all of Angie's school exercise-books, and pointed out time and time again what *beautiful* handwriting Angie had. The Jarvises had, of course, seen plenty of Molly's handwriting on those envelopes whose addresses the post office managed to decipher, and Molly did not doubt that the couple always carried out a careful quasi-forensic analysis of their contents. The Jarvises were, however, also capable of devastating understatement, and Mrs. Jarvis modestly failed to call particular attention to the fact that Angie now addressed her as "Mummy" while neglecting to hang any label at all on Molly.

"You will tell us, won't you, if Christine gets in touch with you?" Mr. Jarvis said, knowing full well that the Social Services would repair any omission on Molly's part as soon as they got wind of it. "She might, you know, even though she'll have to go to some trouble to find out where to look for you. She's such a *resourceful* girl, when she puts her mind to it. We'll let *you* know, of course, if *we* hear anything—that's probably more likely, given that she knows that *we're* always here for her."

Molly decided, right there and then, that she had to get a place of her own, of the kind that might be deemed suitable for bringing up children. That meant she had to get hold of some real money, and not by the usual means. She knew, in any case, that if she didn't find something constructive to occupy her time the Devil would find work for her idle body-parts to do. Having recently met the Devil, she figured that any distractions he threw her way were likely to fuck her up completely, and she couldn't afford that if she hoped to be any use when Christine finally did get in touch.

Given that her qualifications were far outnumbered by her disqualifications, Molly wasn't surprised when the Job Centre couldn't suggest anything better than shelf-stacking or office cleaning. She wouldn't have minded either, because she'd never had a problem with unsocial hours, but when she'd been through six unsuccessful interviews she realised that her current address was a worse handicap than the gaping holes in her CV. It wasn't so much that her immediate neighbours were renegade arch-demons—the DSS weren't officially aware of that—but that the twelve floors below her were packed with enterprising teenage burglars who were always looking for back ways into shops and storerooms, and who couldn't even look at a PC without wanting to strip the chips out of it.

The old Molly would probably have given up after half a dozen knockbacks, but even the Devil had given her credit for *trying* to save the human race from the slough of mediocrity, and she figured that she owed herself no less. She wondered whether it might be easier to get agency work, but the first ones she tried seemed even more paranoid about her record —especially the criminal part of it—than the employers she'd approached directly. It wasn't until she reached the last one on her list that a glimmer of light appeared at the end of the tunnel.

"Actually, Peaslee Pharmaceuticals is looking for single females in your age-bracket," the agency's employment consultant told her, making no secret of her amazement. The woman was really a mere desk clerk; she couldn't have been any more than twenty-five but she was already making conscientious attempts to look younger, which was presumably why she couldn't figure out why anyone in the world could possibly be interested in women over thirty.

"What for?" Molly asked.

"The card doesn't say, but the pay rate's well above minimum, so it must be some kind of testing. It says that they need people in good health, so it's not medical—but it's not badly paid, considering."

Molly didn't have to ask what needed to be considered. The possibility of being poisoned or disfigured was presumably what lifted the pay to a level slightly better than derisory. Molly guessed that the Peaslee boffins were probably testing cosmetics. Human vanity being what it was, there was far more money to be made out of anti-wrinkle creams than cancer cures.

"I'll take it," Molly said.

The employment consultant rang Human Resources at Peaslee and fixed up an appointment for that afternoon. "They'll reimburse your bus fare," the girl told her, disdainfully. Molly couldn't work out whether the disdain was for

people who travelled by bus or people who were so desperate
to be needed that they were prepared to moonlight as laboratory rats.

Peaslee Pharmaceuticals was way out of town. The company occupied four buildings tucked discreetly away in a
corner of a new industrial estate on one of the feeder roads to
the M25. Three of the four were huge windowless blocks
but the guard at the barrier directed Molly to the fourth,
which was an ordinary office-complex. The security was very
tight even there, involving sliding steel doors and shifty-eyed
security-men, but her chit from the agency eventually won
her admission to its cool and sterile corridors.

The woman who met Molly was another artificially-young
item who might have been cloned from the same original as
the agency consultant. She scanned Molly's Oxfam-bought
ensemble with conscientious fashion-blindness, then
switched into hawk-mode in order to scrutinise her face. For
one horrible moment Molly thought that the greys might
have fixed her up so well that her skin was too perfect for
testing cosmetics, but the woman's practised smile was not
unwelcoming.

"Have you done this kind of work before?" she asked.

"Not personally," Molly admitted, "but I used to be
involved with a man who was involved with something similar."

The woman didn't ask for details, which was perhaps as
well, given that Elvis's immortality treatment had gone so
badly awry. "In that case," the fresh-faced woman said,
"you're probably familiar with the procedure. You have to
sign forms giving us permission to administer the injections
and to monitor the effects. I have to warn you that you'll be
waiving your right to take any legal action against us in
respect of any consequence of the trial, but we do provide

insurance cover against death or disability. If we need to keep you here for observation you have to comply, although the particular programme we're recruiting for shouldn't require that. You will, however, have to undertake to be here *on time* for every series of tests. If you refuse any procedure, or if you're late for an appointment, the results become tainted and you'll be deemed to have forfeited all outstanding fees. In order to protect the double blind, you're not permitted to know what the injection is, or what effects we think it might have. If you're unhappy with any of that, there's no point in proceeding."

Molly was unhappy with all of it, especially the bit about the injection, but she wasn't about to back out. The job might turn out to be slightly more hazardous than office cleaning, but at least it promised to be more interesting. She signed all the forms—of which there were a lot—and was promptly whisked away to another room for her preliminary medical and "induction procedure." Nobody said that she'd be bounced if they found any illegal substances in her blood or urine but it didn't matter anyway. Since the greys had cleaned her out she hadn't touched anything more exotic than lager, even though Lilith and Belial had offered to let her partake of one or two of the fiendish concoctions they used to while away their own heavy time.

24

The most gruelling parts of the induction procedure were the IQ test and the personality profile, not because they were unduly challenging—Molly didn't worry overmuch about trying to get the multiple-choice questions right, or even trying to make the fill-in answers legible—but because they were so tediously long-winded. Molly did wonder whether the results of the physical exam would be affected by the DNA that the greys had pumped into her by means of the virus vectors that she'd then started spreading through the population, but it didn't seem to be worth worrying about. By now, half the degenerates in the capital could be carriers, and that was a lot of people. She had every confidence that any stray biochip the aliens might have left lying around her person would pass undetected.

Once Molly had finished the preliminaries she was handed a cheque for the first instalment of her fee. It wasn't as much as she could have earned over a similar period at King's Cross, even after she'd paid the pitch rent, but it was more than she'd have got if she'd spent the time stocking supermarket shelves. Then she was taken to meet the doctor in charge of the test run, who introduced himself as Nathanael Wingate. He looked exactly like a mad scientist out of an old black-and-white movie, right down to the Einsteinian tufts of wispy white hair on either side of his head and the wrongly-fastened buttons on his fawn cardigan.

"You mustn't worry, my dear," he said to her, in what might have been a Canadian or New England accent. "The last thing we want to do is to cause you any distress. We want all our products to do nothing but good. If all is well with the test results, we'll administer the first injection tomorrow afternoon. I can't tell you what it is, but I can say that the effects ought to be slight and subtle—they certainly shouldn't interfere with your everyday routines, although I'll have to ask you not to drink alcohol or take any other drugs, medicinal or recreational. The testing isn't supposed to make you ill, and if it seems to be doing that you should let us know immediately. I'll give you an emergency number to call. If everything goes well, you must return for a check-up and a new shot every third day, no matter what day it happens to be. There are no Sabbaths in science. Are you okay with all that?"

"Sure," Molly said, bravely. She knew that she wasn't supposed to know what was happening in case her expectations polluted the experiment, but she couldn't help wondering. It seemed to her that the "slight and subtle" effects Wingate's employers would be most likely to be interested in were metabolic, but if it was a weight-loss treatment she must be part of the control group—she'd never been fat.

When Molly got back to Arcadia House she immediately set about composing a letter to Christine, just in case her wayward daughter turned up while she was busy being poked and prodded at Peaslee.

It wasn't an easy letter to write, and Mrs. Jarvis's pointed remarks about Angie's beautiful handwriting made Molly even more paranoid than usual about her unruly script. By the time she was done darkness had fallen, although the combination of pollutant haze and reflected street-lighting tinted the darkness red and turned the cratered face of the full moon a curious cooked salmon colour, like a pockmarked Dequadin lozenge. The letter read:

Dear Christine,

I'm very sorry that I couldn't be here. Please wait until I come back. Then we can talk things over and figure out what to do. I'm your mother and I love you very much.

Love,
Mum

When Molly had put the letter in an envelope she took it to Lilith's, and asked her to look after it. She also asked Lilith to make sure that all the other demons knew about its existence, so that they'd know where to send Christine if she turned up. Mephistopheles and Belial were in Lilith's flat at the time, and Belial promised to put the word around. Molly explained to them what she was doing, and why. She expected them to be very pleased, because they still wanted to move another of their company into Molly's flat, but Mephistopheles and Lilith seemed mildly alarmed by Molly's willingness to be injected with unknown substances.

"There are things man was not meant to know," Mephistopheles said, dourly.

"Not any more there aren't," said Lilith, who was one of the few arch-demons to have adapted her outlook to the twentieth century. "I, for one, wouldn't be ungrateful for a reliable wrinkle treatment—ersatz glamour is so much less demanding than the real thing—but I'm not sure I'd want to try out the ones that turned out to have nasty side-effects." All the demons were past masters in the art of illusion, but now that they had retired from active service they found the magical arts very tiring and Lilith was usually content to appear as she was: very old and more-than-slightly wretched.

Because he was one of the demons charged with the duty of shopping for the little community, Belial got out more often than his companions and had a more accurate notion of the value of money, so he was less affrighted by the prospect of work. "I could do that," he observed. "Do you suppose they might give me a job?"

"I'm not sure there are any openings for people in your age-bracket," Molly told him, "let alone for demons." She didn't bother to point out that he didn't even have a national insurance number. None of the demons was registered with the DSS; they supported themselves entirely by magical means, and they tended to be careful in eking out their mundane resources.

"I don't suppose *he'd* approve, in any case," Belial said, regretfully. "I wouldn't want to attract attention." Like his companions, Belial had taken only slight reassurance from Molly's heroically-calculated lies about the Devil's lack of ill-will towards his former minions. The demons knew only too well that even if the Father of Lies had said exactly what she'd told them he'd said, his word couldn't be trusted as far as you could throw a feather into a headwind.

Molly's own anxieties about her new job had less to do with the possibility that she might suffer horrific side-effects than the attitude of Social Services. In theory, having any kind of job was a great leap forward in the direction of respectability, but if and when a case conference were called to decide whether she was ready and able to take charge of Angie—and Christine, if Christine ever condescended to return—the decision-makers might think that being a guinea-pig for unspecified experiments in biochemistry was not quite the kind of work that a good mother ought to be doing.

"It's just a stopgap measure," she told Lilith. "Once I've got something solid on my CV and a better address it'll be a lot easier to get steadier and safer work."

"No good will come of it all," Mephistopheles prophesied—but it was hard to take him seriously when he was wearing spats.

25

The next day, Dr. Wingate collected Molly from the office-building and led her to one of the others via a subterranean passage full of doors that had to be unlocked with a swipe-card. He told Molly that the results of her medical had been very satisfactory, and that she seemed like a perfect subject. He asked her sternly if she had any reservations about continuing, carefully adding that there was no earthly reason why the trials shouldn't be a great success.

Molly was still treading carefully, so she didn't make any sarcastic remarks about unearthly reasons; she just rolled up her sleeve and let Wingate's assistant get on with it. She didn't like injections, but she managed not to faint.

They made her hang about for an hour to make sure that there was no immediate adverse reaction, and then Dr. Wingate took her back to the office building.

"As you know," he said, "I can't tell you exactly what effects we expect, but I can reassure you that they won't be immediate and shouldn't be troublesome—or even unwelcome —when they do make themselves evident."

Well, they say you can never be too rich or too thin, Molly thought, even more convinced than before that the treatment must be something to do with slimming.

Wingate saved his final admonition until they had passed out of the main door on to the forecourt. The furious way he blinked his eyes against the glare of the afternoon sun suggested that he didn't see a lot of daylight.

"No *Thank God it's Friday,* mind," he told her.

"Remember what I said about alcohol and so on. Just eat normally, and be back here Monday morning, at eleven o'clock sharp. You'd better bring an overnight bag, just in case. You've got the emergency number, haven't you?"

Molly nodded. She hadn't told anyone at Peaslee that the chances of any occupant of Arcadia House getting to a working phone in any kind of emergency were a bit slim. All the resident gang members had mobiles, but the one thing gang members had in common with policemen was that there was never one around when you needed one, especially on the thirteenth floor.

As it turned out, though, the emergency number was quite redundant, because that brief nod of the head was the last thing Molly remembered until she woke up at home in bed, naked except for her knickers.

She immediately fished out her wristwatch, and saw that it was nine o'clock. Puzzled by the loss of an entire evening, not to mention the bus trip back from Peaslee, she got up.

A set of clean clothes had been set out, neatly folded, on the kitchen table; there were no dirty ones visible, although the plastic bag she used to ferry her stuff down to the launderette was displaying a slight bulge. There wasn't a dirty dish in sight—not even a coffee-cup—and the last lot of clean ones, which usually hung around in the draining-rack until they were needed again, seemed to have been put away. Molly, who was not normally so tidy, frowned as she put the clean clothes on, wondering if Dr. Wingate's wonder-drug could possibly be intended to turn women into Stepford wives.

Her suspicions were further intensified when she went to the cupboard to get the instant coffee and found it fully-stocked, even though she usually did the weekly shop on a Saturday. The tins were all positioned so that their labels faced outwards, and there was a big packet of bran flakes where the corn flakes usually sat.

When she opened the fridge, she found that it had been so comprehensively tidied up that there was no ice on the element. Six eggs had been taken out of their box and placed in the plastic rack that she had always considered superfluous. When she noticed that the oven had been cleaned and that the kitchen floor had been washed, she realised that the situation was far more serious than she had thought. Apparently, she had been converted into some kind of superefficient household robot.

As soon as she had steadied her nerves with a cup of coffee Molly went to knock on Lilith's door.

"Hello, dear," Lilith said, brightly. "Shouldn't you be on your way to work?"

"Not till Monday," Molly said, finishing the sentence before the horrible sinking feeling hit her in the stomach like a soggy fist. The expression on Lilith's face was enough to tell her that today *was* Monday.

"Oh shit," Molly murmured. "Have you seen me at all since Friday morning?"

"I'm afraid not," Lilith replied. "Belial said that he bumped into you in Kwik-Save on Saturday but that you seemed to be in a world of your own. I knocked on your door a couple of times, but if you were in you were dead to the world."

Those words seemed more ominous than they should have done, but there was no time for Molly to follow up her enquiries, because she knew she'd have to sprint for the bus if she were to have the slightest chance of getting to Peaslee on time.

"Watch out for Christine," she said, as she hurtled on her way.

26

While the bus made its slow way south-west Molly conducted a brief survey of her state of body. She was neither hungry nor hungover and had no suspicious itches or scratches. There were no nasty aftertastes in her mouth and no unwonted fluids leaking from her other orifices. All in all, she was in astonishingly good condition for someone who had lost more than sixty hours. She had obviously been looking after herself as well as her flat.

When Dr. Wingate asked her whether she'd suffered any noteworthy symptoms since receiving the injection Molly hesitated for a moment, but saw no practical alternative to telling him the truth. She half-expected him to nod sagely, because it was exactly what he'd expected, but his astonishment was blatantly honest.

"You can't remember *anything?*" he echoed, excitedly. *"Nothing at all?"*

Once it was established that the lost weekend had not been on the official list of expectable side-effects Molly expected the doctor to be extremely displeased, on the grounds that total amnesia was a pretty serious side-effect for any kind of drug, but he was obviously a back-room boffin whose contacts with Marketing were rare and slight. He was fascinated by her account of the unnaturally tidy flat.

"You gave not the slightest indication of distress as you left the building," he recalled, wonderingly, "and you obviously caught the bus without any difficulty. You've presumably taken adequate nourishment, and you seem to have kept

131

yourself very busy, although you must have gone to bed as normal and slept . . . and you did *everything* without being conscious, like a sleepwalker. Fascinating! Absolutely fascinating!"

Molly wondered briefly whether the greys might have anything to do with it, but rejected the hypothesis. She could hardly have been abducted again if she'd been hard at work scrubbing floors and scouring ingrained stains from her work-surfaces. It was more likely to be a result of her resolution to turn over a leaf and become the kind of mother of whom the Social Services and people like the Jarvises could approve. Perhaps the only way she could bear to do those sorts of things was to go into a trance and blank it out of her memory. She had never quite understood how *anyone* could do those sorts of things without going into a trance and blanking them out of consciousness.

"Did you bring the overnight bag?" Wingate asked her.

Molly shook her head. In her haste, that instruction had slipped her mind.

"Never mind—we'll improvise. We'll have to keep you in from now on, of course. It's quite remarkable! Has anything like this ever happened to you before?"

Molly hesitated, but again she decided that she might as well tell the truth. "Not exactly," she said. "I used to do some stuff, way back when, and I sometimes lost a few hours, even a couple of days—but I used to wake up feeling a hell of a lot worse than I woke up feeling this morning."

"What kind of stuff?"

Molly shrugged. "You name it. More than I could put a name to—the quality control wasn't so hot once the demand for Es began to exceed the supply, and my suppliers weren't the kind to pay much attention to the Trades Descriptions Act."

"Heroin? Amphetamines? LSD?"

"I tried all of them," Molly admitted. "Also poppers, a little angel dust, coke once or twice . . . but I'm clean now, honestly. The people at the Maudsley, last time I was sectioned, told me that my brain chemistry might have been permanently fried, but . . ."

She left it there, regretting that she'd mentioned the Maudsley. She realised that she might have said more than enough to get her booted out of the trial as an atypical subject, but Nathanael Wingate still seemed to be possessed by an altogether unwarranted excitement. Obviously, the experiment hadn't been fucked up too badly by her unusual reaction.

It occurred to Molly then that cosmetics wasn't the only field of research that paid much better than medical. Suddenly, the agency consultant's remark that Peaslee were looking for "single women in her age bracket" began to seem a trifle understated. What other specifications, she wondered, might the job description have contained?

"Are you happy to carry on with the trial, Molly?" Dr. Wingate asked her, his eyes all agleam with recently-glimpsed possibilities. "I'll understand if you want to drop out."

Molly thought about that for a couple of minutes. Any ordinary person, she knew, would have said "No thanks" and resumed the search for that oh-so-elusive cleaning job, but Molly was anything but ordinary. Even if Dr. Wingate *were* working on something whose primary applications were military, he couldn't possibly be looking to do her any serious damage. In any case, she thought, the greys would probably pull her out if she got into *real* trouble. They might not need her active involvement in their own schemes any more, but they still owed her a debt of gratitude.

"If I did agree to carry on," she said, slowly, "we'd have to renegotiate the fees. When I signed on, I was only planning on spending a couple of days a week here. If this going to mop up whole weeks, including all the unsocial hours and the weekends as well—especially if I'm going to lose sixty hours of memory every time I shoot up—I really think we ought to consider the question of double time . . ."

"We'll keep you under close observation, of course," Wingate assured her. "We'll make sure no harm comes to you, and . . ."

". . . or even triple time," Molly continued, casually overriding the interruption. "If I were cleaning offices or stacking shelves, I'd be able to think while I was working, wouldn't I? For this job, I'd be giving up *everything*. That's really heavy, and it *could* be dangerous . . ."

"We'll put you on a salary," Wingate said, his breathless tone revealing the depth as well as the breadth of his interest in Molly's presumably unique case. "Fifteen hundred a month, for a minimum of six weeks."

It was a big hike, but Molly figured that there was nothing to be lost by shooting for the jackpot. "Three thousand a month," she said, without batting an eyelid. Her math wasn't up to the calculation of whether six weeks of that was more than she'd so far earned by legal means in her entire life, but she figured that it must be close. It would surely cover the deposit and six months rent on a thoroughly decent flat.

"Twenty-two fifty," Wingate countered. Like any straight guy, he believed in splitting the difference—but Molly had never operated that way.

"When I say three thousand," she said, flatly, "that's just the basic price. Anything exotic that comes up as we go along will be extra. Take it or leave it. I don't haggle."

"I'll take it," Wingate assured her. "But the conditions remain in place. No questions, no comebacks, no lawsuits."

"I can live with that," Molly said, "but the insurance cover goes up too. The more I'm worth, the more compensation my nearest and dearest deserve—and I'm not talking tens of thousands. My kids may be in care just now, but if I'm not around as back-up, they need an adequate buffer."

"Okay," the mad scientist conceded, gracefully. "I'm confident that it won't be necessary. You'll come out of this as fit as you are now. All you stand to lose by continuing is a little time."

Luckily, he was very nearly right about that, as long as Molly wasn't disposed to quibble about the exact definition of "little." He might have been entirely right if Molly's neighbours hadn't been the cream of Hellspawn, with more than a few tricks up their old-fashioned sleeves in spite of all the wrinkles in their faces.

27

The eight weeks that Molly eventually spent in Peaslee Pharmaceuticals' research labs went more quickly than any other comparable periods of her life—even the five weeks she had spent touring the galaxy. Relativity had only wiped out sixty per cent of that time, but Dr. Wingate's hypodermic cocktails erased more than eighty per cent. It wasn't quite the same, because the time she sold to Peaslee had only been lost subjectively—and not, as it turned out, forever—but from Molly's immediate point of view the days simply sped by, when they bothered to put in an appearance at all.

Most of the time she spent in full possession of her faculties was taken up by careful cross-examinations. Wingate brought in a whole fleet of psychologists in a fruitless attempt to get her to remember what was going on inside while she was under the influence of the drug. He even imported a couple of hypnotists who tried to put her back into the trance-state, but like the hypnotists she'd worked with before they found her unresponsive. She was very glad when they let her alone for a while so that she could slob out watching TV or reading, although that wasn't easy while she was continually hooked up to all kinds of monitoring apparatus, with her head covered in electrodes.

She tried to think of the job as a mere matter of working peculiar shifts, with long weekends in between. Once she got it into that perspective, all the prodding and poking didn't seem so very different from working at King's Cross, although there was a lot less wear and tear on her borrowed bedsprings.

When the experiment reached its conclusion Wingate agreed to let Molly watch some of the video footage of her unremembered activities. She realised then that most of the "work" she'd been doing had been more like office cleaning than honest whoredom, but she took what consolation she could from the thought that if you had to spend every waking minute of four or five days a week obsessing about the neatness and cleanliness of a room that was already almost bare and clinically sterile, it was definitely best to do it in a trance.

"You don't suppose that's the real me, do you?" she asked Nathanael Wingate. "If that's what I've been repressing all these years . . ."

"I doubt it," Wingate told her. "It seems to me more like some kind of *displacement activity*. The EEG traces are all over the place—your brain's been astonishingly active, even while you were asleep, and the activity extends into every region. We're going to have to go back to the drawing-board on this one. It'll need a whole new set of animal experiments before we can even begin to figure out how these neurological effects are generated. After that . . . you *will* come back if we need you, won't you?"

"That depends," Molly said. "If I experience any long-term effects . . . now it's over you can tell me, can't you? What was the damn stuff *supposed* to do?"

"It's still confidential, I'm afraid," Wingate parried.

"In that case," Molly said, "You'll never see me again. From now on, it's informed consent or no co-operation."

Wingate didn't seem unduly surprised by that. He knew by now that Molly was no fool. "You've already signed a confidentiality form," he told her. "It covers *everything*."

"I won't tell a soul," Molly promised.

"Okay," he said. "The stuff was supposed to reverse some of the effects of aging. Not all, but some. If it worked the way it was supposed to as well as the way it wasn't, it might already have added a few years to your expected lifespan. If you're willing to come back when we call you . . . who knows?"

Molly looked at him long and hard, but she couldn't tell whether he was telling her the truth, or whether the Devil had finally got into him.

The first thing Molly did when she got back to Arcadia House after opening her first bank account and depositing her massive cheque was to knock on Lilith's door. Lilith seemed genuinely glad to see that she was fit and well, and dragged her into the flat for a cup of tea.

"I'm sorry, dear," the arch-demon said, as she shuffled off to put the kettle on. "There's been no sign of her. Your letter's still right there on the mantelshelf. Do you want it back?"

Molly shook her head. She hadn't realised until she found herself miserably speechless how disappointed she would be if it turned out that Christine hadn't tried to find her in the fifty-some days she'd been away.

Mephistopheles—who was, as usual, occupying one of Lilith's spare armchairs—said: "How are the mad scientists doing with the things man was never supposed to know?"

"If I were the incurious type, I'd say that it had been an absolute doddle," Molly said, dully, when she had found her voice again. "As things are, though . . . I'll get out of your way as soon as possible, so that you can have the entire floor to yourselves, just the way you want, but I'd really appreciate it if you'd do me a favour first."

"What favour?" Lilith asked.

"I want to know what I was *really* doing while I was blanked out. I've watched the videotapes, but Wingate's right: that was just activity for activity's sake. I want to know what was going on inside my head. Wingate claims that he was working on some kind of rejuvenation serum—which isn't implausible, given that Elvis was involved in something similar not a million miles away—but that's not why he got excited about the amnesia and plastered my head with sensors. He must have started wondering about military applications then, even if he hadn't before. Imagine what the army could do with something that could wipe out memories and turn people into domestic robots! I need to make some sense of this—which is why I need to know where my mind went while my body was getting deeply into trivial housework. I figure that you people are far more likely to be able to help than the hypnotherapists Wingate threw at me, and cheaper too."

"When I say that there are things that man was not meant to know," said Mephistopheles, ominously, "that includes woman, too. Has it occurred to you that your brain might have a very good reason for filtering your memories and rendering them inaccessible?"

"Of course it has," said Molly. "Why do you think I'm so desperate to dig them up? Can you do it?"

"No," said Mephistopheles.

"Of course we can, dear," said Lilith, "But Meph does have a point, you know. Sometimes, ignorance really is bliss."

"Ignorance is intolerable," Molly countered, stubbornly, "and I wouldn't know bliss if it bit my leg."

Lilith sighed. "Tonight, then," she said. "You'd better join us for dinner—I don't suppose you've had time to do any food shopping."

Molly accepted the invitation, and went back to her own flat to change. She'd brought back a plastic bag full of the clothes that she'd been given to wear at Peaslee but it was all

139

casual attire, so she went through her meagre wardrobe in search of something a little more upmarket that wasn't too tarty or too threadbare. There wasn't a lot of choice; all the half way good stuff had disappeared while she'd been absent without leave from the B&B.

Dinner at Lilith's was a grander affair than she'd anticipated. She'd guessed that Belial and Beelzebub would probably be there, as well as Mephistopheles, but she'd hadn't expected Astarte and Belphegor. Apparently, the demons were more interested in the affairs of the human world than they were prepared to let on—unless, for some reason, they thought that what was going on at Peaslee might be of special relevance to them. Molly tried to pump them about that during the meal, but they weren't very forthcoming. The wine was only a Chilean red that had been on special offer in Asda —chock-full of flavinols, if you believed the newspapers, but no use at all for loosening the tongues of demons reared on far harder liquors.

Afterwards, Lilith sat Molly down in an armchair and asked Astarte to do the honours. Because she was one of the demons co-opted from an earlier mythological system, Astarte had a slightly wider repertoire of party tricks than the original products of the Christian imagination.

"First, I'm going to try to put you back into the trance-state," Astarte explained. "If that works, I should be able to give you access to the hidden memories. I'm not going to ask you any questions while you're under, so we won't know anything until you wake up—and then it will be entirely up to you to decide what to tell us. Once the cat's out of the bag, though, it won't be possible to put it back. Whatever it is, you'll have to live with it."

"Fine," said Molly. "And don't worry—I'll tell you everything."

"There are some things that even demons are not meant to know," Mephistopheles said, gloomily, but it was obvious that he was in a minority of one, and he didn't volunteer to leave when Astarte started wiggling her fingers.

For a couple of minutes, Molly thought that it wasn't going to work, and that even demonic magic wouldn't be powerful enough to help her figure out what had been going on—but then she abruptly lost contact with Arcadia House, and remembered *everything*.

28

Molly had expected that the recovered memories would take a relatively ordinary form, at least to begin with, allowing her to recall her body's return trip from Peaslee Pharmaceuticals to 1303 Arcadia House on that first Friday and all the house-work that had occupied her hands thereafter. In fact, the de-luge of memories cut right to the chase and revealed to her exactly what her mind had been doing.

Unfortunately, her mind seemed to have been having a direly difficult time, in a world far more alien than any she had seen on her recent galactic tour.

At first, the only impressions she had been able to glean were of her immediate surroundings, and even they had been vague and distorted. She retained the impression of immense edifices made of some kind of translucent substance, threaded with endless winding corridors and vast spiral stairs, but it had all been horribly confusing at the time, and it was just as confusing now that she had the opportunity to bring hindsight to bear on the task of making sense of it . . .

By day, the walls had been alive with refracted light, col-oured with all the hues of the spectrum; by night they had been filled with dim starlight. These edifices were usually stable, as if built on solid foundations, but she had sometimes had the impression of extremely swift movement, as if they were able to lift themselves from whatever surface they usu-ally stood upon and hurl themselves into the void. When they did so, the alternation of colourful day and glittering night had been replaced with a more complex play of light, and

Molly had felt her own body grow less burdensome.

Because she had toured a tiny fraction of the galaxy with the greys Molly was easily able to guess, now, that the edifices must have been spaceships, and that the alterations in her own self-awareness must have been the result of weight-loss in zero-g—but she had not made that deduction at the time. There was, in any case, something very strange about the remembered sensation, which was markedly different from what she had felt when the greys first took her to their mothership.

As time went by, she recalled, the distortion of her vision had begun to ease somewhat, and she had been able to make out certain shapes more clearly. It was as if she had been seeing through eyes that were not her own, and that she had had to learn to see all over again. She had once read about an experiment in which newborn kittens were reared in an environment in which everything was vertically striped, and had subsequently proved to be unable to distinguish horizontal strips from series of dots. Her own experience had not been exactly like that, because the alien environment in which she found herself had seemed to have no straight lines of *any* kind, vertical or horizontal, and no angles either, but she assumed that something similar must have been going on. At first, her habits of perception had been woefully ill-adapted to the edgeless and un-angular environment, but as time went by she had become a little better adapted to the analysis of its multitudinous curves, circles and spirals.

Molly had eventually been able to make a little more sense of her surroundings, although the first objects that she had been able to pick out clearly were far outside the walls which usually confined her. One was a bluish circle dappled with greens and browns and streaked with white, and this she had eventually recognised as the Earth seen from a distance. The other was a featureless orb whose surface was a uniform polished white. The little she knew about astronomy encouraged her to jump to the conclusion that this must be Venus, and she began to wonder whether she had somehow made telepathic contact with aliens who were engaged in shuttling back and forth between Earth and its inner neighbour on a regular basis.

Molly's improved perceptions had begun to deliver more disturbing news when she began to get a better sense of her own body, and realised that it was not merely her eyes that were not her own. She had gradually realised that certain snaky entities that moved in liquid curves before her were, in fact, parts of her own body. She had never mastered her new sense of touch, but she had eventually been able to manoeuvre her eyes in such a way as to see as much of herself as was readily perceptible by sight alone. So far as she had been able to tell she was still possessed of two eyes, both positioned frontward to produce binocular vision, but they had been set in a huge bulbous mass, more like a torso than a head. She had never managed to obtain a confident count of her tentacular limbs, but there had been at least eight of them arrayed about the lower rim of the fleshy mass.

In brief, she had been metamorphosed into something vaguely resembling a giant octopus.

She had realised fairly soon after coming to terms with that fact that she was not engaged in the kind of activities one might have expected of an octopus. For one thing, she had not been immersed in a liquid medium. For another, her tentacular arms had been continually occupied with various kinds of labour, some of them as thoughtlessly routine as those to which her human body had been consigned. Indeed, while she had been sharing the consciousness of the alien monster her own body had, in effect, been reduced to the status of a few additional appendages. Apparently, this was a species thoroughly accustomed to multi-tasking.

Although she had not been able to make out what food-stuffs her alien symbiote ate or what fluids it drank, she/it had certainly been involved in the routine business of nourishment—but that had only required a couple of her/its limbs. Meanwhile, the others had never ceased to be busy. Some, she felt sure, had been manipulating machinery; others had been involved in some kind of *inscription,* pro-ducing complex designs compounded out of circles and shadowy splashes.

Molly had realised, eventually, that her mind had some-how been made captive. Her personality had been superim-posed upon, or subsumed within, the brain of this monstrous creature, which had made use of it in some fashion that she could not fathom even in retrospect.

Molly realised that the memories which she had of her adventure were entirely passive, and that this was the main reason why they were so ill-formed. Normally, she and every other being with which she was familiar went about her everyday business attentively, picking out certain stimuli for response, noticing items of significance and neglecting others. The memories conventionally secreted into her brain were, in the main, a record of what had captured her atten-tion and what had required response—especially *considered* responses. These newly-recovered memories, by contrast, seemed vague and surreal, partly because they had no such strengthening elements; they were more like the memories of dreams, and might have banished entirely even now had it not been for the fixative power of Astarte's magic.

Even that magic, however, could not put into the memo-ries something that had not been there to begin with: an alert, actively-engaged consciousness.

For this reason, what Molly had recovered remained intensely frustrating even when she came out of her trance. She was alert and actively-engaged *now*, but every time she tried to grasp the fine detail of what had happened to her while she was under the influence of Wingate's drug, it evaded her grasp. It was if as the memories were clouds, which kept forming suggestive shapes but dissipated every time she reached out to try to feel their precise shapes. She discovered a little, but suspected far more, and found it deeply frustrating that she had no way to make her suspicions more concrete. She formed the strong conviction that she had been much more profoundly displaced in time than in space, but when she tried to find firm proof of that conviction she could not find any, at least for the moment.

As the memories continued to unfold, however, she found more and more sense emerging spontaneously within them. The longer her mind had been captive, the more accustomed it had become to its alien habitat, and the more comfortable it had become within the activities directed by the alien consciousness with which it had been fused.

Molly found, in the end, that striving hard to make sense of what she had not been able to make sense of at the time was hopeless, and deduced that her best chance of enlightenment lay in accepting passivity and allowing the development of what she could only conceive as a *flow of intuition*.

Just as her alien powers of sight had become clearer by degrees, so her alien powers of understanding had been slowly augmented, little by little. She had begun to have a vague sense of the exotic mind that had kidnapped and imprisoned hers. She had begun to catch enigmatic glimpses of its stocks of knowledge, its conscious activities, even its intentions and purposes . . .

The work of the handless but inordinately clever limbs

had eventually come to the very edge of meaningfulness, and she had begun to see the *sense* in the patchwork of circles and shadows . . .

But then the flow had been abruptly cut off, as the last of Nathanael Wingate's injections exhausted its effect. She had returned to her body for good. She had, she supposed, been set free, perhaps in the nick of time. Had she progressed just one step further, her mind might actually have fused with its host and been permanently secured within it—but Wingate, perhaps perceiving that she was at breaking-point, had terminated the experiment.

Molly wondered whether Wingate and his colleagues had had the slightest inkling of what had really been happening to her. It seemed more likely that they had only been concerned with observing her from the outside, studying the actions of her mind-deserted body, conceiving of the anomalous activity within her brain as something spontaneous. Wingate probably had not the slightest suspicion of what had really been happening. Even if he had, he certainly could not have been any better placed than Molly was to make sense of it all —and even Molly knew that there was a great deal of work still to be done in *that* respect.

29

"I think it must have been a very long time in the past," Molly told the interested demons, when they pressed their demands for the explanations that remained frustratingly just out of reach. "I think it was billions of years ago—maybe before the beginning of the fossil record."

"Long before *our* time, then," said Lilith. She had already admitted, although some of her companions had not, that Molly had been right about demons being a projection of the human yearning for moral order.

"Long before that," Molly confirmed, speaking rather distractedly because she was still trying hard to connect up the pieces of what she had recalled, hoping to make a little more sense of it. "I think they might have had something to do with the *real* Creation, much further back in time than any mythical Adam. The creation of the first replicator molecule, that is—the ancestor of DNA. Except that it wasn't *creation,* as such, because the organic sludge must already have been here, ensliming the planet. It must have been more like a kind of *nudge:* an evolutionary kick-start."

"You're just making it up," Mephistopheles put in, airily. "It's all confabulation—false memory syndrome, isn't that what the experts on TV call it? The world only began a few thousand years ago."

"You weren't there, Meph," Lilith told him. "I was on the scene, at least in spirit, a long time before you, but I'm not foolish enough to think that was the *beginning.* If you'd only taken the trouble to master the art and science of doubt, you'd know that the so-called Father of Lies was and is a mere apprentice."

"Do you suppose that your mad scientist might have done this deliberately, Molly?" Astarte wanted to know. "Could he have *intended* to put you in touch with these giant octopuses."

"Don't you mean octopi?" said Beelzebub.

"Actually," Mephistopheles put in, eager to regain the intellectual high ground, "*octopus* comes from the Greek, not the Latin, and ought to be rendered octo*pous*. Technically, the plural is *octopodes*, but octopuses is acceptable as an Anglicization. Octopi, on the other hand, is an etymological atrocity."

"Oh, shut up," said Belphegor. "Molly?"

"I can't be *absolutely* sure," Molly admitted, "but I don't think Wingate has any idea what really happened to me. He could see I'd *gone*, of course, and that there was some kind of feedback from wherever I'd gone, but I suspect that what Peaslee are interested in is whether they can figure out how to get rid of people whenever they want to, and bring them back on demand. It's the motives of the aliens that are *really* puzzling. *They* seemed to know what they were doing. I think they even wanted *me* to know what they were doing—and maybe they'd have managed it if they'd had a little more time."

"Maybe your friends the greys can tell you who they are—or were," Astarte suggested.

"I don't think so," Molly said. "The greys evolved intelligence a few million years before we did, and fucked up their own biosphere while we were still busy inventing agriculture, but they belong to the same galactic era—maybe even the same interstellar family, if there *is* an interstellar family."

"You mean that the octopuses might have created them, too?" Lilith said.

"Maybe. Not created, exactly—but the primeval sludge on the greys' homeworld might have been nudged in the same sort of way."

"Well," said Beelzebub, "if they were trying to make the evolution of life on Earth copy evolution on their own world, they certainly made a big mistake. I never heard of a smart octopus."

"Perhaps they weren't," Molly said, still groping for some further insight, some crucial key that would allow her to make that last leap of comprehension. "Perhaps they were trying to make something different, something new. Perhaps that's why they tried to reach forward in time, to establish a link with us. Perhaps . . ."

She trailed off again.

"You need a rest, dear," said Lilith. "It's late. We can talk again in the morning, after you've had a good night's sleep."

"I suppose I do," Molly agreed, although had a nasty suspicion that her dreams might require some time to work their way through the nightmarish revelations that Astarte had just gifted to her. "If I'm going to start flat-hunting tomorrow . . ."

She stood up, her head still spinning with bizarre possibilities. Robbed of the support of Lilith's armchair, she felt weak and dizzy. She wondered if a little fresh air would do her good, and turned reflexively towards the window, which had been behind her while she was telling the demons what she had learned.

Two full lunar months had elapsed since Molly had first gone off to Peaslee, leaving behind the letter that still stood unopened on Lilith's mantelshelf. The moon was full again now, its entire face clearly visible through the thirteenth-floor window, slightly rose-tinted by the atmospheric pollutants that captured the glare of the capital's myriad electric lights.

"Oh shit," said Molly, softly, as another piece of the jigsaw fell belatedly into place. "*That*'s what it was—what we were doing."

"What is it dear?" Lilith asked.

"*Dear Humanit,*" Molly quoted. "*We're very sorry that we couldn't be here. Please wait until we come back. Then we can talk things over and figure out what to do. We're your mother-race, and we love you very much.*"

"What?" said Mephistopheles.

"It wasn't Venus," Molly whispered. "It was the moon."

"What was?" Mephistopheles demanded, his voice sharpening with impatience and incomprehension.

"That other world I saw through alien eyes," Molly explained. "It wasn't Venus—it was the moon, before we wrote the message on its face."

"You can read a message written on the moon's face?" Mephistopheles's tone suggested that Lilith had spoken too soon when she accused him of never having mastered the art and science of doubt. "I never heard of anyone who could do that."

"No," Molly conceded, still speaking very softly. "I don't suppose many others would be able to read it, even if they understood the alien alphabet—but I don't have any difficulty at all. You see, *it's my own handwriting.*"

30

The first-floor flat Molly rented with the Peaslee windfall was in Barnsbury, just off the Caledonian Road. Some people of her acquaintance might have found it a little too close to Holloway for comfort, but Molly preferred to think of it as just a short walk from Camden Market, which had been one of her regular haunts in the days when she was young and not so very far from innocent.

Even the estate agent hadn't dared to describe it as a luxury flat, but it had two bedrooms, one of which was an ample double, and several fixtures that Molly would have put in the luxury category, including the kind of non-bedroom that she felt she could call a sitting-room without feeling silly and a telephone. The wallpaper was fairly new and unblistered by damp, the kitchenette only seemed overcrowded because the fridge-freezer was so big, and the sitting-room furniture hadn't been slotted together from MFI kits whose screws could never be retightened because you could never find the Allen key.

In brief, it had the potential to become a comfortable family home, with all the privileges and responsibilities that concept implied.

The first thing Molly did after the gang's joyrider of the day had helped her transfer her meagre possessions from Arcadia House and bid her a cheery goodbye was to phone the Jarvises. She knew that it was tempting fate, but she couldn't help it. The year was half way through and she felt that she was now making solid progress in the vexatious business of redesigning her life.

"Have you seen her?" screeched the wildly sobbing Mrs. Jarvis, as soon as Molly identified herself.

"Christine?" said Molly. "No, she . . ."

"Not *Christine,*" Mrs. Jarvis yelped, as if no one but a deranged madwoman could have leapt to that conclusion. "Angie! I mean *Angie!*"

"Oh shit," Molly murmured, swiftly inferring that her younger daughter must have followed the elder sister's bad example. Her first impulse, inevitably, was to blame the Jarvises—to lose one foster-daughter might be excused as a misfortune, but losing two reeked of carelessness—but she knew from past experience that all verbal mud flung Jarviswards inevitably rebounded on her. She contented herself with a strangled inquiry as to how long Angie had been missing.

"She set off for school as usual yesterday morning," the calmer but equally censorious voice of Mr. Jarvis reported, "but she never registered, and she didn't come home afterwards. We've notified the police, of course—they should have been to see you by now."

"I'm not at Arcadia House any more," Molly said, numbly. "I've just moved into a new flat." She gave Mr. Jarvis the address, hoping to hear a sharp intake of breath when he heard the postcode, but he was too distracted by what he thought of as his own problems to be astonished by the fact that the mother of his foster children was now living north of the river. "Well, *that's* not much help," was his only comment.

Molly would have continued the conversation if the doorbell hadn't rung, but when it did she immediately leapt to the conclusion that it must be someone who had been told where to look for her by her thirteenth-floor ex-neighbours—possibly Angie, or even Christine, or at the very least a concerned policeperson. She made a hasty excuse and hung up.

When she opened the door she barely had time to notice that the caller was one of the men in black from Croydon before his fist came hurtling into her face. She hadn't time to duck out of the way, although she did manage to lower her head enough to take the blow on her left brow-ridge instead of her nose. That had to be reckoned fortunate, give that her nose would certainly have been broken, but she didn't have time to count her blessings while the momentum of the punch was slamming her back against the corridor wall.

After the second time she had been raped—not counting foul-ups with business procedure at King's Cross and various houses of ill-repute—Molly had taken self defence classes, but one thing they had taught her was that all the tricks in the book can't help you if your opponent is five inches taller, four stone heavier and once did a similar course himself. When the man in black put his massive right hand about Molly's wind-pipe and shoved her so far up the wall that her feet were no longer touching the ground, Molly knew that she was help-less. She made a token attempt to knee him in the balls and stick both her thumbnails into his eyes, but he was ready for both moves. He used his left hand to seize both her arms and twist them around, and leaned forward to pin her securely and suffocatingly against the wall.

"That was very stupid, Molly," he hissed. He didn't mean the knee or the thumbnails—he meant moving away from the thirteenth floor of Arcadia House. Even he would have hesi-tated before throwing his weight about up there, although he probably didn't have a clue who it was that he'd have had to reckon with if he tried.

He was the senior of the two men who'd come to collect her after her abduction by the greys: the one who thought he'd been clever when he left the biochip in her breast first time around, and twice as clever when he fished it out again after she'd been up to the mothership. He was also the first one she had infected with the new DNA that the greys had tucked away inside the protein coats of resident viruses which the men in black had already tagged, and the one to whom she had given the slip when the aliens had taken her on the galactic cruise they'd promised her as a reward. Given all that, Molly figured that she was in for a pretty torrid time. Being a civil servant, he probably wouldn't allow himself to break anything more substantial than her nose, but when she looked into his angry eyes and saw the Devil there she figured that she was all set up for her nastiest raping yet.

"Thought we'd forgotten you, did you?" the man in black sneered, squeezing just hard enough to cut off her breath. "Or maybe you thought that getting into bed with that sparrowfart Wingate would put you out of bounds? Guess again, whore."

Molly had to close her left eye against the blood that ran into its corner but she knew that it would probably close of its own accord when the bruise was ripe. She tried to keep the right one steady, but it wasn't easy. The man in black pulled her off the wall and stepped back, presumably intending to close the door that still gaped open behind him. When she made a second attempt to jab her knee into his groin he hit her in the stomach, and then let her fall into a breathless heap—but when he turned away the door didn't slam shut.

When Molly was able to look up her one-eyed vision was blurred with tears, but she could see that there was now someone else standing in the doorway—someone every bit as tall as her assailant, though not as heavily-built, and likewise dressed entirely in black. She might have taken him for another of the same kind, had he not been wearing a broad-brimmed hat that no officially-sanctioned man in black would ever have been seen dead in.

The newcomer didn't say a word. He simply met the gaze of the man in black, staring him in the face. Molly figured that even someone army-trained was going to have difficulty meeting the disapproving eye of someone who'd just caught him in the act of beating up a woman, and so it proved. The staring-match had barely begun before it was over. The man in black obviously thought about launching his mighty fist at the new target, but just as obviously decided against it, perhaps because he was intimidated by such knowledge as he had of the kinds of company Molly had been keeping lately, and perhaps because he figured that a man in his position could only beat the shit out of so many civilians before endangering his pension.

"I'll see *you* again," he spat at Molly, over his shoulder. Then he pushed past the man in the broad-brimmed hat and left.

31

The man in the hat came in, shut the door behind him and offered Molly his gloved left hand. She took it and levered herself upright. She used her right hand to wipe away the blood and tears so that she could look at him properly—or as properly as was possible with one eye so badly bruised.

Unlike the bully boy from Croydon, the newcomer wasn't wearing a sharp suit. His black jacket and trousers were leather, but not biking leathers—and no biker would ever have worn such a delicate silk shirt, let alone that absurd hat. His boots were leather too, but they looked as soft as his gloves. The reason he hadn't offered her his right hand, apparently, was that there was something wrong with it: the forearm was stunted and the hand itself seemed to be shrivelled, although it was difficult to judge the nature of the injury while he had the gloves on.

"Thanks," Molly said.

"I'm sorry I didn't get here sooner," her saviour said. "You're Molly, I take it? Lilith told me where to find you."

Molly had to wipe her eyes again, but the cut on her eyebrow didn't seem too bad—not bad enough, at any rate, to need stitches. "You know Lilith?" she said, warily.

"Not very well," he admitted, taking off his hat and placing it on one of the hooks set in the wall beside the door. His hair was jet black. "It's more that we have acquaintances in common—as you and I also have."

It was then that Molly remembered the meagre details of what Elizabeth Peach, her social worker, had told her about

Christine's disappearance. Christine had allegedly been seen talking to a man in his fifties who wore a broad-brimmed hat. Molly squinted, trying to figure out how old her visitor might be. *Anywhere between thirty and three hundred* was the answer that sprang by mysterious means to her mind, but she supposed that an observer as limited in his imagination as Mr. Jarvis might have decided that fifty was a safe compromise.

"Who are you?" she asked, sharply.

"Call me Tom," he answered lightly. "Most people do." The addition seemed more than usually gratuitous. His eyes glinted green for a moment, like cat's eyes, but the pupils were round and human.

"Where's Christine?"

"Safe," he assured her, in the manner of a man who expected that his word would be trusted without elaboration. "It's not Christine we have to worry about. It's Angie."

"Okay," said Molly, using the frost in her voice to signify that all the moral credit he'd gained by seeing off the sharp-suited man in black had just been cancelled. "Where's *Angie?*"

"She's been kidnapped by the Queen of the Phase," he said. At least, that's what Molly thought he had said, until he added: "That's eff-ay-why-ess. Some people call them fairies, but they don't like it."

Molly opened her mouth to protest but hesitated, then shut it again. She had to admit that her licence to object to statements like that had accumulated more than enough endorsements to render it invalid. "That being one of the mutual acquaintances you and Lilith have in common, I suppose," she said, after a reasonable pause.

"Just so," he confirmed.

"And that would make you Thomas the Rhymer rather than Puss-in-Boots, I suppose?"

She actually caught him slightly off guard with that one, but he was quick to suppress his smile, which would have been entirely inappropriate despite its ruefulness.

"I wish I could be as specific as that," he said, "but at this point in time, I'm only a mysterious tall dark stranger. I hope that we'll both find out in due course exactly who I am, but for the time being I'm as much at a loss as you are."

"I've had amnesia myself," Molly confessed. "I hate it—my guilt-ridden subconscious always takes advantage of the absence of my ego to make me do housework. *Why* has the Queen of the Fays stolen my twelve-year-old daughter from her loving foster-parents? Is it just that random abduction's the sort of thing she's into, or has she some specific motive for targeting my daughter rather than someone else's?"

"Interesting question," said the man who most people allegedly called Tom. "Given the way things have worked out, I think we can take it for granted that it isn't a coincidence, and that you must have something the Queen wants badly enough to warrant stealing your child. You're probably in a better position to guess what that might be than I am."

Molly sighed. She used the fingers of her left hand to probe the sore spot on her abdomen while she stared at the blood that was streaking the fingers and back of her right. "If I were at my best," she confessed, "I'd be sorely tempted to grab the collar of your silk shirt and twist it hard while I demanded an explanation of what you mean by *given the way things have worked out,* but as things are, I think I'd better make a cup of tea while you explain. Would you care to come through to the sitting-room?"

Tall dark Tom not only came through to the sitting-room but casually made himself comfortable on the non-MFI settee while Molly went into the kitchenette to put the kettle on.

"What I meant," he told her, regretfully, "is that when I found out that the fays were staking out the house in Tooting, I assumed that it was Christine they were after. I . . . well, I needed a *claim*, you see, to get into Faerie, and it seemed to me that if I could only get myself into a position where I had a claim on Christine, I'd be okay when they followed through. That was a mistake, of course. When Christine decided to go missing, I went after her—but the changeling squad went after Angie instead. Now I need a claim on *you*, because you're the only one with a strong enough claim to go after *her*. It might have been okay if Christine had been Angie's full sister, but this is one of those times when half isn't quite enough."

Molly thought back to the moment when she'd first seen Tom on her doorstep. He hadn't exactly thrown himself on the man in black like an outraged hero, but he had nevertheless saved her from a heavy mauling. She had to figure that he'd already established his claim on her, even though he hadn't gone out of his way to say so.

She put two tea bags into two mugs and watched the quietly burbling kettle pensively. If her visitor needed her in order to gain entry to Faerie, the need was probably mutual. It wasn't that she was too stupid to find any place that wasn't on the tube map, but this was one place where she definitely wouldn't be able to find her way around with an A-to-Z.

As for what she might have that the Queen of the Fays might want badly enough to warrant crude extortion—well, that could be any one of several things. She didn't have Elvis's address any more, but she probably had more of the greys' DNA than she'd infected anybody else with, and if she really were the only person in the world who could read what was written on the face of the moon she must be the only one who could read any other messages the planetoid-sized cephalopods might have left lying around back in the pre-Cambrian.

32

"I suppose you know," Molly called out to the tall dark stranger, as she poured boiling water into the mugs, "that you're not much different from the Angel, or Lilith—or the Devil himself for that matter. You're just one more projection of the human yearning for moral order. There are a lot of you about. I put it down to the Millennium, myself. It still has six months to run, you know, even though the mathematically-challenged went ape last New Year's Eve."

"What if I am?" he retorted. "You're not labouring under the delusion that I'm just something your drug-fried brain conjured up, are you? Believe me, Molly, if there were a competition to decide who has the more meaningful existence, I'd win hands down."

"No you wouldn't," she told him, confidently. "The Devil would. I've met him, and I can assure you that he still has us all beat, even if his top arch-demons have gone AWOL. Do you want milk and sugar?"

"Just milk, please."

Molly fished the tea-bag out and dropped it in the sink. Then she added a dash of milk straight from the carton. Jugs, like trays and biscuits, were strictly for Jarvises and social workers.

She took the mugs into the optimistically-titled sitting-room and handed one over before sitting down for the first time in one of her newly-rented armchairs. He took it in his left hand, after pausing to remove his left glove. His useless right hand remained concealed.

161

"What do *you* want from the Queen of the Fays?" Molly demanded.

"That's my business," Tom parried.

"Not any more it isn't," she informed him. "You've just made it *my* business."

His eyes glinted green again, but he nodded to acknowledge that she might have a point. "I don't know, exactly," he confessed. "I suppose I'll find out if and when I find out the rest of it—but to do that, I need a claim on her attention. I have asked others for help, including Lilith, but they all told me the same thing. There are only two places where I might get what I need, and the other one is Hell."

"If the Queen of the Fays wants something from me," Molly said, experimentally, "then I don't really need you, do I? Presumably, she'll send for me soon enough."

"Oh, you definitely need me," he said, with what seemed like ominous overconfidence. "The Queen will make sure that you get into Faerie when *she* figures that the time is ripe, but it's always best to steal a march on her kind, if you get the chance—and if you want to get out again, you'll need as many cards up your sleeve as you can carry. Even the greys can't pull you out of *there*."

"Okay," said Molly, quickly draining her mug to the dregs. "Let's go."

"It's not that simple," tall dark Tom informed her, sparing a couple of moments to glance down meaningfully at his own half-full vessel. "If we're to run a successful bluff, we need to play the game as cleverly as we can. It would help a lot if you looked the part."

"And what part am I supposed to look?" Molly asked, letting her annoyance show.

"Dangerous. A hint of mystery wouldn't hurt, but you certainly need to look like someone who can handle herself a lot better than you were when I arrived. I don't suppose you have anything in your wardrobe that says *I don't know the meaning of fear—mess with me and you'll regret it.*"

"No I don't," said Molly, sourly, "but I know someone who does."

While Tom continued sipping his tea she fished her address-book out of the relevant cardboard box and went back to the phone. When she'd persuaded the answering service to put her on to Torquemadam herself, she said: "Hi, Sylv, it's Molly—yes, *that* Molly. I need to borrow a warrior princess costume. Do you still have one in my size?"

Torquemadam confirmed that she still had Molly's size, but regretfully informed her that she was no longer entitled to a staff discount. Molly assured her that she could pay the hire charge in full. She paused to ask whether tall dark Tom had a car, and on being told that he hadn't—which didn't surprise her in the least—she told Torquemadam that she'd hop on the tube right away.

"How easy is it to get to Faerie from Soho?" she asked the man with the withered arm when she'd hung up. "We can use Leicester Square, Piccadilly Circus or Oxford Circus tube—whichever's most convenient."

"That's okay," he said, putting down his mug at last. "You can get to Faerie from anywhere—but it does involve going underground, after a fashion." He collected his hat as they left the flat.

While they walked to Caledonian Road station Tom explained to Molly that Faerie had certain things in common with the Heaven from which her angel had fallen. Although it was neither timeless or spaceless, it was the kind of place where an awful lot of time could pass unnoticed if you dropped your guard, and the kind of place which fitted so neatly inside ordinary places that it was extremely difficult to perceive or slip into. In order to get into it, they would have to become a lot smaller than they usually were—but this would have certain advantages as well as a few disadvantages, because putting the squeeze on the empty space within their atoms would make their bodies much more solid.

"That might give you a feeling of invulnerability," he told her, while they were riding southwards on the Piccadilly line, "but you mustn't take that too seriously. Packing all your mass into the same sort of volume as a toy soldier certainly makes you *hard,* but everyone else down there is just as hard as you are, and any tiny wound you get is likely to turn into a great big gaping hole when everything goes soft again. If you get into any kind of fight—and you might have to, if things go badly—try to settle it with one blow."

Molly looked pointedly at his right hand as she said: "Why do I have this terrible suspicion that you've already tried that —and failed ignominiously?"

She had never seen eyes glow the way his occasionally did —and this time, they glowed red instead of green. *Ignominiously* had taken the implication beyond the limit of his tolerance. "Anyone can come unstuck," he said, through gritted teeth, "if they don't know what they're doing and won't listen to good advice." He seemed as if he might go into a deep sulk then, but Molly begged him to carry on forewarning her.

He told her that she'd have to do most of the talking once they were in Faerie, and that she mustn't allow herself to be outwitted or intimidated. He told her that she mustn't eat or drink anything the fays offered to her, mustn't accept any gifts, mustn't address the queen as Titania or Gloriana and mustn't assume that anything the Queen told her was actually true.

"And above all else," he said, "*don't dance.* When the music starts—and it will—you have to stay still. It's when people join the dance that time and chance start playing nasty tricks."

Tall dark Tom went on to list so many other things that Molly mustn't do that by the time they arrived at Leicester Square station he seemed positively parental, in a Jarvisy sort of way. Although she refrained from telling him so, she obviously had difficulty seeming sufficiently grateful for all his gnomic advice. He was still a little tight-lipped and frayed around the edges when they got to Torquemadam's dungeon, but he loosened up again when the brothel-keeper laid out the warrior princess costume.

With the black wig and all that leather on, Molly looked completely different: dangerous, uncompromising and *sexy*.

"Do you want the sword and the steel frisbee?" Torquemadam asked her.

Molly looked at her companion, certain that he would have further advice to offer.

"Have you ever actually *used* a sword?" Tom inquired.

"Only for spanking," Molly admitted.

"Is there any kind of weapon you *have* done some real damage with?"

Molly sighed. "Better make it a whip, Sylv," she said, knowing that it would cost extra because it didn't come with the costume. If she continued spending in this lavish vein, her Peaslee Pharmaceuticals nest-egg wasn't going to last very long.

Torquemadam handed over the whip.

Molly had known her sometime employer for years, on and off, and had always thought her the one person in the world who really was unshockable, but tall dark Tom didn't waste any time at all once Molly was properly kitted out, and he made the passes with his arms right there in the dungeon, while Torquemadam was still looking on. The last thing

Molly saw before the grey mists swirled up around her was the expression of utter astonishment on the older woman's face as she realised that there was one kind of vanishing act she hadn't previously encountered.

33

The mist became so thick that Molly lost sight of her companion for a while, but a cool breeze sprang up which seemed to cut through the peculiar fog like a knife. Faerie was just as dimly lit as Torquemadam's dungeon but the quality of the light was very different. As the vapour dissolved around Molly and Tom it exposed a cloudless royal blue sky lit by a sun the colour of an orange—except that the "sky" wasn't really a sky and the "sun" wasn't really a sun. The "sky" was the vaulted roof of a vast cave, and the "sun" was some kind of creature creeping across it, like a vast phosphorescent slime-mould.

Molly saw by the sun-creature's light that they were in a clearing in a wood. She figured that the wood was probably as near to Athens as it was to anywhere else, but it wasn't what the average Shakespearean set-dresser would have provided. The trees were separated from the pool in the middle of the clearing by a considerable mossy margin, but they looked like the kind of willows that were only supposed to live on a river's bank, trailing their leaf-laden branches on the water's surface. Their foliage was green, but it was a darker green than Molly had ever seen on a tree before. Although the regular kind of weeping willows had always looked to Molly as if they'd merely been watching a soppy film, these gave the impression that they were doing some serious grieving.

Even the atmosphere of Faerie was different. Although the vapour had been swallowed up by the mossy ground, the air that remained was strangely soupy, like invisible gazpacho.

Tall dark Tom didn't waste any time before tearing off the glove that he had used to conceal his injured hand. The right arm didn't seem any shorter than the left now, and the dimensions of the hand were in perfect proportion to the rest of him, but Molly could see raw red marks on the wrist, as if a powerful hand had gripped it and squeezed hard. She knew that she'd looked in the right place when he'd warned her that injuries sustained in Faerie's microcosm could be much exaggerated by a return to normal size.

Tom flexed the fingers experimentally, and seemed very relieved when they worked—but he had no sword, nor any other weapon that she could see, and Molly got the impression that the work he wanted those fingers to do was more delicate by far than any fencer or bowman could have required. Assuming that he really was a projection of the human yearning for moral order, Molly thought she could guess what delicate work it was.

She put her own hand up to her right eyebrow, and found that the swelling had gone down. The skin, which should have been very tender, was now as hard as seasoned wood— but it still hurt when pressed by her steely fingers, and she had a nasty suspicion that it was still discoloured. She took what comfort she could from the fact that she could see clearly from both eyes, neither being in the least bit troubled by dribbling blood or leaking tears.

"Let's go," said Tom, having favoured Molly's rig with one more appraising glance.

She didn't have to ask which way; he had already set off. If the direction in which Faerie's sun-creature was creeping was west, tall dark Tom was heading due east.

They were following a path, which was more than broad enough to accommodate them walking abreast, but Molly would have had difficulty keeping up with her companion's capacious stride even if Torquemadam had been able to supply a pair of boots without high heels. The warrior princess costume didn't come with four-inch stilettos, but it hadn't been designed with actual heroics in mind.

The middle of the path had been pounded flat, apparently by the hooves of countless unshod horses, but it was moist enough to take a grip, and Molly was soon struggling. Tom had to stop every thirty yards or so to give her a chance to catch up.

"How far is it?" Molly demanded, when her patience ran out.

"It depends," he replied, unhelpfully. "The court is a movable feast. People have been known to wander here for weeks—but the Queen will know we're here by now, and you're someone she *wants* to see."

It occurred to Molly that the Queen might be in no particular hurry, given that Tom might well be someone she *didn't* want to see, but by the time she'd formulated a sarcastic response it had been rendered redundant. Two lithe forms appeared on the pathway in front of them, so suddenly that Molly wasn't sure whether they had stepped from hiding or manifested themselves by magic.

Tom hadn't had time to amplify his observation that the fays didn't like to be called fairies, but Molly could understand how that might be the case. The image conjured up in her mind by the word *fairy* was that of kiddie-lit illustration and crude photographic trickery: frail ultra-feminine forms embellished with insectile wings and dressed in diaphanous white. These figures were definitely female, but they looked like the Goths who had hung around Camden in the days when Molly had a regular at the market. The rubber and leather in the fays' all-black ensembles might conceivably have been real, but whatever was used in Faerie as a substitute for PVC was definitely surreal, and the patterns woven into their translucent tights had not been produced by any mechanical loom. Their hair made Torquemadam's best black wig look modest, and Molly had the sneaking suspicion that their black lips and spectacular eyes weren't actually *made up* at all.

"Well well," said one, putting an uncannily long black fingernail to her pointed chin. "If it isn't Tom, Tom, the pauper's son, back for sloppy seconds. Long time no see, Tommy."

"But you can't bring your own girlfriends in here, Tommy," said the other. "It's like taking your own booze to a winebar. These are *licensed* premises—we don't do corkage."

Molly stepped forward. She stuck her thumbs in her belt, mainly to draw attention to the whip that was coiled up and fastened there, and said: "Actually, *he*'s with *me*."

"Well, I don't see what difference *that* makes," the first fay drawled, as she advanced towards Molly. "You can't bring boyfriends *either*."

"No," said the other, who stayed where she was. "*That*'s like bringing roast pork to a bar mitzvah."

"He's my guide," Molly said, resisting the temptation to camp up her own manner for the time being. "Also my adviser. I believe your beloved monarch wants to see me, and didn't have time to send me a proper invitation."

"It's not a matter of *time*, darling," said the first fay, who had now arrived in close enough proximity to reach out and touch Molly's chin with her black-painted fingernail. "It's purely a matter of *inclination*."

Molly reached up and took the fay's wrist in her right hand. "Is this how it happened, Tom?" she asked, looking right into the fay's eyes. Although there were intricate patterns of black all around the lashes and lids, the fay's irises were willow-green; they shrank visibly as her pupils dilated.

"You don't have the grip for it, sweetie," the fay murmured, "and I won't be going out again for quite a while so it would have plenty of time to heal even if you had. I *love* the one-black-eyed look, by the way. Your kid's too pale. When it comes to changelings, blondes aren't *my* favourite."

"But you didn't *change* her, did you?" Molly said, still staring into the fay's wide eyes. "You didn't even leave a block of wood behind."

"We only have to do *that* when we're stealing from vigilant mothers," the fay replied, with minutely-calculated contempt. "The lost and abandoned are fair game. Some guide Tom Puss is, if he didn't tell you *that*."

The insult stung. Molly doubted that they had Social Services in Faerie, and she wasn't about to try to explain why having your kids in care wasn't *quite* the same thing as losing or abandoning them.

"Well," Molly said instead, now mimicking the way the fay had used the word, "I've come to find her, and I want her back. Are you going to take me to your precious Queen, or what?" She managed to pronounce the word *what* as if it were a whipcrack.

"Wow," whispered the fay, leaning forward just a little more. "I could *use* a tongue like that. Ditch the bitch, and I'll take you to the Queen right now. I'll even let you call me Honeysuckle."

"No," said Molly, flatly. "Tom stays with me. We're together."

"Whore," said the fay—but she said it lasciviously, as if it were a compliment, and finally conceded the staring-match in order to seek advice from her companion. "What do you think, Peaseblossom?"

"I think we ought to let them find their own way," said the other fay. "*We*'re in no hurry. When she's cold and hungry and the wolves are after her, she'll be in a more constructive mood."

Molly gave some consideration to the possibility of appealing to the fays' better nature, but only for a second or two. There was no point in wearing the costume if she wasn't prepared to play the part. She took a generous handful of the nearer fay's luscious hair in her free hand and she turned her face back to confront her own.

"Listen, *Honeysucker,*" she said, in her best movie-gangster growl. "I'm *already* cold and hungry, and I've dealt with more wolves in my lifetime than *you*'ve ever heard howl. I've sailed to the stars and I've written on the face of the moon, and I've sat in the Devil's lap in the back of a speeding hearse, and I'm *not* the kind of person who can be intimidated by a freaky fucking *fairy,* so why don't you just get your skinny arse in gear and *take me to your leader?*"

The fay's eyes flared bright red, and the pupils shrank to mere dots, but the Devil wasn't in them, and Molly wasn't about to be frightened by the stare of any eyes that didn't have the Devil in them—not after sailing to the stars and writing on the face of the moon. The fay must have seen her certainty, because as soon as she'd carefully detached her hair from Molly's left hand and her wrist from Molly's right, she smiled like a tiger.

"Well, darling," she said, "I reckon you won *that* little contest. I owe you a nice glass of nectar, and a big wet kiss during the slow dance. Can't *wait* for the rematch. Lead on, Peaseblossom. I'll stay with Molly-with-the-one-black-eye." And so saying, the fay linked arms with Molly and drew her into her stride.

The other fay did as she was bid, and led the party away from the beaten path, while tall dark Tom meekly brought up the rear.

34

The wood was uncomfortably dense and the drooping branches of the trees seemed even more anxious to caress Molly as she passed beneath their crowns than they were to touch base with Honeysuckle, but they weren't unduly assertive. Indeed, they felt eerily delicate and cobwebby. Molly put that down to the unnatural hardness of her own compacted flesh. The thick air was even more humid now, but still not very warm. Fortunately, there was no conspicuous increase in its chill when the sun-creature abandoned the microcosm to a brief purple twilight. As darkness fell, their way was lit by hosts of fireflies, which obligingly clustered in the crown of every tree as they passed by.

"What has the cat in the hat been telling you?" Honeysuckle whispered in Molly's ear. "You know you can't trust him, I suppose."

"*He* hasn't stolen my daughter," Molly pointed out, although she wasn't entirely certain that it was true, given that he seemed to know more about Christine's whereabouts than he was letting on, "and *he* came to tell me what was going on before your precious Queen could be bothered to send a summons my way." It didn't seem politic to mention that he'd also saved her from a fate allegedly worse than death —although Molly had long ago decided to suspend judgment on the proverbial comparison until she'd actually tried death.

"He's a man of sorts, darling," the fay observed. "He doesn't *steal* little girls, he just fucks them and throws them away. It wasn't *your* benefit he had in mind when he sprinted to your door."

"It's understandable that a person might want his memories back," Molly said, "not to mention the chance to let a bad hand heal."

"If people really want lost memories back, there are ways and means," the fay pointed out. "*You* know that, darling. As for getting the use of your right hand back—well, that depends on what you want it *for,* wouldn't you say?"

Before she could frame a reply to that, Honeysuckle put a finger to Molly's lips again, this time bidding her to be quiet. The host of fireflies fluttering ahead of them was scattering, as if to plunge them into darkness—but the darkness was abruptly banished by the glare of a million emergent stars. The "stars" in question seemed to be crystals set in the roof of the fays' underworld, and they filled its sky far more profusely than the stars which shone over London filled the vacuous firmament, but they had no moon to help them out.

The glade ahead was three times as broad as the one into which Molly and Tom had stepped when they first entered Faerie. It was crowded with fays—there must have been at least a hundred. Molly had no difficulty picking out the Queen, even though she had no throne and was no taller than her fays-in-waiting. The hooded cloak that she alone wore was a flowing symphony in crushed velvet, lined with silk the colour of blood—and half-hidden within the capacious folds of the cloak was Molly's twelve-year-old daughter, Angie.

Angie had never been a demonstrative child. Many a time, when Molly had visited her at the Jarvises, she had refused even to smile, let alone to be delighted by the sight of her mother. Sometimes, Molly would look at her and Angie would pretend to look right through her, as if to say, *Is that my invisible mother? Is that the person who should be the central sun of my life and isn't? Or is it just a mouldy patch on the wall?* Molly had never been in the least doubt on any such occasion that Angie really could see her—and she was equally certain now of the opposite.

All the fays in the clearing had turned to look at the people approaching, and Angie had turned with them, but whatever it was that Angie saw, it wasn't Molly.

If there's one thing worse than being invisible, Molly thought, *it's feeling irrelevant.* She knew that Angie's recognition was something she was going to have to buy or win. She didn't know yet if she could pay the price, let alone put up a show in any kind of contest that required more than bluster and bravado.

"Molly, darling!" said the Queen of the Fays, feigning delight. "How good of you to come—and so promptly, too. Honeysuckle, you're an absolute angel for finding her so quickly. Fetch Molly a glass of nectar and a bowl of fruit, Peaseblossom?"

All the while, Angie was staring at Molly without a flicker of recognition.

"No thanks," said Molly.

"You've been warned about tasting *forbidden fruit,* haven't you?" said the Queen of the Fays, with a chuckle. "I suppose that's your doing, Tom. You mustn't pay any attention to Tom Tiddler, Molly. He's got a teensy-weensy chip on his shoulder. I suppose he even told you not to dance. What a spoilsport he is!"

"Let's cut the crap," Molly said, squaring her shoulders and wishing that she'd been able to carry off one of the extra-large warrior princess costumes that Torquemadam reserved for the drag queens of Kensington and Westminster. "I want my daughter back. What will it take?"

"Oh dear," said the Queen. "He's really got to you, hasn't

he? I suppose he pulled that old trick of arriving in the nick of time to save you from some nasty rapist. Men have *no* imagination, have they? To tell you the truth, Molly, I was rather hoping that Angie could stay with us permanently. Perhaps you might agree to stay too—we can bring Christine over any time you like."

"Why would I want to stay here?" Molly asked, trying hard to imply that it was the most ridiculous proposition she'd ever heard.

"Well, dear," said the Fay Queen, "I can think of a lot of reasons, but two will probably do to be going on with. For one thing, it's the quickest and easiest way to be reunited with your daughters—and the only way that's *guaranteed* to happen. For another, Faerie will be the only safe place to be when your world comes to an end in six months' time."

Molly blinked at that one, and couldn't help darting a sideways glance at her silent guide.

"Ah!" said the Queen of the Fays, softly. "He didn't tell you about *that,* did he?"

"It's the first I've heard about it!" Tom was quick to put in.

"Of course it is, Tommikins," said the Queen of the Fays, triumphantly. "*You*'re not the *he* I mean." She didn't elaborate, but she didn't have to. Molly knew exactly which he she meant. She meant the Devil.

"She's lying," said Tom hastily. "I warned you that she might. Remember what you told the angel. If you don't get back up again while you can still do it under your own steam, you might not be able to get back up at all—not in one piece, at any rate."

"Still sore about that hand, Tom?" The Queen laughed, in a way that seemed to Molly to be less than pleasant. "It's fine now, isn't it? Or is it? Peaseblossom, would you fetch that guitar Tom left behind last time he was here—I think he wants to find out whether he's lost his knack."

The fay who'd led Tom and Molly to the court had already turned away once, when she'd been asked to bring fruit and nectar, but she'd turned back when Molly had refused them. This time, she disappeared into the crowd. Honeysuckle, by contrast, leaned close enough to Molly to whisper in her ear again. "He doesn't care about *you,* darling. If he gets what *he* wants, he'll sell you as soon as look at you. He's a man of sorts, remember."

The slanders sounded more convincing than Molly might have wished, but she reminded herself that she'd been robbed, ratted out and generally fucked over by a lot of women too—mostly ones who'd claimed to be her friends and sisters. She knew that she had to pull herself together, and make what preparation she could for the coming contest.

35

"Angie," Molly said to her daughter, as calmly as she could, "I've come to take you home. I know you've never seen it, but it's okay. It'll be the first real home we've ever had. I know it's way too late to be starting a first real home, and I'm sorry, but we can't go back to the beginning. All we can do is start from where we are and try to make it work. I really believe that we can do that. I refuse to believe that it's too late. It's *not* the end of the world, Angie. It's time to come home. Will you do that, Angie? Will you trust me enough to come home with me?"

Angie looked at her as if she were a stranger, and a madwoman to boot.

Molly took three steps forward, which brought her close enough to the Queen of the Fays to let her look deep into her eyes, just as she'd earlier looked into Honeysuckle's. As soon as the returning stare locked on to hers, she knew that the contest had been joined.

"I don't think she can hear you, dear," said the Queen of the Fays. Molly noticed that she pronounced the word "dear" in exactly the same contemptuous fashion as Mrs. Jarvis.

Molly was not going to beg the Queen of the Fays to let Angie hear her. "She will," she said, trying to sound confident.

"Did Tom Kitten tell you to dress up like that, dear?" the Queen countered. "I suppose you realise that it makes you look like a *cheap* whore."

"We both wanted to make sure that I'd fit in hereabouts,"

Molly replied, deftly. "I'll quote you my price if you'll quote me yours."

"You're being very foolish, dear," said the Queen.

"I know," Molly admitted. "It's always been my strong suit. A sensible person wouldn't ever have found her way here, but I came at a mad rush. I even brought a friend. I don't have a plan—but *he* does, and it's a bloody good one. I don't know how long he's had to think it out, but I'm sure that it was time *enough*. People who don't understand the value of time are prone to underestimate people who do, and sometimes underestimate their goodness too. If there's something you want from me, *your majesty,* you'd better tell me quickly, before you lose the chance."

Before the Queen could formulate a reply to that, Peaseblossom returned to the glade carrying an old guitar. Until she saw it, Molly had been thinking in terms of Elvis and the bands she had seen play at the Batcave and the Underworld, but now she realised that Thomas the Rhymer had been much nearer the mark. The guitar was an antique, at least a hundred years old—perhaps a thousand, if guitars had been invented that long ago.

"Well done, Molly," Tom said, softly. "You got it exactly right."

Molly knew that he wasn't really congratulating her—that it was just another move in the game—but the Queen of the Fays didn't. The Queen was convinced, if only for the moment, that her visitors *had* a plan, and that it was working out exactly as they'd expected.

"NO!" howled the Queen of the Fays, so loudly that her voice seemed to rip right through the star-studded cloth of the unnatural night. "This is MY court, and I call the tunes!"

"Then tell me what you want for Angie!" Molly shouted back. "What have I got that you want that badly?"

The strangest thing, or so it seemed to Molly, was that the Devil *still* wasn't in the Queen's flaring eyes. Molly realised, a little belatedly, that whatever Tom might be, the fays were different. They had nothing to do with the world's moral order, or lack of it, or humanity's collective desire to make good the lack. They were outside and beyond that, or inside and beneath it. If the Devil really did have the power to bring about an Apocalypse of Evil, whether in six months' time or in six million years, the fays' microcosm really would sail straight through it, utterly untroubled.

Maybe, Molly thought, Faerie really was the safest place to be, if the fays were willing to let her in—but it was too much to believe that they'd let her in without a price, and once they had whatever it was they wanted, could they be trusted to play fair? Could anyone *ever* be trusted to play fair, once they had what they wanted?

"I can take it all," said the Queen of the Fays, ominously. "If you want to play rough, *I can take it all!*" As soon as she said it, though, there was a slight flicker in Angie's eyes: a flicker which said that something important was getting through.

Molly figured that if foolishness was working, she might as well take it all the way. She plucked the handle of Torquemadam's whip from her warrior princess belt and she let the coils fall to the floor. Then she shoved the clinging Honeysuckle hard enough to thrust her away. Honeysuckle hissed in petulant annoyance as she stumbled and fell sprawling on the soft moist ground.

"All right, bitch," Molly said, with a sneer of which the Devil himself might have felt proud. "If you think you're hard enough, *take it all!*"

She had been expecting a full frontal assault, which she hoped to settle with a single blow, but that wasn't what happened. She had to wonder whether she had overplayed her hand, but she couldn't be sure. She hadn't a clue what was going on when the Queen of the Fays turned abruptly aside, directing her deadly gaze at the waiting guitarist.

"What are you waiting for, pretty boy?" she snarled at him. "You came to play, so *play*."

Tom didn't smile, as Molly might have expected him to if he really had been a bloody good man with a bloody good plan. He just did as he was told.

He began to play—and Molly realised that it wasn't just the trees, the air, the sun and stars that were different in the Land of Faerie. The music was different too—different, and yet strangely familiar.

Whenever Molly had looked back over her life and asked herself how it had all gone wrong, she had been forced to put the blame on the music. Before the sex, and long before the drugs, it had been the music which had lured her up the primrose path: fairy music, tempting her to dance if not to sing. If, as generally alleged, it had all *gone wrong* when she stopped listening to her teachers at the comp, when she decided that there were better things to do than apply her moderately good brain to the things she was supposed to apply it to, then the wrong that had reached out to claim her had been somewhere in the beat of the music, somewhere in the siren song of the lyrics.

The truly surprising thing about where she had finally arrived, after the sex and the drugs and the sectioning, and even after the dates with Elvis and the alien abduction and the little *tête-à-tête* with the Devil in the back seat of poor Dean's stolen car, was not that she had lost her daughters and most of her self-respect but that she no longer possessed a record-player, or even a radio. Somehow, having lost the thread of her life, she had never managed to upgrade to CD, and all her precious vinyl had been scattered by the wayside as she fell and fell and fell, towards and through the wild parties of 1999, into that strange margin for redemption provided by the year that all the world's maladapted machines had calculated as double-zero.

36

In the beginning, there had been the music: the music to which Molly had always danced. Before she had ever tasted any other kind of forbidden fruit, the music had led her astray.

All that Molly really knew about Thomas the Rhymer was that Steeleye Span had once sung a song about him, and she had always got him confused with Tam Lin, although that had been Fairport Convention. But the essence of his tale, she knew—because she still had, even after all her attempts to fry it, a moderately good brain—was that it was all about being seduced by the fairies and sucked out of phase and marooned on the other side of time. She also knew that no matter how the balladeers might have sexed the story up, at bottom it was all about music.

In her own world, long before she had caught the midnight train, Elvis had started it running—but Elvis had only been an instrument himself; in essence, the music had played him, because that was the way that siren songs invariably worked.

And so it was in Faerie, only more so. Tall dark Tom, who only thought he wanted his memories back because he didn't know what they were worth, drew his regenerated fingers across the strings of his recovered guitar, but he wasn't the player at all, because it wasn't his game. Here in Faerie, which had a roof instead of a sky, a slime-mould instead of a sun and crystals instead of stars, the music was the one and only master and everyone else—*everyone* else—was its whore.

Molly wasn't sure how many lies Tom had told her, but as

soon as the music sounded, coming into its own as it did so, she knew that there was one item of pseudoparental advice that she had to heed.

She must not dance.

This time, if she was to remake her life, she must not dance.

She couldn't go back to the beginning any more than Tom could, but she could make a new start, provided only that she could resist the siren song and keep her head while all around her were losing theirs.

The fays danced, because that was what they did. The fays couldn't have stood still if they'd tried, including and most especially their Queen—and Angie danced with the Queen, because she didn't know enough to help herself—but Molly stood firm. No matter how beautiful the fays were, she was not to be moved. As they glided around their enchanted glade, lit by a sky of diamonds and moved by the ultimate Lord of the Dance, they were very beautiful indeed, but Molly was not to be moved. For once in her life, she was determined that her own gratification would be delayed, unless and until she got the price that she was worth.

Honeysuckle reached out to her, and the Queen reached out to her, but Molly stood firm. She was in the middle of the dance but not of the dance. She remained aloof from its seductiveness, its wildness, its ecstasy. Even the lights in the sky reached out to her, and the liquid air kissed her mouth and tongue as it soothed her bloodied brow, but Molly would not be drawn.

Molly understood, now, why Tom had told her to borrow the warrior princess outfit. It was not so much to impress the fays as to help her into her own role. She understood, too, why Tom had told her to bring the whip rather than the sword or the symbolic circlet. It was not because she was going to have to use it in a fight, but because she was going to have to play the ringmaster in a circus. She even understood what it was that the Queen of the Fays wanted from her, on behalf of the underworldly heartbeat whose fleshly envelope she was. It was no mere item of information, nor even the art of reading the script that was inscribed on every gargantuan tablet of stone in the solar system. It was something far deeper and far more meaningful than that.

It was the music of the spheres.

The fays had targeted the supposedly-impregnable Castle Jarvis when she had made her deal with the greys. Perhaps they had assumed, or hoped, that she would see and hear far more than she actually had, but that wasn't the heart of the matter. The point was that she had left the solar system and gone into the wilderness, where very different voices murmured and sang, and she had brought something of that murmurous melody back, even though she wasn't consciously aware of it. She had experienced the universe, not as an earthbound grub looking up at the stars through the murky and polluted atmosphere, nor even as an armchair voyager contemplating the marvels of radio-astronomy and the spangled chaos of galaxies photographed by the Hubble telescope. She had experienced the true loneliness of the space between the stars, and heard the restless purr of the virtual particles which seethed and sang in the void—and from the point of view of the master of the fays, the Lord of the Dance, that was a prize well worth stealing children for.

Had she danced, Molly would have given it all away, but this was year double zero, and she was not the person she had been at twelve or fourteen. She was qualified now to pick her way through the blizzard of pseudoparental advice, able to select the essential and discard the superfluous. She was grown up, even though she had never upgraded to CD. So she struck her warrior princess pose, with her dominatrix whip in her hand, and she refused to dance.

Tom didn't refuse, in spite of his own good advice, but that was only to be expected. People who had lost themselves as entirely as he had were always likely to be disappointed when they found themselves again—but there was a sense in which he had got what he wanted anyway. The regeneration of his hand had allowed him to be part of the music again, and like all true musicians he longed to be played. For him, the dance itself was reward enough, far better compensation than any mere *name* could ever be, in Earth or any other sky-bridged world.

The star of the dance was, of course, the Queen of the Fays. That was how she came to be the Queen. Molly had never seen anyone dance so gracefully, so wildly, so freely, so ecstatically—but every time the Queen reached out to her, no matter how lovingly, Molly refused to take her hand.

It would all have been easy if it hadn't been for Angie, but the Queen had Angie and Angie was far more tempting than any mere hand. Angie was dancing too, and she could see her mother plainly enough now that anger and the music had given her the power of sight. Angie was reaching out to her mother now, wanting her to join the dance, unable to understand why Molly couldn't just fall into step.

Molly knew that the real contest couldn't be engaged, let alone won, by looking into Honeysuckle's eyes, or the Queen's eyes. The real competition had to be joined and won by looking into Angie's eyes and forcing a way past all the hurt and all the misunderstanding. Somehow, Molly had to make Angie see that she had to come to her real mother now, because no substitute would do—and until Molly had made her daughter see that, she had to prevent the music of Faerie stealing the music of the spheres from wherever it was hidden in her unconsulted memory.

Tom was only one ten-fingered man, but his six-stringed guitar wasn't just a guitar. It was more akin to a synthesizer, with samples of every sound known to fay and man embedded in its memory. His fingers were doing more than plucking strings; they were reaching into the heart of the instrument, which had a lead running straight into the heart of the world. With the master of the underworld to accompany him, Tom was more than an orchestra, more than Orpheus and more than Apollo himself. Whatever magic it was that gave music the power to stir emotion, Tom had it all —and he aimed it all at Molly.

If the only defence that Molly had had was a mother's love, she'd have been well and truly blasted, because she'd had that from the moment she'd given birth to Christine, and it hadn't ever been enough—but she had something better now. She had stubbornness, and the knowledge that the Devil himself had respected her as an adversary. The fays couldn't make a dent in that. So Molly held on to what it was she had, and *she* reached out for Angie.

And in the end, the Queen of the Fays had no alternative but to let Angie reach out in return. There was far too much distance separating them, of course, but that didn't matter. All Molly had to do was flick her whip and send the end snaking out into the vortex of air that was thick as blood, where it cracked like a wry smile—and when Angie took hold of it, Molly began to reel her in.

Molly could read, not merely in Angie's pale blue eyes but in the Queen's bright red ones, that she had made her deal and won her game. Even so, she waited until she actually had Angie's hand in hers before she began to let the hidden music out.

She had expected something symphonic, classical and

grand, but it wasn't like that at all. It was all drum and bass, brutal and elementary—the kind of music no one had ever thought to compose before computers. When it melted into the music of Tom's guitar, though, it merged with the melody far more smoothly than she would ever have imagined possible.

Molly knew then that the vast spacefaring cephalopods who had kick-started humankind's evolutionary ascent from the cyanobacterial slime had not simply been messing about. They had had a plan, and it was probably working, after a fashion.

37

As Molly dropped the whip and clasped Angie to her bosom she saw the Queen of the Fays and all her minions flee into the grieving trees. The forest swallowed them up, but as they faded into its shadows they took the precious music with them.

All the stars of Faerie went out, except for the scattered fireflies. As the living lights flared and died Molly caught the briefest glimpse of a big black cat sawing away at a Stradivarius, whose eyes gleamed as brightly green and as full of life as any vivid star she had ever seen or could ever have imagined.

There was ecstasy in those eyes, but there was something plaintive too. Molly had often heard it said that you should be careful for what you wished for, in case you got it, and she felt that everything that had happened to her since she had stepped out of the world she knew was proof of that—except in her own case. All she had wanted was to free Angie from the Queen of the Fays, and there was no curse in winning *that* objective. However cunning fate might have cheated her guide or her adversary, Molly felt certain that she had come out of it well.

When she had picked herself up from the stone-clad floor and dusted herself down, Molly found that all she was holding was a wooden doll. She wasn't unduly disappointed by that. After all, the fays had to give you a token of your vigilance if your kids weren't really lost and abandoned, and Molly's weren't. There would undoubtedly be formalities to go through before she got them all the way back, but they weren't lost and they weren't abandoned and the final deal was as good as cut and dried.

"The punter's gone, dear," said Torquemadam, who was lounging in the doorway. "You can take the outfit off now." The lazy expression on her face held not the slightest echo of the astonishment that had been there when Tom had pulled his vanishing trick. The brothel-keeper had obviously managed to persuade herself that she *had* seen everything, even though she obviously hadn't.

Molly patiently divested herself of the warrior princess outfit and began to put her own clothes back on.

"Weren't thinking of coming back full time, were you, Moll?" Torquemadam asked, in a carefully neutral tone that wasn't an invitation but nevertheless held out the possibility of mutually-beneficial negotiation.

"No," said Molly, shortly.

"Perhaps as well," the dungeon-keeper said, effortlessly switching into calculated insult mode for purposes of provocation. "You're probably getting too old for this kind of lark."

Torquemadam wasn't a day under fifty herself, but she was just a ringmaster nowadays. She was a dominatrix's dominatrix.

Molly picked up the whip and coiled it before handing it back to its owner. "You could leave me your phone number if you like, though," the whoremistress added, not entirely unhopefully. "Experience counts for something, after all. I'd give it a week or two, of course—make sure that eye's as good as new again. There's something about a black eye that says *victim,* and that's not the sort of image my clients pay good money for."

"Sorry, Sylv," Molly told her. "I really am out of it for good."

"Straight too, I bet," said Torquemadam sceptically.

"I've even kicked the Prozac," Molly told her.

"You need to be careful, dear," the whoremistress told her, not unkindly or unseriously. "If you give up too many of the things that used to turn you on, you can soon end up where it's awfully dark and lonely. Believe me, love—I've seen it happen too many times."

"Not to me," Molly assured her, as she picked up the doll that was her token of Angie's safe delivery. "I've still got enough spare cash to buy some equipment of my own."

"Not *this* kind of equipment, I hope," Torquemadam said, with unfeigned coldness. The specialized market to which she catered had always been substantial, but there were too many amateurs about nowadays as well as too many freelancers and she'd been feeling the cold winds of economic depression ever since the golden days of the Lawson boom. If things had been better, she'd never have shown Molly the door in the first place—the smack had just been an excuse.

"Not this kind of equipment," Molly assured her. "My days as a warrior princess are over. It's September of year zero, and it's time for me to start dancing to a different tune. One way and another, I've *got* to upgrade to CD."

38

When Lilith rang Molly on a borrowed mobile to say that someone had just called at her old flat in Arcadia House and had left an envelope for collection Molly wasted no time in hopping on a bus. Unfortunately, she had nothing else to do; it had not been as easy as she had hoped to find the kind of job of which Social Services might have approved. There was plenty of cash-in-hand work available in the environs of Camden Lock but Molly knew that she had to steer clear of the black economy, as well as the kinds of legitimate labour that would require her to be out of the new flat at the times when children might be expected to be in it.

Molly hardly dared to hope that the envelope might contain news of Christine, but she couldn't imagine why anyone else would use such a roundabout method of getting in touch with her now that she had her own phone. At least the journey released her, if only for a while, from the awful restlessness of wanting to do something but not having a clue where to start.

"Hello, dear," Lilith said, as she unlocked the metal security-gate guarding her door. "The envelope's on the mantelpiece. I'll put the kettle on. Have you had any news?"

"Angie's still safe and sound at the Jarvises," Molly said. "She hasn't shown any sign of doing another runner, and they're watching her like hawks in any case. Liz Peach isn't happy, though. Because Angie won't say a word to the shrink about what happened, all the child abuse warning bells are ringing, and that's blocked the processing pipeline that's supposed to be delivering her back to me. At least she's got the sense not to tell them that she was snatched by the Queen of the Fays because the bitch wanted a souvenir of my galactic holiday—that would have put a *real* twist in the psych brigade's knickers. Oh shit."

"What is it?" Lilith asked. She was still in the kitchenette waiting for the kettle to boil.

"It's from Wingate," Molly said, dully. "The freak at Peaslee Pharmaceuticals who cooks up rejuvenation serums with unfortunate side effects."

"A passion for housework isn't so very unfortunate," Lilith observed, casting a critical eye around her as she carried the tea-tray into the living room. Lilith was a conspicuous subscriber to the Quentin Crisp school of housework, which held that the dust didn't get any worse after the first four years. Given that she'd been Adam's rebellious first wife, ousted in favour of the domestically-minded Eve, Molly wouldn't have expected Lilith to feel in the least guilty about the state of her flat, but the old lady probably took a certain amount of stick from the pernickety Mephistopheles, who seemed to spend more time here than in his own pad.

"It wasn't the housework I was thinking about," Molly said, accepting a cup of tea but refusing a home-made biscuit. "It was the mind-meld with the giant octopus at the dawn of time."

"Well," said Lilith, judiciously, "if you'd let well alone, you wouldn't even know about that. The trouble with you humans is that you just can't resist temptation."

Molly thought that was a bit rich, considering that the entire crew of Arcadia House's thirteenth floor tenants had spent thousands of years in the temptation and supernatural retribution business, but she had to admit that Lilith made a super cup of tea. She was almost tempted to ask what the secret ingredient was that the arch-demon mixed with the

PG-tips, but she had a suspicion that it might only add one more item to the catalogue of her discontents. The reason she'd refused the biscuit was that she knew that Lilith tended to lace all her home baking with something far sweeter than honest cane sugar.

"What does it say?" Lilith asked, nodding in the direction of the note.

"He wants to meet me. Six o'clock in the Atlantis Bookshop in Museum Street. He wants me to make sure I'm not being followed." Molly double-checked the scientist's seemingly-hasty scribble, just to make sure that this unlikely congeries of instructions was indeed the gist of the missive.

"That's nice," said Lilith. "He must fancy you."

"Somehow," Molly said, with a sigh, "I don't think it's a date he has in mind." She looked at Lilith speculatively, trying to imagine what the old lady might have looked like when she was young, beautiful and—if rumour could be trusted—utterly vicious. Having seen what happened to an angel who's been lost on Earth for less than a week, Molly wasn't in the least astonished that Lilith's outward appearance had run to seed once she had opted out of the role of ultimate *femme fatale* and baby-murderer, but she suspected that there was still a very sharp mind lurking behind the mask of absolute inoffensiveness. Beelzebub was an honest dolt and Mephistopheles a transparent fusspot, but Molly had always known that there was more to Lilith than met the eye.

"Spit it out, dear," said the arch-demon, as if she were able to read Molly's mind. "Even if I don't know the answer, two heads can chew a question better than one."

"I lied to you," Molly said, by way of laying a little groundwork. "About what the Devil said to me in the back of that car, I mean. He was a lot nastier than I let on. I wasn't really trying to fool you, or even to put your minds at rest—it was more a matter of feeling bolshie. He'd ordered me to give you a message calculated to upset you, so I thought I'd give you one that wouldn't, just to spite him."

"It's not usually a good idea to try to cheat the Devil," Lilith said, shaking her head pensively. "Why tell me now?"

"Because the Queen of the Fays said that there was something even nastier that he *didn't* tell me, and I'd rather like to know whether it's true."

"Well," said Lilith, "I hate to say it of a sister in spirit, but the Queen of the Fays is almost as big a liar as the Old Man, especially when she wants something. I presume that what she told you fitted in uncomfortably with what the Devil told you—what he *really* told you, rather than what you told us."

Molly nodded. "She said that the world is going to end at the end of the year. And what the Devil really told me to tell you is that he doesn't need you and wouldn't take you back if you wanted to come back, because he has some *real* soldiers now. He threw in a few extra insults, but that's the bottom line. I didn't think much about it until I put it together with what the Queen said—and then I began to ask myself what he might want a brand new army *for*. I know that he's only a metaphor made flesh, a grab bag of human terrors—but as tall dark Tom pointed out to me, that makes entities like him a lot more real than any mere person. I understand that anything he does is only a representation of what we do to ourselves, and that no one really expects the world to end on December 31st, especially after the Y2K thing proved to be such a damp squib, but I just . . . well, you're supposed to know him as well as anyone ever has."

"The rumour-mongers who made me Queen of Hell were far too extravagant," Lilith told her, dismissively. "Nick and I were never that close. Like Adam, he always preferred Eve. Men have no taste at all, have they? I have to admit, though, that laying on an apocalypse for the day on which every madman in the world is expecting one is very much his sort of thing—especially after he let last December 31st alone on pedantic grounds, thus lulling the unwary into a false sense of security. He always had a wicked sense of humour. He didn't give you any clue, I suppose, as to who these *real soldiers* might be?"

"None that I noticed," Molly admitted. "My first thought was the greys, even though they seemed perfectly benign to me. I suppose that story they fed me about wanting to make a new world but not wanting merely to recreate the old one might be a load of old cobblers, especially if they're in the pocket of the Father of Lies, but . . . I can't buy it. On due reflection, definitely not."

"Why so definite?" Lilith inquired.

"Well," said Molly, hoping that her hostess wouldn't feel insulted, "it was that cosmic pleasure-cruise that did it. We didn't get any further than Altair—which is just around the corner, galactically speaking—but it was far enough from Earth for me to realise just how big and strange the universe is. To be perfectly honest, it made the terrors of the human condition seem rather petty and the myth-building capacities of the human imagination a trifle pathetic. And if *that* hadn't been enough to convince me that it wouldn't matter a damn, on a cosmic scale, if the human race did gobble itself up in some kind of evil apocalypse, what I eventually remembered about the asteroid-sized octopuses put the icing on the cake. I've seen the *real* writing on the wall of infinity. No matter how big a cheese he is down here, the greys and the octopuses are a whole lot bigger than the Devil *out there*. They aren't his soldiers and they never will be. Whoever—or *what*ever—he's recruited, I think he's done it right here."

Lilith nibbled a biscuit appreciatively, with a faraway look in her eye. "I think I'll have to take your word for all that, dear," she said, softly. "So far as I'm concerned, there's only ever been Eden and the wilderness beyond its hedge. Plus Hell and Pandemonium, of course. The Devil's exactly the same. Bad dreams have bounded him in a nutshell, with infinite space forever beyond his reach. The reason we both became redundant—although he hasn't admitted it yet—is that humans discovered far better excuses for their sins. Who needs demons when you have genes? We haven't entirely vanished from the scene, but even we're not *proud* of the fact that we've mostly retired to the top floor of a third-rate tower block on a sink estate that everyone refers to as the Waste-Disposal Unit. What you call the human yearning for moral order has moved into the laboratory, at least in these parts."

Molly had already returned her curious gaze to the piece of paper she was holding in her hand. "Wingate's laboratory," she said, nodding her head, "and all the other ones where genetic engineers are working on biological warfare and software engineers on computer viruses. According to the machines we built to run things for us, this wasn't scheduled as the year two thousand—it was marked down as year double-zero, the year that didn't make sense. I met a man not so long ago who told me that the machines were right and we were wrong—that it really is *year zero,* and that it's ridiculous to pretend otherwise. I think that's what finally persuaded me that I had to make a new start."

"Nick would probably like that argument," Lilith observed. She was becoming more spaced out by the minute, having nibbled her way through yet another biscuit.

"But what does he want with *me?*" Molly asked. She was still looking down at the ill-written message—the *he* she meant was Nathanael Wingate, not the Devil.

"You can find out in two hours' time," Lilith pointed out.

"But there is one thing you might care to bear in mind."

"What's that?" Molly asked, suffering a slight pang of regret now that it was too late to change her mind about the biscuits.

"The Queen of the Fays is no kitten, despite what shaky Will and the Victorian cutie-pie brigade did to her reputation," Lilith told her. "She and I used to be so similar you could have taken her for my reflection in a looking-glass, and it seems that she's held faster to her roots than I have to mine. If you sold the music of the spheres to the Queen of the Fays, you're no mere pawn in this game. You might not be a player, but you're definitely a *piece*. Wingate might think of you as a scatty Stepford wife, and you might think of yourself as someone who only ever pretended to be a warrior princess to give a few ex-public-school wankers a pathetic thrill, but even the Devil took time out to throw a scare into you and it probably wasn't by pure chance that the octopuses from the dawn of time picked you out to help them scrawl graffiti on the moon. Better be careful out there, girl—you probably have more enemies than you imagine."

"*I'm* not important," Molly said, wishing with all her heart that it were stating the obvious but remembering only too clearly what had happened the last time she had answered her door without looking to see who it was. "All I want is a new start, my kids and a quiet life."

"Maybe so," said Lilith, "but if the Apocalypse of Evil really is scheduled for the week after Christmas, the opposition ought to be starting to take shape by now. You might not be cut out to *be* the Anti-Antichrist, but if I were him, taking recent form into account, I'd certainly want you on my team."

39

Molly took the Victoria line to Oxford Circus and changed to the Central line for Tottenham Court Road. She still had half an hour to spare so she popped into the basement of Forbidden Planet to kill some time, but she didn't buy anything. The Atlantis Bookshop was still open when she got to Museum Street and there was no sign of Wingate, so she set about scanning the shelves. Their contents seemed slightly more relevant to her recent exploits and dire expectations to those in *Forbidden Planet*, but there was nothing at all to be found on the subject of the Anti-Antichrist.

She became so engrossed that she didn't notice Nathanael Wingate sneak into the shop, and had no idea he was there until he tapped her on the shoulder.

The balding scientist was wearing designer sunglasses that clashed horribly with his appalling tweed jacket—whose tastelessness wasn't in the least improved by the flashy mobile phone ostentatiously displayed in the breast pocket. Molly had to concede, though, that the shades probably hadn't seemed quite as ridiculous outside the shop as they did inside. Although it was nearly October, the weather was warm, sky was clear and the West End was lousy with Ray-banned wannabe It girls.

Wingate was carrying a rigid-framed black briefcase with a combination lock. He flicked the catches, opened it by the barest crack and carefully manoeuvred a grey wallet-file from the inside.

"We've been taken over," he whispered, melodramatically.

"Have we?" Molly said, slightly nonplussed.

"Not everybody," he explained, testily, "just *us*. Peaslee Pharmaceuticals. Swallowed up by Chiliad Science Inc—but they're just a front for some colossal multinational. It's supposed to be a secret but our share price has been going up like a rocket for a fortnight, so the City insiders knew beforehand. My work's been subject to an *intensive review* for the last three days."

"That's nice," Molly said, although she knew it probably wasn't.

"The Chiliad people have gone through all my reports with a fine-toothed comb," Wingate said, sourly. "They've impounded my notebooks. Told me I had to relocate to Yorkshire to join *their* rejuvenation team. Not a demotion, they said, but it's pretty obvious that I'll just be *gobbled up*. No credit, no patent, no share-options, no glory."

"Oh dear," said Molly, colourlessly. "Why tell me?"

"The suit who went through my results seemed particularly interested in you. Asked some *very* odd questions. It just so happens that I know my old line-manager's computer password, and *he*'s been upped three grades, so I figure he's been in on the takeover since it was just a gleam in an accountant's eye. Last night I took the opportunity to nip into his office and into a few files. Most of the databases into which our new masters have been integrating our data are locked up tight, but I got into *your* file easily enough. The stuff in it is so far off the wall that you'd need a telescope to find the light-switch, but it still triggered an alarm when I started printing it off. I had to get out PDQ. In theory, there's no way they can trace the intrusion back to me, but if my ex-boss can convince them it wasn't him, there are only a handful of people likely to have illicit knowledge of his password. I figured that it was best to start preparing a fallback position, so I went straight to the embassy."

"Which embassy?" Molly asked absent-mindedly. She was still trying to calculate the import of what Wingate had told her.

"The *American* embassy. I'm still a US citizen, you know."

"Oh," said Molly, disdainfully. "Your accent is so mild I assumed you were Canadian." Even as she was putting him down though, it occurred to her that what he probably meant by going "to the embassy" was ratting out Peaslee Pharmaceuticals' new owners to the CIA.

Wingate obviously wasn't in any hurry to show her the entire contents of the file he was still clutching to his bosom, but he did pull out a single piece of paper. Like all photographs printed from a computer by a bubble-jet the quality was lousy, but it probably hadn't been very good to start with. It appeared to have been taken by a supermarket security camera trained on the speciality cheeses section. Molly's heart leapt in astonishment as she saw it, and then sank swiftly as she realised what its presence in the files of a multinational colossus might signify.

"That's you," Wingate said, pointing to one of the two people captured by the image.

"It might be," Molly agreed, guardedly.

"Who's the man you're talking to?" Wingate wanted to know.

"Can't remember," Molly lied. "It was way back in January. I don't normally shop in Sainsbury's so I didn't even know they had a singles night."

"It looks like Elvis Presley," Wingate said, ominously.

"It looks like Elvis Presley, circa 1964," Molly pointed out. "Logically, it couldn't actually *be* him, could it? This doesn't prove anything."

"Oddly enough," Wingate said, mournfully, "that's exactly what the embassy said. They're not prepared to lay on a safety-net unless I can give them something much more convincing."

"You think *I'm* more convincing?" Molly said, in frank astonishment.

"Don't be silly," the scientist countered, curling his lip contemptuously. "It's not your testimony I want. If I'm going to get more, I need some back-up. I thought you might like to volunteer."

Molly decided to ignore the curled lip for the time being. "You want me to help you prove that Elvis Presley is alive and rejuvenated?" she said, carefully.

"I've been in the rejuvenation business for thirty-five years," Wingate told her, earnestly. "I've poured my heart and soul into the quest for the Holy Grail of biotechnology. I've worked day and night, year in and year out, with nothing to sustain me but peanut-butter sandwiches and the *vision*. I always played by the rules, because that's the way I was taught to play and that's what I believed in. How do you think it feels, having got within sight of the end, to have a bunch of corporate suits from some multinational leviathan waltz into my lab and tell me that I've got to relocate to Yorkshire and wash out test-tubes for some jumped-up Frankenstein? The same jumped-up Frankenstein, that is, who's been running *his* secret programme in parallel to mine, ten steps ahead every inch of the way because he *hasn't* been playing by the rules. *He* hasn't been putting in grant applications and taking begging bowls to board meetings. *He's* been shopping for humungous backhanders, persuading the rich and stupid to hand over vast slices of their ill-gotten fortunes and fake their deaths in return for the privilege of joining a conspiracy of secret immortals intent on running the world."

It was obvious that Wingate's hacking had been slightly more productive than he'd let on, even if the embassy wouldn't accept it as proof. "What I was looking for," Molly told him, tiredly, "was an explanation of why you think I ought to help you."

"You *knew* about it!" he said, as if it were obvious that she owed him something. "I levelled with you. I told you what the injection was for, and you just smiled and went on your way. You just couldn't be bothered to tell me that I was running a bad second to the opposition, just as you couldn't be bothered to mention that the commonplace virus coats sloshing around in your bloodstream were full of exotic DNA allegedly deposited there by *little grey men in flying saucers.*"

Molly could understand why Wingate was a trifle overwrought, but she wasn't about to stand any nonsense. "And if I'd told you all that," she said, "how much of it would you have believed?"

"Well, none of it, I suppose," Wingate admitted. "But I hadn't seen your file then. Do you think we ought to buy something? The lady at the till is giving us funny looks."

Molly plucked a psychic self-help manual from the shelf and dumped it on top of Wingate's wallet-file. "There's a Pizza Hut just up the road," she said. "I'm not saying that I'll help you, but I'll hear you out if you think it'll do any good—just so long as you buy me dinner."

Wingate hesitated, but then he nodded meekly. He paid for the book and they went back out into the sultry twilight. They walked back along New Oxford Street to Pizza Hut.

40

Molly wondered as they walked whether Nathanael Wingate could possibly be the Anti-Antichrist, if there really were any such thing. It didn't seem likely. She also wondered what else was lurking in the wallet file. He'd obviously seen some sort of account of her adventures in darkest Croydon, but there was no way anyone other than Lilith and her friends could know about what had *really* happened to her under the influence of his miracle drug and it was unlikely that anyone had found anything suspicious in any pictures that might have been taken in the streets through which she'd walked with the angel. Given that he'd happily gone traipsing up to the thirteenth floor of Arcadia House to leave her a note, he presumably didn't know that it was the secret refuge of the former hierarchy of Hell. The puzzling thing was that he knew anything about her at all—and that he had found it in a computer file that had set off an alarm when he started to print it out.

"I find it hard to believe that your new employers had a file on me *before* you started telling them about me," she observed, suspiciously, when the waiter had taken their order. "I find it even harder to believe that the file had *that* photograph in it."

"So did I," he replied, drily. "Unsettling, isn't it? All the more so when you look Chiliad up in the dictionary. I was *this* close to the elixir of life, you know—and *mine* didn't start population explosions of immortal nematodes in the experimental subjects. Chiliad's suits issued me with a user-ID and took a palm-print, and they gave me a swipecard that will get me past the automated security—but they're not expecting me till Monday. With any luck, we can get in and out again early tomorrow morning—*very* early. It's Sunday, so it's unlikely that there'll be anyone around. If there is, we'll just have to bluff our way."

"Who's this *we?*" Molly wanted to know. "Why on earth should I help you pull some kind of industrial espionage caper for the CIA?"

"I think they're holding your daughter there," Wingate said, with the air of a man playing an unbeatable trump.

Molly didn't believe him—but she wasn't sure that she dared to call his bluff. "Why would they be holding Christine anywhere?" she asked, sharply

"Because they're worried about you," Wingate told her. "For some reason, they seem to be taking this little grey men crap seriously. They put it together with the photograph, and added two and two to make God knows what. The embassy thinks it's all flimflam—but they're prepared to listen if I can provide hard evidence of any wrongdoing. They can help you, too, if the need arises."

"Somehow," Molly said, faintly, "I can't quite imagine the kind of need that would make the CIA put in a good word for me with the men in black. What *does* the dictionary say about Chiliad?"

"It means much the same as Millennium, in the religious sense. Chiliasm is the belief that Christ will return to Earth to institute an empire of righteousness. Which makes *Chiliad Science* into a bit of a joke, don't you think?"

"It's a bit on the optimistic side," Molly said, evenly. "According to my information, it's the Devil who intends to be on top when the world ends in December."

Wingate looked at her as if he wanted to look at her as if she were completely mad but didn't quite have enough confidence to do it. Molly was reassured to learn that they might both be in a position to run bluffs. "Did the little grey men tell you that?" he asked.

"No. It was another reliable source. I think she was using the word *end* fairly loosely, but I guess it'll be some kind of end-of-civilization-as-we-know-it scenario. Survivable, after a fashion, but the ones who survive might figure that the ones who didn't were the lucky ones. I talked it over with a friend, and we suspect that it might be something cooked up by the kind of scientists who don't play by the rules—maybe the kind who'd think that Chiliad Science is a neat joke. I don't suppose you know what *else* is going on at this establishment in Yorkshire, apart from rejuvenation research?"

She was testing him to see how far he was willing to go to humour her, and she was perversely reassured by the fact that his credulity couldn't stand the strain any longer. "So far off the wall you'd need binoculars to see the light-switch," he repeated, shaking his head sadly. "Completely crazy." He brightened up considerably, though, when his medium Hawaiian and Molly's small deep-pan BMT arrived.

"If I'm crazy, Dr. Wingate," Molly said, as she worked her way through the pizza "how crazy does that make you? How crazy does it make the people who hung alarm bells on my file? I may talk to Elvis in supermarkets, but *they* sent him out to do the shopping and *you* came begging for my help on the basis of a blurred photograph and a mess of rumours. I'm just a clapped-out whore trying to find a minimum-wage job and get my kids back, but *you*'re paranoid about losing the patent on the elixir of life and *they*'re planning to take over the world. What makes you think they've got Christine?"

Wingate was too careful to be taken by surprise. He took a slow swig of Red Rock cider before answering, but he was just procrastinating. He couldn't read the writing on the moon, but he seemed to know well enough which side his bread was buttered on. Molly only wished that she could be as sure of her own situation.

"It says so in the file," he told her. "So—are you in or out?"

"You'll have to show me," Molly countered.

Wingate rooted around in the file and brought out another single sheet. It was headed by the tail end of what seemed to be an analysis of the rogue DNA in her bloodstream. That was followed by a series of notes. The first stated that "operatives" had attempted to interview her again but had been "thwarted"—the date was the day she had set off on her interstellar tour. Her recent changes of address were both recorded, but there was no mention of the visit which an "operative" had paid her on the day she had moved to the new flat. There was a note about "A" having gone AWOL from her foster-home, and another to say that she'd returned. The last note on the page bore a date less than a week old. It said: *C located and neutralised; moved to Bingley.*

Strictly speaking, there was no proof that this referred to Christine, but Molly was more worried about the use of the word "neutralised." What could *that* mean, in this particular context?

"You could have typed that in yourself," she said, warily. "Presumably the other stuff told you that I have a daughter named Christine and that she'd done a runner from her foster-home."

"I could," Wingate admitted. "but I didn't." He met her stare with the steady eye of a man who knew that she couldn't afford to tell him to go to hell.

"What do you want me to do?" she asked, defeatedly.

Wingate unbuttoned his shirt. When he got to the fourth button she saw that he had something taped to his belly. She had to suppose that it was what the TV cop shows called a "wire," presumably attached by "the embassy." He showed her that the tiny mike was attached to the souped-up mobile phone in his jacket pocket. "All I have to do is hit the REDIAL button," he said. "The call connects it to a computer that will record every word spoken in its presence."

"Lovely," said Molly, unenthusiastically. "So why do you need two?"

"I don't," he said. "But I will need both my hands free, and that means that somebody else has to take the pictures." He reached into the file yet again and pulled out a camera the size of a matchbox, a second souped-up Nokia, and a long plastic-sheathed lead. "It's digital," he explained. "You just hit REDIAL, and it'll hook up to a second line on the same computer. All you have to do is point and click, every time I tell you to."

"And this is supposed to help me get Christine out?"

"If she's in there and we find her," Wingate told her, "we can *bring* her out."

"And what if we get caught?" Molly wanted to know.

"What if we do?" the scientist countered. "If we've got enough information out, we'll have leverage. If we haven't . . . you've saved yourself a few days of twiddling your thumbs. They're going to come for you again anyway. What can you lose by trying to get your retaliation in first?"

She had to concede that one. It was the first really good point he'd made. The man in black had told her that he'd be back when he blacked her eye, and the possibility of bringing off a pre-emptive strike was definitely appealing.

"I want to see the rest of my file," she said, to prove that she was no pushover. "Everything you printed off."

"Sure," he said, immediately. "You can look through it while we're on the train. We can be on our way right now—unless you want a dessert."

Molly decided that even though Wingate was paying it wasn't worth holding out for a dessert.

41

They took a taxi to King's Cross. Oddly enough, it was the first time in Molly's life that she'd ever gone there to catch a train. Wingate was the kind of obsessive-compulsive who always kept an emergency supply of twenty-pound notes concealed about his person in case a pickpocket lifted his wallet, and he explained to Molly that didn't want to put two tickets to Bingley on his credit card, just in case his new employers were keeping tabs on him. They had half an hour to wait for the express to Bradford, and Wingate handed over the wallet-file while they waited in the queue to board it.

Molly was perversely disappointed by the contents of her file. There were extensive documents of a supposedly-confidential sort, culled from various sources. Their statistical sum was an account of her entire life since the age of eleven, lavishly decorated with all the discomfitingly slanderous comments that various schoolteachers, social workers, medical practitioners and probation officers had felt it incumbent on them to place on her record. There was also an exhaustive transcript of her various interviews with the Croydon cowboys, but this had been carefully sanitized so as to imply that the men in black were scrupulous boy scouts who treated their interrogatees with all possible politeness and consideration. There were elaborate appendices listing the results of various tests to which she had been subjected at Croydon. So far as she could tell, as she skimmed over the gnomic symbols, there was nothing in that section to indicate the nature of the object they had ripped out of her breast or any information recovered therefrom.

"According to the Extra-Special Branch," Wingate pointed out, a little breathlessly, when they were finally allowed on to the platform to join the mad rush for seats, "the only possibly-apocalyptic threat in the offing is the one concealed in your Trojan Horse viruses. If all that stuff can be taken seriously, you're the new Typhoid Mary—except that their analysts can't seem to figure out what the exotic DNA you've been spreading so generously is supposed to do, outside of cocking up my experiments by introducing a rogue unknown into the sample."

"It's not supposed to do us any *harm*," Molly assured him, wishing that she could be absolutely certain of that herself. "It's not a disease, as such."

"According to the ESB, it's worse," Wingate insisted. "They reckon the viruses are vectors, like the mosaics we sometimes use to modify crop-plants. They suggest that the aim was to *transform* your clients—and they aren't certain yet that it didn't work. They hypothesize there might be some kind of activating trigger: maybe something to be taken orally, maybe something even simpler, like a spoken sentence or a musical tone. We're talking *Invasion of the Body Snatchers* here." She could tell by his tone that he didn't believe a word of it, even though the new owners of Peaslee Pharmaceuticals seemed to be taking it seriously. He was obviously still uncertain as to how much *she* believed.

"If the greys wanted to snatch our bodies," Molly said, "they'd have done it way back in 1897, when *The War of the Worlds* didn't happen. They're sophisticated people, even if they do look like the saddest cliché on the sci-fi market. Anyway, they aren't even the biggest kids on the block, and they'd probably have to reckon with our mother-race if they tried to fuck us up. Forget the ETs, Dr. Wingate—it's our own mad scientists we have to worry about. They're the ones with the Devil in their eyes and up their arses." She figured that if they were testing one another out, she might as well get as much early retaliation in as she could.

"Actually," said Wingate, as the northbound train drew away from the station, "I bitterly resent the demonization of scientists, and genetic engineers in particular. We're the ones who are working to *ensure* the future of the human race. We ought to be the heroes of popular fiction. I'm sick to death of seeing all of us cast as malevolent monster-creators. It's stupid and it's childish."

"Sure," Molly agreed, sarcastically, "but it makes good melodrama. Anyway, *you*'re on the side of the angels. If Hollywood ever gets to tell the tale of our great adventure, you'll be the male lead. They'll forget all about the bad haircut and the horrid tweed jacket—all they'll remember is the stratospheric IQ and the grail quest. I'll probably get relegated to the love interest. Not, of course, that you actually have to do anything about that. I could really do with an action-hero type to take care of that part of the plot, but the only tall dark and handsome man I've met all year turned out to be a pussycat. Do you really think we can achieve anything in Bingley, Doc? This is going to be a hell of a washout if they won't even let us in."

"By the time we go in the last night-owls will have gone home," Wingate said. "The night-security's fully computerised, so the only thing that can possibly go wrong is that my palmprint hasn't been fed into the system and my swipecard won't work."

"You don't have much imagination, do you?" Molly said. "I can think of a dozen other ways things could go *very badly* wrong. On the other hand, I have the consolation of knowing that if we get into *real* trouble the greys will beam us both up into orbit. Probably."

He wasn't even a little bit convinced. "Just make sure you click that camera shutter whenever I give you the word," he said. "I don't care how barking mad you are, just as long as we get the pictures back to the embassy."

Molly decided that she might as well kill time by taking offence at that. He was a captive audience, so she spent the next couple of hours explaining to him exactly how "barking mad" she really was. She told him about the angel, and her interstellar tour, and who lived on the thirteenth floor of Arcadia House, and her meeting with the Devil, and why the Queen of the Fays had kidnapped Angie. She even told him what had really happened to her while his drug had thrown her lower brain functions into Stepford wife mode. It took a long time; she didn't finish until after they'd changed trains at Bradford and boarded the local hopper that would take them to Bingley. By that time, Wingate had gone quite pale.

"I always played it by the rules," he said, faintly, "until last night, at least—and a little self-defensive hacking is hardly a major infraction. You have to play by the rules, you see, because if you don't have science you don't have sanity. If you can't stay within the bounds of reason, *anything* goes. I never understood why people didn't like science, because I never understood how anyone could bear to live in a universe where *anything goes*. I never understood why anyone would want to live in a universe without rules, without science, without sanity."

"What's *want* got do with it?" Molly asked—although she knew, in her heart of hearts, that there was a manner of speaking in which *want* had everything to do with it.

For want of a nail, according to the poem, a battle had been lost and a nation with it. Two kids had to be worth immeasurably more than a nail—more than enough to lose a universe that was not only queerer than one supposed but queerer than one *could* suppose. She didn't say that to Wingate, though. She had told him more than enough already, and he was genuinely distressed by what he had heard, even though he didn't believe a word of it. From his point of view, this adventure was a desperate attempt to hang on to a sense of reality that he couldn't bear or afford to lose —and he hadn't the slightest idea how far away from that goal he had already strayed.

42

Wingate paid for a room in the Cottingley Beck Hotel from his supply of ready cash. The desk-clerk obviously thought he had immoral purposes in mind, but Wingate hadn't taken advantage of her while he had her in his power at Peaslee and he didn't try anything now. He didn't have to ask Molly to undress in order to set up her equipment, and he was apologetically embarrassed about the modest rooting around that he did have to do. They didn't even sit on the bed together while they watched late night TV, waiting for the week's most unsocial hour to arrive.

They started walking at two, but it was after three when they reached their destination on the bank of the canal. Wingate was still clutching his briefcase as if it were some kind of security blanket, and the whiteness of his clenched knuckles betrayed his deep-seated unease. Molly guessed that this really was the first time in fifty-some years that he had ever stepped out of line.

The outer shell of the edifice that had been made over into Chiliad Science's northern headquarters had been erected in the nineteenth century, presumably as a woollen mill, but it had recently been fitted with an inner tegument of dull metal whose resolute opacity was clearly visible through all of the glassless windows. As Wingate had promised, there were no human attendants at the car-park barrier or the main door. Nor was there an intercom connected to some internal security-post—just a pad on which Wingate had to place his palm and a slot for his swipecard.

When the swipecard passed through successfully, the door opened and they passed through into a vestibule whose lights came on automatically. The security camera on the wall dutifully recorded Molly's unauthorised presence as well as Wingate's but it seemed that nobody was watching the live broadcast, and that no one would be any the wiser until they played back the tape. Wingate had to repeat the procedure to let them through the inner door, but it worked as well the second time as it had the first.

Again, the lights came on as they passed through. They found themselves in a corridor with half a dozen side-doors and a steel-clad lift at the far end. Wingate made straight for the lift.

"Get that camera ready," he said, plucking his mobile phone from his breast-pocket. Molly's phone was discreetly fastened to her belt. The lead connecting it to the camera was tucked inside her blouse, whose ample sleeves hid the connection to the camera. She had to be careful to keep the connection in place as she took the camera out of the pocket of her jeans.

Molly followed Wingate along the corridor. Neither of them heard the door that must have slid open soundlessly behind them, and the first Molly knew of anything amiss was the gloved hand that reached around her from behind and closed upon her mouth. A muffled voice in her ear whispered: "Gotcha!"

The whisper was purely for melodramatic effect. Wingate heard it anyway, and whirled around—but a second man in black was already moving past Molly, holding an obscenely large pistol before him. It was the one with the unkempt moustache who'd had a nasty run-in with Gloria that might well have cost him his faith in the deterrent power of pump-action shotguns.

Molly saw Wingate's thumb close on the REDIAL button of his phone before he said: "What on Earth are officers of British military intelligence doing here? How dare you point that gun at me! I'm an employee of Chiliad Science Inc, going about my legitimate business."

"Sure you are," said the man who had hold of Molly. Now that he was speaking normally she had no difficulty recognising his voice. She'd heard it often enough. "And this is your star research subject. Can't thank you enough for bringing her in safe and sound. We might have had trouble, given the ease with which she's slipped through our fingers in the past, but now she's in a lead-lined building she won't find it quite so easy to float away—and there's not a soul in London who knows where she is! Incidentally, Dr. Wingate, there's not the least point in your aiming that phone at me. It was broadcasting long before you hit REDIAL, and I expect the battery's stone dead by now. We *did* have fun listening to your conversation on the train, though. You've exceeded all our expectations—couldn't have done better if you were a trained interrogator."

Wingate's face was as white as a fay's. It was pathetically obvious that he hadn't been in on the set up. "I'm an American citizen," he said, defiantly, "and the people at my embassy know that I'm here."

"Of course they do," said the man in black. "Who do you think told us you were coming?"

The lift doors slid smoothly aside behind Wingate. The man who stepped out was as tall as the one who held Molly but his smart suit was grey and his tie was silver. Only his hair was black. He was accompanied by a woman, so much older than he was that her blonde hair was certainly dyed. She was wearing a lab coat but if she was in the rejuvenation-serum business she certainly wasn't much given to

217

testing her own products.

Wingate was still catching up. "The CIA tipped you off?" he said, wonderingly. "Chiliad Science has been working for the CIA all along?"

"Don't be ridiculous, Dr. Wingate," said the man who'd come out of the lift. "It's the CIA and all its parallel organizations that work *for us*. We're a global corporation with employees in fifty-two countries. We're the taxpayers, voters and citizens of the world."

Molly half-expected Wingate to collapse like a punctured balloon, but she wasn't entirely surprised when he went crazy instead. People stepping out of line for the first time after half a century of repression often went way over the top, in her experience.

Wingate slammed the black briefcase into the groin of the man holding the gun. It must have been a lucky shot—from Wingate's point of view—because his complexion turned lily white before he dropped the gun, clutched himself in agony and toppled like a dynamited factory chimney.

Wingate immediately hurled himself at the second man in black, but this time he had to raise the briefcase as if it were a battle-axe because Molly was in his way. Molly heard her captor chuckle as he cleverly deployed the only weapon ready to hand: her. The briefcase caught the tall man at the side of the head and sent him staggering back against the wall, but Molly and Wingate fell over in a terrible tangle.

Molly's opinion of Wingate went up by an entire order of magnitude as he put his lips very close to her ear and whispered: "There's a second feed the company doesn't know about. Take the pictures. Same time same place." Molly assumed that this meant that Wingate had jiggered the mobile phone so that it would send its digital signal to more than one computer, and had done so without the CIA's

knowledge, and that he would meet her in the Atlantis Book-
shop on the following Saturday if circumstances permitted.
She slipped the tiny camera back into her pocket while they
were still sprawled in an ungainly heap

By the time Molly and Wingate got back to their feet,
everyone was laughing except the man whose balls had been
crushed.

"There's really no need for that, Dr. Wingate," said the
black-haired taxpayer. "You're a little early for work, but I
think we can forgive that. We can talk about it on Monday.
We'll instruct the computer that you aren't to be readmitted
before then, of course. Don't worry about Molly—Dr.
De'Ath and I will give her the grand tour."

The grey-haired woman smiled bloodlessly as her name
was mentioned, but it was the black-haired man who offered
Molly a hand to help her up. "I'm Edward Hyde," he said. "I
thought about changing it to Jekyll, or even Moreau, but that
would have seemed like hiding my true self—and once I
teamed up with Marjorie I realised that there were worse sur-
names in the world."

The man in black who'd been holding Molly until Wingate
forced him to let go stepped forward as if to receive her into
his custody again, but Hyde shook his head. "Please see that
Dr. Wingate gets out safely, Mr. Wilson. You can leave Molly
to us now."

The man in black looked as if he wanted to scowl at Hyde
but couldn't quite muster the necessary irreverence. While
his associate was still gasping for breath, Wilson took
Wingate by the arm and guided him back the way he had
come. Edward Hyde and Marjorie De'Ath stood aside to let
Molly precede them into the lift, and when Hyde gestured
expansively Molly did as she was bid. She still wanted to see
the inside of the factory, although what Wilson had said

about the greys being unable to levitate her out of a lead-lined building was a trifle worrying.

"Do I get to see Elvis?" she asked, by way of testing the water.

The lift doors closed. Hyde punched a button and the car headed downwards. If the buttons could be trusted there were no less than seven subterranean floors.

"My dear," said Dr. De'Ath, "you get to see *everything*."

"Including Christine?"

"Ah," said Dr. Hyde. "There, I'm afraid, we can't oblige. We have tried to find her—you can't imagine how hard we've tried—but we've drawn a blank. We knew that you couldn't be inveigled into a trap for anything less, so we doctored the record for Dr. Wingate's benefit. I'm sorry—but sending Mr. Wilson to pick you up didn't seem safe, considering that you slipped through his fingers on the last two occasions."

While Hyde was talking Molly looked him squarely in the eyes, fully expecting to see the Devil therein, but the scientist had more style than that. If the Devil were in him, he'd never let it show. When she turned away he obviously thought he'd won the contest, but she was only shielding her mobile phone while she hit REDIAL.

The doors opened again at the uppermost of the seven basements, and Hyde flourished his manicured hand yet again to indicate that she should go on.

The light was more muted down here, and instead of conventional doors the corridor that curved away into the bowels of the ex-mill, apparently following the arc of a great circle, was studded with great wedges of steel like the entrances to time-locked bank vaults. Each door was, however, equipped with a round observation portal at head height—head height, that is, for a man. Molly knew that she'd have to stand on tiptoe and crane her neck to get a clear sight of whatever was within each chamber.

"Please go ahead," said Hyde, politely. "We really would like your honest opinion on the merits of our work."

So Molly went ahead, with the tiny camera still clutched in the right hand that she had thrust into the pocket of her jeans—and even though Edward Hyde didn't have the Devil in his eyes, she found herself embarked on a tour so thoroughly Infernal that even Dante might have fainted in horror at the imagination of it.

43

Beyond the first set of observation portals Molly saw:

gargantuan mice with giant human ears grafted on to their backs;

pigs with the wings of bats, birds and angels;

the heads and spinal cords of gorillas and cattle mounted on hectic assemblies of glass and rubber tubing, through which red and blue fluids circulated endlessly;

sheep whose thick fleeces were brightly patterned in pink and blue;

thick-boled conifers whose boles were covered with leopard-skin and mink-fur instead of bark;

cacti whose many-spiked bodies were sculpted into humanoid form, like legions of Saint Sebastians;

and bushes whose vibrating flower-heads emitted musical notes of amazing purity and timbre.

Behind the second set of ultra-thick doors Molly saw:

a series of huge bicep-like muscles six or eight feet long, flexing continuously to pull two huge metal bars together and drive them apart again;

an array of hearts the size of basketballs pumping luminous fluids through three-dimensional mazes of transparent tubing;

a row of transparent artificial wombs within which dozens of unrecognisable embryos slept;

a million staring eyes, some cyclopean, others grouped in pairs and others gathered into compound masses;

a flock of peacocks whose multicoloured tails swirled with bronze and silver, gold and imperial purple;

a battery of headless, featherless and footless chickens with plastic tubes carrying nutrients disappearing into their necks and others carrying waste products away at the rear;

and a multi-layered pyramidal assembly of brains in bell-jars, of many different sizes.

Through the third set of observation windows Molly saw:

classrooms in which cheetahs, mandrills, warthogs, tapirs, spider-monkeys, capybaras and hyenas whose bodies had been surgically modified into humanoid form were sitting before computerized blackboards learning the eight times table;

nurseries full of baby chimeras, some with the bodies of cats, the wings of parrots and the heads of snakes, others with the bodies of iguanas, the wings of dragonflies and the heads of bushbabies, and others with the bodies of natterjack toads, the wings of ostriches and the heads of wasps;

gardens in which thorny bushes grew within the flesh of human beings planted waist-deep;

sweatshops in which children with plastic-covered wires sprouting from their shaven skulls were working sewing machines at a furious rate, their tiny hands flying hither and yon as they processed bolts of gossamer cloth into garments;

hospital wards in which the flesh of every patient was rippled and undulated by the squirming of larvae beneath the skin;

studios in which half-humans from which everything beneath the navel had been removed and substituted with the nether parts of goats, horses and wildebeests were painting in oils, producing masterpieces of which Hieronymus Bosch would not have been ashamed, had he only had the opportunity to paint from life;

and workshops in which the cadavers of non-functional cyborgs were laid out on tables like mortuary slabs while multitudinous robot ants and plastic centipedes carried spare parts of metal or flesh, where steel fireflies flared and fumed as they settled to make spot-welds.

In the fourth set of isolation-chambers Molly saw:

marine aquaria in which teams of busy cuttlefish were patiently erecting submarine apartment-blocks, communicating between themselves by changing colour, while gigantic sea anemones trawled the water for edible debris;

festoons of spiderwebs through which hairy black arachnids moved with sinister grace, clotted here and there with ragged clusters of yellow eggs;

patchworks of four-foot-long cocoons from some few of which moth-winged humanoids were struggling to escape;

trees whose globoid fruits were bowls full of turgid liquid in which long frilly worms twisted themselves into improbable knots;

vivaria in which the two heads of brightly coloured bifurcate snakes competed for the privilege of swallowing their own tails;

shallow pools where somnolent turtles with jewelled shells lay, staring back at her with heavy-lidded but preternaturally intelligent eyes;

and grottoes whose walls were lavishly decorated with redistributed human flesh, sprouting arms, legs and genitalia more-or-less at random but manifesting far more faces than the limbs and other accoutrements could ever have been coupled with under normal circumstances.

Within the fifth set of vaults Molly saw:

Elvis, looking exactly as he had at the very end of his life, bloated and dazed and but deeply troubled, as if mourning some lost love;

Robert Maxwell, looking like a corpse which had been immersed in the sea for a very long time, attended all the while by shoals of greedy fish, but still striding back and forth like a man with a mission;

Gilles de Rais and Erszabet Bathory, looking hideously raddled and half-melted, commiserating with one another on the monstrous injustice of having been framed by such immoderate enemies;

Jeffrey Dahmer and Ed Gein, sharing a meal;

Marilyn Monroe and Patsy Cline, dancing on puppet-strings controlled by a huge computer and weeping constantly for a series of long-lost loves;

Boris Karloff made up as Frankenstein's monster, hunting for a bolt that had come adrift from his neck;

and a gymnasium in which thirty-three clones of Adolf Hitler, steroidally overloaded in spite of having only one ball apiece, were working out furiously, zealously cultivating muscles fit for finalists in the Mr. Universe contest.

The sixth circular array of rooms contained laboratories in which:

the skeletons of half a dozen angels of various sizes were strung together with steel wire;

six-foot-high glass tubes full of formaldehyde were crowded, within which floated the preserved corpses of greys and at least a hundred other alien species, only a few of which Molly had glimpsed during her selective tour of the inhabited worlds of the Orion Arm;

doleful demons were confined in narrow cages, their wings covered in purulating sores and their horns broken by the convulsive battering of their heads against the bars;

octopuses of a very ordinary size were busy inscribing circles, ellipses and amoeboid symbols on tablets of stone, using acetylene torches clasped in their many tentacles;

Honeysuckle and Peaseblossom were laid out with arms and legs at full stretch, with giant bradawls through their wrists and ankles, and their torsos carefully cut away to reveal the neatly rearranged delicately pink organs within;

an Abyssinian cat was practising the delicate art of walking in high-heeled black PVC boots;

and multiple clones of Edward Hyde and Marjorie De'Ath involved themselves shamelessly in all the multitudinous forms of sexual intercourse that Molly had been privileged to witness in the course of her chequered career.

Through the last set of portholes Molly saw:

a drill-square on which a legion of zombie soldiers were being put through their paces by a howling sergeant who bore more than a passing resemblance to a younger and fitter Beelzebub;

a swimming-pool full of boiling blood in which dozens of men and women were immersed as far as the neck;

a maternity-unit in which dozens of headless, armless and legless female torsos were straining to give simultaneous birth to deformed infants;

a mortuary block from which the badly-burned body of a young black boy was struggling to rise, although the tortured expression in his eyes testified that he would far rather rest in peace;

a vast block of ice enclosing an entity which might have been Beelzebub's fatter and unhealthier brother;

a wind-tunnel in which tiny naked humans with Molly's own face and the wings of hummingbirds were secured by massive blobs of glue to rigid vertical wires while the artificial tempest forced them to fly faster and faster without ever making progress;

and a dissecting-room whose slab was quite bare, although a tray containing a host of gleaming stainless steel instruments was ready beside it.

44

Molly clicked her camera at every appalling sight, hoping that whatever digital cameras had instead of rolls of film wasn't as readily exhaustible. Drs. Hyde and De'Ath didn't appear to notice the camera in her hand as she lifted it again and again. They seemed far more concerned with noting her facial reactions. She tried not to give them the satisfaction of seeing how distressed she really was, but she knew that the dereliction of her soul and desolation of her spirit must be showing.

She wasn't entirely surprised when Dr. Hyde unlocked the last vault-door of all and swung it open. She turned to run, but Mr. Wilson had caught up with them by now, and he was only too eager to grab her.

Beam me up! she cried, silently—but she knew now that the flying saucers would never be able to reach her down here. Wilson carried her to the dissecting table and laid her out. He lifted a device like a gargantuan staple-gun from the tray and shot four huge pins into her hands and heels. Only then did Dr. De'Ath pick up an obscenely large hypodermic syringe and ram its point into her windpipe. Molly choked on the liquid which flowed into her throat but it didn't knock her out and it didn't numb the pain.

It was Dr. Hyde who cut her clothes off, piece by piece. He threw the scraps into the corner of the room. The mobile phone and the camera—which she had hidden once again within her pocket—went with them. It occurred to Molly, rather belatedly, that they probably hadn't stopped her taking the pictures because they knew she wasn't going to get out of the building and hadn't given a damn what she did. They didn't know abut Wingate's extra insurance policy, but whatever good that might do him, it seemed that it wasn't going to be any help to *her*.

When she was completely naked, Wilson pointed out the part of her breast from which he'd taken the greys' biochip, and then he tapped her sternum ominously. Hyde nodded, and took up a circular saw. When he switched it on it hummed like a hive-full of angry bees. De'Ath and Wilson stepped clear to allow him room to operate. He started at the neck and cut along the entire length of the sternum, then continued sawing through the softer tissues of her abdomen until he reached her clitoris. Then he took the loose flaps of skin in his hands and wrenched them apart, splitting her as Honeysuckle and Peaseblossom had been split.

Hyde turned to De'Ath and pointed at something in Molly's belly, in the vicinity of her womb. "*That*'s what we need," he said, in a tone that mingled modest relief with smug self-satisfaction. "Better make sure that she doesn't see *this*."

Wilson took up two mounted needles, and plunged them into Molly's eyes. She presumed that the points must have gone all the way through to her brain, because that was the moment at which she finally, and mercifully, blacked out.

45

When Molly woke up to find her unclothed body sandwiched between a medium-hard mattress and a floral-patterned duvet the first thing she did was check her hands and the space between her breasts.

There were no wounds, nor even any tangible scars. Her immediate assumption was that she must be on the alien mothership and that the greys had fixed her up again, just like last time, but somehow it just didn't seem plausible. The walls were papered and there were framed pictures hanging on them. Molly recognised a photograph of Albert Einstein and a portrait of Charles Darwin, but the others were unfamiliar. The bedside table was unvarnished pine, the chair beside the bed was grey plastic with an aluminium frame and the wardrobe had been fitted together from an MFI flat-pack. The greys had had far better taste than that.

The implausibility of Molly's situation increased by a further order of magnitude when Marjorie De'Ath walked into the room, smiling. The smile seemed strangely warm and welcoming.

The grey-haired woman was carrying a tray which she set down on the bedside table. It contained a mug of white coffee and a plate of Jaffa cakes.

"Hello Molly," said Dr. De'Ath, sitting down beside the bed and handing Molly the coffee-mug. "How do you feel?"

"What day is it?" Molly asked, suspiciously.

"Friday. I'm sorry that we had to keep you out so long, but we had to make sure that every last trace of the trigger-drug was flushed out of your system. You wouldn't believe the trouble we had scouring your flat. We didn't bother with 1303 Arcadia House, on the grounds that the new tenant almost certainly isn't carrying any rogue viruses."

"You cleaned my flat?" Molly said, warily, as she sipped the coffee. If her taste-buds could be trusted, it wasn't instant. Molly was still a little confused, but she knew that cleaning flats wasn't the kind of thing the Devil's minions were supposed to do.

"Yes. It should be safe now. Wilson's men are watching it round the clock. I'm sorry that we had to lure you away from London like that, and that we had to take you so close to the edge, but we were pretty certain that you'd pull through. How *do* you feel—I really would like to know."

"Not bad," Molly confessed.

"I'll send for your clothes in a little while. First, you're entitled to an explanation."

"Am I?" Molly parried, jesuitically.

"The file that Wingate showed you wasn't complete. Apart from the reference to Christine, however, it *was* accurate. Minutely accurate." She paused, as if waiting to be contradicted. Molly knew that the older woman must be referring to the transcripts of her interviews with the men in black —the ones that had shown them in such a flattering light. Molly wasn't tempted to observe that pigs might fly.

"May I tell you what else we know about you?" Dr. De'Ath asked, politely.

"Feel free."

"On December thirteenth, 1999," the old woman recited, somewhat after the fashion of a policeman giving evidence in a particularly boring court case, "you asked your social worker, Elizabeth Peach, whether your two daughters could spend New Year's Eve with you and then go with you to Trafalgar Square to see in the year 2000. Their foster-parents, Mr. and Mrs. Jarvis, objected on the grounds that Angie was too young to be out so late and that Trafalgar Square was likely to be a dangerous environment on that particular night. After some negotiation, the compromise decision was that Angie would remain in Tooting with Mrs. Jarvis while you and Christine spent the evening together at your then residence, a Bed and Breakfast hotel in Brixton—but that Mr. Jarvis would collect Christine from the B&B at one a.m. precisely.

"Because almost all the other residents of the hotel wanted to go to Trafalgar Square, you volunteered to listen for any signs of distress from the young children they left behind. Two others remained behind, but Anne Hawksley was not generally considered fit to baby-sit and Francine Docherty was busy entertaining her boyfriend, known to her and to you as Adam. However, all of these others gathered in the ground floor room where the television was kept in order to take part in what two of them considered to be the countdown to a new millennium. When the chimes of Big Ben had sounded, Anne Hawksley returned to bed and Francine Docherty fell into a drunken stupor, while you and the man calling himself Adam engaged in a mildly self-congratulatory discussion occasioned by the fact that both of you held fast to the pedantic opinion that the new Millennium would not actually begin until January the first, 2001. Christine listened, until Mr. Jarvis picked her up in his car, as arranged.

"Francine's boyfriend then favoured you with a long speech regarding the measures employed to combat the so-called Y2K problem, arguing that the inaptly programmed machines were actually right, and that the new year would be far better thought of as year zero than year 2000. He argued, too flamboyantly to be taken entirely seriously, that a glorious opportunity had been missed—that the world could have and should have shaken off the burden of the past and set itself to start from scratch, to make a new beginning. He suggested that it had been ridiculous to persuade the machines to continue dragging the burden of 1999 years of historical folly and error, and that the wise thing to do would have been to let civilization grind to a halt, pause for reflection, and then begin anew without all the social and psychological luggage that would be better discarded. Is that a fair summary, do you think?"

"You had a lousy B&B that was doubling as a home for fallen women *bugged?*" Molly said, incredulously. "Why?"

"There were no hidden microphones in the B&B, at that stage," Marjorie De'Ath told her. "Mr. Wilson was, however, stationed in a car across the street, with a directional mike trained on the front room window, picking up every little vibration. He had been following the pseudonymous Adam for some weeks."

"Why?" Molly said, uncomfortably aware that she was becoming repetitive.

"Because Mr. Wilson suspected that the man in question was about to launch an illicit field trial of what we assumed at the time to be a new psychotropic drug—although it now seems that this was an underestimation of the complexity of his scheme. We do know, however, that he exposed all four of the people who were with him as midnight approached to a biohazardous compound. Two of its victims were dead within a matter of weeks, having failed to negotiate stage two of the programme, but the other two survived. You, Molly, have been living the consequences of the illicit experiment for more than eight months. We believe that Christine has been following in your footsteps, and may have been deemed the more interesting of the two remaining subjects. We assume, of course, that she is currently with the experimenters. We don't know where, but we intend to do everything possible to find out."

Molly thought hard about all this while she worked her way through one Jaffa cake after another, as grateful for the glucose shot as she was for the taste of oranges. "You're saying that I've been drugged for the last eight months?" she said, finally.

"On and off," said Dr. De'Ath. "They didn't give you the second part of the cocktail until March, of course—when you were persuaded to believe that you'd been abducted by aliens."

"Persuaded to believe?"

"You've been in a more-or-less constant state of induced paranoia," Dr. De'Ath amplified, less helpfully than she seemed to think. "That has affected your perception of quite ordinary situations—but in addition to that, you've been taken in for further treatment on three occasions, not counting the one when we directed you to Peaslee Pharmaceuticals so that we could give you a more thorough examination than Wilson's people could contrive. We used poor Wingate shamefully, of course, but we had permission from his embassy. We'd have set him straight by now if the silly idiot hadn't taken it into his head to go underground—but we're not displeased about that, because we may be able to use him again. The opposition will undoubtedly be after him too. While you've been in their untender care, they've manipulated your perceptions very carefully indeed, depositing amazingly elaborate confabulations in your memory—amazingly persuasive ones, too, if what you told Wingate on the train is true. They must have been trying to push you further and further each time, to see how far you'd go before you refused to accept the supposed evidence of your own senses.

Judging by your expression when we gave you the tour last Sunday morning they'd got you into a condition where you were prepared to believe absolutely anything. When you're dressed, I'll take you around again, so that you can see the dull reality that the drugs wouldn't let you see before."

Molly put the mug down and took another long, hard look at the palms of her hands. Then she raised the duvet so that she could look down at the line where Hyde had appeared to slit her from throat to vagina before drawing her two halves apart.

It hadn't been real. None of it had actually happened—and now she knew that it hadn't been real, it seemed absurd that she could have been deluded into thinking that it *was* happening. She had *thought* that she was feeling pain, but how could anyone have stood the kind of pain that such horrors would have generated? How could she have been so foolish?

It had been going on since the very moment she resolved to make her "new start." What an understatement that seemed, now! She had made a new start all right: her mind had been cast adrift in year zero, to fall in with Elvis and an angel, greys and gargantuan octopuses, demons and fays and cats in human form. She had swallowed it all, hook, line and sinker, even while she had felt dutifully bound to inform the Devil that he was nothing more than a projection of humanity's fears and moral anxieties. She had been in the grip of the ultimate chemical Antichrist, from which she had now been delivered by Chiliad Science Incorporated.

Or had she?

The only real evidence she had of former delusion, she realised, was that which had accumulated since she had set foot inside this strange building. Her vivisection had obviously been a delusion, and what she had seen on her tour of

Chiliad Science might indeed be far too difficult to swallow—but what if she had only been given the psychotropic when she stepped across Dr. De'Ath's threshold? Or—and this was, in its way, an even more ominous thought—what if everything Dr. De'Ath said were true, except for the allegation that Chiliad Science and Francine's Adam were on opposite sides. Maybe this was just one more phase in the experiment, one more insidious attempt to fuck with her mind?

Dr. De'Ath must have seen the uncertainty in her face. The old woman reached out and pressed a bell-push situated in the wall above the bedhead. Within half a minute a much younger woman appeared, carrying Molly's clothes. They were the same clothes she had seen cut to ribbons while she lay pinned to the dissecting-table, but they were whole, and they had been recently washed and ironed. They were very faintly scented with lavender. The mobile phone and the miniature camera were, however, missing.

Molly got out of bed and dressed herself, slowly. She didn't feel giddy or weak—her "not bad" had carefully under-estimated her feeling of well-being—but she did feel more than a little paranoid. That wasn't entirely surprising. After all, whether Drs. De'Ath and Hyde could be trusted or not, *somebody* was definitely out to get her.

Dr. De'Ath was as good as her word. She took Molly on a tour of the building, showing her all the doors that weren't in the least like bank-vaults, and all the busy people behind them, working away in all apparent health and happiness. There were a few areas marked with biohazard signs, where methodical young men were using big gloves and mechanical manipulators to work with cultures in sealed containers, and there was an animal room full of caged rats and mice, but there were no monsters, no chimeras, no obscenely detached body-parts and no dead superstars. The only laboratory Molly had previously spent time in was Wingate's, but those of Chiliad Science looked exactly as she might have expected the labs of a thoroughly reputable, honest-to-goodness, cutting edge biotech research establishment.

"Okay," said Molly, when she had wound her way through the corridors of all three subterranean floors. "I'll buy it. Who's the opposition? Who, exactly, was Francine's Adam working for?"

"All we're certain of," said Edward Hyde, who'd just emerged from an office to join them outside the steel-clad lift, "is that they're local and relatively small-scale. They're not agents of any foreign power, and they're not tied up with any major player in the global cartel. They're obviously not amateurs, but they're not true professionals either. They have their own agenda—and we're as enthusiastic to know what it is as you are."

"Am I?" Molly countered. "Maybe I just want out."

"Don't be silly," said Edward Hyde. "While Christine's in, *you*'re in. Your interests and ours coincide. It's just a matter of your agreeing to play it *our* way." The lift doors opened and Hyde politely ushered Molly inside.

"And your way is?" Molly wanted to know.

"The double bluff. We'll probably have to let them take you again, without them realising that we want them to take you. We'd have to persuade them to think that you're completely under their spell—but you'd have to resist the worst effects of the drug. You'd have to play along, but you'd have to hang on, in your heart of hearts, to the knowledge that none of it is real. You'd have to get all the way to the inside—and then you'd have to let us come in after you. I don't say it wouldn't be dangerous, but it might be the only chance you have of getting out of this in one piece, with your daughter by your side." The lift ascended while he spoke, and by the time he had finished the doors were opening again. He lingered long enough to add: "But there might be a way of avoiding that necessity, if you don't mind helping us to activate another *agent provocateur*."

Molly had been expecting something of this sort, but she put on an act of mulling in over as they moved into the corridor and paused again. She wasn't certain whether all this really was a double bluff, or whether it might amount to a triple or a quadruple, but she figured that once you got *that* far into a tangled web of deception there wasn't much point in trying to keep count. The one thing she knew beyond a shadow of a doubt was that she wanted out of *here* with all her options intact.

"Okay," she said, finally. "What do you want me to do, exactly?"

46

This time it was Wingate who had got to the Atlantis Book-shop ahead of time and was deeply immersed in scanning the shelves when Molly arrived. He was still carrying his black-clad lethal weapon, but he looked perfectly harmless. Without the sunglasses his weary eyes seemed uncommonly pale and watery, and he blinked hard when he turned to look at her.

"Thank God," he said. "I thought they might have done something to you. What happened?"

"Thanks for worrying," Molly said, taking some comfort from the fact that the thanks were sincere even if sincerity had to stop at that point. "Nothing much. A thorough examination and a few more samples. I think they've got all they need, now."

"I didn't dare go back on Monday," Wingate confessed, unnecessarily. "I caught the first train back to London. I've been staying with my ex-sister-in-law."

"Did you get the pictures?" Molly asked.

She already knew that the reason Hyde and De'Ath hadn't stopped her taking the pictures was that they knew full well that they'd show the labs as she had seen them on Friday, not as she'd seen them in the early hours of Sunday. So she wasn't in the least surprised by the contents of the file that Wingate eased out of his briefcase and didn't bother to pretend.

"There's nothing I can take to the embassy," he said. "Which isn't altogether surprising, given that they knew we were coming. Even if they didn't know about the second download, they had time enough and sense enough to hide anything incriminating. Did you find out anything at all? Anything I can *use?*" He sounded like a man who knew that his hopefulness was absurd.

"Even if I had," Molly pointed out, "Who would believe me, after all that stuff I told you on the train?"

Wingate nodded sorrowfully. "But *something*'s going on!" he complained. "They're hiding *something.*"

"Well," said Molly, following her instructions to the letter, "it seems to me that you've only one chance left to find out what it is."

Wingate had to consider the possibilities for a few minutes, but he was a methodical thinker and the conclusion was foregone. "I've got to hack in again," he said. "I've got to go back to Peaslee in the early hours of tomorrow, and I've got to get through those firewalls. It's possible. It's desperate, but if I don't try, I'm finished. I'll never get back on track. No credit, no glory, no patents, no share options, *no rejuvenation.* I've got to strip what I can out of the systems and shop around for a higher bidder."

Molly was deeply impressed by the accuracy of Edward Hyde's psych-profiling. She had always thought that forensic psychology was fashionable mumbo-jumbo, but Hyde had Wingate's reactions mapped like those of a lab rat. All Molly had had to do was press the trigger; the rest would follow like a row of tumbling dominoes.

Molly knew that she didn't owe Wingate anything. He hadn't been exactly scrupulous in persuading her to serve as his camera-carrier. On the other hand, he hadn't taken advantage of her mental absence while she was under the influence of his serum to have his wicked way with her, and he had actually blushed while feeding the camera-lead through her sleeve. He was, after his own pathetic fashion, a gentleman—and, she supposed, a scholar. Given that she had no idea who was who in this war of illusions, Molly didn't want to be one more nail in the poor fool's coffin.

"Don't do it," she said, mentally tearing up the script and throwing it away.

"What?" Wingate was suddenly very uneasy. He had obviously picked up on her confusion, perhaps even on the fact that she had been sent to prompt and provoke him. Three words could convey a lot, if spoken in the right tone of voice.

"They want you to do it," she told him. "They have a booby-trapped package all wrapped up and waiting for you. They want you to take it to the opposition. They want the opposition to think you're worth hijacking. You're bait in a trap, just like me. They're even playing us off one against the other. I don't know if we can save our skins, but I feel fairly certain that they only way we'll save our souls is to opt out of the game. Don't go back to Peaslee. Wherever you do decide to go, don't go *there*."

She saw as she stared at Wingate's furtive eyes that it wasn't going to work. She had no credibility. It didn't matter whether she told him a pack of lies or the truth, he couldn't believe her. All he could do was react to the triggers she provided—and her mere presence was probably trigger enough. If she had stayed away . . . but she hadn't dared or wanted to do that. She had been worried about him, too—and she had needed to see the pictures, just in case. No one as paranoid as she was could have left such a tempting stone unturned.

Edward Hyde must have known that, Molly realised. He and De'Ath were quite a team.

Molly leaned a little closer to Wingate. "They don't know everything," she whispered. "They don't even know as much as they think they do. They're convinced that Francine's boyfriend is local, but their whole theoretical edifice might be founded on the wrong brick. *What if it's the greys who are real, Wingate? What if the greys are calling the whole bloody tune?"*

He looked at her as he'd looked at her once before, like a man who wanted to look at her as if she were mad but couldn't quite contrive the requisite expression with his facial muscles. She didn't need to be an expert psych-profiler to know that he was never going to believe that the greys were the real players behind the scenes, the real choreographers of the whole bizarre fandango. He was a scientist, and he wasn't mad. He needed rules, and imaginative boundaries. He needed sanity, and intellectual safety. He needed to believe that the truth was manifest, if only one could hack through the firewalls. He would never in a million years be able to read the writing on the moon.

Molly knew, however, that she was different. She had spent the greater part of her life embracing the unembrace-able, and thinking the unthinkable was only one small step beyond. It had been proved to her that some of what she'd seen and thought these last few months wasn't real—but some of it was, and she didn't have to accept anybody's word for which was which.

"Don't play their game, Nat," she said, softly. "Leave it to the experts."

"What experts?" he asked.

"Those of us who've been to Hell and back at least a dozen times. Those of us who know that anybody who isn't para-noid in a year that doesn't make sense is crazy. Those of us who've touched base with the mother-race of the Orion Arm civilizations and the big wheels in the land of Faerie. Let me be the Judas goat, Nat. I don't need you. I can do it on my own."

"You don't understand," he said, with all the confidence

of a man who couldn't even conceive of the possibility that he might be the one who didn't understand.

Molly took a psychic self-help book off the shelf, barely pausing to check that it wasn't the same one he'd bought before, and thrust it into Wingate's hand. "You'd better pay for that," she said. "The lady at the till is giving us funny looks again."

Nathanael Wingate blinked, and then said: "I don't suppose you fancy a pizza, by any chance?" The tone of his voice seemed to have turned to boyish jelly.

"You have to steer clear of me from now on," Molly told him, sternly. "It really isn't good for you. You're just a pawn, but I'm a piece. You have to let me tackle this in my own way. Can you do that? Can you let it go?"

He didn't answer. He hadn't made up his mind—but at least he didn't protest that he wanted to stay with her, to save her from whatever worse-than-death fate was lurking around the corner. He was prepared to let her go. He was a scientist, after all, and by no means mad.

Wingate went to the till to pay for his book, and Molly went home to await the Apocalypse of Evil at her leisure.

47

Given that the world was due to end in a matter of weeks Molly didn't think it was worth knocking herself out searching for the kind of job that might lead to better things. Elizabeth Peach had made it abundantly clear that she stood no chance of recovering custody of Angie before the end of the year, so Molly figured that she might as well fill in as best she could until she found out exactly what the Devil had planned for the week after Christmas. In keeping with the spirit of her new start, however, she decided to work behind the bar in a brand new pub in Camden rather than one of the older establishments on the Caledonian Road.

Following the ignoble precedents set by others of its ilk, the pub bore the mock-ironic name of the Laydownyer Arms. Its clientele consisted almost entirely of the kind of young unmarried professionals who used their flats solely for bedding down, spending all their waking hours at work or "networking"—a mysterious process which always seemed to involve getting drunk. The institution of this new way of life had gifted a minor economic boom to the likes of brewers, distillers, publicans and white van men.

Molly had entertained hundreds of yuppies back in the 1980s and had naively supposed them to be the ultimate dregs of corporate humankind's devolution, but a fortnight in the Laydownyer Arms revealed depths of imaginative degradation whose existence she had never suspected. The shock of its discovery appalled and discomfited her, but her co-workers were so completely inured to the new reality that they did not even notice the advent of the zombies.

At first, Molly wasn't absolutely sure about the zombies herself, all the more so because Drs. Hyde and De'Ath had warned her to be on her guard against the inevitable return of her paranoid illusions. Eventually, however, Molly plucked up the courage to ask the bar manager whether a particular group of closely-huddled patrons seemed as unusually pale, dispirited and waxy of complexion to him as they did to her.

"It's a bug that's going round," he assured her. "Some kind of flu. The symptoms aren't severe but it drags on a bit. Dulls the mind, but looks worse than it feels. Hardly noticeable by day, apparently, but muted light enhances the look and makes sufferers more emotional."

"Emotional?" Molly queried, eyeing the huddle sceptically.

"Not amorous, if that's what you're thinking," the manager said, with a slight hint of regret. "Huggy, not sexy. We'll both catch it soon enough—working in a place like this, we come down with everything that's in the neighbourhood. Like I said, the word is that it's not serious. Just lingering."

It seemed unnecessary as well as impolitic to introduce a word like "zombie" into that sort of conversation, so Molly didn't.

The bar work soaked up all of Molly's evenings and some of her days, but it left her free to start trawling charity shops and market stalls for second-hand books. Given that the world was approaching its end she could have started hanging out in Compendium and buying at full-price, but she figured that she ought to make some attempt to keep her principles intact and she couldn't quite bring herself to take it for granted that money would be valueless once the Apocalypse of Evil got into full swing. It was one invention that had never let the Devil down in the past, so why would he abandon it if and when he were able to usher in his Millennium of Malevolence?

Occasionally, as she was walking home from work after midnight, Molly would catch sight of the pencil-moustached man in black she now knew as Mr. Wilson watching her from the driving seat of a black Volvo—a car that would have been far more discreet than his usual choice in a more suburban environment but which still tended to stick out a bit in Barnsbury. If she chose to wave to the man in black he would offer her a mock salute by way of reply, but he was no more inclined to approach her and strike up a conversation than she was. He obviously had his orders and was sticking to them.

Before the advent of the zombies, Wilson's seeming ever-presence had been the only firm evidence Molly had that the world was not exactly as it seemed to be. Like her flat, she had allegedly been thoroughly disinfected, and she was mildly surprised to discover how little natural paranoia she seemed to have. Presumably, pharmaceutical paranoia was like heroin in the sense that while you were on it your body didn't bother producing its natural defences against the pain and indignity of everyday existence, so that when you came off it you had to give your own systems time to kick in again.

Even the knowledge that Wilson or one of his men was always close at hand and her temporary dearth of natural paranoia hadn't prevented Molly from taking great care as she walked home in the early hours, but it wasn't until she started noticing the zombies in the pub that the journey became truly nerve-racking. There had always been some funny people around at that sort of hour, but as soon as the zombie flu started doing the rounds their numbers began to increase nightly. Most of them were harmless, being the phantom kinds of homeless who used darkness as a cover for rooting surreptitiously around in the waste-bins of restaurants and pubs, but even the shyest phantoms sometimes strayed over the schizo line and couldn't help becoming a danger to themselves and everybody else. Molly wore high heels at work, as she was obliged to do for the edification of the customers, but she always changed into trainers when she started out for home in case she had to run.

She had been followed from the pub several times before the advent of the zombies, but stalkers of that tentative kind had tended to give up long before she reached home, being unable to match her pace while brim-full of lager. It was not until the flu epidemic had built up momentum that people who must have been lying in wait for her actually began to lurch out of the shadows into her path, groping inarticulately.

The first time this happened Molly was glad that the reaching figure was moving so slowly and awkwardly, because it made evasion that much easier—but when it happened again, and then a third time, she realised that the bar manager's observations about the effect of muted light on the victims of the epidemic did not tell the whole story. The darker it was, the more fully the symptoms were brought out and it was only in the faintest light of all that the sufferers revealed the true current extent of their physical and psychological degradation.

Their skin was not merely mushroom-white but palpably rotten; the pupils of their colourless eyes were shrivelled to mere dots in defiance of the normal reflex; their movements were not merely dulled but afflicted by a strangely jerky slow-motion; and their desire to enfold other people in their asexual but coldly affectionate embrace, as if they were long-lost children, displaced every other motive and every qualm of conscience or common sense.

The spread of the disease through the capital soon became

obvious to everyone, but it failed to generate any widespread alarm. TV news programmes, reflecting a solidly suburban view of life and spectrum of concerns, were unprepared to devote anything more than grudging token attention to the existence of an epidemic which had not yet caused a single fatality, and such items were always reassuring. It might have made a difference if cinematic zombies had not had the characteristics of ghouls unfairly foisted upon them in the name of melodrama, but no one who had seen *Night of the Living Dead* or any of its sequels was likely to get too excited about such mild-mannered zombies as the ones the new flu was creating.

Once Molly had convinced herself that it was frustrated affection and not addictive hunger that was motivating the *avant garde* living dead she decided that she ought to investigate the phenomenon a little more carefully, while always retaining the distance appropriate to an objective scientific inquiry.

48

The next day, when Molly left work at one in the morning, she caught sight of Wilson sitting in his Volvo reading a copy of the *Telegraph*. She marched over and tapped on his window. He lowered it and said: "No, I can't stop following you around. It's my job."

"I know," she said. "I just wanted to compare notes on the zombies."

"What zombies?" he repeated, warily.

"The ones who come out at night and try to hug people. Come on, Wilson, you've been out here two or three nights a week, and when you haven't been here in person you've had one of your legmen filling in. Their reports must have mentioned that the numbers of the local vagrants seem to be increasing exponentially, although the increase isn't putting any undue pressure on the supplies of scavenger-fare."

"Oh," said Wilson. "*Those* zombies."

"Something weird's going on, isn't it? Come on—you're a senior man in black. You know about these things."

"On the contrary," Wilson retorted, smoothly. "I *used* to know about these things, in the days when they were nice and simple, but that was before Chiliad Science took over. Now, I'm just one of the suckers who has to hang around waiting for you to flip. You *are* flipping, aren't you Molly? You're not just winding me up?"

Molly sighed. She almost wished that she had come up with the story herself, just for the sake of a practical joke. "I think it's beginning," she said, firmly. "I don't know exactly

what it is, but it's started. The Devil's plan has been acti-
vated. I know there are still seven shopping days to Christmas, but the Antichrist is up and running, and if our side
really is the Anti-Antichrist we'd better get our arses into
gear. If Chiliad Science Incorporated can't cope with a lousy
fake flu epidemic, what use are they to you, me or the world?"

"Couldn't have put it better myself," said Wilson, with
weakly-feigned enthusiasm. "I have to hand it to you, Molly,
when you flip, you flip all the way. You want to get in, or
what?"

"I don't think so," Molly said. "I'm tired and I need some
sleep. If I were you, I'd call for some back-up and round up a
few of the zombies. They won't be able to tell you anything—
they're only zombies, after all—but Hyde and De'Ath can get
started on the job of figuring out how and why they tick."

Wilson opened the door of the Volvo and got out, tow-
ering above her as was his wont. His capacious chest bulged
alarmingly. He walked round the bonnet to the passenger
door and wrenched it open, then stood waiting beside it.

"Get in, Molly," he said. Oddly enough, he didn't say it as
if he expected to be obeyed; he said it like a man who knew
perfectly well that the menacing tone he'd worked so hard to
cultivate was a broken tool.

"I don't want to," said Molly, although she had moved
round the front of the car herself so that she could stand face
to face with him on the pavement.

"I know," he said. "I know how it works by now. I have to
force you, so you can blow your mind all the way from here to
nowhere. How about this?" He reached out for her, almost as
clumsily as a zombie—although his eyes couldn't begin to
match the deadness of a real zombie's eyes and mere laziness
was no substitute for authentic awkwardness. Molly evaded
him easily enough and kicked him on the inside of the left

knee, more in irritation than in anger.

"Damn it, Wilson," she said, "I'm trying to *help* you! We're supposed to be on the same side now!"

The kick must have shocked the ganglion, because Wilson started hopping as if his left leg would no longer support him. Molly seized the open door and slammed it shut with a bang.

"We've *always* been on the same side, you stupid cunt!" Wilson yelled. Molly knew that he wasn't going to include *that* in his official report. She would have stalked off up the road in the direction of the Caledonian Road, but she suddenly realised that the pavement was blocked by half a dozen zombies who had appeared as if out of nowhere. She was some distance from the darkest stretch of her homeward journey, but Wilson's training always made him park his car in a well of shadow, and the zombies seemed pretty far gone.

It only required one hasty glance behind to assure Molly that she and Wilson were completely surrounded and cut off. She began to regret the reckless kick. Even an expert martial artist wasn't going to be much use against an army of the living dead if he had to fight them standing on one leg.

"Wilson," she said, faintly. "Is that a gun or a mobile phone tucked under your arm?"

Wilson's scepticism on the subject of zombies had not only evaporated but turned to frank alarm. He reached into his jacket and pulled his weapon out of his shoulder-holster. The automatic pistol didn't look nearly as big as Molly had expected but the matt black metal of its barrel was reassuringly businesslike. Because these were not cinematic zombies but people who still turned up to work by the cold light of day, Molly assumed that shooting holes in them would do enormous and bloody damage, but because they were real zombies the individuals making up the crowd did not seem to be in the least intimidated by this prospect. Every last one of them wanted to give Molly and Wilson a great big hug, and the fact that he was threatening them with messy death was simply not getting through to their benumbed brains. They continued their lumbering advance.

"I *told* you to call for back-up," Molly said. "You left your phone in the car, didn't you?"

"And who was it that slammed the fucking door?" Wilson retorted, reaching out as if to pull it open again.

It was too late; the zombies were already pressing forward, and there seemed to be nearly a hundred of them now. Even if the man in black had got to the phone, no help he summoned could possibly have got to them in time to prevent . . .

What?

As Molly backed up against the wing of the Volvo, she realised that the zombies didn't seem in the least bit *hostile*. Their eyes and complexions were as dead as eyes and complexions could be, but there was no animosity in them, and no hunger. They were not going to eat anybody, or even crush anybody to death. All they were programmed to do was embrace the uninitiated, presumably in order to pass on their infection.

Wilson screeched in annoyance as the first gripping hand touched the jacket of his suit and left a distinct smear of putrid flesh on the sleeve. He retaliated by pressing the muzzle of his gun to the zombie's shrivelled nose and pressing the trigger.

The zombie's head exploded in a bloodless cascade of oily grey matter, and the body obligingly fell away. Had the members of the mob been *compos mentis* they would have scattered immediately, but the zombies knew no fear. The rest continued to reach out with their avid arms towards Molly and Mr. Wilson, as generous and loving as ever.

Molly knew that the only thing that could possibly save the

two of them was light—and suddenly, there *was* light!

There was, in fact, a veritable torrent of light which fell from above, lighting up the faces and the minds of the zombies, persuading them on the instant that there were more important things to do than cluster about these particular lost children.

Molly looked up gratefully into the luminous cascade, bathing in the eerie radiance. Mr. Wilson had obviously not been the only one delegated to keep close watch on her.

Unfortunately, Wilson had already given way to panic. As the zombies backed away and gave him room to manoeuvre he fired his gun again, and again, and again. More heads exploded.

A beam of even greater intensity stabbed down from the underbelly of the spaceship, and Molly felt herself growing lighter and lighter, until she was unable to keep her feet on the ground. She floated up into the air, and up and up, until she could see all the lights of north London laid out beneath her like a vast fairground. Because of the pollution-haze that never seemed to lift nowadays, the yellow lights seemed even yellower than usual; their glow was so sulphurous as to be suggestive of the fires of Hell.

The last thing Molly heard before the light soothed her consciousness away was Mr. Wilson's extremely distant voice saying; "Oh, *shit!*" She could not quite make out whether the aggrieved tone was that of a man whose suit had just been irredeemably ruined, a secret agent who had just blown his promotion prospects by losing the person he had been keeping tabs on, or an officer of the crown who had just committed four totally unnecessary murders in the line of duty.

49

"It's been a while," said Molly to the grey who was bending over her. "We've got a lot of catching up to do." They were in the kind of bland white-walled and white-curtained room that the greys usually employed for intercourse with their abductees, because they knew that if and when the abductees told their stories sceptics would take its blandness and whiteness as evidence of a simple failure of the abductees' delusional imaginations. She was, however, laid out on a guest bed, not one of the unforgiving examination-tables.

"Things aren't working out quite as we expected," the grey replied, rather sternly. "There's a complication."

"Is that *my* fault?" Molly countered, combatively.

"To be perfectly frank, we rather think it might be. You made us certain promises."

"I made certain *suggestions,*" Molly pointed out. "The instruments were all yours. I just offered you a strategy that might be worth trying—you were the ones who were supposed to put the plan into effective operation. If it's screwed up, you're the ones who've screwed it."

"There seem to be certain factors in the equation of which we knew nothing," the grey came back. "We take the view that we should have been warned. We had not realised that human belief in God and the Devil was so widespread, or so powerful."

"Well, *I* take the view that your methods of enquiry were seriously flawed," Molly told the grey, determined not to give an inch. "If you'd spent a lot less time abducting people and subjecting them to minute physical examinations and a lot more talking to them about their hopes and fears you'd know everything you could possibly need to know about God and the Devil and all their works. You're too hung up on *facts*. You think you know everything about us because you've been through our bodies with a fine-toothed comb, but you don't know *anything* about our inner lives. I tried to help you over that as best I could, but I couldn't tell you *everything* in a mere matter of weeks, could I? I'm sorry I didn't mention the Devil, but I hadn't even *met* him back then and I didn't find out about the impending Apocalypse of Evil until I went to Faerie. I'm even sorrier than you are if that's what's getting in the way of *your* schemes for the evolutionary perfection of humankind, but the question isn't who's to blame—it's *what do we do about the zombies?*"

"What zombies?" asked the grey, innocently.

"The zombies you just saved me from," Molly said, weakly. She had been knocked right out of her conversational stride.

"Oh, *those* zombies," said the grey. "They wouldn't have hurt you. It's just some sort of flu bug that's going round—we've pulled samples out of half a dozen of our abductees. The symptoms are trivial but it does seem to drag on a bit. That's not why we pulled you up."

Molly recalled that the greys always examined their experimental subjects in *very* bright light. They hadn't seen the zombies the way she'd seen them. "Well then," she said, "why *did* you pull me up?"

"Because we've got someone here who says that you can confirm his identity. We can't quite believe he's who he says he is, you see, although our usual methods of analysis have turned up a few anomalies that might support his story. Either way, he's a complication."

Molly furrowed her brow. This was a turn of events for which she was completely unprepared. "Who does he say he is?" she asked, warily.

The grey levitated her from the bed—which wasn't particularly difficult, given that they were obviously back in orbit and quite weightless—and directed her out into the corridor. He floated her around the sinuous arteries of the ship, without pausing to let her enjoy the gloriously starry view from any of the portholes they passed *en route*. Eventually, they came to another white room, not quite as bland or as barely-furnished as the other but still not the kind of place the greys liked to relax in when they were on their own time. Its central feature was an unusually brutal cage with thick steel bars.

"Have you ever seen this person before?" asked the grey, pointing a slender finger at the human figure confined within the cage.

It was the last person Molly had expected to see, on or off Earth, and she was distressed to see that he was in a worse condition than he had been when she had last seen him. Dilapidation was too mild a word for his state of being, although he didn't seem in the least zombified.

"Hello, Molly," the angel said. "I'm truly glad to see you."

"I thought you'd gone back to Heaven," Molly said. "I honestly thought you'd made it—that I'd saved you from suffering the consequences of your fall."

"You did," said the angel, "and I'm very grateful. I was sent down again as a messenger, on a special mission. It was only supposed to last a matter of hours, and I shouldn't really have had time to lose my wings and fade to near-human, but you have no idea how long it takes to get an appointment with a major religious leader these days. Time was that when an angel turned up in all his glory on the Vatican steps, *everybody* jumped to it, but now even God himself would have to go through channels and kick His heels in waiting-room after waiting-room. Would you believe that the only one I got in to see the first time of asking was the Dalai Lama?"

"The Dalai Lama doesn't believe in angels," Molly pointed out.

"Considering the state I was in by the time I got around to him, he's seen nothing to shake his scepticism," the angel admitted. "He didn't believe that the world was about to end either, but at least he was *polite*. I should have gone home right then, but I had one last courtesy call to make. Salt Lake City, for Heaven's sake! Why didn't He just go the whole hog and add East Grinstead to the itinerary?"

"I *said*, do you *know* this person?" the grey interrupted, having obviously become tired of being ignored.

"Of course I do," Molly said. "He's an angel. He fell once already, but he got right back up again. I assume that you've contrived to prevent him from doing that again?"

"There is no such thing as an angel," the grey told her, firmly.

"There's no such thing as little grey men in flying saucers, either," Molly told him. "You really haven't got the hang of this business at all, have you? He's a projection of the human yearning for moral order, but the fact that he's imaginary doesn't make him any less *important*. Why do you want to stop him going back to Heaven?"

"We don't, if that's really what he is and where he's going. We thought he was a transformed human—an unexpected side-effect of the little experiment you talked us into. We thought that the uplift process might have been spontane-ously triggered and then gone way off course."

"He's an angel," said Molly, firmly. "Trust me on this." She turned back to the caged angel. "You came back to give

257

the world's religious leaders notice of the Apocalypse?" she said, to make sure that she'd understood him correctly. "Not just the Catholics, but all of them."

"A matter of professional courtesy," the angel said. "Thanks to TV, all humans live in a multicultural society now, whether they like it or not. Everyone has had a chance to hear the good news and win salvation. Strictly speaking, it wasn't necessary to give any sort of notice to anyone, as the required warnings had already been officially posted within the scriptures, but it seemed only polite even though He knew it would be futile. Heaven's outside time and space, you see. Everyone who's there always has been there and always will be there, in a manner of speaking, so we already know exactly how many people are due to come over during the Moment of Rapture on Christmas Day."

This speech gave rise to all manner of questions, but Molly knew that she'd never forgive herself if she didn't go straight for the jackpot. "And how many people *are* going to Heaven when the world ends this Christmas?" she wanted to know.

"Thirty-seven," the angel told her. "Seen from the perspective of Earthly time, it will double our human population at a stroke, but as there's no time in Heaven . . ."

"Thirty-seven!" Molly repeated, incredulously. "Two thousand years of religious wars, crusades, witch-hunts, revivals. Reformations, Counter-Reformations and God only knows what else, and the number of people deemed fit for Heaven is *thirty-seven!* One would be severely tempted to ask whether it was worth it, were there not a more urgent question to address. *What's supposed to happen to the rest of us?"*

"In theory," the angel said, seemingly unembarrassed by the caustic manner of her criticisms of the Heavenly Order, "you ought to be bound for Hell *en masse*—but it seems that's not going to happen. The Devil's had enough of the palace of Pandemonium and bleak infernal landscapes, so he's moving his entire operation—or what's left of it, at any rate—to Earth. We don't know what he plans to do there, although he seems to be intent on a thorough shake-up of worldly affairs. Not our business, you see. Our dealings with humanity close at noon on Christmas Day. Not that the hour has any cosmic significance, of course—but because there's no time in Heaven, we've always been prepared to be liberal in calendrical matters."

"You're abandoning us," Molly said, flatly.

"Strictly speaking," the angel replied, fixing her with his remarkable celestial blue eyes, "*you*'re abandoning *us*. And the fact that the Devil's sticking around says as much again about your capacities and preferences. Hey—I'm just the messenger. If I'd got my deliveries done in time, I'd have paid you a call. You should be pleased that the greys held me up. It gives me a second chance to give you the present I brought you, by way of thanks for what you did for me last time I was down."

"Present?" said Molly, trying to remember the last time somebody had given her a present without expecting a *quid pro quo*. "What present?"

The angel reached into his right armpit with the same practised dexterity as Mr. Wilson, with what looked like a similar result.

"A *gun?*" said Molly, incredulously. "Since when do angels carry guns?"

"It's not a gun," said the angel, holding out his arm to slide the device between the bars. At closer range, Molly saw that although it was structurally identical to Wilson's weapon it was much shinier, not merely because it was polished but because it actually radiated a silvery light of its own: a halo of sorts. Wilson's matt black weapon had looked brutal and businesslike, but this one looked very different. It was far too bright to be mistaken for a real gun by anyone who judged by appearances, once it was clearly in view.

"It's a *deus ex* machine," the angel told her. "It's only good for one shot, but that single shot is miraculous. It's not Aladdin's magic lamp, mind. It doesn't grant wishes. You have to aim it *very carefully indeed,* but if you can get the right target in your sights and hit it fair and square . . . well, there *are* limits to what it can do, but I certainly don't know what they are."

Molly reached out as if to take the *deus ex* machine, but the grey got there first. The angel didn't try to stop the alien taking it. He and Molly waited patiently while the grey broke the ammunition clip out of the handle and held it up for their inspection.

"Empty," said the grey. "Useless."

"That's what *you* think," retorted the angel. "You haven't got the requisite eyesight to see the seed of a miracle. Let Molly have it, will you? I brought it for her."

The grey shrugged his slender shoulders and replaced the seemingly-empty ammunition clip before passing the weapon to Molly.

Molly didn't like to admit that the ammunition clip had looked empty to her too. She'd never been strong on faith.

50

"This is a very unfortunate turn of events," the grey said, turning his back on the angel in order to speak more sternly to Molly. "When we put our plans into operation, we had no idea that these kinds of factors required consideration. This so-called Devil is, of course, merely a mental symbol of instinctive impulses rooted in the human hind-brain which consciousness rightly deplores but has never managed to obliterate. God and the angels are antithetical symbols of cerebral opposition to the anarchic appetites of the hind-brain. The fact that such ideas exercise sufficient power to make these symbols incarnate will almost certainly compromise our transformative enhancement of the abilities of the human mind. When we allowed our various agents to communicate the transformative viruses to their peers, we took it for granted that the abilities that would be enhanced when they were eventually triggered would be under responsible conscious control, directed to entirely rational and Utopian ends, but if belief in angels and demons can have real material consequences it is possible that such beliefs might warp the effects of the transformative viruses into something very weird and scary.

"There is, of course, no harm in delivering an empty gun into the hands of an idiot individual—but what we greys may innocently have done at *your* suggestion might, in effect, have delivered a far deadlier weapon into the hands of an idiot species. If the vestigial instinctive impulses of the human hind-brain are augmented by our scheme as well as—or, far

worse, instead of—the cerebral faculties, the result will be
very different from what we intended. The fact that we might
be robbed of the valuable lesson which you suggested to us is
a very minor irritation compared with the tragedy that could
befall the human race itself. Unfortunately, I am not certain
that our experiment can be halted. Even if we abort the
formal trigger mechanism, this new data suggests that there
will be spontaneous transformations, some of which could
well have occurred already—and the activity of the enhanced
minds might be sufficient in itself to start a domino effect."

"Well," said the angel, undeterred by the fact that the grey
was ignoring him, "I hate to say this, but they all had their
chance to go to Heaven. Having blown that, it's difficult for
Him to attach much relevance to the question of what might
become of them instead."

"You know," Molly told the angel, "I think I liked you a
little better when you'd fallen. Now that you're back on
God's team, you've become smug and censorious."

"What did you expect?" the angel countered. "So, are
your diminutive friends going to let me out of this cage so that
I can go home, or do I have to wait for the Moment of Rapture? It's not that I don't have the patience of a saint, of
course, but time is *such* a drag. I'll be glad when I've turned
my back on it forever."

"Let him go," Molly said to the grey.

The grey's huge almond eyes stared back at her for a while
as if to say, *Who are you to give me orders?* In the end, though,
the child-like shoulders shrugged again and the alien reached
out to unlock the door of the cage. He opened it wide, and
gestured to indicate that the angel was free to go.

The angel stepped out, with an expression of perfect bliss
on his face. Then he closed his eyes, raised his hands above
his head, and sprouted wings: vast white wings twice as big as

he was. An aureole as bright as the sun appeared around his head, dazzling Molly so thoroughly that she didn't see him vanish. By the time her eyes had recovered from the shock he was gone.

"I'm surprised you were able to hold the angel at all," Molly observed, when she and the grey had retired to more comfortable and less relentlessly white surroundings. "Especially when he had the *deus ex* machine up his sleeve all the time."

"Even angels are fallible," the grey retorted, sourly, "and that fake gun is worthless against anyone who doesn't believe in it. You'll have to save it for the Devil or some other creature of superstition—and even he might call your bluff. We extra-terrestrials come from an entirely different framework of understanding. Heaven's rules don't apply to us and its silly tricks have no effect on grey power."

"According to Drs. Hyde and De'Ath, you're just as imaginary as the angel," Molly pointed out. "You're an example of the versatility of modern paranoia, but at the end of the day you're just one more image reflecting the same old archetypes."

"Drs. Hyde and De'Ath have climbed into a mental cage with thicker bars than the one in which we kept the angel, and they've locked the door behind them," the grey replied. "They couldn't admit the reality of flying saucers now if they were under threat of torture. You're more flexible than that, Molly. You know that it was us all along, not Chiliad Science's hypothetical multinational rival, who were active in and around the B&B from January on. You know perfectly well what *really* happened to Annie and Francine— and what really happened to *you*. So does Wilson, although he has to play along with his new bosses for the time being."

"So where does Francine's boyfriend Adam fit in?" Molly wanted to know.

"He doesn't," the grey informed her. "Not into our plans, at any rate. He's strictly your problem."

"My problem! Why is he *my* problem?"

"Because he's the one who ran off with your daughter, of course. Or did you think it was *you* he was chatting up with all that florid talk after Francine passed out."

"It *was* me," Molly objected. "He carried on for hours after Mr. Jarvis picked up Christine."

"Inertia and the lack of anything better to do," the grey informed her cruelly. "It was Christine he began to show off for—and by the time she left, he had her address."

"But she's only fifteen! Adam must have been . . ."

"The kind of predator who picks up drug-addicted whores and other assorted losers. He was with Annie before Francine. Maybe if Christine hadn't been there he'd have hit on you instead, but she was. Can we get back to the *real* problem now?"

"No we can't. *Where is she?*"

"How should I know?" the grey retorted. "Maybe you should have asked your friend the angel before you told me to cut him loose. He's the one with a hotline to the All-Seeing Eye. I'm just a scrupulous scientific observer and logician."

Molly refused to wilt beneath the sarcasm. "So give me the benefit of your logic," she said, tautly. "Given your new-found insight into the perversities of the human hind-brain, tell me how to go about finding my daughter."

The grey sighed. "It won't make any difference whether you find her or not, will it?" he said, crushingly. "She hasn't been kidnapped, has she? She went willingly—a sucker for temptation, just like her mother. What have you got to offer her that could possibly persuade her to give it up?"

It was a good question—sadistic, but good.

"The real point at issue," the grey reminded her, "is the fate of our plan to uplift the abilities of the human mind. Can we still go ahead with the next phase? If not, should we simply let events unwind or should we take steps to defuse the situation? To be perfectly honest, I'm not sure that your input is going to be much help, but having listened to you once we think it only fair and reasonable to hear what you have to say. What's happening on Earth, Molly? What's *really* happening, underneath the absurd confusion of conflicting imaginative representations?"

The length of this speech gave Molly time to calm down again. She knew that she had to co-operate with the greys, for her own sake as well as theirs.

"Conflicting imaginative representations," she echoed, pensively. "Neat phrase. Believers have always argued that the Devil's greatest triumph was persuading us that he doesn't exist, but they might have got it backwards, upside-down or wrong way around. Maybe the hind-brain's greatest triumph was persuading the cerebrum that it was just a mess of anarchic appetites. Maybe the reality behind the Devil pulled a fast one by disguising itself as the Emperor of Hell. Maybe it doesn't matter what symbols and labels we use, as long as we realise that we have a genuine fight on our hands. Nobody seems to be taking the plague of zombies seriously, because the progress of the disease is so gradual and nobody is dying from it, but the Devil told me that he didn't need his army of demons any more because he had some *real* soldiers lined up for the big push. You're a genetic engineer, so tell me —what would be the characteristics of the ideal biological army?"

"You know as well as I do," the grey told her. "In order to be universally infective, the bioweapon has to be harmless in its early phases and highly contagious. Once the secondary phase is triggered, however that's accomplished, it has to move very swiftly and aggressively—to kill, if that's the objective, or . . ."

The alternative the grey went on to map out was, of course, the kind of benign enhancement that his own generous "weapon" was intended to bestow upon its "victims"— but Molly didn't think it was necessary to listen to the detail. Instead, she wondered now what other possibilities might lie between the two extremes. The real intention of war was, of course, conquest rather than mere slaughter, and if the instinctive power of the human hind-brain really were great enough to subvert the transformative effects of the greys' cerebrum-aimed viruses, they wouldn't necessarily turn them into mere killing machines.

"Is it possible," she asked, when the grey gave her a chance, "that one of the viruses I and others like me spread so liberally on your behalf is responsible for the zombie plague?"

"No," said the grey, flatly. "It's packaged as flu. We never used that kind of coat."

"Then it's somebody else's. It has to be the Devil's. No matter what kind of intermediary he's using, it's the Devil's. Is there any possibility that the transformative DNA you've introduced might be an effective countermeasure against it?"

"It's impossible to say," the grey replied, although Molly could see that he was intrigued by the possibility. "Even if we knew exactly what the ultimate effects of the new virus would be, and even if we knew that our own transformers would work as intended . . . the experiments could take *years*. Maybe centuries."

"We don't have years," Molly said. "Chiliad Science must be working on the new virus, assuming that it isn't one of their own that's contrived an escape. They and half a dozen other biotech companies may already be working on an immunization serum, even if they think it's fairly harmless . . ."

"Oh, we can knock up one of *those* for you in no time, if that's all you're worried about," the grey put in, disingenuously. "In fact, we can go one better. We can make up shots of ready-manufactured antibodies. You'd probably need them at this stage, because the virus is already so widespread that there wouldn't be time for an uninfected person's own immune system to produce antibodies to the blanks before running into live ammunition."

"Will you do that?" Molly asked, breathlessly.

"Sure. As I keep trying to remind you, that's not the real problem. The problem is that once we grant the Devil an effective existence, even if he's no more than a glorified metaphor for something more numinous, there's a possibility that our uplift programme might go horribly wrong—and might, in fact, be already in the process of going horribly wrong. If what the angel said can be taken at face value—again, even if only as a set of metaphors, then it seems that the elements of cerebral consciousness that were existentially alienated into the concept of God are being withdrawn from the ego-arena, in which case . . ."

"In which case," Molly said, "the Devil is going to assume full control of his empire during the week after Christmas. The plague is his Antichrist, preparing his intended subjects for their new state of being. Calling them the living dead is putting the cart before the horse. What they really are is the dying alive, and I have a nasty suspicion that they could be dying alive for a *very* long time. He's tired of Hell, so he's making something else on Earth—something different, but just as bad. We have to stop him. We *all* have to stop him. First, we have to get the Anti-Antichrist into play. If you make me up some sample shots of your antidote, and a formula for mass-production, I can take them to Chiliad Science. Then you have to trigger your uplift viruses, hoping that they'll work as planned at least on the unzombified. Even then, it'll probably take a miracle—but we have one up our sleeves. I suspect that the Devil hasn't factored the *deus ex machine* into his calculations—and that could be just the edge we need."

"I can see that this is a way of talking about things which is neither uninteresting nor unappealing, if you're that way inclined," the grey admitted, wearily. "But if I may say so, it really doesn't *help*. Let's accept, for a moment, that there really *is* a God, and a Devil, and as many kinds of fairyland as you like. If we take it *all* aboard, what situation are we facing? God is withdrawing entirely from human affairs and Heaven is closing down. The Devil is about to precipitate an Apocalypse of Evil. A great plague is turning the entire human population into zombies. All that stands between the Devil and victory is a handful of scientists who don't believe in flying saucers, a handful of saucers whose flyers only believe in science, and a broken-down whore with an empty gun who's prepared to believe in absolutely anything. The race may not always be to the swift, nor the chess-game to the clever, but how would you calculate the spread if *you* were a bookmaker?"

"We still have to try," said Molly.

"You were wrong about the Devil's greatest triumph," the grey told her, bleakly. "The Devil's greatest triumph wasn't persuading people that he didn't exist, but ensuring that every single attempt to fight him ultimately worked to his advantage. Why do you think there are only thirty-seven living humans fitted for Heaven, when there are millions who've devoted their lives to fighting the Devil?"

"I think I liked you a little better when you didn't believe in the Devil," Molly said, wishing that she had the energy to summon up a better reply.

"I think I liked Earth and humankind a whole lot better when I didn't have to," the grey replied, with deadly neutrality. "Thanks for your input, Molly—I'll take it to the board meeting, and give you their decision in due course."

51

By the time the greys sent Molly back to Earth it was Saturday, the day before Christmas Eve, and the plague of zombies
had spread much further than when she'd left, although the
vast majority of Britain's citizens had not yet noticed it.

The greys were putting in some hectic overtime in their
routine abduction-and-examination work, in order to figure
out how effective their transformative DNA was likely to be
in the circumstances, but they had been reluctant to bring
forward their own plans until they had a better understanding
of the Devil's.

"The powers-that-be reckon that it's not our job to save
humankind from the consequences of its own self-loathing,"
her dutiful informant had informed Molly, after the relevant
board meeting. "Some of them figure that it might be rather
interesting to see how this zombification process works out—
they take the view that we can always find another species,
preferably with a few less hang-ups, to serve as guinea-pigs
for the uplift scheme. They don't have a majority yet, but
they currently outnumber those of us who think that your
plan might be worth a shot. Until the don't-knows have made
up their minds, by which time it might be too late anyway . . ."

Molly had got the picture. She had argued, of course, but
she was talking to one of the converted, and mere repetition
couldn't possibly prevail against the logical might of the
greys. In the end, and strictly as an interim measure, the
aliens had agreed to make her up half a dozen hypodermics
full of artificial antibodies against the zombie plague, to make

use of as she chose, and a formula for making more that she could pass on to Chiliad Science. In the interests of fairness, however, they had also ordered that she be given a lecture pointing out the possible advantages of the zombie condition, based on their most recent researches.

"It's true that they become increasingly intellectually and imaginatively challenged," their spokesman had admitted, "but that takes a lot of weight off their minds. They're still capable of love, and the fact that they're not capable of much else means that their love is displayed far more generously and consistently than the love of the easily-distracted. The fact that they're so much more interested in drinking than in eating means that they might gradually pine away to nothing, but the process will take longer than most of them had to live anyway and it won't involve any messy *moment of death*. Think of it as a process like supercooling, whereby a crypro-tected liquid never actually freezes but slips unobtrusively into vitrification. Having no awareness of mortality, you see, zombies don't suffer the burden of existential *angst* . . ."

"Oh, shut up and give me the needles," Molly had said.

The second thing Molly did when she got back to Earth, having been landed on the roof of Arcadia House so that she could pay a flying visit to the thirteenth floor, was to head for Tooting. The passengers on the Northern Line train were evenly divided between zombies and the unconverted, but the bright light that seemed to hide the zombies' true nature from the incurious eyes of their fellow-travellers also made the zombies' physical and behaviour symptoms much less obtrusive. Molly could see that their twitching hands were longing to start hugging people, but they stuck to their seats and their straps with the same stern resolve as any other com-muters, while their pinpoint-pupilled eyes stared fixedly into the same infinitely-distant void.

When Mr. Jarvis opened the door, Molly felt a stab of panic go clean through the chambers of her heart. Mr. Jarvis was a zombie already—a recent convert, to judge by the unspoiled nature of his pallid skin, but a convert nevertheless.

"I've come to see Angie," Molly said.

"Now, Molly," said Mr. Jarvis, in the same patronisingly treacly voice he had always employed in addressing her, even when he had been human. "You know that you can only do that by *arrangement*. There are *proper procedures* that are meant to make things easier for all of us."

"Let me in," Molly said, flatly.

"Now, Molly," Mr. Jarvis repeated, in exactly the same fashion. "You know that you can only do that . . ." Zombies, it seemed, were not capable of overmuch versatility in speech or manner.

Molly knew that time was pressing. If Mr. Jarvis was a zombie, then Mrs. Jarvis was a zombie, and Angie was in great danger.

She hauled out the *deus ex* machine and stuck the barrel in Jarvis's face, saying: "Let me in, motherfucker, or I'll blow your face into the middle of next week." She knew as she said it that she had finally crossed the line, and that if rumour of this adventure ever got back to Elizabeth Peach her chances of getting Angie back would evaporate completely—but the end of the world was nigh and Angie's foster-parents were zombies, so that seemed slightly irrelevant.

Mr. Jarvis crossed his eyes slightly as he focused on the gunsight. The reflexive effort seemed to confuse his thoughts considerably, but he managed a lop-sided smile. He didn't know that the apparent gun wasn't a gun at all, of course, but his zombified brain wasn't as prone to terror as a normal one.

"N-n-now, Molly . . ." he began.

Molly didn't think there was much point in kicking him in

the balls so she lowered her head and charged forward, butting him in the stomach. The momentum of the thrust sent him cannoning back into the square-sectioned post at the foot of the stairs which led to the upper floor of the Jarvises' semi-detached. The post was topped by a rounded piece the size of a football, with which Mr. Jarvis's head made very satisfying contact. He fell over. He didn't lose what consciousness he had left but Molly could see that efficient motor control would be way beyond him for at least a quarter of an hour.

There was no sign of Angie or Mrs. Jarvis in the sitting-room or the kitchen, so Molly hurried back towards the staircase. The recently-zombified Mrs. Jarvis was already half way down by this time, and Molly stuck her hand between the banisters to grip the older woman's ankle. Mrs. Jarvis obligingly fell the rest of the way, but she fell so limply that she didn't seem to break any bones. Like Mr. Jarvis, she didn't lose consciousness but she became temporarily incapable of any movement more complex than a facial tic.

Angie was in her bedroom playing *Tomb Raider*. She looked okay, but Molly wasn't taking any chances.

"Roll up your sleeve, darling," Molly said.

Angie took one look at the syringe whose sterile covering Molly was already tearing apart and said: "No way. You *know* I hate injections."

"It's for your own good, sweetie," Molly assured her. "For once in your life, you have to trust me. You'll see what I mean as soon as we get outside, but *there's no time to waste*. It's not just a matter of life and death—it's got beyond that now."

"No," said Angie, trembling on the brink of panic. "Where's M-M-Mrs. Jarvis?"

Even though it was Molly, not Mrs. Jarvis, who'd rescued her from the Queen of the Fays, Angie had almost given into habit and referred to Mrs. Jarvis as "Mummy," only contriving in the nick of time to turn the mistake into a zombie-like stammer that was almost as disturbing. It was, at any rate, too much for Molly. "*I'm* your mother!" she screeched. "*I'm* the one who loves you—*me*. Mrs. Jarvis is a fucking *zombie*. If you don't believe me, *go and look!*"

Molly stood aside to let Angie leave the room, but didn't follow her. She heard her own words echoing in her head, wincing at the shrewish tone and the crudity of the sentiment. She couldn't help remembering what the grey had said about the love of zombies being so generous and so consistent because it was uncomplicated by other motives.

After a minute and a half, Angie came back. She was already rolling up her right sleeve.

"Shit, Mum," she said. "What did you *do* to them?"

"They did it to themselves, darling," Molly said, as Angie squeezed her eyes tight shut in anticipation of the pain. "We all did it to ourselves—the whole human race. And please don't swear. I know I did, but I shouldn't have. I've been under a lot of pressure lately." She found a vein and slipped the needle in. She hadn't had much practice, but she wasn't a novice either, and she didn't think any trained nurse could have done better.

When Angie opened her eyes again she immediately directed her gaze at the other hypodermics that Molly had set down on the bed. She also saw the *deus ex* machine. "Cool," she said. "Mrs. Jarvis always said that it was only a matter of time before you became a pusher. Christine used to drive her mad by saying that at least you'd get to carry a gun."

"I'm not a pusher," Molly told her, "and the gun's not real. I don't suppose you've heard from Christine at all?"

"No. You'd think the cow would at least have apologised for leaving me all alone in this hell-hole, but no. Mrs. Jarvis said that she's probably gone to the Devil, just like . . ."

"I haven't," Molly said, "and if Christine has, we're going to get her back."

"You mean we're going to Hell?" Angie said, smiling to show that she didn't really mean it, although a girl who'd been kidnapped by the Queen of the Fays shouldn't have been capable of such smugness.

"No point," Molly told her. "Hell's finished. The Devil is moving to London. Don't ask me why—in his place I'd have picked Paris or Vienna—but Mephistopheles and Lilith are back in touch with the infernal grapevine and they're pretty certain that he's moving to the City. I really need to get Chiliad Science moving on the antidote to the plague, but for the time being, we're heading back to Barnsbury. If the men in black aren't staking the place out, I'll get on the phone to Hyde and De'Ath. You'd better pack everything you need—however this turns out, you won't be coming back here."

Molly became uncomfortably aware that Angie was looking at her as if she were completely mad.

"I know what I'm doing, darling," Molly assured her— and then, for the first time, was overtaken by a sudden vast rush of black doubt. Marjorie De'Ath had warned her to be on her guard against further delusion, and to be careful always to keep something of herself in reserve so that she might subject everything she saw and felt to a measure of studious scepticism. She hadn't done that. She hadn't even stopped to consider the possibility that everything that had befallen her since she caught sight of the first zombies in the Laydownyer Arms might be a paranoid nightmare—and now it was too late.

"We have to save the world, Angie," she said, defiantly. What she didn't say, although the thought had struck her very forcibly, was that if she couldn't, she certainly wouldn't be able to save herself.

52

Molly spent the journey north explaining the situation to Angie as best she could, and detailing all the matters that Angie must be careful not to mention while the wrong people were listening. Angie was only just thirteen, but she had a lot of imagination and a healthy quota of common sense. Whoever her father had been, his genes had coupled more productively with Molly's than could ever have been the case with the vast majority of the men she'd fucked.

The men in black were waiting for her outside her flat. There were three of them in the big limousine, and their leader was not in a good mood. He wasn't showing the slightest sign of zombification, but Molly guessed that even if he understood what a lucky escape he'd had, he would have attributed his good fortune to the shots he'd fired rather than the light beamed down by the flying saucer.

"This is getting out of hand, Molly," Wilson told her, when he saw that she wasn't alone. "Kidnapping is over the line." He looked as if he would rather have thumped her, but didn't think it would be seemly behaviour with a twelve-year-old looking on.

"I'm her mother," Molly told the man with the pencil moustache. "She won't be any trouble. I need to see De'Ath and Hyde, and I assume that they're equally keen to have a word with me. Given that you lost me yet again and shot four people in the process, they must be rather annoyed. I suppose they have to hope that they primed me well enough to keep my head straight even in the remoter reaches of the abduction delusion."

"That's about the size of it," Wilson conceded, with an ominous edge to his voice.

"Can I wash and change first?"

"As long as you're quick," Wilson conceded.

Molly was as quick as she could be. She put all but one of the hypodermics and the formula into a plastic bag, then carefully concealed the *deus ex* machine and the last hypodermic within the folds of her clean clothes.

The subsequent car-journey didn't take long; like the Devil, the directors of Chiliad Science Inc had decided that London was where the hottest action was just now. Their current hidey-hole was a first-floor room in the Excelsior Hotel, which was nearer to the city centre than the Peaslee Pharmaceuticals complex on the North Circular, although it was more Highgate than Hampstead.

"There you are, Molly," said Marjorie De'Ath, who seemed almost as pleased to see her as Molly was to see that the grey-haired woman was still unzombified. "We were very worried. I wish I knew how the opposition pulls that vanishing trick."

"It's a bit late for that," Molly pointed out. "In fact, it may also be a bit late for anything else you have in mind, but I've got something here that will allow you to start fighting back." She handed over the plastic bag and Dr. De'Ath peered inside, uncertainly.

"What is it?" The question came from Edward Hyde.

"It's a serum containing artificial antibodies and a formula for making more. It's not important how I came by them— the point is that they'll work. I don't know how much help they'll be to the existing zombies, but they'll prevent anyone who's been inoculated from becoming one."

"Zombies?" said Dr. De'Ath, frowning. "What zombies?"

For a moment, Molly was struck by the desperate fear that she might have over-reached herself already—but then the older woman's expression suddenly cleared and she added: "Oh—*those* zombies. We haven't been able to keep track of the vulgar terminology. Our best medical personnel are working flat out to determine the pathology of the condition, of course, but it's early days and it's only another mutant flu virus. We're still hoping that the condition might be temporary and that all the sufferers might make a full recovery. It doesn't seem to be causing any fatalities, even among the very old. It's an unfortunate complication, but it's definitely not the result of the transformative DNA you're carrying. That's still our primary concern. Now, what can you tell us about where you were taken and what happened there?"

"Not much," Molly said, truthfully. She had decided that the one thing she couldn't tell De'Ath and Hyde was that what they thought of as a carefully-implanted paranoid confabulation was anything but.

"But you did retain some awareness that the illusion was an illusion, didn't you?" Edward Hyde put in. "We did prove to you that you couldn't rely on your senses, didn't we?"

"I kept my wits about me as best I could," Molly assured him, not entirely hypocritically. "But even if you're a hundred per cent convinced that what you see as an alien spaceship in orbit can't possibly be anything of the sort, that still doesn't give you the power to see it as anything else."

"I suppose not," said Hyde, openly contemptuous of her failure, "but you must have picked up *some* clue to what was really happening. Didn't you?"

"Yes I did," Molly said, as positively. "I picked up the *very* strong impression that the DNA I'm carrying isn't the real problem—not the most urgent problem, at any rate. I know that the new thing looks like a new flu virus, and that familiarity has bred a certain contempt for all bugs of that kind, and I know that it hasn't caused any fatalities so far, but there's worse to come—and I mean *much* worse. You have to get started on that stuff right away. By all means leave Mr. Wilson to carry on debriefing me, but there really is no time to lose. You have to do your part."

"What make you think so?" said Dr. De'Ath, peering into the plastic bag yet again, but holding it at a greater distance now, as if it might contain something dangerous.

"You don't have to believe me," Molly said, patiently. "All you have to do is accept that there's a slim possibility that I *might* be right. You have to get that formula into manufacture as quickly as possible—immediately is by no means too soon. The zombie flu is manufactured. It's a weapon. If you don't act *now* the whole world might be lost by New Year's Eve—but you don't have to take my word for that. All you have to believe is that I found out *something*. Check it out."

While Molly was speaking Hyde and Wilson moved slightly to one side so that Wilson could put his head close to the scientist's and whisper in his ear. Dr. De'Ath seemed hopelessly indecisive all of a sudden, even though she must have been the one who'd suggested that Molly could be useful, if only they could persuade her of the extent to which she'd been deluded. Molly wondered whether there was anything else she could possibly say that might move Chiliad Science Inc to action. Perhaps she would have thought of something if the door hadn't flown open at that particular moment to reveal an angry man wielding a menacing gun.

53

As gunmen went, the newcomer was not nearly as convincing in the role as Mr. Wilson. Molly had to admit that his dumpy stature, wispy white hair and terrible dress-sense made him look rather absurd—but he did have the physical advantage of having his gun already in his hand, while Mr. Wilson's was still in its shoulder-holster. He also had the psychological advantage of knowing that everyone in the room was intelligent enough to have deduced that he must already have taken care of at least two of Mr. Wilson's henchmen in order to get to the door.

Everyone else was utterly dumbstruck, so it was left to Molly to say: "Wingate! What on earth do you think you're *doing?*"

"I want out," was Wingate's reply. "Right out of the country. I'm in the business and I *know* what's going on. I don't know if it was an accident or a deliberate release, but I don't need an electron microscope to tell me that it certainly didn't jump over from any Hong Kong chicken and there's no way I'm sticking around to see how it all unwinds. I want out —but *I'm taking my work with me.* All of it. No carefully-prepared booby-trapped packages—the real McCoy. To get it out of the machines I need a better password than the one I've got, so I figure I'll have to use *yours.*"

The last remark was directed, with feeling, at Edward Hyde. Hyde had been busy matching the reproachful look that Mr. Wilson had been directing at Molly, who had blown their earlier plan to use Wingate as a mule by telling him about the booby-trap, but now he turned his whole attention to Wingate.

"What the hell are you talking about, Wingate?" he said, hotly.

Molly didn't know whether to feel terrified or relieved. "He's talking about the zombie flu!" she said, excitedly. "He's twigged, even if the rest of you are too bloody slow or too bloody distracted. I was just trying to explain it to them, Nat. I *told* them it was manufactured! De'Ath's got an immunization serum right there in that plastic bag."

"Pull the other one, Judas," Wingate told her. "You can't possibly think I'm stupid enough to fall for *that* one!" It wasn't until he spared her that one vicious glance that Molly caught sight of the Devil in Wingate's eyes. She had never seen the Devil there before, but there was no doubt in her mind—the Devil had got to Wingate, and had turned him into a spanner to be thrown into Chiliad Science's works.

"This isn't necessary, Nat," Hyde said, having collected his scattered wits and moderated his tone "and your timing could hardly be worse. We're all on the same side, you know."

"We could have been," said Wingate, bitterly, "but you blew that—so don't blame me for my *timing*. Now move out of the door, Hyde—I don't have any more time to waste."

Molly had seen Wilson's hand edging towards his shoulder, but she didn't think that Wingate had. Nor did she suppose that Wingate was capable of doing anything about it even if he had, having presumed on the basis of his ultra-nerdish appearance that he had probably never held a gun in his life, let alone fired one. Wilson presumably felt the same way, but he too had forgotten that Wingate was an American, and that British standards of likelihood didn't apply to his particular case.

When Wilson made his move he did so with practised efficiency, but the man in black was only half way through the draw when Wingate blew a neat little hole in the middle of his forehead. As the back of Wilson's head blew out, blood and globs of tissue spattered the wall behind him. Molly winced as the half-drawn gun was released from Wilson's disturbed grasp and soared through the air towards her, but it fell to the carpet six inches short of her left trainer.

Angie screamed and Marjorie De'Ath turned zombie-white, but Molly was curiously unmoved. She still hadn't forgiven Wilson for the mangled tit and the black eye, let alone the intention he'd been harbouring before tall dark Tom had interrupted him—and she had watched him mete out exactly this treatment to four zombies whose only crime was to want to give him a hug. She watched his black-suited body go down in a heap as bits of his brains redistributed themselves in a series of slow downward trajectories across the patter of the hotel wallpaper.

"Wingate . . ." she began, uncertainly.

"I can't take you with me, Molly," the scientist said, curtly. "You'll have to make your own arrangements for getting out. Take my advice and start now. Even if these motherfuckers didn't start the war, they're sure as hell not going to stop it. Britain's finished, maybe all of Europe. Africa and Asia will go down like dominoes. North America is where any comeback will come from, if it comes at all, but you might be better off on some small island, the more remote the better—Madeira or St Helena. Now, *move.*"

Again he addressed his final admonition to Edward Hyde —and this time, Hyde made shift to obey. It had presumably occurred to him that for as long Marjorie De'Ath was still available to take his place, even he was disposable. He might even have had enough heroism in his soul to realise that if he went with Wingate, Dr. De'Ath might be able to get on with the business of getting the immunization serum into manufacture—a business whose seriousness and urgency could no longer be plausibly doubted.

It wasn't until Wingate closed the door behind him that everyone relaxed. Molly knelt down to take Angie in her arms as the twelve-year-old said: "What did he mean about getting out, Mummy?"

Marjorie De'Ath was busy drawing a deep breath of relief, but she didn't seem to need any physical support, so Molly stayed where she was and answered the question.

"He's figured out that the plague is something cooked up in a genetic engineering lab, sweetie," Molly explained. "He doesn't think it can be stopped before it causes a complete collapse of civilization. He didn't believe me when I told him about the serum." She didn't think it necessary to mention that she'd seen the Devil in Wingate's eyes, and that he was probably far more dangerous than he seemed.

"He's gone mad!" snapped Dr. De'Ath, biliously. "Completely off his head! He thinks it's ours! He thinks *we* let it out. He doesn't have the sense to realise that even if we *were* developing such weapons—which we aren't, by the way—we'd have the sense to manufacture an immunization serum in tandem with the attack agent, so that we could protect our own."

Molly sighed. She released Angie and came slowly erect, purloining Wilson's gun as she stood. She tucked it away as unobtrusively as she could. Marjorie De'Ath was too preoccupied to notice, although Angie saw it all. "But he's not one of *your own*, is he?" Molly said, quietly. "He doesn't belong to anyone any more. He's a loose cannon."

The door opened again, and two men in black burst through, wielding pump-action shotguns. They groaned theatrically when they saw that Wingate was gone and that their former superior was dead.

"He's headed for Peaslee," Dr. De'Ath told them, having recovered most of her composure. "We'd best get after him. If you can take him out without risking Edward, do it—but he's an experienced shooter. Don't give him any chances."

The two men in black nodded curtly and hurried on their way.

"Come on," Dr. De'Ath said to Molly, as she headed towards the main staircase. "We can get to work on this stuff as soon as Wingate's out of the way."

"Actually," Molly said, as meekly as she could, "my little girl's had a terrible shock, and it *is* nearly Christmas. I think I'd rather go home and rest, for now. Things will probably look a great deal brighter in the morning. You can send someone to pick me up then, if you still need me. Nine o'clock?"

Dr. De'Ath had had a terrible shock too, and she must have thought that Moll and Angie would only get in the way of the siege. "Fine," she said. "Hopefully, Dr. Hyde will be safe by then, and we'll be on the way to figuring out exactly what this stuff you've given us can do."

"Somebody has to save the world, Dr. De'Ath," Molly said, earnestly. "If not us, who? If not now, when?"

"You can be sure that I'll do my very best," De'Ath replied, her homiletic reflexes clicking into gear in spite of the situation, "but science isn't an individualistic business, as you well know. There are thousands of people already working on every aspect of this problem, with the best intentions in the world. The *method* will pull us through, just as it always has. It's the one dependable thing in the universe. Science will save the world, not you or I."

Having said that, the grey-haired genius hurried off down

the staircase and through the lobby.

Angie looked up at Molly. "Can I mention the Devil now, Mummy?" she asked.

"Yes, darling," Molly replied, "it's safe to mention the Devil again, now."

"They weren't ever going to help us, were they? Not against the Devil."

"No," Molly said. "They have their own area of expertise, but people like us always have to face the Devil on our own."

54

It was very late when they got back to the flat, but they didn't have any real difficulty making the journey. The buses had virtually stopped running but creeping zombification had improved the manners, if not the motor co-ordination, of the majority of taxi-drivers, so London aboveground wasn't yet paralysed. The tube still seemed to be functioning normally, a triumphant testimonial to the value of automation.

The hours of darkness presumably saw a further deterioration in the situation, but Molly and Angie spent the night locked up tight in the precious privacy of their own home. If the zombie Jarvises had had sufficient presence of mind to report Angie missing they obviously hadn't had enough to mention the gun—with the result that the misdemeanour was far too low on the ever-inflating register of Social Services priorities even to warrant a phone call. Given that the next day was both Sunday and Christmas Eve, Molly reckoned that they were now safe from any official intervention until the world had actually ended—or not, if the Anti-Antichrist could be put into production in time.

Molly and Angie got up at seven so that they'd have plenty of time to eat and compose themselves before leaving the flat at eight. Molly stowed Mr. Wilson's gun in her knicker-drawer, estimating that things hadn't yet become *that* dangerous on the streets, but she kept the *deus ex* machine about her person because she didn't dare take the slightest risk of mislaying it. In any case, the *deus ex* machine was probably a more reliable defence against the enemy she had to go to see.

Paying a call on the Devil seemed like a more profitable use of her time than twiddling her thumbs at Peaslee while Marjorie De'Ath's minions started work on the serum—assuming that they were now able to do so.

When they came out on to the Caledonian Road Angie pointed south-westwards at something in the far distance, partly obscured by the morning haze, and said: "What's that?"

It looked like a raggedly-tapering cone whose slender tip was lost in the clouds.

"I don't know," said Molly. "I don't think it was there yesterday—but I think we're going to find out soon enough."

Molly was glad to find that it was not merely possible but easy to catch a tube from Camden Town to Moorgate. The train wasn't even crowded—the vast majority of the commuters who would normally have been packed in like sardines had either been so comprehensively zombified as to have failed to get out of bed, or so comprehensively spooked by the increasingly-obvious plague that they had decided to take whatever kind of leave they could get and head out of town.

Ironically, the Moorgate-bound diehards who had refused to compromise their sense of duty found their good intentions firmly frustrated when they emerged from the station by the sole remaining exit to find themselves facing a looming forty-foot wall of bleak black stone that had divided New Union Street into two and had reduced Finsbury Circus to the status of a mere Crescent. Even at this close range Molly could see that within the first wall was another, far higher, and within that, a third. There seemed to be six walls in all, surrounding a central tower so incredibly high that its heights vanished into the clouds.

Even the unzombified brokers and bankers were so stupefied by the sight of this astonishing construction that they were reduced to standing helplessly by, unable to bestir themselves. Molly, by contrast, took Angie by the hand and started walking round the circular wall in search of the main gate. The fact that the Devil had raised such a vast edifice several days ahead of the due date of the Apocalypse obviously wasn't a good sign; it implied that he was feeling very confident of his new World Empire.

It turned out to be a long walk, although it wouldn't have been any quicker if they'd gone round the other way. The main gate turned out to be almost exactly opposite her starting-point, on Queen Street Place facing Southwark Bridge. The gate was twenty feet tall. It appeared to have been made from planks of *lignum vitae,* abundantly reinforced by ornately-wrought bars and studs of titanium, but Molly knew that it was mere art-work rather than serious siege-craft. The Devil did not expect to have to defend this citadel against any ordinary army.

Molly was surprised to discover that the sentry posted at the gate was tall dark Tom, back in human form and black leather. He still had the same flamboyant taste in hats.

"I thought you'd found your niche in Faerie," Molly said.

"So did I," he said, with a sigh, "but the best-laid plans of mice and cats . . . it turned out that the Queen wanted the music of the spheres in order to swing a deal with Old Nick. She figures that Faerie has no future, and sees no payoff in hiding away in a timewarp for ever and ever. She wants a place in the New World Order. This, apparently, is my share. No boots, no guitar, no nookie. A real dog's life."

"You are going to let us in, aren't you?" Molly said.

"Oh yes," said Tom. "You're *expected.* I even have instructions to guide you through the labyrinth, to save time." His green eyes narrowed thoughtfully before he added: "If I had to guess, I'd say that you have something else they want.

Maybe something you didn't have before. You've been back to the saucer, I suppose?"

"I've got nothing special," Molly lied.

Tom looked down at Angie as she said that. "Are you sure you want to take the little one in with you?"

"Quite sure," Molly said.

"I'm not so little," Angie observed.

"In here," Tom said, as the great black door swung open, "*everybody*'s little—but some are even littler than others."

It was easy to see what he meant. The gap separating the outer wall from the next one in was criss-crossed by so many hollow arches and covered bridges that no part of the interior ground level of the Devil's citadel was open to the sky. Beyond the gateway was a gloomy space whose crowded vault extended crazily into darkness. The next wall was so close that Molly felt distinctly cramped as well as humiliatingly small.

Tom led them away into a maze of corridors full of abrupt left- and right-turns and upward- and downward-leading stairways. There were dozens of doors, all made of the same black wood as the main gate, many of which had to be unlocked using keys selected from the multitude attached to the huge iron ring through which Tom's belt was looped. The lighting was uniformly dismal, although the torches which smouldered in their high-set brackets were closely akin to the fake "log fires" favoured by British Gas.

"You'd think he'd have made a few more concessions to modernity," Molly commented.

"It's very different from his last place," Tom informed her. "Pandemonium was a cross between a Tunisian brothel and Las Vegas. Anyhow, modernity is dead, and even post-modernity is past it. This is Year Zero."

"I know what year it is," Molly retorted.

When Tom opened the next door, Molly saw that there were people waiting for them in the corridor beyond—but the Devil wasn't among them.

"Hi, Moll!" said the first of the two female figures, grinning as she'd never grinned before. "Great to have you back, even out of uniform—and you've brought little Angie, too! *Lovely* girl."

Molly felt Angie draw closer to her side.

"Hello, *Honeysucker*," Molly said. "If I were you, I'd get a new dentist."

Honeysuckle's costume hadn't changed in any conspicuous detail but she was sporting a magnificent pair of extended canines. The first time she and Molly had met she'd merely been a Gothic fay, but now she'd graduated into a fully-fledged lamia.

"I've lost my taste for *honey,* honey," the ex-fay said, licking her scarlet lips, "but I could still give you a *real thrill.*"

Behind her, the similarly-transmogrified Peaseblossom gave a delicate little laugh.

"You'd need more than joke-shop teeth to do that," Molly assured her. "Don't even think about trying to get in our way. You know what happened last time."

"Only those who fail to learn from history are condemned to repeat it," Honeysuckle assured her. "That's a human thing, don't you think. *Oh my! Done the tragedy, done the farce! Whatever's next?* You're caught in the web, darlings, and Mummy Spider's on her way. Easy-Peasy and I wanted to say hello and goodbye, but we can't come with you today. Catch you later, I don't think."

Molly pushed past the chortling vampires, drawing Angie along with her.

Although they turned every which way at least a hundred times, Molly knew that their effective directions were northwards and upwards, towards the top of the central tower which stood on the site of the Old Lady of Threadneedle Street. She was very weary by the time they reached the elevator which took them up the last few hundred floors.

"I'm afraid of heights, Mummy," said Angie, who was smart enough to realise where they were headed.

"So am I, darling," Molly said, less calmly than she could have wished. "Let's not go near the edge, shall we?"

She was profoundly glad, when the car doors opened, to find that they were not on a platform open to the sky but a glass-clad rotunda. The ceiling was glass too, but there were metal shutters beyond the glass that hid the greater part of the sky. There were other rooms—or kiosks, at any rate— grouped around the elevator shaft, but the difference between the inner and outer diameters of the rotunda was at least twenty feet. The open space was lushly carpeted in red.

Molly was not surprised to discover that there was a lone male figure awaiting them at the window opposite the lift doors, who turned when she made no move to go to join him. She was, however, very surprised to see the face he wore. It was not the same one that he had presented to her in the back of poor Dean's stolen car, but she recognised it just the same.

It was Adam, seducer of Annie, Francine and—so rumour had it—Christine: the man who had persuaded her that this was Year Zero, the year when the past could and ought to be obliterated so that history could be born anew.

Hyde and De'Ath had assumed, not unnaturally, given their limited powers of imagination, that the mysterious Adam—whose sojourn in the B&B had initiated a flood of alleged delusions—had been working for a rival biotech company. They had been wrong about that, just as they had been wrong about the reality of the greys. Adam had been the Devil all along.

"Hello, Molly," said Adam the Devil, mockingly. "Have you come to give me a Christmas present?"

For a moment or two, Molly wasn't sure whether he meant the *deus ex* machine or Angie. "No," she said, becoming suddenly very clear in her own mind as to exactly why she *had* come. "I've come to give you the opportunity to give one to me."

55

"Won't you come and see the view, Molly?" the Devil asked, unctuously. "It's quite spectacular. Even on a clear day, you can't see much of Earth, but if you look up, you can see forever. It's glorious by night—we're way above the primary pollution-layer here."

"Heights scare me," Molly said, flatly. The windows of the rotunda extended all the way from the shuttered ceiling to the red-carpeted floor. If she'd gone to stand by the window it would have been like standing on the lip of a precipice.

"Really?" said the Devil. "I *love* heights. I know all about the *deus ex* machine, by the way. In fact, I know rather more about it than you do, because I can see slightly more of the future than you can. Not that anyone can see the future clearly, of course, except for entities that elect to live in timeless Heavens where issues of causality simply don't arise. Personally, I've always considered that a bit of a cheat. Those of us who would rather live in lovely, delicious, precious time can only see the possibilities which exist and can only guess the likelihood of their emerging into solid fact, because the future is yet to be made, sculpted, and *nailed down*. So far, the only thing that's absolutely certain about your future and mine is that thirty-seven of those pathetic little creatures way down there are Heaven-bound. As to what becomes of the rest of us . . . well, Molly, I'd like to say that it depends on me, but it doesn't. It *really* depends on you. Some responsibility! Would you like a drink, by the way?"

"No thanks," said Molly, shortly. The lift doors had long

since closed behind her, carrying tall dark Tom back down into the bowels of the citadel, but she hadn't moved an inch. Nor had Angie.

The Devil seemed to be in a tolerant mood. Accepting that she wasn't going to cross the blood-red carpet to stand with him, he meekly came to her—but he didn't try to get too close. He stopped at a perfectly respectful distance, and the blue eyes with which he looked into Molly's were as mild as milk, with none of his usual flare and fury. He was wearing a salmon-pink sweater, brown slacks and flat shoes. He looked as if he'd just played nine holes of non-competitive golf for the sake of practising his swing.

"You don't believe me, do you?" he said, with a sigh. "You have no idea how inconvenient it is to be the Father of Lies. It's a title to be proud of, no doubt, but it makes it very hard to have a straight talk with anyone. Every time I tell the truth, people assume the opposite, so even when I'm being perfectly honest—*especially* when I'm being perfectly honest—the effect is confusingly deceptive. Perverse, or what? But I do need to be straight with you, Molly, because if I can't persuade you to do the right thing on New Year's Eve, all of this could come to nothing. *All* of it. I don't want that to happen, Molly—and deep down, neither do you. I know that for a fact, by the way. It's one thing of which we can both be certain."

"Where's Christine?" Molly asked, bluntly.

The Devil raised his eyebrows and spread his arms slightly as if to indicate that he couldn't possibly be hiding anything. "She's around," he said. "She knows you're here. To tell the truth, I think she's secretly just as keen to see you as you are to see her, but she won't admit it to herself, so she'll hang on as long as she dares before putting in an appearance. Teenagers, eh! I haven't done her any harm, Molly. I've looked after her very well. I suppose, technically speaking, that it was statutory rape, but I *am* the Devil after all—no sin, no fun. Don't bother to reach suggestively towards the *deus ex machine*. We both know perfectly well that it's not a gun, and you're not going to point it at me and pull the trigger in a fit of mere petulance. In fact, we both know that you're not going to use it until midnight on New Year's Eve. That's what I want to talk to you about—and what you actually came here to talk to me about, whether you're prepared to admit it to yourself or not. We can settle this business sensibly, you know, if we just put our heads together and talk it through. We want the same things, Molly—none of this could have happened if we didn't."

"I don't think so," Molly said.

"And you won't believe anything I tell you, because I'm the Father of Lies. Well, Molly, I have more faith in you than that—which incidentally, is more faith than you've ever had in yourself. I think that if I tell you the truth now, so that you can chew it over at your leisure, you'll eventually see it for what it is. You'll leave here is a state of utter confusion and uncertainty, but when the deadline arrives, you'll have weighed everything very carefully indeed, and you'll have understood that there's only one possible explanation for everything that's happened this last year. I think you've already figured out that what Dr. De'Ath told you up in Bingley is balderdash, and that the little grey men don't really have a clue what's what. As for the giant octopuses scrawling graffiti on the moon—you *must* have seen that for the quirky wish-fulfilment fantasy it was. You're *so* close to working it out for yourself that you only need one last clue before it all falls into place. In a way, I'm sorry it has to be me that provides it, because I'm sure you'd have taken it better from the angel or dear old Lilith, but I'm the male lead in this little melodrama and we all have to play our parts."

He paused, as if waiting for permission to continue. "Go on," said Molly, obligingly.

"Well, Molly," the Father of Lies went on, "it really did start last New Year's Eve, at the B&B. Whatever De'Ath and Hyde may think, though, it certainly wasn't started by any paranoia-inducing drug—and much as I'd love to take credit for *everything,* it certainly wasn't started by me. It was *you,* Molly. It's always been you. You must have known that, even though you couldn't quite admit it to yourself. You started it —you and nobody else. Now it's up to you to finish it, either by sealing the circle or breaking it. Personally, I think you should break it. Trust your instincts, not your intellect."

"And how exactly, did *I* start it off, without the aid of any wonder drug?" Molly wanted to know.

"With the *deus ex* machine, of course. You don't actually fire it until New Year's Eve, but when you do fire it there's nothing whatsoever to stop its effects extending back in time, not merely to the beginning of the year but the beginning of time. In fact, if you think about it carefully, you'll see that it could hardly be otherwise. If the machine didn't reach back to the beginning of time *and* to the beginning of the year, how else could it set up the circumstances by which it could come into being as well as the circumstances of its firing? The only way it can establish itself within the universe and to credit itself with the power it needs to remake that universe is to put all their essential elements in their proper places *primordially:* God, Heaven, me, the giant octopuses, the greys, Chiliad Science, the angel, Elvis, Wingate, the Queen of the Fays, the men in black . . . and *you,* Molly. You above all."

"Why me *above all?*" Molly demanded.

"Because somebody has to aim the device *very carefully* and pull the trigger," the Devil told her, "and somebody has to provide an appropriate target. That's you. You're the one who has to solve the angel's little riddle—and I think you've probably worked out by now what the answer seems to be. Unfortunately, you're wrong. You've been wrong all along. You've been wrong since the beginning of time, even though you haven't actually done it yet."

56

"What's all that supposed to mean?" Molly asked, warily. She knew, though, that the Devil was right. She *had* worked out to her own satisfaction exactly where the *deus ex* machine would have to be aimed if it were to complete year zero's new year resolution and give her what she needed. The last thing she needed was to have doubts cast upon her tentative decision—but she knew only too well that she could be wrong.

"Oh, come on," said the Devil. "Do you really think I'm stupid enough to believe that you're going to aim it at *me?* I'd try to tempt you to do that, of course, if I thought it would work, but I know it wouldn't. It would just make you suspicious. You've already spent all the time you could spare going over the angel's instructions in your mind, trying to figure out exactly what he meant by having to *aim it very carefully indeed* —and we both know that you've already come to the conclusion that there's only one person at whom you can effectively aim it, because we both know that there's only one person who can be profoundly affected by it. It wasn't an easy decision, of course, and it wouldn't be easy to hold to it even if I let the matter ride, because we could be in the middle of a really tense climax if I cared to string things out that way. In the end, though, you'd stick to your guns—if you'll pardon the pun. You'd put the barrel of the *deus ex* machine in your mouth and point it at your hind-brain, and pull the trigger, so that it would blow you all the way back to the beginning of the year, in your brand new role as Molly the miracle-worker, Molly the Warrior Princess, Molly the saviour of the world.

"In a sense, of course, that's already happened, because the assumption that that's what you'll do is already built into the way year zero has been unfolding—but the future still lies ahead of us, Molly, unformed and uncertain. There's still time to change your mind and make a fool of fate. You're not a prisoner of the assumptions that have foisted themselves upon you—it's still up to you to decide which of them will be set in historical stone and which of them will turn out to have been illusory phantoms of improbability. It's still year zero, Molly. The final question is still to be asked and answered and the final decision still has to be made—and *deus ex* machines are far too powerful for their action to be troubled by petty paradoxes. Everything is still possible, Molly, if only you're prepared to question your deepest assumptions, and figure out what you really and truly *want*."

"And what *do* I really and truly want?" Molly wanted to know.

"I may be the Devil, Molly," the Devil said, leaning forward seductively and smiling like a snake, "but I'm *your* Devil. You made me, in your own image. I may be the Father of Lies, but they're the lies to which *you* gave birth. We both know that I can't take the *deus ex* machine off you, by persuasion or by force, but we both know that you can agree to hand it over, as a gift—and we both know, deep down, that I'm the only one who can make proper use of it. I'm the better part of you, Molly—the instinctive, emotional, ambitious part. You might doubt my motives, but without me, you'd have no motives at all. You know better than to take Heavenly propaganda on trust, or you'd be one of the timeless thirty-seven. You're wise enough to know that you can't defeat evil by fire and flame or a retreat into claustrophobic sanctity; you have to work to transform it, to accept what can and must be accepted while controlling the rest. Listen to your heart,

Molly. Listen to your heart—and give me the Christmas present I want more than anything else in the world. Give me the chance to work *my* miracle."

Molly remembered, dimly, that she had really fancied Francine's Adam during that magical couple of hours after the midnight that had divided 1999 from year zero. He could have had her for the asking—but he hadn't asked. It had taken her the best part of a year to figure out why. She heard the lift doors slide open behind her, but she didn't turn around. She was still looking deep into the guileful and guilty eyes of the Father of Lies. It was left to Angie to say: "Chris! Mum, it's Chris!"

Molly waited for Christine to walk around her and take her defiant stand beside her unsuitable lover.

"Hello Mum," Christine said dully. "I'm not coming with you, you know."

"Yes," said Molly, dully. "I know. How've you been, sweetie?"

"Never better," Christine said, unsurprisingly, "but not so sweet. You?"

"As well as can be expected," Molly said, "and not quite so sour. I've still got a spare dose of the immunization serum against the zombie flu, if you want it."

"I don't need it," Christine assured her. "Adam can take care of all that—can't you, Adam?"

"Absolutely," said the Devil. "Nobody gets the zombie flu without my say-so. Depend on it. We don't need your serum *here,* Molly. Angie would have been safe enough with the Jarvises, by the way, no matter how far and fast they rotted down. In any case, zombies are more sinned against than sinning. You should have listened to the greys—they'd begun to see the advantages of a world of zombies. They're not going to go ahead with the mass uplift, you know. They've accepted the logic of my pre-emptive strike. By this time, my favourite loose cannon should have blown Peaslee Pharmaceuticals sky high, and Edward Hyde, Marjorie De'Ath and your precious immunization serum with it. It's just you and me, Molly, as you and the *deus ex* machine always intended. We had to get here by the scenic route, but we had to get here. You could stay, if you wanted to, but I know you don't. You want to go back home and play happy families for a few precious days, until the Apocalypse of Evil falls due. I'm sorry that Christine prefers to stay here, but she's a free agent—I can't order her to go with you. I'll give you our mobile phone number, though. You can get through to us any time, day or night. She *will* talk to you, won't you, Christine?"

"I suppose so," Christine said, dully. She seemed slightly disappointed that things hadn't taken a more argumentative turn. She obviously had a lot of confused feelings bottled up inside.

"Thanks," said Molly. "I'll give you mine, darling. Please call, when you feel like it." She found an old receipt in her jacket pocket and used a pencil-stub to write her number on the back, then stuck her hand out in Christine's direction. After a moment's hesitation, Christine took the receipt.

"Even miracles don't happen overnight," the Devil said, letting a sarcastic gleam show in his eye for the first time. "In fact, every single one of them requires the reconstruction of eternity. We'll see you on Sunday anyway, of course—it'll be quite a party. Are you absolutely *sure* that you wouldn't like to take a look at the view, Molly? It's traditional, you know— kingdoms of the world, and all that."

"I don't like heights," Molly said, again.

"Pity," said the Devil, as Molly heard the doors of the lift slide open again behind her. "Acrophobia is a strictly cerebral failing, you know—a folly of consciousness. If we could only trust our instincts . . . our hind-brains *love* heights, because they're not prey to any discomfiting delusions of grandeur." He chuckled self-indulgently.

It was Angie who said to Christine: "*Please,* Chris!"

It was to Molly that Christine said: "I can't, Ange. This is where I belong now."

"Going down," said tall dark Tom, holding the elevator doors apart as they vainly attempted to follow the mechanical instinct urging them to slide shut. Molly put her hand on Angie's shoulder and guided her into the car.

"Think it over," said the Devil, amiably. "Then go with your instincts."

57

Molly and Angie took the tube back home. Molly was glad that the system was still working, and doubly glad that she didn't have to watch the collapse of civilization that was taking place above her head. There was something comforting about always travelling in tunnels, with nothing beyond the windows but blank and carefully-constructed walls. Tunnels were the antithesis of vertigo-inducing heights. From dizzy heights you couldn't help seeing the kingdoms of the world in all their horrid, crawling expanse, but when you looked into the window of a tube-train all you could see was your own face staring back from a reflected carriage, with nothing behind it but nothing. There was safety in reflection, duplication and circularity . . . at least until you started thinking.

Molly had no difficulty in imagining what it was like up above. By now, seven out of every ten Londoners would be zombies. By tomorrow it would be eight, and by Boxing Day —assuming that the Devil was right about Wingate having blown himself up and the serum with him—it would be ten. They wouldn't all be equally far gone, of course, and most of them would be ready and eager to continue the traditional binge of false generosity and honest self-indulgence all the way through to the new year. Even zombies could get stinking drunk, probably more easily than ordinary folk. The world wouldn't actually dissolve into mere atoms on the thirty-first, but by then the completion of the process would be assured. Nothing but a miracle would be able to prevent it—which wasn't surprising if, as the Devil alleged, it was a version of the very same miracle that had created the conditions for the world's possible salvation.

There was safety in reflection, duplication and circularity, Molly thought, but none at all in an open-ended universe that merely went on and on forever, with one thing leading to another, never recoiling on itself to erase mistakes and offer second chances.

"Is the world really going to end, Mummy?" Angie asked, as the train drew away from King's Cross, heading for Camden Town.

"No, love," Molly said. "That's just a manner of speaking. The world never ends, even if you put a gun to your head and take yourself out of it by blowing your brain to smithereens. But it's never the same world from one year to the next, let alone one century to the next or one millennium to the next. It changes, and you can't hold it back."

Too true, she added, silently, to her herself. *You have your kids, you lose your kids, you try to get them back, but you can't ever really get them back, because they're not the same kids from one year to the next, and they stop being yours as soon as they become themselves, and no matter how well you try to protect them, you can't choose for them whether they'll be zombies or real people, brides of Christ or mistresses of the Devil, scientists or fools. All you can hope for is the possibility that they might learn from your mistakes without having to repeat them—that they'll never have to get to the same old end of the same old line with nowhere to go to but nowhere. Done the tragedy, done the farce—what's next?*

"I'd give you a Christmas present," Angie said, "if I had any money to buy one—but I haven't."

"I'd give you the world," Molly assured her, "if I had it to give—but I'm not quite sure how that particular trick's supposed to work. I almost was, but now the Devil's sown the seeds of doubt again, I really don't know what to do."

Camden High Street was as busy as it usually was on Christmas Eve, but it was difficult to think of any location to which a plague of zombies would have made less difference, at least in daylight. Before starting on the heavy shopping, Molly took time out to drop into the Laydownyer Arms to apologise for her long absence.

"That's okay," said the slightly-zombified bar manager. "Some tall guy in a black suit dropped in to say that you might not be in for a while. He said something about your being attacked on the way home—it was the same night four locals got their heads blown off in some kind of firefight. Drug war, they said, but rumour has it that they were all shot in the face with the same .44 automatic. You can come back on shift any time. It's been slow for Christmas so far, but it's bound to pick up tonight. If New Year's Eve's half as good as last year I could really use you then."

"I can't," Molly said. "My kid's staying with me." She nodded in Angie's direction and the zombie barman winked at the child.

"Okay," he said. "If you change your mind, though, just give me a ring."

Since moving to Barnsbury Molly had got out of the habit of doing a whole week's shopping in one go, but with Angie along to help out with the carrier bags it was easy enough to lay in abundant supplies. Sainsbury's was crowded, but under the glare of neon striplights zombies were sticklers for trolley etiquette and patient queuers at the check-out. When you got right down to it, Molly thought, that was what zombiedom was all about: queuing in an orderly, patient and supercool manner for the ultimate check-out.

"We'll be okay," Molly assured her daughter, as she let the two of them back into the flat. "There's plenty on TV. We'll be fine."

It sounded a trifle hollow, and when she actually turned on the TV it began to seem even more hollow. The zombie newsreader reported the rumour that the new flu epidemic was a biological weapon escaped from a military laboratory with all the contempt his lax face muscles could muster, and stressed that as the disease had not yet claimed a single fatal casualty it could not possibly be reckoned as anything more than a minor nuisance. He also assured north Londoners that the fire burning in the laboratories of Peaslee Pharmaceuticals was at last under control and that the North Circular Road would be reopened as soon as possible. Fire investigators would begin to investigate the source of the explosion that had ripped through the lab complex as soon as possible, and would also be able to confirm the final death-toll, currently estimated at thirty-seven, including world-famous genetic engineers Marjorie De'Ath, Edward Hyde and Nathanael Wingate.

"I should have done what Hyde told me to do," Molly murmured, when the weatherman finally came on. "If Wingate had gone in and picked up that package when he was supposed to . . . but no, I had to feed his paranoia one last biscuit."

"Have you still got the big man's gun, Mummy?" Angie asked, curiously. "Will you get into trouble for taking it? Are you going to use it?"

"Yes I have," Molly admitted. "I don't think I'll get into trouble, because the other men in black will probably assume that Wingate took it. I'm not going to use it unless I have to, and I'm pretty sure I won't. The men in black probably won't come calling again now that Wilson, De'Ath and Hyde are all out of the picture—not until the holidays are over, at any rate —and the zombies can't do us any harm."

58

The phone didn't ring that evening, and Molly didn't try to ring out. It didn't ring on Christmas Day either. Molly picked up the receiver of her own phone half a dozen times, but she always put it back down again, because she knew full well that if she dialled she'd only get the Devil's mocking voice on the other end, saying that *of course* she could speak to Christine, insinuating all the while that he'd won yet again.

Molly and Angie had Christmas dinner *à deux* and they both tried hard to pretend that it was a festive occasion, but they couldn't muster the requisite conviction. They both knew that Christine preferred dancing with the Devil and that the world was due to end in a week, and this patchwork pall of depression was more than adequate to take the edge off the turkey breast-roast.

The Moment of Rapture passed without any unusual display of Heavenly Light in Camden, and it didn't make the early evening news—but that wasn't surprising. Nothing ever did make the early evening news on Christmas Day except the Queen's speech, whose banality would hardly have been affected by the defection of the Heavenbound even if it hadn't been pre-recorded.

Molly made no attempt to ring Christine on Boxing Day either, but she resolved that if Christine hadn't made the first move by seven o'clock on Wednesday, she'd take the bull by the horns and give the little cow and her diabolical boyfriend the satisfaction of savouring the extent of her desperation.

At six-thirty-five on Wednesday, the phone finally rang.

Angie picked it up before Molly could get there, but she had sense enough not to hang on to it. "Yes," "Hi" and "Okay" were the only words she spoke before handing the receiver to her mother, saying, "It's Chris. She says she wants to explain."

"Hello, Chris," Molly said, trying not to sound tearful. "I was just about to call you. You don't have to explain anything. I was fifteen myself once. I know how these things happen."

"I know you think he's the Devil incarnate," Christine said, "but that's because you don't understand him. That's what I want to explain."

"You don't have to," Molly said, again.

"But I *do*. You think it's the end of the world, and it's not. It's the beginning of something new, something wonderful."

"You're pregnant," Molly immediately inferred. She couldn't help remembering the old *aide memoire:* Mars implies; Venus infers. She'd quote it to Torquemadam once, but poor Sylv hadn't been able to see the joke. "What are plies?" she'd asked, mystified.

"No I'm not," Christine. "Or—well, actually, yes I am, but that's not the point. The point is that he's not really *evil* at all. That was just scapegoating. He's taken the blame for an awful lot of things that *weren't his fault*. All he needs is a chance to prove himself. That's what this whole thing is, to him—a chance to prove that he can look after the world far better than God ever did. All that temptation and torment business is behind him now. He's completely fed up with being a collection of negatives. He wants to do something *positive* now. He wants to remake the world, not just to pull it out of the horrible mess that the all God squads have left it in but to make it better—better than the likes of the little grey men could ever imagine, let alone contrive. You should never have listened to them, Mum. They're clever enough, but they're just scientists. They don't understand *love*. Those weirdos at Chiliad Science were just as bad—no different, really. They're all just *androids,* Mum—none of them understands what it is to have *feelings*. But you're a *mother*. You could understand, if you'd only try. If you'd only open your mind . . . if you could only see him the way I see him, and really listen to what he has to say . . . if you could only accept him for what he is, instead of thinking of him as the Devil . . ."

"Chris," said Molly, softly. "He actually *is* the Devil. And I have seen him for what he really is, in the back of poor Dean's car."

"Well, he's sorry about that now," Christine said. "He was a bit pissed off because you were getting so chummy with his old friends—they *let him down,* you know—and he hadn't seen enough of the future at that stage to realise how important you were. He hadn't been the Devil for very long, you know. Well, in one sense, of course, he'd *always* been the Devil, but in another sense, he'd spent the first thirty years of his life as some perfectly ordinary bloke who just happened to bump into your friend Annie when she was at a low ebb, and then got tangled up with your friend Francine, and then just happened to be sitting on the couch in the front room of the B&B when *zap!*—eternity unwinds and the fallout from *your* miracle-machine sends him straight back to central casting for the role of the villain to end all villains. I mean, Mum, you're at least *partly* responsible for all this, and I know you're a bit jealous because you fancied him too, but *have a heart, Mum. It's not my fault!*"

"No, love," said Molly, very softly indeed. "It's not."

"They're just zombies, Mum," Christine went on, hardly having paused for breath. "They're not suffering any pain. They aren't even going to die, *as such*. They're just going to sort of *biodegrade,* peacefully and usefully, feeling nothing but love and joy and all that sort of stuff. The world doesn't need them, Mum—in fact, what the world needs more than anything else is to be without them. Chiliad Science never understood that, and nor did the greys. What the world needs, desperately, is a *new start.* A new Eden, a new humanity. It needs *cleansing,* Mum. Next time around, we'll do far, far better. We'll get a proper start, and we'll all have eaten the fruit of the Tree of Knowledge. It'll be great, Mum. Absolutely great. He doesn't even need the gun-thing for himself—all he really needs is for you to point it in the right direction. All he needs is for you to refrain from *destroying him.* He really likes you, Mum, and he really, like, *respects* you, but he's just a little bit worried that you won't do the right thing. People are only human, he says, and sometimes they can't help getting their knickers in a twist. If only you'd think about it, he says, you'd see what you ought to do . . . what you *have* to do. He's not really the Father of Lies, Mum, but he *is* the father of my child and I don't want to lose him the way you lost *my* dad, and Angie's. You do understand that, don't you? You do understand?"

"Oh yes," Molly whispered, while the tears ran silently down her cheeks. "I understand."

59

Thursday's post brought Molly and Angie a gaudy invitation to a big party on New Year's Eve. It was accompanied by a hand-written note which informed them that a car would be sent to deliver their costumes at eight, and would wait to carry them to the venue when they were ready. It wasn't signed, but the RSVP phone-number was the same one that the Devil had given Molly. There was also a belated card from the thirteenth floor of Arcadia House, signed by the entire ex-Hierarchy of Hell. That too had a hand-written note enclosed, signed by Lilith alone, which simply said: "Sorry it's late. We've had a lot on our minds."

The lunchtime news on TV still had no mention of the Rapture or of any mysterious disappearances. It seemed that the thirty-seven humans qualified for Heaven had lived lives of such quiet obscurity that no one had yet noticed that they were gone. The zombie newsreader did, however, report unusual activity on the part of the US Air Force in several different locations, including the Iraqi no-fly zone, New Mexico and Guam. It seemed that missiles had been fired at a number of targets but no hits had yet been confirmed nor any reason given for the action.

"Oh shit!" said Molly. "That wasn't in the script."

"What wasn't?" Angie wanted to know.

"He's going after the greys. He's actually mobilised the US Air Force to go after the saucers."

"Is that bad?"

"It is if the action's successful. I was relying on the greys to pull our chestnuts out of the fire if all else failed. I thought that might be the Devil's only weakness—the fact that he's terrestrial and they're not. They perform on a much bigger stage, you see. They could have put the whole problem into a different and more productive context. Also, they could have beamed us up if things got really sticky. He's already taken out Chiliad Science—if he takes out the greys, we really are on our own."

The six o'clock news confirmed Molly's worst fears. Three extraterrestrial vehicles had been shot down. One had fallen into the Pacific and one into the inaccessible desert close to the ruins of ancient Babylon, but there was abundant footage of the inhabitants of Roswell dancing among the wreckage that was liberally scattered over four square miles. Senior USAF officers were queuing up to talk to CNN about the relief they felt at finally having completed Operation Softly Softly, which had begun fifty-two years before. The BBC was, however, careful to point out that it had been the British who had first alerted the initially-sceptical Americans to the fact that Earth was under observation by aliens, following the now-legendary Woking Encounter of 1897.

It wasn't until the ITN news at eleven that Molly finally obtained the one piece of information she had been desperate to hear. The US president had made a live broadcast announcing that the alien mothership had fled the system. It had gone into warp drive, he assured his rapt listeners, somewhere beyond the orbit of Mars. America—acting, of course, on behalf of all mankind—had just won the first interstellar war, so comprehensively that the enemy had not been able to fire a single shot. This, according to the president, boded well for the future conquest of the galaxy, which would provide the greatest challenge of the next thousand years. It might have sounded even better had the president not been in an advanced phase of the zombie flu.

By this time, Molly had put Angie to bed, so she had no alternative but to brood alone. She knew that with the greys out of the picture her last chance of an easy escape had gone. While they could have lifted her out of the nightmare at any moment the question of whether the nightmare was subjective or objective hadn't seemed to be of paramount importance, but now it was. Now she finally had to confront the question that Marjorie De'Ath had insisted she retain at the back of her mind: the question of whether all of this might be a drug-induced paranoid delusion.

It was, Molly knew, by far the simplest explanation. It was also the most comforting explanation. If all of this *was* happening inside her head, then the human race had not actually been turned into zombies, the presiding geniuses of Chiliad Science had not been immolated, Angie had enjoyed a quiet family Christmas with the Jarvises and Christine was not living with the Devil in a new Tower of Babel erected on the site of the Bank of England. If all of this *was* happening inside her head then the Moment of Rapture had not passed unnoticed on Christmas Day, Elvis was sleeping the peaceful sleep of the dead in Graceland and any little grey men that happened to be passing through the solar system would do so unintercepted by tomahawk missiles. Molly knew, however, that no matter how hard she might hope for this to be the truth of the matter, it was not something she could simply take on trust. She had never been easy prey to the temptations of faith, and she knew that no good evidence of the world's safety—let alone proof thereof—could possibly present itself to her senses if she were really as crazy as that hypothesis implied.

Whether her predicament were objectively real or not, she decided, she had no alternative but to play it straight. If the world did not need saving, all well and good, but if it did—and *she* would still require saving in either case—then it was up to her to do it. The Devil had carefully stacked all the cards in his own favour, but whatever else he had lied about he must have told the truth about the future being as yet unmade. His scheme could still be undone, if only she could figure out a way to undo it. Unfortunately, he had already anticipated the possibility that she might turn the *deus ex* machine upon herself—and by letting her know that he had already factored the possibility into his plan he had thrown the value of the move into doubt. Was he bluffing, or double bluffing, or triple bluffing? Did he really want to prevent her from doing what the universe had already assumed she would do, or was he trying to ensure, in his inimitably sly fashion, that she *would* do it, repeating a mistake that had already turned tragedy into farce and moving on to something even stranger?

It was quite a problem, and it was not obvious that she could ever work her way through it by logic alone. Unfortunately, it was equally hard to believe that she could obtain an appropriate result if she simply threw logic aside and trusted to her instincts and spontaneous impulses. If she had not trusted her instincts and spontaneous impulses far too much already, she wouldn't have been in this mess in the first place —and if the Devil were merely a projection of some wicked and unruly part of herself, he was instinct and spontaneous impulse through and through. If he had a weakness, that weakness had to be approached via the cerebrum, by rational thought and cleverness.

"The race is not always to the swift, nor the poker-game to the clever," she murmured, "but you'd have to be a complete idiot to bet any other way. Whether it's the whole world that'll comprehensively buggered, or only me, I'd have to say that the odds don't look good."

But that, she realised, was what *deus ex* machines were for. To them, million-to-one chances were routine. As long as she had the *deus ex* machine, the odds didn't really figure in the equation at all.

60

When the Devil's car turned up at eight o'clock on New Year's Eve, Molly wasn't entirely surprised to find that the driver was Elvis, looking somewhat older than when she'd first met him at Sainsbury's singles night, but not as old as he'd seemed when she'd glimpsed him in Chiliad Science's delusion-dressed research lab.

"It's good to see you again," she told him, sincerely. "How have you been?"

"Feelin's mutual, ma'am," he said, ruefully. "Not so bad, considering. In Pandemonium, I was part of the floor show, but that's all closed down now. Now I'm just the Devil's driver. Needs must and all. I hope you like your costumes—I told the boss you might like a choice, but he said that it was his party, and that these were the only ones he had that were guaranteed to fit."

The larger of the two outfits was a cowgirl costume complete with fringed waistcoat and mock-Stetson hat. Elvis told Molly that it was modelled on one from *Annie Get Your Gun*, with the obvious exception of the black mask, but Molly had only seen *Even Cowgirls Get the Blues* and she remembered only too well what had happened to the head cowgirl in that movie. It did fit, though—and the holster was exactly the right size to accommodate the *deus ex* machine.

"What the hell," she said, gathering it up so that she could change in the bedroom.

Angie's costume was a miniature Harlequin which rendered her peculiarly androgynous. She liked it, except for the little black hat.

"I'll be a joker, won't I?" she said, having only seen the bastardized kind of Harlequin you could sometimes find in a pack of cards.

"Sure you will," Molly told her. "You use the bathroom, sweetie. Better take a seat, Elvis—this could take some time."

"No hurry, ma'am," Elvis assured them both.

It didn't take as long as it might have, but Molly made no attempt to rush. Like Cinderella, she didn't intend staying at the party after midnight, but that didn't mean that she was in a hurry to get there.

Elvis hummed the tune of "Heartbreak Hotel" while he drove south along roads that were eerily devoid of traffic, but Molly wasn't tempted to sing along and Angie was too young to know the words.

When they stopped outside the gate of the Devil's new palace, Elvis leapt out to open the door for his passengers. "That costume looks pretty good on you, ma'am," he lied, gallantly, "but if you'll forgive me sayin' so, that gun doesn't look real. Too shiny."

"It's not a gun," she told him. "It just looks like one."

Tom was no longer manning the door. Mephistopheles was there instead, sporting a garish *major domo*'s uniform.

"I tried to get my *old* job back, of course," he said, mournfully, "but it doesn't exist any more. This was all that was on offer."

"I understand," Molly said, gently. "There's no point retiring to the world of men if the world of men is finished. I suppose the others are all inside?"

"Serving drinks, mostly," Mephistopheles confessed, with a tiny tear in his eye. "Poor Beelzebub's on duty in the GENTS."

"It could be worse," Molly assured him, thinking of the greys shot down in flames and the scientists blown to smithereens—but Mephistopheles' wan smile suggested that he couldn't find it in his heart to agree. He guided them as far as the lift, then delivered them into the charge of Belphegor, who was manning the car. Belphegor seemed slightly more philosophical about his fate. "At least it's not one of those glass-sided things that goes up and down the outside of the building," he said. "I *hate* heights."

"Me too," said Angie.

Although time was getting on, the party still seemed to be in the warming-up phase. Neither the Devil nor Christine had yet put in an appearance, so Molly and Angie drifted aimlessly away from the lift. Molly didn't much want to talk to anyone, and was rather pleased when the vast majority of the guests seemed to be avoiding her, but Honeysuckle and Peaseblossom were prepared to be exceptions to almost any rule.

"*So* glad you could make it," said Honeysuckle, forgetting all about her last parting shot. "There are so few designated victims around that I was afraid we'd have to go thirsty. You have no idea how *boring* the Devil's friends are. International financiers, arms-dealers, boardroom creeps . . . honestly, darling, I'd expected *gangsters* and *psychopaths!* And their floozies. You just wouldn't *believe* that there were so many dead straight sluts in the world. Oh for the days when *femme fatale* actually meant something. No disrespect, darling, but that bulge . . . it's so obviously not a real gun that it's not even worth making catty jokes about your being pleased to see me. *Way* too shiny."

"It's not a gun," Molly assured the lamia. "It just looks like one."

"You really ought to give it to the cloakroom attendant,"

Peaseblossom suggested nodding in the direction of the utterly glum Astarte, who was leaning on a wooden counter in one of the booths adjacent to the lift-doors.

"Somehow," Molly told the one-time fay, "I think that might be a bad move. I'll hang on to it, if you don't mind."

"*We* don't mind," Honeysuckle assured her, gently stroking Molly's chin with a long black fingernail, "but we know a man who does. I don't suppose we could borrow your daughter, could we?"

"Lay a finger on her," Molly said, "and I'll hammer a stake through your heart here and now."

"We wouldn't *hurt* her," Honeysuckle retorted, insouciantly. "We just wanted a little taste. We've already tried the *other* one—and *she* didn't mind *at all*. I do hope you're not going to turn out to be *no fun*. This is supposed to be the party to end all parties, but it's a real drag so far."

When Molly finally managed to get away from the lamias she saw that there was indeed a lot of real drag around, but she had to agree with Honeysuckle about the disappointing calibre of the Devil's friends. Even in fancy dress they seemed unutterably banal. If these were to be the fathers and mothers of a new humanity, Molly thought, they certainly weren't going to produce a race of giants. Most of them looked at her with suspicion and contempt, if they looked at her at all. They didn't seem to have the least idea who she was or why she was here, but they knew that she didn't *fit in*. She wasn't the only person accompanied by a child, but she was the only one who looked like a mother—and perhaps that was enough in itself to qualify her as a spectre at *this* feast. Given that the other guests included at least half a dozen figures costumed as the Red Death and three as the King in Yellow, Molly felt that this was a bit of an insult, but she would have felt worse if people of this sort had welcomed her as a kindred spirit.

Molly's isolation wouldn't have been so conspicuous if she'd been able to turn her back on the crowd and pretend that she was looking at something else, but in order to do that she'd have had to go to the window-wall circling the rotunda, and there was no way she was going to go that close to the apparent edge. It was something of a relief when Lilith finally decided that it was safe to take a break from waitress service and took Molly aside for a surreptitious chat.

"I don't know what he has planned, dear," the old lady said, "but you'll have to be careful. I think he told you the truth when he said that he can't simply take the *deus ex machine* off you, but he'll get it by trickery if he possibly can. I don't know where he intends to aim it, but I'm sure he wants to be the one who pulls the trigger."

"It's okay, Lil," Molly said. "You don't have to put yourself on the line for me. I think I have it all figured out—the only possible problem is Christine. From my viewpoint, she's the one and only loose cannon. As long as she stays out of it, I'll be fine."

61

Christine made her entrance some time after eleven. She looked magnificent, clad not in fabulous billows of red or black but in contemptuous bridal white. She didn't have any visible bulge yet, but she wouldn't have passed for a virgin anyway, given the smile on her face. She was radiant, but not with purity.

Molly wasn't entirely surprised. Everyone qualified for Heaven was long gone, and those who were not no longer had the slightest need to pretend.

Molly tried to move across the room to talk to her elder daughter, but Christine seemed just as intent as all the Red Deaths and Kings in Yellow on cutting her dead. Only the vampire fays were willing to trade conversation with cowgirls, it seemed, and only for the purpose of mockery. Unfortunately, it was very easy for Christine to avoid her mother; all she had to do when Molly drifted close was to make a bee-line for the windows, to set her ethereal whiteness against the starry dark and the sulphurous light-carpet that was Zombie London.

"This is boring," Angie complained.

"It's just cheap tactics," Molly informed her. "The Devil wants me good and rattled by the time the witching hour arrives—but it's not going to work. I've come to spoil the party, and I'm going to spoil it. He can't wait forever—one way or another, midnight will roll around, and then the Millennium ends."

"Mr. Jarvis said that it ended last December," Angie

observed. "He said that people like you were just idiot pedants."

"And none of his machines clapped out," Molly snapped, "because they were all like him, *Y2K compliant*. Nobody here thinks that anything's over and done with. They all know that year zero has yet to expire, and that everything's still up for grabs."

"Not exactly, my dear," said the Vampire Queen of the Fays, who had just materialised at Molly's elbow. "We already have the music of the spheres, and the secret of life. This time, everything's *in place*. There won't be any undignified grabbing."

"Is that why you didn't let Elvis provide the cabaret?" Molly asked. "But you're not actually *playing* the music of the spheres, are you? No matter how tall the tower is, it can't touch the stars."

"Not yet, dear," said the Queen, smugly. "But we *shall* play the music of the spheres, and the tower *will* touch the stars. You can depend on it."

"You can't," Molly countered, defiantly. "You may think you can, but you can't."

It was at that moment that the Devil finally appeared amid the throng, wearing a dinner jacket of whose severity and simplicity Beau Brummell would have been proud. When Molly sneaked a look at her wristwatch she was astonished to see that there were only a few minutes to go till midnight.

"Doesn't time fly when you're having fun?" she murmured, far too softly for the Devil to hear—except that he did.

"No, my dear," he said, his voice cutting through the chatter like a knife. "It gets stolen—by procrastination. Which suggests to me, Molly, that you haven't yet made up your mind exactly what you're going to do."

"Oh but I have," said Molly, hauling the *deus ex* machine out of its holster and letting the glory of the haloed barrel show clearly for the first time. "I'm going to aim it at the place where your heart would be, if you had one, and I'm going to turn back time without you. I'm going to secure the rule of the head, and damn the heart!"

As she levelled the gleaming machine, which caught the light so brilliantly that it seemed to burn with holy fire, the crowd which stood between her and the Devil split into two and melted sideways, leaving her the clearest of shots.

"That would be a mistake, my love," the Devil said, lightly. "What you *ought* to do, as I suggested to you, is to aim it at yourself. You're the only person here qualified to be the beneficiary of a miracle, after all. But you think I'm lying, don't you? You think it's a double bluff—that I'm advising you to do it because I assume that you'll assume that my encouragement to do something else is a ploy—but you're still not sure, are you? Perhaps it's a triple bluff, you think, or maybe a quadruple. You're hesitating, Molly. If you had *really* made up your mind, you'd have taken the shot by now."

"It's not quite midnight," Molly said, pugnaciously. "I'm waiting for the first stroke of Big Ben. The angel said that I had to aim very carefully, you see—and I think timing is as important as direction. But as soon as I hear that first stroke, you're dead and gone forever. Eternity unwinds without you. And you can't take it off me, can you? *That* much is true. There's nothing you can do but stand there and wait."

"You know *that*'s not true, Molly," the Devil said. "You might not be able to think more than one move ahead, but I *know* you've got that one covered."

He snapped his fingers, and a single figure emerged from the crowd to move gracefully into the line of fire.

"I can't let you do it, Mum," Christine said.

"Yes you can, darling," Molly countered. The Devil was right, of course. She'd anticipated *this* move. Now she really had to start talking. Everything depended on Christine's willingness or unwillingness to step aside.

"Give me the gun, Mum," Christine said, taking the first tentative step towards her mother while keeping the Devil's immaculate dinner jacket carefully shielded.

"It's not a gun, sweetie," Molly said. "It only looks like one. It's a *deus ex* machine. It has the power to put everything right, if we only let it. It can unwind time, remake the past, erase all our mistakes. Yours, mine, the world's. It can do *anything,* if it's only aimed well. All we have to do is take out the Devil. Just that—no more and no less. You have to trust me, Chris. I'm your mother. I've been a lousy mother, I admit, but all that will change if you only let it. We can begin again, and this time we can get it right. You have to do it, Christine. I'm your mother. You have to trust me. In spite of everything, *you have to trust me.*"

As she pronounced the last words, Big Ben struck for the first time, beginning the twelve-part count-down to midnight. The sulphurous carpet that was London was lit up twice as brightly by the first wave of celebratory fireworks. The zombies didn't care that they had already welcomed the new Millennium once—they were more than prepared to do it all over again, for auld lang syne.

"Oh, give it a rest, Mum," Christine said, "and give me the fucking gun."

Big Ben seemed to go into overdrive, as if the fireworks had driven him into a frenzy. Suddenly, there was nothing stately about the procession of his chimes. Suddenly, time itself seemed to be coming apart.

62

Christine surged forward, without ever once exposing the Devil to the barrel of the *deus ex* machine, and she snatched the weapon out of Molly's hand. Molly could have fired, in spite of all the confusion, but she'd only have hit Christine. She'd already given serious consideration to the possibility that Christine ought to be the target, the agent of the miracle —but she'd rejected it.

"*I* can't take it off you," she heard the Devil say, "but I know someone who can!"

"Sorry, dear," Lilith's voice whispered in her ear, as Molly stood dumbfounded. "I had to tell him what you said. You know how these things are."

I sure do, Molly said to herself—but she said it silently, lest anyone should understand.

Christine gave the *deus ex* machine to the Devil, and Big Ben's panic attack died away. Time now seemed to have been suspended, between the eleventh stroke and the twelfth. The Devil wanted to enjoy the moment of his triumph to the full.

Until now, the Devil had carefully maintained his appearance as Francine's Adam, the apprentice ponce, but now he let his true colours show. Molly saw him now as she'd seen him in the back of Dean's Devil-driven car, in all his horrible glory. He was the foulest thing that she could imagine, and his eyes were ablaze with malice.

"You stupid little cunt!" he sneered. "Did you really think that you could save the world? Did you really think that you could even save yourself? Did you ever really *think* at all?"

Molly said nothing.

"You're worthless, Molly," the Devil sneered. "Utterly and completely worthless. You've never done anything right in your entire fucking life. Nothing. Do you know what this has always been about? No—of course you don't. You don't know *anything*. Well, I'll tell you. I'll tell you why I wanted this little toy, why I *needed* it, and why I had to reconstruct the whole fucking universe just to make sure that it would be delivered to my care. Heaven would never have let it go otherwise, you see—I had to make sure that He'd not only feel the obligation to leave it behind but to leave it in the custody of the biggest fool in all Creation, the one person guaranteed to bring it here tonight and let it be plucked from her feeble fingers. The one *nothing* in all the world stupid enough to think she actually had a chance of turning the tables on *me!*

"The reason I wanted the *deus ex* machine, you stupid cunt, is because I've spent all eternity in Pandemonium, with nothing else to reach for but the Earth. It wasn't *enough,* Molly—to be bound in a nutshell by nightmare, while infinite space lay without. I wanted the *stars,* Molly. I wanted the galaxies, and the universe entire—and you've given it to me!"

As he spoke, he raised a scaly arm. The metal plates that had been covering the glass ceiling withdrew into their beds above the tower's central shaft, so that the outer part of the crown of the Devil's citadel became entirely transparent. Then the lights were dimmed, so that the stars could be seen in all their naked glory. The fireworks down below, frozen within the moment, seemed direly vulgar by comparison. The only other thing which glowed as bright was the barrel of the *deus ex* machine: the key to eternity.

It was a clear night, and the tower was *very* tall, but Molly had seen the stars shine even more brightly, and in much greater profusion, from the observation deck of the greys' mothership. She had seen them shine on alien skies, tinted and distorted by exotic atmospheres. There was nothing here to excite or appal *her*, except for her awareness of the tower's height.

The moon loomed over poisoned London, the message on its face half-obliterated by shadow, but the stars and galaxies were above and beyond it, filling infinity.

"All mine," said the Devil. "All mine, at last."

The delayed stroke of Big Ben sounded in slow motion as the Devil put the *deus ex* machine into his mouth, aiming upwards at his cerebrum, the seat of his wisdom and ambition: the device by which he intended to encompass *everything* this time around.

He pulled the trigger.

The bang was incredibly loud.

The top of the Devil's head exploded, and a vast cloud of bloody shards slowly expanded, separating into particles as it spattered the carefully-angled panes of glass. The Devil's guests could still see the stars, but they were red now, as if all the matter in the universe had been turned to luminous blood.

If the Devil had been merely human, he would have crumpled up like Mr. Wilson, albeit more slowly, but he wasn't. He continued to stand there, his unspeakable eyes wide with astonishment.

If he had been capable of speech, he would probably have asked Molly what she'd done, and she didn't want him to perish in ignorance, so she reached into her sleeve and brought out what looked like an empty ammunition clip. She knew that if there were anyone in the world capable of seeing beyond the apparent emptiness to the charge that was still contained within the clip, the Devil would be the one.

"Sometimes," she said, blandly, "you don't need a miracle. Sometimes, an ordinary bullet is all it takes to do the job."

The Devil just had time to look into her eyes, with awful realization dawning in his suddenly-ineffectual stare, before he finally began to fall.

Christine screamed, and hurled herself upon his crumpled body, covering her lovely white dress in sticky scarlet blood. Then she straightened up again, with the glowing *deus ex machine* clutched in her right hand and Hellish fury written all over her face.

"You fucking bitch!" she yelled, and fired.

The bullet hit Molly just to the right of her navel. Its subsequent trajectory was such that the shock wave trashed her small and large intestines and several minor organs before pulverising her right kidney.

"Oh shit," said Molly, with feeling, as she was overcome by a sudden urgent need to sit down. "*That* wasn't in the script."

63

It was Angie who took over. Somebody had to, because Molly was no longer capable of purposive action and none of the party guests had moved an inch since their host's brain had been distributed all over the inside of the crystal cupola. Molly had the impression that the tower might already have begun to collapse into itself, folding up like a telescope, but she wasn't sure that she could still trust her intuitions.

Angie plucked the seemingly-empty ammunition clip from Molly's nerveless fingers and marched over to the spot where Christine stood, doubly horrorstruck and frozen stiff.

"Give me the gun, Chris," Angie said.

Christine meekly handed over the shining device—which was indeed, for the moment, no more and no less than a gun. Angie released the ammunition clip that Molly had taken from Mr. Wilson's gun and threw it away. Then she replaced the one that the angel had originally put into the weapon. Then she offered it back to Christine.

"No," said Christine.

"You have to," Angie said. "You shot her. It's up to you to put her out of her misery."

Molly wondered what time it was. Was the new Millennium already ticking away in its ordinary course, or had the Devil's time-freezing tricks outlasted his blasted intelligence? Were they all still trapped in the unrapturous moment of midnight? Is so, could they ever escape?

The outflow of her blood was making her very faint, but Molly tried to hang on. She desperately wanted to see what, if anything, would happen next.

Christine took the shining gun from Angie—except that she knew that it was no longer a gun. Christine knew that the *deus ex* machine was loaded with a miracle now, and that the only matter to be settled was how carefully and effectively it could be aimed.

Molly, speechless with shock, couldn't advise her. It was up to Angie to steer her sister through.

Christine looked down at the blood on her beautiful white dress, and turned towards her dead lover. She pointed the gun at the Devil's shattered head.

Angie stepped between them.

"No, Chris," Angie said. "There's plenty more where *he* came from. You don't need a miracle for that. It'd be a waste."

Christine thought about that for what might have been two minutes or no time at all. Then she turned back to Molly.

"Sorry, Mum," she said. "I guess it wasn't your fault."

They sounded like the sweetest words in the universe, sweeter even than the legend written on the moon. After they'd been spoken, Molly's need for a miracle seemed to have receded, but she knew perfectly well that you couldn't have a *deus ex* machine in a plot without having it go off, so she wasn't in the least surprised to see Christine level it again.

This time, Molly was glad and proud to see, Christine took very careful aim before she fired.

64

"You took your time," said the gigantic not-quite-octopus with far too many eyes. "For a while there, I thought you weren't going to make it."

Molly flexed her tentacles experimentally. Her suckers were itching to get on with the job.

"We're way back in the Proterozoic," she said. "What's a few million years between friends? The cyanobacterial sludge doesn't care when we start work on it."

"*We* have other Creations to supervise," the alien cephalopod with whom she was mind-melded assured her. "Our horizons are, of necessity, much broader than yours."

"I may be just the local help," Molly told her host, "but I'm working within a cosmic perspective. I take it we're done with all the signwriting, and that it's time to get down to *business*."

"Absolutely. There's nothing more you can do with the old script, but the new one is capable of *much* greater subtlety. It may look simple, having only four letters, but you'd be surprised what you can do with four letters."

"No I wouldn't," Molly said. "When you've seen as much as I have, nothing much surprises you any more. There's just one thing I need to know, before we get on with the writing."

"We're mind-melded," the moon-sized cephalopod pointed out. "What I know, you know."

"Well, I need reassurance. I need to be reassured that this isn't just some stupid dream, from which I'll wake up tomorrow, having done nothing but housework."

"Hark at you!" said the monster in whose body Molly was cosily prisoned. "Nothing but housework! Do you have the slightest idea how long it's going to get this baby into shape? Can you *imagine* how long it's going to take us to make the atmosphere breathable and turn all that stinking sludge into lands and oceans fit for Eros? Believe me, darling, this is *not* the work of a single night, and dreaming is *not* the way to get the job done. This will take nearly forever, and you'll be on the job every second of every day."

"That's what I thought," Molly said, with some satisfaction. "I just needed to be sure."

"Miracles take time," the cephalopod informed her. "They have to be very carefully planned, and very carefully inscribed—and even then there are a million ways in which they can go wrong. The only way to do these things properly is the hard way. You have to start from year zero, and it takes as long as it takes. It's hard work."

"Sure," said Molly, "but once you've shot the Devil, it's not as hard as all that. At least, I hope it's not."

About the Author

Brian Stableford has long been recognized as one of Great Britain's premier hard science fiction authors, particularly in the area of biotechnology. The sixth and final volume of his "future history" series from Tor, *The Omega Expedition*, will be published in December 2002; the earlier volumes in the series are *Inherit the Earth* (1998), *Architects of Emortality* (1999), *The Fountains of Youth* (2000), *The Cassandra Complex* (2001) and *Dark Ararat* (2002). He is currently employed as a 0.25 lecturer in Creative Writing at King Alfred's College Winchester, teaching on an M.A. course in "Writing for Children".

Born in 1948 in Shipley, Yorkshire, Brian was educated at Manchester Grammar School and the University of York (B.A. in Biology; D.Phil. in Sociology). From 1976 to 1988 he was a Lecturer in the Sociology Department of the University of Reading, teaching courses in the philosophy of social science and the sociology of literature and the mass media. He has also taught at the University of the West of England, on a B.A. in "Science, Society and the Media". He has been active as a professional writer since 1965, publishing more than 50 novels and 200 short stories as well as several nonfiction books; he is also a prolific writer of articles for reference books, mainly in the area of literary history.

The employees of Five Star hope you have enjoyed this book. All our books are made to last. Other Five Star books are available at your library, through selected bookstores, or directly from us.

For more information about titles, please call:

(800) 223-1244

or visit our Web site at:

www.gale.com/fivestar

To share your comments, please write:

Publisher
Five Star
295 Kennedy Memorial Drive
Waterville, ME 04901